'[...] *[...]en the Dead Come Calling* tracks the toxin which se[...] [...] [...]f y[...] [...] closer y[...] will see who the "key workers' are. Helen Sedgwick saw into the future and that future is now! It's an incredible book! READ IT.'

Lemn Sissay, author of *My Name Is Why*

'Creepy, atmospheric and spine-tingling, *When the Dead Come Calling* is the kind of mystery so deviously plotted it left me reeling. Brilliant.'

Chris Whitaker, author of *We Begin at the End*

'*When the Dead Come Calling* confirms what many of us already knew: Helen Sedgwick is one of Scotland's finest contemporary storytellers.'

Claire Askew, author of *All the Hidden Truths*

'Beautifully written, beguiling and mysterious, the sort of book that would reward a second (and third) read.'

Fiona Erskine, author of *The Chemical Detective*

'A multi-layered tale from a range of viewpoints that reaches back into history and poses as many questions as it answers... A thumpingly good read shot through with some beautiful prose.'

Herald on Sunday

'By combining up-to-the-minute themes, well-tuned dialogue and warm and witty details of everyday life with a deep, impressionistic sense of dread, Sedgwick produces a mystery as addictive as it is anxiety-inducing... Deserves to be a stonking series with wide appeal that should run and run.'

Molly Flatt, author of *The Charmed Life of Alex Moore*

'The dense narrative moves back and forth, incorporating horrors from the past and fears and resentments from the present.

The final twist works well and adds an extra layer to the story that is both surprising and moving.'

Literary Review

'Sedgwick's writing is minutely observational, clever and warm. One minute you are transported by her descriptions of the landscape, the next she is raising the hairs on the back of your neck with her dreamlike descriptions of whatever lurks in the cave at the foot of the cliffs. It is her portrayal of the closed world of a remote community, however, that will chill you to the bone.'

Scotsman

'This is a stunning, complex, out-of-the mainstream novel that's completely immersive.'

Mystery People

'Helen Sedgwick weaves a clever combination of psychological suspense and low-key police procedural.'

Crime Review

'*When the Dead Come Calling* is assured, engaging and beautifully layered. Intriguing characters meet contemporary issues, and historical whispers, in a haunting landscape. A must-read!'

Scottish Book Trust, picked as a 2020 Great Scottish Novel

'It's the poetic quality of her writing that makes this a moodily engrossing, and rather uneasy, opening to the series.'

Peterborough Telegraph

'An ethereal, supernatural take on the crime genre.'

Huntly Express

'Sedgwick trusts her readers to understand and dispenses with tedious explaining: it's a truly exceptional book.'

The Book Bag blog

WHAT DOESN'T BREAK US

HELEN SEDGWICK

POINT BLANK

A Point Blank Book

First published in Great Britain, Australia and the Republic of Ireland
by Point Blank, an imprint of Oneworld Publications, 2022

ISBN 978-0-86154-194-2 (paperback)
ISBN 978-08-6154-195-9 (ebook)

Printed and bound in Great Britain by Clays Ltd, Elcograf S.p.A.

Oneworld Publications
10 Bloomsbury Street
London WC1B 3SR
England

For Brigit

Falkirk Council	
30124 03167375 1	
Askews & Holts	
AF C	£8.99
MK	

CHARACTERS

THE POLICE

DI Georgie Strachan – in charge of Burrowhead police station

DC Trish Mackie – a local girl through and through

PC Simon Hunter – still reeling from the murder of his boyfriend Alexis Cosse

DS Daniel Frazer – a city officer sent to investigate the Abigail Moss disappearance

Dr Cal Dover – head of the forensics lab in Crackenbridge

PC Susan White, aka Suze – a PC from the larger station in Crackenbridge

Jacob Prowle (deceased) – ran Burrowhead police station before Georgie's time

THE OUTSIDERS

Pamali Patel – Georgie's best friend, who runs the Spar

Fergus Strachan – Georgie's husband, who likes to consider himself a local

Orlando Joyce – a rich student from the city

Julie Alperstein – from the city too, working on Ricky Barr's farm for the summer

Deborah-Jane Barr – Ricky Barr's estranged sister, recently returned to Burrowhead

Betty Marshall – an old lady who lives in a care home in the city

Pauly and Rachel (deceased) – technically local kids, died in a presumed suicide pact

Sonny Riley (deceased) – a little boy fostered by Nora and Jacob Prowle, found buried in Ricky Barr's field

Dr Alexis Cosse (deceased) – Simon Hunter's boyfriend, murdered by Bobby Helmsteading

Abigail Moss – no one knows who she is

THE LOCALS

Shona Jones – a local girl, writes for the local press

Kevin Taylor – Shona's boyfriend, got a bit of an attitude

Andy Barr – awkward kid, been in a fair bit of trouble

Ricky Barr – local farmer, bully, Andy Barr's father

Natalie Prowle – head of the community council, always keeping an eye

Nora Prowle (deceased) – Natalie's aunt and Jacob Prowle's wife

Lee Prowle – Natalie's younger son

Aaron Prowle – Natalie's older son

A little girl in tattered clothes (?) – only Georgie can see her

Walt Mackie (deceased) – Trish Mackie's great-uncle, raised her as his own

Amanda Mackie (deceased) – Trish Mackie's mam, died when Trish was a girl

Art Robertson (deceased) – friend of Walt Mackie

Elise Robertson – Art Robertson's daughter, well acquainted with Trish and Suze

Jack Helmsteading (deceased) – friend of Walt Mackie and Art Robertson

Mrs Helmsteading – Jack's wife, Dawn and Bobby's mam, currently in prison

Dawn Helmsteading – escaped Burrowhead, current whereabouts unknown

Bobby Helmsteading (deceased) – killed Alexis Cosse, was killed by his mam in return

Penny-Ann Taylor – one of Kevin Taylor's sisters

Camellia Taylor – Kevin Taylor's mam

June and Whelan Rogers – a middle-aged couple from Burrowhead who grow roses

Terry from the garage and Ben from the pub – a couple of the younger locals

Bessie Wilkie and Colin Spence – locals from the neighbouring village of Warphill

Mrs Smyth – an old lady, lived in Burrowhead all her life

Mrs Dover – likewise

THEN, AND BEFORE THEN

A few days ago

Trish Mackie attended her Uncle Walt's funeral

The week before last

Fergus Strachan moved out of his and Georgie's house

And during the few days before that

A black mare was ritually sacrificed on the cup-and-ring stone in
the woods
    Sonny Riley's bones were discovered in Ricky Barr's field
        An archaeological dig found Iron Age remains in the motte

---

Nearly six months back

Alexis Cosse was murdered by Bobby Helmsteading
    Bobby was killed by his mam because of what he did
        Lee Prowle and Andy Barr attacked Pamali in the Spar

Twenty years ago, give or take

Georgie married Fergus Strachan, and they moved to Burrowhead

But before they did

A mass livestock cull was ordered to stop the spread of foot-and-mouth
    Dawn Helmsteading was almost sacrificed on a stone altar on the cliffs
        Trish's mam disappeared and was presumed drowned at sea

Forty years ago, heading for thirty

Deborah-Jane Barr witnessed Jacob and Nora Prowle murder Sonny Riley
    The first cases of the mad cow disease crisis were reported
        Ricky Barr's dog was sacrificed by a threefold death in the woods

Sixty years ago, still in living memory

Mosley's right-wing rallies prompted race riots across the country
    The Beatles released their first single, *Love Me Do*
        Betty Marshall saw Abigail Moss on a stone altar in the woods

250 years ago

The old minister murdered his slave as the villagers watched on
   The villagers hung the old minister from his cherry tree
      The old church was abandoned to ruin

2,000 years ago, in the Iron Age, things getting hazy now

Crops failed and the villagers starved
   A young girl refused to name the father of her child
      A whole family was sacrificed and buried in the motte

Around 5,000 years ago, sometime in the Neolithic

Now we don't really know how, and we certainly don't know why, but a circle of standing stones was positioned within a wide circular ditch, banked around its outer edge. This created a stone henge that would later be lost; and began the story of a village that would later be broken.

AIR

LAST YEAR

The corridors of Warphill Academy are a failure of white and blue, the white turned grey and speckled with yellowing lumps of chewing gum and the blue, lower down, scuffed with boot marks and the occasional smear of what looks like it could be blood. These are the halls where Pauly walks, eyes straight ahead, stubborn look on his face, all through lunch 'cause if he keeps moving the teachers and kids alike leave him alone, and the shadows have no way to follow.

He carries with him the smell of stale cigarettes and something older, too, something most of the other kids can't place. There's a gang of them in the common room, girls smirking and boys glaring, the door kicked closed soon as someone on the inside sees him passing by. As he pushes through the fire escape to the off-limits car park, the salted smell of midsummer replaces the stale smell of sweat and for a second he imagines himself alone out there, back against the wall, smoking a fag, being still for a minute. Then he spots them out by the brown gate: Lee and Andy, Kev, Shona. He steps back through the fire escape and trudges on.

He doesn't know why he came in, except that he didn't know where else to go. Rachel said she needed some time on her own first, and when he's without Rachel he doesn't much care where he is anyway. He wants that fag though, so he walks right out the front door and doesn't care who sees him go, walks straight out of Warphill and makes his own track through the fields, picking blackcurrants from the wild fruit bushes he passes, sitting at the edge of the woods for a smoke. He can feel them now. The scratching on the back of his neck, the hiss of the breeze through leaves. Then he sees a single swift wheeling its way over the trees and heading for the coast.

That's his way, too.

Time to go.

Rachel is waiting for him, sitting on her mam's old tartan blanket on the clifftop outside Burrowhead, wearing her long, flowing blue skirt with the embroidered golden flowers. Pauly sits beside her without a word when he arrives, their eyes knowing each other, knowing this moment. Then he opens his rucksack. It's in there, what he's made, but that comes later. First, he pulls out a tub of blackcurrants he's collected through the afternoon.

'Raspberry,' he says, starting the game off.

Her face warms to a smile. 'Gooseberry.'

'Loganberry.'

He has dimples; they glitter.

'Strawberry.'

Their words coming faster now.

'Blackberry.'

'Not quite.'

'But close.'

'Give me one then.'

So he reaches forwards, gently places a blackcurrant into her open mouth, and moves round to sit behind her. She leans her head back against his chest.

'Blueberry,' she says slowly, her hands on his legs.

'Red berry,' he whispers in her ear.

'That's not even a thing.'

'Is too.'

A brush of his lips against her cheek, the lazy heat of the evening sun. He lights a rollie, passes it to her, lights another for himself.

They're overlooking the pebble bay that you can only reach by scrambling along the coast at low tide. It's their place, hidden and sacred, though the fact it's hidden and sacred to others as well is one of those things they feel lingering over their shoulders but refuse to turn around and see. It's not where they're choosing to look. But they are looking for something, Rachel and Pauly, out here on the cliffs at midsummer, with the sea a deep turquoise over the sand bed half a mile out and the rocks glinting golden and pink. Pauly kisses her neck; Rachel scrunches her shoulder up against the tickle then reaches back and pops another blackcurrant into his mouth. He catches her chin, holds her face to his. The flask is beside them now, waiting on the blanket.

'You sure you want to do this?' he says.

'I've never been so sure of anything in my life.'

'Then we do it together.'

'Always.'

Later, Rachel's hand strays off the picnic blanket to the grass, feather-like between her fingers. She looks down: swathes of the deepest emerald green, each blade perfect, dancing in the breeze. Her fingertips follow their roots into the ground, through red soil, through pillars of stone to the worlds under the surface as their picnic blanket flutters over the cliffs and down to the glinting rock pools, to snag on barnacles and twist like seaweed. They don't notice it go.

Rachel is thinking of her mam, the way she died, the way she said goodbye, and she's flooded with forgiveness. She can hear her now, humming to herself while she prepares fish fingers for tea; she can see her cascade of curly hair, her bare feet. She feels again the way it felt to look across the kitchen and watch her, to hug her mam's legs as she did the washing-up and know her mam would never tell her to go away. She knows it wasn't like that for Pauly.

Pauly is saying 'I love you,' and it carries across the patchwork fields of green and yellow satin, over the rusted Burrowhead playground and the overgrown lane that passes the Barrs' farm. It fills the empty fountain at the top of Main Street and water at last glistens the stones. It flees through the old church ruin and abandons itself to the breeze from the coast that carries it up through the purple haze condensing over the sea and away. Away from the footsteps, edging closer. Away from the dragging footsteps and the circle surrounding them on the cliffs.

It is cold, where the shadow falls, but it's the sound they know first. They're still lying on the grass, Rachel stroking Pauly's chest and the mist gathering around them. It is a rasping on the edge of words; a nail faintly scratching their skin. Then the shape elongates above them and they know.

They stand together, Rachel and Pauly, on the clifftop outside Burrowhead.

Rachel feels the warmth of her mam's hand gently touch her face.

Pauly says 'I love you,' as the purple overhead deepens, and their fingers intertwine.

Then salt air is streaming around them and soon their bones shatter through their bodies and what's left is only the slow hiss of breath through cracked teeth, lingering somewhere beneath the silence.

LAST NIGHT

'Fuck,' Andy's saying over and over but Aaron's so out of it he's not even opened his fucking eyes and 'fuck fuck fuck' and Andy's the only one who can see it, the rest of them, they're away, they're gone, all but Lee on the floor making that gurgling noise as blood bubbles out his mouth and his leg twitches at the knee with spasms that put Andy in mind of the way a chicken dies. He's seen them die often enough, his da taught him to kill them when he was a kid. Phone Trish, he thinks, or Pami? 999? Ambulance? Fuck.

Aaron is making this noise like he's fucking humming or something, like there's a tune playing in his head, his body swaying with the rain on the roof, with whatever the fuck he thinks he can hear. He's singing along with this blissful look in his eyes and fuck. Lee's face is covered with sweat, his skin glistening. The blood's coming out mixed with spit now, frothy. There's a pool of it on the brown caravan floor, reflecting the light, glistening like the sweat on his forehead. Beside him, the girls are curled up together. Terry's slumped against the wall, mouth open, eyes darting back and forth across the window like he's following a bee desperately trying to find a way out. Andy gets that.

He's dialling though. 999. Instinct taking over and there's a noise outside, low and pure, like an owl calling in the constant rain. It's ringing through the caravan park, screeching up into a siren, and he thinks about running, he didn't give his name, he's not even sure what he said – they're coming though, they're here, moving him out the way and surrounding Lee on the floor there with tubes and masks and his leg is still twitching, that jerking at the knee like a kick, like he's vicious even in the way he's dying. Maybe he'd like that, or maybe he'd rather be alive.

Maybe they'd all rather that.

Sitting on the wet metal steps of the caravan next to the one where Lee's spewing blood, the sky overhead is deep purple and Andy knows he's not going to run. The sky is making him dizzy, the rain barely washing the sweat from his face, so he forces his gaze down the track and across his da's field to Burrowhead police station. Bars on the windows. Damp in the walls. They're bringing Lee out now, strapped to a stretcher, his foot twitching. An oxygen mask over his face. Does that mean he's still alive? Fuck.

Andy's not alone.

In that caravan behind him, through the door he's leaning against as he reaches into his jeans pocket for a fag, he knows Kev's watching through the rain-streamed window, and Shona's in there with him. That means they're all here now, in a way: Shona and Kev, Andy and Lee, Rachel and Pauly. He's leaning back to get some shelter, cupping his hand and flicking at his light, but he's no getting a flame. Fucking thing. He gives up, thinks about chucking it into the shadows – he'd a done that, a few months back – but instead he slips it into his pocket, cigarette hanging from his lips unlit and turning soggy in the rain.

Then there's a shape coming out of the dark. It's slipping between the caravans and stopping beside him. A wheezing, a rasping in the back of the throat and a match grating against the strike strip and held out towards him, sheltered by hunched shoulders, a cupped hand. Andy turns, leans forward with the cigarette in his mouth and inhales against the light. Through the flickering of the flame his da's face looks like an old tree trunk, etched rough and ridged, furrowed as an ancient ash. His eyes avoid Andy's own as he puts the matchbox away in his shirt pocket and wipes the back of his hand against his mouth. They've nothing to say to one another, Andy and Ricky Barr. They're sitting together though, on the steps that lead up to Kev and Shona's caravan, where Kev and Shona are standing at the window watching them; they're sitting together as more bodies on stretchers with oxygen masks are loaded into the ambulance, and as the ambulance drives away into the dark red spill of the sunrise.

THIS MORNING

Georgie is conscious of the sound of her shoes, their wet rubber soles squeaking as she follows the nurse down the hospital corridor. Her forehead is damp, either from rain or sweat – she's given up trying to tell the difference. This weather, so muggy she can feel the weight of the air in her lungs. The last time she was in this hospital, she had Fergus. Her stomach twists at the thought, at the knowledge of what people are saying. In the corner of her eye she glimpses filthy matted hair, feels a tugging on her shirt cuff but this is not happening again; she won't let it. She keeps her eyes staring straight ahead and folds her arms. *You're sensitive, aren't you, Georgie?* That's what old Walt Mackie said before he died.

'Ma'am?'

It's DS Frazer, he's here with her. HQ agreed for him to stay, for another week or two at least, to keep following his leads, investigating the Abigail Moss murder – or whatever it was old Betty Marshall witnessed in the woods when she was a girl. Abigail Moss: a name with no records attached to it, a memory from sixty years ago, and a dedication on the bench by the village playground. It's not much to go on, but it could be the last crime for Burrowhead police before the station is closed for good.

Unless there's a crime she needs to investigate here too.

'You talk to those four,' she says, nodding her head down the corridor to where Aaron Prowle, Penny-Ann Taylor, Terry Dodd and Julie Alperstein are being kept in for observation for a few more hours. Three locals and one student from the city: Julie Alperstein, here to work on Ricky's farm for the summer. Frazer straightens his shoulders in that formal way he has and heads off. Simon's on his way to the caravan park, though he sounded groggy when Georgie phoned him first thing, and she knows it's a bad day for him, was always going to be a bad day. Alexis's birthday. The first since his death.

Trish is not coming in though. Trish has handed in her notice. 'Jumping before I'm pushed,' she'd said, and Georgie had wanted to say that she'd no intention of pushing anyone anywhere, that she'd been trying to help, secure her another posting, but there'd been that tightness in her jaw and she'd paused when she should have spoken and Trish filled the silence with 'D'you need me to work the notice?' Georgie only knew she didn't want anyone staying where they didn't want to be, and she's thinking about Fergus again, as she stands at the door to the room just along from intensive care – where Lee Prowle was treated last night, where they saved his life. A monitor is beeping beside the bed and he's covered in a thin hospital sheet, eyes closed. Except his eyes flick open and he's staring at her. She's still holding the door frame. She drops her hands. Returns his stare.

There's a blade of white light coming in under the closed blind, sharp enough to cut through the clouds, though the rain's still pelting the glass and the heat in the room is sticky and thick. A week it's been going, this storm, clinging to the village, refusing to stop once it started; a week of Georgie living alone and wondering if she was going to see Fergus everywhere she went, the cliffs, the Spar, but she saw him nowhere. She phoned but didn't leave messages. He texted once. *It's like you said, a break.* That was all she got. And what could she accuse him of, not speaking to her before he ran away? But he'd tried, he'd tried so many times and she'd been—

'Lee,' she says, surprised at the severity in her own voice.

The room looks like the one Pamali was in, less than six months ago. Maybe that's why Georgie's angry. She remembers the way Pamali looked up from the hospital bed with such warmth in her eyes – even through the pain of that dislocated shoulder Lee had given her. Pami always seemed able to keep hold of her own kindness. The night Fergus left, Pamali was the only one Georgie had been able to speak to; when was that, not much more than a week ago? Pamali had walked Georgie home, insisted on coming in so Georgie wouldn't have to be alone, stayed over so Georgie wouldn't have to wake up alone the next morning either. The morning it all became real: Fergus was gone and everything was changed and she still feels sick with it, even standing here with a job to do. She could use some of Pami's warmth now. There's no warmth to be found in Lee's eyes, though there's less spite than there used to be, and if she's not mistaken there's some doubt in there too. After this, she'll have to go and speak to Natalie. Lee's mother, Natalie Prowle.

The villagers have been talking about her, about Fergus, about Natalie Prowle.

Small fingers curl around her wrist and she grabs her hand away.

'Lee,' she says again, forcing herself into the room and blocking out everything else. 'I need to ask you a few questions.'

ALONG THE CORRIDOR

'You lot need to know your rights,' Julie says from the bed where she's sitting, her legs stretched out and her ankles crossed on top of the covers, fully dressed, skinny jeans and white T-shirt, ready for the second they get discharged. 'You don't need to say anything, you got that? We've done nothing wrong, and don't you forget it.'

'I don't know...' Terry is mumbling from the chair opposite, coat on, Cat boots laced. 'I thought the whole point was that we—'

'The point,' Julie says, 'is that we have rights.'

Standing over by the window Aaron Prowle doesn't even turn round, though they can all hear the gruff noise he makes in the back of his throat.

Julie would like him to face her if he's got something to say. He never says much though, Aaron Prowle, just darkens every room he's in, like a sustained bass beneath the chatter of these kids she hardly knows really, except for Penny-Ann, but whom she likes anyway. Except for Aaron Prowle. It's hard to imagine anyone liking Aaron Prowle.

'I need to talk to Lee,' Terry's saying and Julie grins at him, prompting that flush that covers Terry's neck every time someone looks him in the eye.

'He's going to be okay.'

'That's not what I asked.'

Penny-Ann has noticed his blush though, misread it in the cutest way, and Julie shifts over so Penny can join her on the bed. Penny-Ann Taylor, from Burrowhead.

'Look, I'm just saying, time to wise up.'

Aaron still hasn't moved.

'They can't force us to give samples without our consent, and they can't arrest us, they've got no right to arrest us and I know having rights doesn't stop the police, not here and not anywhere, but if *we* know, if we make them see that we know—'

There's a noise outside the door and she stops, eyes flicking across the room. No one else heard it. Beside her, Penny's checking her phone.

'What?'

'My brother—'

'Kev's here?'

'No, he's texting. What?'

The noise comes again, movement beyond the door, then a loud double knock and Penny drops her phone. 'Shit.'

'You lot heard me, right?' hisses Julie as the door opens.

'DS Frazer,' says the cop standing there in Dolce & Gabbana, holding out his hand. 'Can I ask you all a few questions about last night, please?'

His accent, his tone of voice, fuck, that suit – Julie knows his type. He's not from Burrowhead. She needs to handle this. She swings her legs off the bed, strides forward, smiles, reaches for his hand and shakes it warmly before telling him that she knows her rights and so do they all and they do not, in fact, feel like answering any of his questions today.

INFORMAL INTERVIEW WITH
LEE PROWLE, 8 A.M.

'What is it you want to know?' Lee's voice cuts through the room.

Georgie reaches for the chair, pulls it away from the bed before sitting down. A small hand fleetingly clasps at her ankle. She presses her forehead, forces herself into the present, the hospital room with its lingering smell of lentil soup.

Lee's eyes are bloodshot, raw around the edges. As she looks, he starts scratching at them and Georgie has to stop herself from pulling his arm away.

'What was it that you took, Lee?'

That scratching at his eyes, it's excruciating to watch.

'Do you need...will I call the nurse, get you some eye drops or something?'

He sniffs, and she can hear the rattle of something in the back of his throat. His eyes dart over her shoulder, to the door, the corridor. She turns. There's no one there.

'They've taken plenty samples,' he says, finally pulling away from his eyes and starting to scratch at the IV in the back of his hand instead. She can see him aggravating it, and there's a bruise there already from when the needle went in. She wonders if he bruises easy, Lee Prowle. He's a small boy, five foot five and pretty with it, or he was before the skin became stretched over his cheekbones, the way it's done these last few months. Lips scabbed over from where he's been biting them. Georgie can remember when he was a cute kid. 'So you'll be telling me what it was, I imagine, DI Strachan.'

'You're saying you don't know?'

He clamps his jaw tight at that. Georgie's not sure if any of them are going to talk, but she certainly wasn't expecting to get much out of Lee. He's had a scare though. He might not be ready to talk to the police, but he's got to be blaming someone. His eyes, darting over to the door again. He's right about the samples, of course, Cal will be able to tell her exactly what it was. Cal's been good to her this past week, since Fergus left, and she appreciates it. Especially with Trish not speaking to her either. A bit of company over dinner helped more than she'd imagined it would, stopped her thinking about Fergus for a few hours, about what he's doing, where he's staying. Cal's good company, and he's good at his job too. So yes, Cal will be analysing Lee's stomach contents. He's got bloods, urine, even swabs of his sweat, and he'll be going through the caravan too. Cal will find out what they all took.

It's not anything she recognises, though, and that's not good.

She checked the toxicology report for Rachel and Pauly before she came here. Not that she could have forgotten what it said. They'd taken something before they died, too, something unknown. This past year, under all of it, under what Bobby Helmsteading did to Alexis, before Sonny Riley's bones rose up from the soil after decades of staying buried, under it all she'd never forget Rachel and Pauly last year. The suicide pact. Two lives that should have been so much more, whose end never made any sense. The state of their bodies when she found them: that haunting look in their wide-open eyes. Bones smashed from the fall. Their stomach contents: tree bark, plant root, raw animal blood. Their hands clasped together. Their fingers gently, lovingly, intertwined.

WHEN THINGS ARE SPOKEN

The flimsy curtains across the caravan window are closed and Simon knows it's early, for a Sunday, but he needs to talk to them: Shona Jones and Kevin Taylor. He knocks again, lightly but several times. Remembers Shona knocking on his door once, a lifetime ago, just days after Alexis died.

'Mate.' It's Kevin's voice, from inside, though he must have seen him through the curtains – they wouldn't block much of anything out, right enough. The door opens and he's standing there, jeans hurriedly pulled on, bare feet, T-shirt in his hands. 'You do know we were up all night with that.' He gestures over to Aaron and Lee's caravan. His sister's one of the kids in the hospital, you'd think he'd be a bit more concerned.

'You can sleep later,' Si says.

Kev pushes his hand through his hair.

'And I'm told Penny-Ann's doing fine.'

'Found that out myself, thanks.'

Shona appears at the door behind him, one of Kev's T-shirts over a denim skirt.

'Ease up, Kev. It's Sunday,' she says. She has a kindness to her voice, Shona, always has. 'Come on in, Si.'

Her arm is on Kevin's shoulder and Kev steps back to let Simon in. Soon he's perched on the narrow bench facing the bed where Shona and Kev sit side by side, sheets tangled beneath them.

'Do you want a drink?' Shona says. 'Tea, water?'

'I'm alright, thanks.'

'I need a water,' she says, getting up again, retrieving a glass from a cupboard overhanging the sink and filling it. 'Is everyone okay?' she asks, her back still to him, like she can't face turning around until she knows whatever he came here to say.

'Yeah, they're okay. They'll all be fine.'

Si sees her shoulders relax at that. Then Kev pipes up, like he reckons his role in all this is to undermine every bit of decency Shona shows.

'How's Orlando?'

Simon drove back to Burrowhead the second he got Georgie's call and what the fuck does Kevin Taylor know about anything?

'You're a dark horse.' Kev, still smirking at him.

'Can you not.'

Silence then and all Simon can see is Alexis, smiling softly, and it makes him ache so bad he has to press his hands over his eyes.

'Sorry mate,' Kev says.

But Simon's here for a reason. He needs to know what they know – he has a job to do and it's not about him or Alexis. It's about the suicide of two kids last year and another in intensive care. There's something that connects them, he's sure of that.

'You knew...' Simon clears his throat, sits up a bit straighter. 'You knew Rachel and Pauly, didn't you?'

Kevin's face changes and for a second he looks older than the teenager he is, and there's something flitting behind his eyes – is that regret?

'Known them for years,' he says. 'Since we were at primary together.'

Shona's back on the bed, holding her glass of water with both hands.

'Are you finally reopening their case?'

'Shona—'

'You think it's connected to that lot?' She flicks her head over towards Aaron and Lee's caravan.

'Please,' Si says, though he knows what Shona thinks, knows she's been trying to follow the supply of drugs all year to find whoever's responsible. Maybe to write another article, maybe for something else. 'Tell me about Rachel and Pauly.'

'I knew Rachel first,' Kev says. 'Shona and Pauly were at Warphill Primary, see, but we were at Burrowhead. There's photos of us playing on the beach and that.'

He pauses then, blinks a couple of times, as though he'd forgotten she was dead and then it hit him again. Her suicide.

'So you stayed close then, as you got older?'

'For a while,' he says. 'I mean, aye. Her and Shona were—'

'We were best friends,' Shona says. 'I met Kev through Rachel. But then...'

They look at each other and Si feels things they're not saying, hidden in the gaps.

'The last couple of years had got a bit weird,' Shona says.

In the silence Simon hears Alexis's voice, his gentleness: *Just describe what you see.*

'I mean, Pauly,' Kev says, shaking his head. 'You couldn't say anyone was friends with him. He didn't want friends. No one knew what to say around him. What are you supposed to do with someone like that, who won't...'

He doesn't finish the sentence, so Simon tries instead. 'Play the game?'

Kev shrugs. 'They were both getting secretive too. I tried to ask Rachel what was going on, but she didn't want me around. The two of them were close though, properly close. And they were into some weird stuff, the pair of them.'

'What do you mean?'

Shona puts her hand on Kev's leg and he doesn't say any more.

'Are you reopening their case?' she says.

'Kevin,' Simon tries again, 'what do you mean, weird stuff?'

'Look, they were getting seriously into drugs, alright? I mean, we all…you know what it's like. But they were on a different level. That's what I reckon, anyway.'

This is it, this is why Simon's here. But Kev's looking at Shona and she's refusing to look back at him. Something changes in the light coming in through the curtains, the colour shifts from white to something softer, almost golden.

'I saw them once,' Shona says, and the tone of her voice makes Simon wonder if she's been waiting for him to ask, if she was needing to say it. 'They were dancing out by the standing stone in the middle of a storm. Spinning round in circles with their arms wide, reaching up for something like they were crazy. They weren't in their right minds, towards the end. Rachel's mam had died, see. She was that cut up about it.'

Simon frowns, like there's something worse than the light making him squint.

'But she'd always been a bit weird.' Kevin again, not wanting to be left behind. 'She tried to rope us into some nonsense about summoning spirits one time.'

'You mean like Ouija boards and that?'

'Nah, more like graveyards and chanting. She was always hanging about at the church ruin. When I asked her what the fuck she was doing, she said she wanted to know the true world. They were off their heads, the pair of them.'

'And Lee and Aaron were getting the same way?'

'Fuck no, nothing like.'

'But then…do you know what Rachel and Pauly were taking?'

'No clue, mate.'

He looks at Shona and she shakes her head sadly. There's something tugging at Simon's mind though, something Shona said.

Something Frazer's witness claims to have seen decades ago. It wasn't only Abigail Moss she saw in the woods that night. He'd always thought Rachel and Pauly's death had something to do with drugs, but maybe there's a different connection he should be following.

THE DIFFERENT WAYS OF BEING ABANDONED

Everything Uncle Walt had is strewn on the floor, room after small, square room, and Trish is in the middle of it all. She couldn't bring herself to sit in his old comfy chair, she never could, not since she was a little girl and she'd climb up onto his knee, cuddle into him and glance at her mam like it was a victory. No, she's sitting at the kitchen table where all the files, letters and bills she's found are haphazardly piled. Uncle Walt wasn't one for order, not of the filing-his-tax-returns kind, not of keeping a record of his pension or his doctor's visits or...what is it she's looking for?

She's not been able to sleep much since the funeral. Lying awake every night in Uncle Walt's house, in the room that was her room as a kid, she feels the emptiness of it dragging her down and she understands how her mam must have felt, lying on the sofa for hours, staring at nothing. She never understood why someone would do that before, but she understands now.

The white light coming in through the dirty window is dappling the small square table beneath the small square window in the small square room. It's one of the old cottages, Uncle Walt's – hers now, it's all hers now, she's the only one left – thick stone walls and low doors, something heavy about it, barely masked by the plants on every surface, in every corner. Uncle Walt loved his plants. Trish hasn't a clue what to do with them. She'd probably kill them if she tried and they're looking bad enough as it is, droopy, brown and lethargic. There's a succulent in the living room dropping whole branches off itself, if branch is the word for the strings of fleshy leaves it's made of. It used to flower every Christmas, that one, bright red flowers bursting from the tips, cascading like water from a fountain. Now it has the plant version of leprosy.

What is it he's not telling her? Uncle Walt, her Uncle Walt. It can't really have been a heart attack, can it? But everyone's telling her so. His big heart giving in after all that love he showed her when she had no one else; enough love to compensate for a whole family. Then she sees it again: Uncle Walt clasping at his throat, pain shooting through his body as Ricky Barr stands above him.

They say it was a heart attack. But heart attacks can be provoked.

She presses the heels of her hands into her eyes. What is she doing? What is she *going* to do? How's she even going to earn money? She needs to think.

But the soil is still fresh above him, there in the new graveyard where he's buried. Her Uncle Walt. It's been less than a week but sometimes it feels like a year, sometimes an hour. She asked for him to be buried in the graveyard of the old church ruin, he'd have liked that, but there was no space. Apparently they'd closed it for burials last year. She hadn't known that. Turns out there was a lot Trish hadn't known.

When her mam disappeared – died, she tells herself sternly – she was too young to manage anything. It all fell to Uncle Walt. It all went to him, too, everything her mam had. It wasn't much, but there must have been a day like this, Uncle Walt going through her mam's things. Finding something in her mam's things. Is that what she's hoping for? Old photos, her birth certificate maybe, an old dress of her mam's, a diary, explaining? But there's nothing. No photo albums she's been able to find, nothing about when her mam died. Just the weight of knowing her Uncle Walt is gone too.

Georgie was at the funeral. They all were. Simon had given Trish a hug but when Georgie tried to do the same, Trish stepped away.

'I'm so sorry—' Georgie started.

'Why did you have to question him like that?'

Georgie was shocked, she could see that, but Trish had resigned. She didn't have to be DC Mackie any more; she'd never be DC Mackie again.

'You scared him!'

'I was doing my job, Trish.' Georgie's voice was gentle, but Trish didn't want to hear it.

'You kept suspecting him and upsetting him and he wasn't in his right mind, was he? If you hadn't kept pushing, he wouldn't have run away from the care home to confront Ricky and he'd still be—'

She'd stopped short of saying he'd still be alive, but it was true. Sometimes she thinks it was true. And what was Uncle Walt guilty of, really? He'd killed a dog forty years ago. Trish isn't proud of it, but at the end of the day it was only a dog. Uncle Walt had believed that a sacrifice would summon the ancestors, the Others, to save the village. Trish doesn't believe it, of course, but Uncle Walt had. Natalie did, too, and that was why she'd copied him by sacrificing Ricky's horse two weeks ago. Would she have still done it without Uncle Walt's help? Yes. Did Uncle Walt help her? Trish presses her fists into her eyes again, but she knows: yes, he did. Was that why Georgie blamed him?

But it wasn't Georgie who'd watched as Uncle Walt died. It was Ricky Barr. He was there, watching. Then he'd *dared* to come to the funeral and she'd not been able to stop him and when Trish had got back here, to Uncle Walt's house afterwards, that carved wooden face still sitting in the window was glaring at her. The vines threaded through the eyes and mouth were a vivid green and she thought for a second it had been a furious self-portrait, that Uncle Walt knew he'd be gone and wanted to leave his image staring out at the village. Judging her for not protecting him. Then something in her snapped and she rushed inside, pulled the carved face from the windowsill and threw it in the kitchen bin. There was no bag inside. He must have emptied the bins before going to the care home. Still, that's where she left the wooden face he'd carved with his own hands, the trails of vines twisting around the back of it, and she let the lid swing shut and hasn't been near it since.

There's someone here, though. Outside. Beyond the metal lines running through the leaded window, fracturing the street beyond: a shadow moving. A person. Georgie's here, at her house, come to see her, but for what? Then the shadow moves and it's not Georgie at all, it's a different face beyond the glass. Andy Barr is looking in at her, his expression all concern and nervousness and he's pointing as if to say *Do you want me to come in, or do you want me to go away?* She invites him in with a flick of her head and he gets it, heads to the door and pushes it open slowly.

'Trish?' he says, stooping to get inside – the door frames are low in these old houses and Andy's lanky as can be. 'Trish?'

'Come and sit down, Andy.'

Trish realises that's the first time she's spoken this morning, and her voice feels awkward in her throat.

Andy stands and looks at her as though he wants to give her a hug, then folds himself into the kitchen chair. He's carried a flask in with him, seems to be trying to balance it on his knee before giving up and placing it on the table. Christ, she'd have made him a cup of coffee. Mind you, she's not sure there's any milk. Or coffee.

'Are you alright, Trish?' he says, then thinks better of it, scratches at his cheek. 'I mean. Not alright, but you know.'

Trish nods. 'I've got to sort all this out,' she says, realising she's sorted nothing, emptied cupboards and drawers and found only out-of-date tins of tuna, dusty cassette tapes of folk music that hadn't been played in years – he'd nothing to play them on – bills and demands for payment, his old clothes, his name stitched into the back of every shirt in case he went a wander. She had tried to keep him safe. She'd tried.

'The thing is, Trish…' Andy clears his throat. His eyes look fresh and alert, unlike hers. 'The thing is…' His voice trailing off, his hands anxiously folding around the flask then releasing again.

'What is it, Andy?'

'This morning, well last night really, I don't know if you've heard but there was a thing and I was the one that called the ambulance see, and I've been waiting but—'

This morning, last night, in that shimmering space between night and dawn, Trish had been at Uncle Walt's graveside. There were shapes hanging from tree branches and shadows moving beyond the gates and she'd known that there was something wrong in the way he died, that she couldn't let it go; she mustn't let it go. She has a sudden urge to take the carved face back out of the bin.

'—so I thought maybe I should come to you, 'cause I can trust you, right, and no one else came to see me but I've got something, see?'

'What are you talking about, Andy?'

He startles and she remembers how he used to cringe away from his dad, how afraid he was. Trish doesn't know exactly what Ricky has done to him over the years, but Ricky is a bully of a man and that she knows with no doubt.

'We were all in the caravan. Me and Lee and Aaron and Penny-Ann and Terry and the new girl, Julie, and her and Penny-Ann are like, at it—'

'Andy, can you start from the beginning? I'm going to need some help here. What were you doing in the caravan?' Then it dawns on her that these kids, Andy too, are taking whatever it is Ricky's dealing through the village and on up the coast—

'Lee had a reaction to it, that's what I'm saying, a bad one and I thought he was dying, so that's why I called them.'

'Wait, Andy, what did you take?'

'No,' he says, shaking his head. 'Not me, that's what I'm saying. It looked disgusting. It were something new, they were all excited see so I faked it and I thought, I'll see what happens here and then I'll talk to Trish.'

'And you got this from your da?'

'Nah, Aaron was passing it round and none of us know where he gets it from, well, maybe Lee but maybe not and I don't know if the hospital called Georgie but—'

'They must have called her,' Trish says, because when she couldn't take kneeling by Uncle Walt's grave any more, she'd seen Georgie on her way home. Driving towards the village at first light, with DS Frazer in the car beside her. They must have been on their way back from the hospital. They didn't see her, and that was how she'd wanted it. It wasn't only Georgie she couldn't face; it was Frazer too. The way he'd looked at her when she handed in her notice. He'd come out of the station after her, calling her name, not DC Mackie as usual, but Trish, Trish please.

'Please what?' she snapped, for once not caring what he saw in her face.

'Let me explain. I—'

'No,' she interrupted. 'I don't want to hear about it right now.'

Even as she walked away, he was still trying to be kind to her, in that way he has, the formality mixed with pity that makes her want to scream.

'I'm here,' he was saying. 'Trish, if you need...'

What she needs is not to need anyone at all.

But there *was* something wrong in the way Uncle Walt died. She knows it as well as she knows this coast. Her Uncle Walt dying there on Ricky Barr's land with Ricky Barr watching. She's on her feet, walking to the bin, lifting the lid.

'What the fuck is that?'

'Uncle Walt carved it,' she says, placing it on the table beside Andy's flask.

Uncle Walt who died on Ricky Barr's land and now there's kids in the hospital from something they took in Ricky Barr's caravan, something she suspects came from Ricky Barr himself and so what she needs, it turns out, is exactly what Andy is offering her right now.

'Right,' Georgie says, back in her office at last, away from the hospital, away from her empty home, with a mug of coffee in her hands. 'We need to get this all straight. We have three...'

She glances at Simon and he offers, 'and counting?'

'Three cases that may or may not be linked. Three cases and counting.' She manages a smile, and Simon gives her one back. They're short-staffed for this, with Trish gone. She feels another spike of loss. Trish is so angry with her; she's not sure anyone has been so angry with her, except perhaps her father in the weeks after Errol died. Or Fergus?

No, Fergus isn't angry, Fergus is feeling something else. She just wished she knew what.

'Georgie?'

She nods, puts her coffee down and picks up the marker pen. Pulls off the lid then pushes it back on. She's asked for Suze back from the Crackenbridge station, an extra pair of hands to help out, a temporary transfer for the week, maybe a couple. Well, a couple of weeks is all any of them have, with the station closure looming. She takes a deep breath before she speaks.

'First, we have Lee Prowle and the others, taking something that put them in the hospital last night.'

Behind her on the whiteboard she has three columns, each with a title, one in black, one in blue, one in red.

'They got it from Aaron Prowle who is, predictably, refusing to say where he got it from, despite it nearly killing his kid brother. We're waiting on toxicology and forensics from Cal. They were in one of Ricky Barr's caravans at the time, and they're all still in the hospital, where they'll be kept for the morning at least. Except for Andy Barr, who was there but not partaking, and who called the police. So *this* is today's case. The new one.'

She points to the whiteboard, to the column written in black.

'Everyone who was there is being uncooperative, so far. The new girl, Julie Alperstein, persuaded them not to talk to the police and has accused DS Frazer of being a corporate city cop she can see right through.' She lets a smile flicker across her face.

Frazer grins at her.

'And speaking of DS Frazer...' She moves her finger to the blue column, to the name Abigail Moss. 'We have case number two. Frazer, an update?'

He stands, taking her place in front of the whiteboard, allowing Georgie to sit.

'I know I've been on this case for a couple of weeks now, but I think we're finally about to make some progress,' he says.

From her chair she can see out of the window to the sky that's gone white with heat, to the wet, glistening paving slabs stretching from the wall of the station out towards the lane of soggy grass that leads, eventually, to Ricky Barr's farm. That's where they found Sonny Riley, the little boy whose burial decades ago feels as raw to Georgie as though he'd been killed yesterday. She feels a child's hand on her knee and suddenly she can't move; a little girl's sore grey eyes are reflected in the window, staring at her, staring until Frazer clears his throat and the image vanishes. She needs to breathe.

'When Betty Marshall made her statement from the care home, she claimed to have witnessed a murder, out here, when she was a teenager in the 1960s. I've made copies of her full statement, and you've all got one on your desk.'

Georgie looks at her desk: it's true. It helps her focus, to take another breath. And it's efficient of him, seeing as their printer has been broken for months now. Has he paid for this from the print shop in Crackenbridge out of his own pocket?

'The pertinent points being—'

He holds up his hand to list them on his fingers and for the first time since meeting him at the start of the year Georgie wonders if he might be a little bit of an arse. She can see what might have got Julie Alperstein so defensive. She likes him though, despite it. He catches her eye and relaxes his shoulders a bit.

'On 24 June 1962, sometime during the night, Betty Marshall saw a group of people in the woods beyond the grounds of Wyndham Manor. They appeared to be dancing and chanting in a language she didn't recognise, and she believes she saw one of them – a young girl named Abigail Moss – lying on a stone slab and being killed. At least, Betty Marshall claims it looked like she was being killed. She says her eyes were rolling back in her head and there was blood on her neck as though her throat had been cut. She says she saw "at least" a dozen people circling Abigail—'

When he says 'at least' his fingers make neat quotation marks either side of his head.

'Though it might have been more than that. She would have been significantly outnumbered had she approached them.'

'But none of them saw her?'

'She was hiding in the bushes and scared enough to creep away while the sacrifice or whatever it was continued. She herself had taken LSD – along with many of the staff that night, which was the night of their midsummer party – and she tried to convince herself she'd hallucinated the whole thing.'

'But she went looking for Abigail Moss the next morning?'

'Yes, exactly. She clearly didn't believe it was a hallucination even then. Abigail's room had been cleared out and the house-keeper, Mrs Pettigrew, told her Abigail had left her job and wouldn't be coming back. Betty Marshall never saw Abigail Moss again. She has spent her life fearing she witnessed a murder but thinking no one would believe her.'

'And do we believe her?' Georgie says.

'I believe her,' Frazer replies. 'At least, I believe she saw *something*. The group, chanting, dancing in the middle of the night—'

'They could have taken LSD as well,' Georgie says. 'Betty was in the woods with a group of staff, and Abigail was staff too. Could it have been her friends she saw?'

Frazer holds out his hands. 'Could be. We don't know. She says she didn't see their faces. She was scared. She was high.'

'So,' Georgie says. 'Next steps.'

'Our best lead is the bench dedicated to Abigail Moss at the playground. I've spent the last week interviewing residents of Burrowhead and Warphill, but no one has even admitted to recognising the name.'

'Then we need a list of companies that supply benches and plaques,' Georgie says. 'Start with local places.'

'Yes, ma'am.'

'We need to know who dedicated a bench on the cliffs to our unknown Abigail Moss.' That's where Georgie was sitting, the first time she glimpsed the little girl with the matted hair, the pleading eyes. 'Then there's Abigail herself. There must be some records?'

'I'll keep looking.'

He looks a little deflated. Georgie knows he's found no sign of her anywhere, no birth certificate, no police reports, no missing person – no Abigail Moss.

'For as long as I can, ma'am.'

He means for as long as his boss will let him stay here. Georgie's the one being closed down; Frazer has a job waiting for him back at HQ. That tugging on her sleeve. She ignores it.

'And then we have a third line of—' Georgie pulls her hand away from her side, grasps it at the wrist. There's nothing there. It's just her skin, the heat in this office. 'Well, potentially a third case,' she says. 'Simon?'

It's Simon's turn to stand, though Frazer doesn't sit back down, and the two men end up facing Georgie together. They're both tall, both young, both fit. It's obvious enough in Simon, you couldn't miss the blue-eyed bulk of him, but it's there for Frazer too; under his suit and tie there's muscle and tone. She's not surprised Trish fell for him. But Trish is gone and Georgie's an odd one out again. No longer the only person of colour in the room, not now Frazer's here, but the only woman.

'Betty Marshall's description of the way the group of them were dancing,' Simon begins. 'Their heads back, eyes staring at the sky, arms out, the whole image of them is similar to something Shona Jones has described to me. She saw Rachel and Pauly doing the same thing. Before their suicides, long before you first stepped foot up here, DS Frazer, Shona saw Rachel and Pauly dancing around the standing stone, at midnight.'

'It resonates with what Betty Marshall described,' Frazer says.

'But without what she thought was a murder.'

'Followed instead, days later, by their suicide.'

'And that is why we're reopening Rachel and Pauly's case too,' Georgie says, standing at last, pointing to the third column on the white board. In red.

'We need to find out what really happened to them, before we...' Si glances at Georgie. 'Before we're closed down. I can't believe it was a suicide.'

'What we *know*,' Georgie corrects him, 'is their stomach contents from the night they died. Animal blood. So much it suggests they were drinking it.' She points at the list on the board. 'Plant-based materials, roots from some shrubs, tree bark. But no drugs, not as such, in Rachel and Pauly's systems—'

'Maybe not that night, but they'd been taking something, according to Kevin Taylor. Were they taking the same drug Lee Prowle and the others took last night?'

'We don't know,' Georgie says. 'Yet.'

'But for now,' says Frazer, 'we can perhaps connect Rachel and Pauly back to Betty Marshall and Abigail Moss, through what sounds like some kind of ritualistic behaviour – dancing around in the dead of night, chanting.' He pauses to look at Georgie. 'And there's something we haven't mentioned yet. The series of animal sacrifices that have been taking place in these villages for generations.'

'You mean Walt Mackie, Jack Helmsteading, Art Robertson and Nora Prowle killing Ricky Barr's dog decades ago,' Georgie says.

'And Natalie Prowle killing his horse two weeks ago.'

'The threefold death, she called it.'

'But the question is if, and how, that's related to our three cases,' Georgie says. 'And I'm not so sure about that.'

'You think it's unconnected?' Frazer says.

'I think we should put the animal sacrifices to one side, for now. Walt Mackie and his friends were killing animals with an ancient dagger, supposedly to summon their ancestors. In reality, it was to scare outsiders – to bully people they didn't like. But they weren't murdering anyone, and I certainly can't imagine them taking drugs and dancing around at midnight.'

'Ma'am.'

'What we need is the stomach contents analysis from Lee Prowle and the others. They weren't performing any kind of ritual, they were sat in a caravan getting high, and *they* are our current and priority case. Then we might be able to stop guessing and start connecting these crimes.'

She stands then, and they both watch her.

'One: The drugs. Lee and Aaron Prowle and whatever they are up to right now. Two: What, if anything, Betty Marshall witnessed sixty years ago, and how that connects to the missing girl, Abigail Moss. And three: What really happened to Rachel and Pauly last year. One. Two. Three.'

And four, Georgie thinks but doesn't say. Four: why can she feel that small hand wrapping around her index finger even now, even here in the office where it's perfectly clear there's no little girl at all.

LAST WEEK, AFTER THE FUNERAL

The new graveyard outside Burrowhead is a long, wide plot that was empty and used for nothing before becoming a graveyard. Most of it is still neatly mown grass. Georgie can feel the expanse of it, waiting, behind her, while past the wall is the potholed road to Warphill, and on the other side, beyond the overgrown scrub of gorse and thorned bramble, is the jagged line of the cliffs.

Georgie's hanging back from the graveside, after what Trish said to her. The way she'd glared at her with those piercing eyes of hers. The way she'd shouted.

You scared him!

Had she scared Walt Mackie? It had never been her intention, but he had seemed frail in that care home, lost and frightened, and she had asked questions.

If you hadn't kept pushing, he wouldn't have run away from the care home to confront Ricky and he'd still be—

Alive, that's what Trish had wanted to say. If it wasn't for Georgie, her Uncle Walt would still be alive.

The air's so still today, even here, there's no breeze from the sea to shift the heat. Georgie looks up and the sky seems white and vast above her. Simon's left already, but he did his best. It can't have been easy for him, another funeral after the year he's had. Everyone else is milling around, some placing flowers, some talking, most looking like they don't know what to do. There's no reception – Trish hadn't wanted that. Nowhere for the villagers to sit down for tea and sandwiches, to talk out of the sun, so they're whispering here in the new graveyard instead. Elise Robertson's over there with Terry from the garage. Some of the staff from the care home are clustered around the grave. It was good of them to come along. June and Whelan are here, brought some of their own roses to leave. And on the other side of the grave: Fergus.

He's wearing his suit, must be sweltering in that.

His hair looks dishevelled.

They'd arrived separately. But they'd both arrived alone.

Everyone knows he's moved out. Everyone's watching them. Georgie hadn't meant to look at him, but she must have because now he's giving an uncomfortable half-wave and turning away, walking towards Trish, who's over there with Pamali, giving her a hug.

Georgie thinks maybe she needs to leave. Trish doesn't want her here. She told her as much. Georgie only came here to help Trish, to support Trish; she'd thought she might be able to do that, but she shouldn't have come. Trish has other people to look out for her. Besides, you can't help people who don't want to be helped.

Uncle Walt's grave is the first in a new row, but they've put it right in the middle and Georgie doesn't know why. Nothing but grass either side, the long stretch of it carved by the brown soil of his single plot. He's got a tall, upright, rectangular gravestone, simple but solid, and she thinks he'd have liked that at least. There's a tree in the corner that's been there far longer than the graveyard, a wide scraggly oak, branches twisting and weighed down with leaves. Mrs Dover and Mrs Smyth are standing under there for a bit of shade away from the crowd. And Georgie can hear the waves, even on a day so still as this: Walt will always be near the sea, he'll always be able to hear the waves.

Though a voice is carrying over them now.

As she listens, a car arrives in the car park out front but it's Fergus's words she's focused on. He's trying to defend her.

'She never would have meant that.'

Oh God, he's trying to defend her to Trish and Trish pushes him away with a shove to the shoulders and Fergus almost stumbles back with the shock of it. Then Trish is storming away towards the car park where Natalie Prowle has just pulled up and Cal is watching it all unfold and that's it then. Georgie standing alone all the way over here as Cal deliberately makes his way towards her. Fergus beyond the row of older graves, waiting for Natalie Prowle to collect him. And Trish walking away from them both, from them all, leaving them separated by the freshly dug earth of Walt Mackie's grave.

A FEW YEARS BACK, IN A
DIFFERENT GRAVEYARD

Rachel knows things look different, hereabouts, after dark. It's not something the adults of the village speak of, but the kids know it, the teenagers, the ones who grew up here. Rachel knows it in the same way she knows her mam is her mam, her own face is her face. She's felt it calling to her, the old ruin where she sits on her own, after school, running her fingers over the weathered names on the gravestones. She brings flowers with her, wildflowers that she picks on the walk over, bluebells or daffodils, sprigs of holly, the ruffled purple heads of wild rhododendron, and places them on a different grave each time. She wants the recipient to feel special, to know they are the only one, that day. Everyone needs to feel special sometimes. And at night, she's seen their petals catch the silver moonlight. At night, the walls have not tumbled to the ground but have grown, from buried stones to majestic archways that invite her in. She's been here many nights on her own, but tonight she is not alone. Tonight she needs more power than she has on her own; she needs a circle of the living.

She asked Shona first, because she knew she'd come even if it was for the wrong reasons – Shona likes to break the rules, though the truth is she and Rachel always recognised different sets of rules in the first place. Shona's come with some weed, a flask of peach schnapps and lemonade she nicked from her parents' drinks cabinet, and Kevin Taylor. Andy and Lee make it five, though with the smart-arse jokes they've been telling on the way over she's starting to regret inviting them already. For the sixth, she's got Pauly. He's the only one who truly believes in what she's doing. He's afraid.

It's warm, for an autumn night, the harvest moon coinciding with the alignment of three planets, and as she steps over the crumbled stones in the entrance to the old church, the moon is bisected by two entangled branches that grow from the single hawthorn tree beyond the ruins. In the graveyard, there are cherry trees and birch trees, an apple tree that never produces fruit, but the only hawthorn is through the pillars where arched windows must once have been, and Rachel chooses her seat so that she can see both the tree and the moon. The others are standing about, hands in pockets. Shona's lighting a cigarette, Lee asking to bum one, Andy leaning against the remnants of a pew that's too low for him – he tries too hard, Andy, makes him seem younger than the rest of them, and Rachel feels a pang of sympathy watching him. But they're no use to her standing around like that.

'Sit down,' she says, her voice resonating between the collapsed walls, and it's not until she's spoken that she realises the others were all whispering, and that maybe this place has power over them, too.

'What, on the ground?' Lee scuffs his boot into the mud – no grass grows in here, it never has, though there's no roof any more.

'Yes, on the ground.'

Somehow she can command them, even though she's sitting already, her long skirt sinking in the mud, her hair tangling around her face. One by one they sit down, instinctively forming a circle of six inside the church ruin at the approach to midnight.

Pauly's eyes. She's not going to forget them in a hurry.

He never says much about his parents, but she knows they're believers – the kind of believers who want to save him and don't care how much they hurt him in the process. Rachel doesn't believe in their devil or their God, though Pauly might; it can be hard to rid yourself of something forced into you when you're too young to fight back. He does fight back though, in his way, running from them every chance he gets, hiding in the woods, in the cave in the cliffs, stealing food when he has to, eventually getting dragged home by the police or his parents themselves, only to run again. He'll have climbed out of his window to be here, they'd never have let him out, though the same is probably true of Andy and he's got his own demons to deal with, so maybe they all need this. Maybe they are the right six people, in the right place, on the right night.

For Rachel's part, she told her mam exactly where she was going and her mam gave her blessing. Rachel is struck by how rare that is as she pulls six tall white candles from her bag.

In the centre of their circle she places a frayed square of purple silk, and she lays the candles on it before lifting the first one and passing it to her left. Shona takes it then passes it to Kev, who thrusts it at Andy, who holds it out to Lee – it's as though none of them are willing to claim it yet – until it reaches Pauly. He holds it in both hands before pushing the end deep into the ground and looking at Rachel with that intense gaze of his, and she's glad of the darkness for hiding the reddening of her face. She breathes deeply, finding coolness in the air, the sea breeze travelling in from the waves they can hear from where they sit. She passes round the next candle, and the next, until there are six candles in the ground, and she lights her own and nods at the others to do the same.

None of them speak.

Their ancestors had their own language once. Something like Gaelic, or Welsh, but also entirely unlike any other. It's been forgotten except for fragments lingering in the strange lines of folk songs her grandma used to sing, in untranslatable words muttered for protection by old people afraid of what the village has become. Rachel has added her own words, too, words that came to her when she was a child, a secret language that whispered when she played barefoot on the beach, trying to catch the tiny black fish that darted through the rock pools. So when she starts to speak, her voice melodic and pure, she works hard to bury her fear that the others will laugh at her. They don't, though – perhaps because the wind dies, leaving the silence of no waves crashing, like the sea itself is holding its breath – and her words flow as naturally as if they were her own language, an ancient summons to the dead.

She has tried calling them before, but never like this. Never on a night of the harvest moon with six souls and six candles, never when she could feel every hair on her arms prickle with static. The flickering flames cast Shona's features in amber, shimmering in the candlelight; Andy's skinny shoulders are hunched, carved inwards like a rock eroded by the sea. Then there's Pauly, eyes glowing in the dark, his breathing heavy. Each inhale sounds like a struggle, and when she looks closer she can see he's shaking, his body shuddering with effort. His lips are moving but she can't hear any sound. All she can hear is her own voice chanting until Pauly clasps his hand around his candle's flame and whispers at her, 'Stop, stop, not like this, stop—'

Lee suddenly kicks his own candle in the mud and gives that sharp laugh of his.

'Talk about killing the fucking mood,' he says. 'Freak.'

Pauly is still whispering: 'Not here, please, not like this, stop, they're—'

'I need a fag,' Lee says. 'Fuck. Andy?'

Andy unwraps himself from his crunched position on the ground and stands, locates a crumpled packet of cigarettes in his pocket, and the circle is broken. Rachel's words are gone and the others are themselves again, even Shona, flicking her hair over her shoulder in that way she has. But as Rachel reaches over to take Pauly's hand, he clasps onto her like there is nothing but her grip keeping him alive.

LOOKING BEYOND
WHAT YOU CAN SEE

Shona wakes, again, with Kevin's arm lying across her hips, his face pressed against the back of her neck. Her own bare legs are curled away from him to the air beyond the tangled covers. It's roasting in here but she daren't open a window – the insects fly in to escape the drenching rain and they'll be everywhere, in her hair, under her clothes. She's never managed to sleep a full night even on her own in one of these caravan beds, let alone with Kev beside her. Whatever keeps her awake doesn't bother him, though. He sleeps deep as can be, his body wrapped around hers. Even this morning, after what Simon was asking, what happened in the night, he's sleeping soundly.

When the ambulance left they'd stayed up for a while, talking in whispers – Andy and Ricky were sat outside, they'd seen them from the window and been seen in return. Ricky doesn't seem to mind Shona staying here, in Kev's caravan, even though she quit her summer job. Kevin's still working for him till the end of the season, so he still gets the living quarters, and Shona's his guest these days, when she's not back at her mam's writing for the paper. Her article about Sonny Riley and his hidden burial got more clicks than anything in their website's history – it was even quoted nationally in a couple of newspapers. She wrote it sensitively; she feels a connection to that little boy. The local paper is small-time, though. Shona wants something bigger.

Last night she was at the community council meeting. Trish Mackie's first meeting as chair. Shona preferred it when Natalie Prowle was in charge, but Natalie got herself arrested for killing Ricky's horse and even though she's out, awaiting trial, she's lost something far as the villagers are concerned. Not that they care about Ricky's horse. But Natalie was never supposed to get caught. And so what if she's taken the fall for the rest of them? They're so dismissive of her now Shona almost feels sorry for her.

Feeling sorry for Natalie Prowle; what the fuck next.

Trish Mackie though, Shona didn't see that coming. Trish Mackie has a streak of anger running through her that made Shona anxious at the meeting, made her sit that bit straighter, focus on every word. It's not that she thinks Trish is dangerous, though what exactly it is she can't put her finger on.

'Shona?'

Kev's waking up slowly, the way he does. He's affectionate before he's awake enough to put on his act. It's there even when he's with Shona, most of the time, but she loves him in these few minutes before the Kevin Taylor that everyone else knows appears. He stretches out his legs, his back.

'What's that yoga thing you do?'

'What's wrong?'

'My back. It's these beds I reckon. Show me...' Though as he's saying that he's nuzzling into her neck, his breath warm and sweet and his hand moving up underneath her vest top.

'You'll have to give me some space if you want yoga,' she says, a smile in her voice, and he obediently rolls over onto his back and watches intently as she shows him. There's admiration in his eyes; no one ever did look at Shona quite the way Kev does in the minutes after he wakes.

'One foot over the other knee first,' she tells him, 'then reach around your thigh.'

He copies her movements, the two of them just about fitting side by side on their backs on Ricky Barr's caravan's bed.

'Now pull your knee up to your chest and hold the stretch.'

'Damn, that's good—'

Shona can't help it: she lets the laughter in, feels light and free at first, then selfish after everything that's happened, and it dies away fast as it arrived. Kev's still holding the pose and she remembers that fight Aaron and Lee had the other day. The way the two of them ended up on the ground so punched out they looked like a tangle of limbs. She purses her lips, sits up and pulls her arms away from Kev.

'I think I need to attend a class,' he says, after a minute. 'Take this yoga serious, am I right?'

'Well, my mam's starting her course again after the summer,' Shona says. 'You'd be the only man, mind.'

'Doesn't bother me.'

But as he says it he releases the pose and straightens out his legs and they both know that whether it bothers him or not is not the point. Kevin Taylor can't be seen going to yoga, Kevin Taylor can only be seen smoking and drinking, fighting down the pub, chatting to Lee, voices hushed, working for Ricky on the farm. Kevin Taylor can't do anything that might make any of them suspicious, not if he's going to get Aaron's contact – Aaron's just taking orders, Aaron's a nobody – and get a meeting with whoever's supplying. Whoever it was supplied Pauly and Rachel last year. Whoever it is Aaron's so fucking afraid of.

At the community council meeting last night Trish Mackie was talking about Ricky Barr like it was a done deal. Ricky Barr is the one supplying the drugs, the one killing these villages, Trish is sure of it. Shona's sure of no such thing. Then there's the way Fergus Strachan arrived at the meeting again, with his own key, the one Natalie gave him. He didn't say much this time – none of the usual nervous laughter and apologies and chit-chat you'd expect from the old Fergus Strachan, the one who hadn't walked out on his wife. But he *has* walked out on his wife. He's walked out on Georgie and everyone knows it, and he was sat at the back of the community council meeting and all the while, as Trish talked about Ricky Barr and the drugs moving up the coast and how she's going to save the villages, Shona could feel his presence like an itch on the back of her neck.

'What is it, Shona?' Kev says.

'I think…' She glances at him. 'We must have missed something.'

'You mean Rachel and Pauly?'

The trouble is, she doesn't know – and this is what's been eating away at her since Simon was here – she doesn't know what it was that made Rachel and Pauly do what they did. Maybe it was drugs. Maybe it was something else. Someone else. She's been chasing the answer since last year, watching Ricky, watching Aaron, watching and waiting, but she's got nothing.

'I think we need to go back to the start.'

She hears Kev shift on the bed beside her. 'Back to the church ruin?'

'No,' Shona says. 'I want to go to the place where they died.'

'To the cliffs, then?'

Shona shakes her head again. 'To the beach.'

'We tried. There's nothing down there.'

She shakes her head. 'Then I need to try again. Look, Kev…' She rests her hand against his chin. 'You've heard the stories about the cave, haven't you? Rachel used to tell them, and she believed in them.'

'Okay.' Kev shrugs. 'Can I come with you?'

'Course you can.'

He grins, pushes himself up. 'Right then, let's go.'

'No, not now,' she says. 'Tonight. After dark.'

Her hand has left his face and the sun must have gone behind a cloud or something because the heat has dimmed and there's a breeze coming under the door.

'What is it you think we're going to find, Shona?'

'I don't know,' she says. 'I just need to stand where they fell.'

ON THE OTHER SIDE
OF THE ROAD

Fergus is not someone who struggles to get out of bed; he likes to get up fast and meet the morning with a smile, a clap of the hands even. Who knows what a new day might bring? The sun streaming in the window, warming his face the way it does. Yes, Fergus is someone who likes to have a gaze at the sky, appreciate the beauty of it first thing, and it's so beautiful out here, one of the reasons they moved here, him and—

Then it hits him again.

Every morning. Every single one.

He's not at home. He's not in their bed, he can't turn over and find Georgie there, waiting for him to roll into a hug. It's all gone. He doesn't even know if he's done the right thing, only knows he can't go back now he's left. Something's holding him here. Though Fergus isn't one to believe in invisible forces, well, except the invisible forces of physics, the way electromagnetism can attract or repel, the pull of gravity. Gravity then, he'll go with that. The gravity that held him to Georgie is holding him here now instead – and it does feel like a weight, a mass he's not strong enough to move beyond. He's heard people say he and Natalie are having an affair but that's not it, of course not. Natalie's his friend, that's all, how could she ever be anything more when Georgie... He could never hurt Georgie. He just has this unshakable feeling that she doesn't love him any more. What she said, what she accused him of. He can barely find the energy to move his legs out of the bed, to push himself up into a sitting position. It's a physical pain, this missing of Georgie, this doubt.

But Fergus has so much to be grateful for. Friends, when he needed them. He hadn't really known who his friends were before. Natalie, offering him a room in her home, despite everything she's going through with her arrest, a trial on the horizon. He thinks about how she could have done it, sometimes. How she could have killed that horse, an innocent creature; Fergus could never have done that. But it wasn't only Natalie, was it, there was a group of them, and Natalie is taking the blame because that's what Natalie does. Like how she takes the blame for her boys going off the rails, sees it as her job to find the people responsible and hold them to account; to save her boys. He's told her they're grown men, more or less, and you can't save someone who doesn't want to be saved, but she'll never stop trying. From the way she touches the urn of her Aunt Nora's ashes every morning, Fergus knows she can't stop trying to save the people she loves any more than she can stop remembering those who are gone. Folk are complicated, that's what Fergus thinks, and there's always good to be found in them if you look right.

That's better now, he's out of bed. Letting his knees click, his back – he's still sore from the excavation even after a week of rest. Natalie's orders. And despite the deep crunch in his gut of missing Georgie there is a reason to get up, to face another day. The university have sent back his iron figurine.

He showed Natalie as soon as he opened it up. Well, he returned it to Natalie. It was never really his to keep. She wanted to know what they'd found out, but all they'd told him was that it was genuine, after all, from the Iron Age, even though it was Natalie who'd recently reburied it in the motte. Now she can put it back where she found it – down in the basement of the museum along with all the boxes folk have donated over the years. Although this morning it's still sitting on the desk by the window and Fergus looks at it, takes a moment to imagine everything it's seen. Beneath the bodies buried in the motte, the archaeologists found an ancient stone with etchings similar to the menhir, but broken, shattered into pieces. It could have been a sort of signpost, like the cup and ring and the standing stone itself. It means the motte had been something else, before it was a motte, and before it was a grave.

Then there's the henge, he's going to discover the henge soon: a broad, circular, banked ditch around some kind of monument – could it be an actual stone circle, buried somewhere for him to find? Is that what all the stones are pointing to? The standing stone outside Warphill, the woodland stone of the cup and ring, and the smashed stone buried in the motte. They're pointing to something and he's going to follow their lead all the way to Burrowhead and there, somewhere, is the ancient henge. In the village, or on the edge of the village, or beyond—

There's a knock on his door.

That'll be Natalie with his cuppa now. She brings him one in every morning, says it's nice to be useful again, been years since her boys appreciated a cup of tea in the morning. He's staying in Aaron's room, while Aaron is away working for Ricky Barr. There are no band posters or anything like that, though. Fergus doesn't know what a teenage boy's room would look like really, these days, but he'd not have expected the clean white walls, the duck-egg blue curtains, the freshness of it all. He wonders if Natalie needs to see a smiling face when she walks into this room; if she needs him to be here as much as he needs somewhere to be. It's a comfort, helps him not to feel like a burden. But he needs to work out what he's going to do. For now, he's back on the tills, afternoon shift, and he's trying to sleep through the nights and get his head straight.

Then he sees Natalie's face, her eyes.

'Milk and two,' she says, hand shaking as she places his cup on the bedside table. Something's wrong.

'Natalie, what is it?'

'You've not heard?'

From the way she looks at him he realises it's late, it's coffee she's brought. He looks at his watch, flushes with shame. It's gone half eleven.

'Heard what?'

He's sitting on the bed wearing his green squirrel T-shirt – faded and marked around the armpits, tight round the middle – and pyjama bottoms, and it feels so painfully inappropriate.

'Lee... Lee's in the hospital.'

'Why?'

'They say he overdosed.'

'Oh God, on what?'

She's shaking her head, though he's not sure if that's because she doesn't have an answer or doesn't want any more questions.

'I had to collect some things but I'm going back to the hospital now.'

'So you've seen him? He's okay—?'

'You have to fend for yourself today.'

'No, wait, I'll come with you.'

'No, Fergus.'

'But Natalie—' She's gone though, closed the door behind her and left him there on his own with a coffee and a feeling of utter uselessness.

Of course he can fend for himself. He wants to help, that's all. Is it serious? Her son's in the hospital, it must be serious. He walks over to the window and there she is, getting into her car, driving away without so much as a glance back up at him and he just stays there, useless Fergus, and imagines what Georgie must be doing this morning, if she was the one who called Natalie. He's standing there staring out of the window when old Bessie Wilkie waves up at him from over the road. The tarmac has turned a reflective black in the heat and the rain, deep puddles gathering where potholes have been inadequately filled with gravel. He is suddenly struck by the ugliness of the rain-soaked pebbledash of Bessie's house opposite.

No. He's not going to start thinking like that.

These houses have character. Yes, they're blocky and plain, but still, there's character. Look at the roses in Natalie's front garden, so red and vibrant everyone comments on them. When they're not commenting on the other things: on Natalie and how she's sick with worry for her boys – it's convenient, to blame the dead horse on someone like her – and him, everyone talking about him, how he left Georgie. It's more complicated than that, though, isn't it? It's always more complicated.

Then he sees DS Frazer striding along.

A few weeks ago Fergus would have pushed open the window to call out a hello. He doesn't do that today. What is Frazer doing here, in Warphill, again? He's always around, these past couple of weeks, knocking on doors or walking the streets with that purposeful stride of his. Fergus doesn't know why it's getting his back up. He likes DS Frazer, always did, but it's starting to feel like he's testing them or something, asking his questions over and over, waiting for someone to slip up. He's with Georgie sometimes. Fergus was ashamed of how ill it made him feel to see them – they're just colleagues, after all, and he's not a jealous person, he doesn't want to be that man. He should wave. He's got nothing to hide, has he? But as he raises his hand it knocks into the iron figurine, which topples sideways, and his marriage is no one's business anyway and suddenly he's looking up and down the street to see a glimpse of Georgie's face.

She's not here though. It's DS Frazer on his own and whatever he was doing he seems to have finished doing it. He glances up at the window and Fergus steps back, stays out of sight until he hears the slam of a car door and looks out again to see DS Frazer driving back towards Burrowhead. Fergus feels like his legs might collapse. He has to sit back down on the bed and put his head between his knees for a minute. Then he straightens himself up and feels that kick to his stomach again, that lurch of missing Georgie so badly that if she were here now he'd beg her to take him back. He'd fall on his knees if that would help. He'd tell her that he loves her and he's never going to stop.

WORDS AND NOT SAYING THEM, PART ONE

Frazer is not one hundred percent sure, but it seems fairly likely that he just saw Fergus Strachan hiding from him in Natalie Prowle's top room.

Poor Georgie. She's covering it well but he can tell how upset she is. It's like the thing that was rooting her to the goodness in the world has frayed and broken. Mind you, Frazer would not have chosen Fergus Strachan to hold a rope or to be one. He always seemed a little too oblivious. There's a line between looking on the bright side and burying your head in the sand and he was never sure Fergus was on the right side of it.

Here's Burrowhead now. Strange how the miles between here and Warphill always seem to vanish in a haze of not quite feeling himself, not quite being able to focus on the road in front of him through the spitting rain. He should tell Georgie he saw Fergus in Warphill. Or should he? Maybe not. She's got enough to be worrying about, with her station closing. And she was out with Cal the other night, apparently. He wouldn't want to interfere. Besides, she's effectively his boss, with him posted here for the case, and DS Frazer is not someone who'd bring his personal life into work. He knows what it's like to have someone remind you of it when you're doing all you can to focus on the task at hand. Simon's been a support though, since he realised the truth about

Frazer's wife. He understands the grief, the way it ages you. Makes it impossible to see the innocence in things.

PC Hunter, not Simon.

Frazer's not sure how it's happened, but he seems to have slipped into using everyone's first names out here and he's not sure he likes the habit. Best to keep himself separate from Burrowhead police and the locals, if he can; remember why he's here.

How is it that Trish Mackie literally appears every time he's managed not to think about her? But there she is, sitting in the rain on the edge of the fountain in Burrowhead village square – if you could call that overgrown patch of weeds a square – and looking for all the world like she's running her hand through the non-existent water in the basin.

Trish Mackie. Seeing her is like a shock of static every time. Leaves his pulse beating that bit too fast, his neck feeling hot. God but he's tried to forget that kiss. When she resigned from the police she seemed furious with Georgie, with all of them, for her Uncle Walt's passing away. A heart attack like that, scrambling for breath in the middle of the night in an excavated grave – no wonder she's in a mess. No one wanted that to happen. He's pulled to a stop outside Spar and he's sitting in the car because he wants to see Trish for a minute, peaceful like this.

He's here to interview Mrs Dover again. She's probably watching him through the window from behind those net curtains of hers. In the city he'd go striding up to her door right now. In the city there's no Trish Mackie though, is there.

As soon as they lock eyes he feels it. His legs have a mind of their own, they're taking him out of the car and leading him over to where she's sitting, to where she doesn't get up. He smiles, looks down, looks away. She's soaking, her clothes and her hair. He holds out his umbrella then feels like an arse for carrying it. She's watching him all the while, that strange smile on her face, like she knows something about him, like she can see right through him. Maybe she can.

'Trish,' he says.

'Just Trish now.' She smiles at him and he has absolutely no idea what it means; that she's pleased to no longer be DC Mackie, that she's glad he called her Trish, or that she's laughing at him? She always did find his formality annoying, was that it? Oh, not this again, not this constant second guessing and flustering and—

'Are you going to sit down, DS Frazer?'

'Daniel,' he says.

'Daniel.'

'Or...Dan.'

He resists the urge to wipe down the fountain, to find a plastic bag or something to sit on, and the stone is cool. Her face is gleaming in the rain. She's got freckles and he's sure she didn't have them before, just beyond-pale skin and that spiky hair of hers. She doesn't look anything like a police officer now, in her soaking vest top and jeans, her tattoos visible along her arms: bees on one side, flying between her wrist and elbow, an elegant twist of gorse rising to her shoulder on the other, dappled with rain.

'You have any?' she asks him.

He shakes his head.

'Wouldn't look good for the job?'

'You have no idea.'

She goes quiet at that, but not for long.

'I think you'd suit one, actually.'

His shoulders fall, his body relaxes. He casts his mind back over the last week to separate reality from imagination and yes, this is the first time they've spoken, properly spoken – not him calling her name and her yelling at him – since the day her uncle died. Uncle Walt, the only family she had left, Georgie told him. He hadn't known, the night before. He'd still have had to question him though. He's a police officer. He follows the rules.

'Will you have lunch with me, Trish?'

She looks over her shoulder, waves her arm to point from one end of Burrowhead to the other. There's nowhere to go for lunch, not without driving back to Warphill, not without Trish inviting him to her house, to her Uncle Walt's old house, and she's not doing that.

'Where?' she says, her eyes still mocking him, but not unkindly.

'Here.'

'Under your brolly?'

He's got sandwiches in his car, he says. He could share them. He wants to share them more than anything – he doesn't say that out loud, of course.

Sometimes, before she died, his wife would come and meet him on her lunch break. It never seemed like anything much, until it was gone.

Then Trish is saying, 'Tell me about her,' as though she can read his thoughts and knows that every silence that falls between them is because he's thinking about his wife and he can't help it, it's the way his mind has decided to torture him. His heart.

'I need to hear you talk about her. You want to have lunch with me, so talk.'

He says nothing.

'Please.'

He can't help it, he falls back into another memory of how easy it was, how—

'Say something.'

In their kitchen, back in the city, bright and crisp and light, he's pouring the red wine and she's sitting on the stool by the breakfast bar in that way she has. It must be the violinist in her, the way her back's always straight, not forced, just poised and elegant, in her long deep red dress. He's dreading the do they've got to go to, awards being given to people who don't particularly deserve them, police congratulating themselves, and he'll be expected to mingle and chat and charm and he hates it, he really does.

'What am I supposed to say to them all?'

She's laughing, his wife, she's laughing at him in that gentle way of hers.

'I've not got any charm in me,' he says.

'Come on, you're a right chatterbox at home. Can't get a word in...'

His arms slip around her waist, the way she's the perfect height, up on that bar stool, for him to kiss her neck as she whispers, 'You're right, you're a lost cause.'

'Don't know why I bother,' Trish says.

He blinks and he's back, the fountain, the village, Trish Mackie. She speaks with an edge to her voice but then there's something else, a softening in her eyes – she's remembering their kiss, he's sure of it.

'I'm sorry about your uncle.'

'That's talking about my loss,' she says, 'not yours.'

His mouth is dry suddenly, the air too clammy, the heat and moisture on his skin.

'I never, ever, wanted him to get hurt, Trish. I promise you that. I wanted to find out what had happened, that's all.'

'Well, now everyone knows. Old Walt Mackie killed Ricky Barr's dog. Everyone can blame him for everything.'

'I'm not blaming him for anything.'

'And again we are talking about my loss, not yours.'

She's steely, all of a sudden, Trish Mackie, prickly, like she can be.

'Tell me about your wife.'

Something in Frazer shifts and he's powerless to stop it.

'What do you want to know?'

'Tell me her name.'

'Nia.'

When was the last time he spoke it?

'Her name was Nia.'

EVERYWHERE CAN MAKE SENSE
IF YOU LOOK CLOSE ENOUGH

'I can see perfectly well,' Julie Alperstein says, her arm sweeping the length of the high street.

'But you're not from round here—'

'Dear Lord, Penny, not you too—'

'Let me finish!'

Julie's walking her fingers up Penny-Ann's spine though, under her top, and Penny's laughing and half-running to get away and whisper-screaming, 'You do know people are going to see you doing that.'

'And?'

'We are literally on the high street.'

'Twitching curtains?'

'I'm serious.'

Penny, finally clasping both Julie's hands in her own, and the two of them testing their strength, refusing to let the other go.

'But why did you come here, Julie? I mean, of all the places.'

'Not much work in the city I fancied doing.'

'Didn't you want to go travelling or—'

'You think I've got money?'

'I didn't mean—'

'Because if that's what you're after, Penny-Ann Taylor, you're going to be sorely disappointed.'

Julie lets Penny win, stops fighting to get her hands back and lets Penny do with them whatever she wants. She doesn't let go, though.

'Believe me,' Penny says, 'money is not what I'm after.'

Penny-Ann Taylor, with her black hair and white skin, her wonky teeth, her slight overbite and the dimples she gets before she smiles.

'But what Lee says about us, the names he calls us,' Penny says. 'Doesn't that bother you?'

'Alright, so Lee called me a dyke and your brother punched him in the jaw—'

'Not a bad moment for Kev, I'll give him that.'

'Bit of an about-turn, from what you've said. And then Lee and Aaron invited us to their caravan, did they not.'

'But still, why would you want to be here?'

'Look, with the choice between working on a farm and being stuck in a call centre all summer, give me the country *any* day of the week.'

The hospital released them all, except Lee, though even he is on the mend, they said. Of course they released them, they had to, there was nothing wrong with any of them. Julie's never felt so good. It's like she's aware of her feet meeting the ground, the soil beneath the paving stones connecting with the fields and woods beyond the village, the trees reaching up to gather the rain and that same rain landing on Penny's hair, on the tip of her nose, running down from her fringe into her eyes. If she wants to wipe that away, she's going to have to let go of Julie's hands, and it's turned into a game of not-letting-go now. They were heading back to the caravan park but they've stopped here instead. The Spar is the next block down, the fountain in the village square just ahead of them. Julie nods to let Penny know someone's there.

'That's Trish Mackie,' Penny whispers, pulling Julie closer now. So she doesn't care who sees them after all.

'And the other one I know from the hospital,' Julie says. 'That's DS Frazer again, suit and all. Now *he's* not from around here.'

'Stop making fun of me.'

'That's not what I'm doing.'

Julie pulls her hand away at last, strokes Penny-Ann's fringe away from her eyes.

'What are you doing?'

'Living my life.'

'But here?'

'Why not here.'

'I get that you want to understand, right, unravel what happens in the villages, make sense of...this.'

She waves her arm around as though there were something here Julie should be afraid of. It's a pretty street though, that's what Julie sees. A poor village but a living one, a street with homes, a broken fountain, cobblestoned alleyways and old trees with gnarled trunks, their branches still covered in glistening summer leaves. True, there are net curtains. There are also feathers hanging in some of the windows, and to Julie they look like dreamcatchers.

'But I grew up with this shit,' Penny-Ann says.

'And I grew up with other shit.'

'I know—'

'So what's your point?'

'That it's shit here.'

She laughs then, they both do; today does not feel shit.

'There are reasons,' Julie says.

'You always say that.'

'There are always reasons.'

Julie kisses her then, right in full view of every house on the street.

'The folk round here, they're not running the country, are they? The problem isn't Burrowhead. The problems are not *coming* from here.'

'I guess not.'

'I know not. And for what it's worth, I think Burrowhead is beautiful.'

'Then I'd better take you to the woods.'

'What's in the woods?'

Penny-Ann grins, shakes her head in secrecy.

'Things start in the woods.'

And their foreheads are resting together in their bubble of two and across the street from where Trish is sitting she catches Julie's laughter and wishes she was her, just for a moment.

WORDS AND NOT SAYING THEM,
PART TWO

The way he's talking about Nia makes Trish ache. She wants to hold her arms tight around her own body, she's that certain no one has ever loved her the way Dan Frazer loved his wife.

She did it to herself, too. Forced him to talk. Good one, Trish. She doesn't even know why, only knows that when she saw him she felt like smiling for the first time in days and she wanted to get past his barriers – and the man has some, that's for sure. Something has changed now, though.

She was a violinist, apparently. His wife. Nia. She used to play with the symphony orchestra. He's talking a lot now, describing the tone of the notes she made sing from her violin; his body moves as he talks about it, the music his wife played, as though he can hear it and can't help but respond. And she was graceful, he says, and tall, she was taller than him, the umbrella rising high above them as he reaches up – and Trish is short and always ready to fight and she knows it – and he says that people looked at her everywhere she went and she hated that, never wanted the attention. She used to say she wanted out of the city, dreamed of moving to the country. Frazer says he doubts they'd have done it. But she loved the autumn. Winter too – she'd wear big, knitted jumpers that she made herself – but she loved autumn colours the best. She'd never been to Burrowhead, but they used to go hiking inland,

65

and then he says it, they were going to have kids, they were talking about it before she got ill and it all...

Trish doesn't know where it's coming from but she's leaning forward into the rain as though her stomach is cramping and her eyes are stinging with tears that she absolutely please fuck God does not want him to see. A week of this, of thinking she's okay, of being okay, being strong, spiky Trish and then suddenly her body collapses in on itself and she's gasping with grief and when was the last time she felt anything like this, this piercing pain running through her stomach and her heart – her mam, disappearing, leaving her, heading out in a disused old boat for the sea to swallow her up and never even spit her out again and Trish falling into Uncle Walt's arms as he told her that he would look after her, that he would spend his whole life looking after her, until now, because now he is gone. They're all gone. Her da when she was a baby, her mam, her Uncle Walt and she is the last of their family, the last one and fuck he's putting his arm round her shoulders now.

'I'm so sorry,' he's saying. 'I know, nothing helps, words just...'

Rain, pouring on her, splashing the paving stones, filling the fountain.

'It gets better with time, Trish. I mean, not better but you can manage it, you learn to manage it. Sorry, I'm not...you'd think I'd know what to say.'

Rain, on her neck, down the back of her top, cooling her. She's pulling herself together again. Straightening up.

'Nothing helps really... Shit.'

'You're alright,' she laughs. 'You're doing better than the last person who tried.'

'Si?'

She smiles, shakes her head. 'Young Andy, first thing this morning.'

His body straightens, she can feel it instantly.

'Andy Barr?'

Trish, you fucking idiot.

'He came round to see how I was doing.'

The way he pauses then, the change in his eyes. She can see his thoughts forming, rising up between them again.

'First thing?'

He probably knows already. Maybe if she says something, gives him something.

'He was the one called the ambulance.'

His eyes, on hers.

'I know.'

He sounds almost sad as he says it.

'So then he called round on me,' she blurts out. 'So what?'

'Does DI Strachan' – Trish feels her shoulders tense – 'know this?'

'Of course she does, fuck!' Though Georgie probably doesn't know, not yet. 'I told you, he called the ambulance. He's a good kid.'

Frazer is staring at her in a way that's making her regret it all, regret willing him to see her, to get out of his car, to come and sit with her, regret pushing him to talk so that they could feel close, so that she could feel close to someone, when any closeness can turn to this, this – what is it, judgement? He probably thinks Andy's a racist, Georgie will have been feeding him all that and he's still police, fuck's sake, what was she thinking?

'Do you know what they took, Trish?'

She hates that stern voice of his.

'Did Andy tell you? I'm serious. We don't know what it was. Something like DMT's my best guess, but it's not that, they couldn't recognise it in the hospital—'

'I have no idea,' she snaps. 'And you need to remember I'm no one of the police any more.'

Then the hurt look on his face. Trish could scream.

'But you still care, Trish,' he says, quiet and soft. 'I know you do.'

'Maybe I've just realised there's better ways to care than being a police officer.'

'Like what?'

She doesn't reply to that. None of his business what she's doing.

'Tell me you're being careful, Trish.'

She snorts. Trish never did find it easy to get her back down once it was up.

'You sound like you're planning to take the law into your own hands,' he says.

'Take the law into my own hands,' she says, mimicking his voice.

'I'm serious.'

'So what if I did?'

'Then I'd arrest you.'

'I'd better watch my step then, hadn't I, DS Frazer.'

She doesn't mean it like a threat, but she's hardly going to be helping Georgie and the police now she's finally free of them, is she, not now she can do things her own way and the rest of the village are with her. He's not returning her smile though. He looks worried. That frown, crinkling his forehead. For a second she wants to reach forward and rub it away. But she doesn't. If she touched him she's not sure she'd be able to walk away at all, and she is – she's up and glancing back and Frazer is still there, sitting on the edge of the fountain. His head is down, his umbrella low, his eyes on the ground and his hand in the basin of Burrowhead fountain as though he were running his fingertips through cool, fresh water instead of getting his precious shirt cuffs soaked with the dirt and the rain.

14:30

'You okay there, Georgie?' Cal's voice is as cheerful as ever.

'Give me the list over the phone,' she says, aiming for professionalism but sounding unnecessarily stern. 'I mean, you can follow up with the official report.'

'Right you are, Georgie.'

The heat is stifling in here but she can't open the window, the clinging rain is carrying thousands of tiny, microscopic insects, she can sense them, almost hear the noise of them like an insistent hissing—

'To start with, there was plenty of booze in the lot of them. They've happily admitted they were drinking all night, so no surprises there. You'll be wanting the full list of Lee Prowle's stomach contents.'

'Yes. Please.'

'Well, the alcohol was lager. Found empty cans in the caravan too, piles a them.'

'Lager?'

'Aye.'

But it's not a hiss, that noise, it's got more shape than that—

'Nothing stronger?' Georgie manages.

It's a whisper.

'That's all I'm afraid, Georgie. There were crisps as well, so he'd been snacking earlier in the evening.'

Cal chuckles and Georgie feels a flare of irritation and that noise, it's still there, right by her ear.

'Well,' Cal continues, 'they were tortilla chips, to be specific.'

Georgie clenches her teeth, crosses out *crisps* and writes *tortilla chips*.

'Be specific from the start, Cal.'

He doesn't reply to that. He's not used to her snapping at him.

'Please,' she adds, then hates herself for it.

Please—

Did she really hear that? A child's voice, her own word whispered back at her?

'Now, let's get on to the weird stuff, shall we?'

Georgie swallows. There's no one here. No whispering. And this is important.

'We have a bunch of unidentified plant materials. Roots mostly, and some tree bark.'

'Are you sure, Cal?'

It sounds similar to Pauly and Rachel.

'His body couldn't digest it. I literally have a lump of regurgitated bark in a Petri dish in the lab. The roots are from a large shrub, I'd say, something substantial.'

'Will you be able to tell me what?'

'With a bit of time, aye.'

'And you're saying there were lumps of it? How did he swallow it?'

'I didn't say large lumps, Georgie. They're macroscopic but only just. I'd say they'd been roughly crushed, maybe mixed in a drink. You can see from the edges it's no been cut neatly – like I say, crushed.'

'Why would anyone be drinking crushed-up tree bark?'

'There's more.'

As he talks, she writes it all down. A list of Lee Prowle's stomach contents, both from having his stomach pumped and from the vomit found at the scene. She wants to know everything in his system, legal and illegal. All of it. Except there's nothing illegal in there. He's eighteen now. He can drink if he wants to. He can eat the entire contents of Mungrid Woods if he wants to.

Eighteen years old. What is that, a child or a man?

It's older than Errol ever got.

Lee is still in hospital, being monitored, on IV for fluids. Recovering, though. No longer unconscious. Recovering but with a fever, shivering, confused, dehydrated. They don't know what caused the unconsciousness yet. Seizure, most likely. Allergic reaction? Poisoning? It looks like a poisoning, that's why they pumped his stomach. She has to go and talk to Natalie soon. Her pen bites through the paper. She's written:

Tree bark, macroscopic but only just. Crushed? Coarse.

Shrub roots.

Nettles.

Animal fur.

She puts her pen down, presses her hand into her head.

'Good God, Cal. Fur?'

'Small amounts,' he says, with a kindness to his voice, as though that could possibly make it okay. 'We're getting it analysed.'

'But why would anyone willingly ingest animal fur?'

Small fingers curl around her wrist.

'We don't know if it was willingly ingested,' he says.

'Willing or not, *why?*'

That insistent tugging; she grabs her arm away.

'I'd guess, if I had to guess—'

'Take a bloody guess.' Her voice makes her ashamed. 'Shit, Cal, I'm sorry.'

'Look, are you alright, Georgie?'

His voice is different. He's worried about her. What is she doing? Maybe they could talk outside of work again. Is she waiting for him to suggest it?

'I'm...yes, I'm fine. Sorry, Cal. Please, carry on.'

'Well, I'd guess,' he continues, taking his time with it, 'that the animal fur was a mistake, got in there along with the final item for your list.'

'And what's that?'

'Blood, Georgie,' he says. 'Animal blood.'

And there it is: the connection.

The stomach contents match Lee and the others with Rachel and Pauly, and the dancing and chanting at midnight lead from Rachel and Pauly to Abigail Moss.

'And before you ask,' Cal says, 'I'm getting the blood analysed. But it was raw, I can tell you that now, and there was lots of it.'

A tattered dress and matted hair. Raw, pleading eyes. It's the little girl Georgie saw on the cliffs the day Fergus left. Her lips are moving but no sound is coming out.

'So, seeing as I'm taking guesses now—'

It's not so much that Georgie ignores the smile in Cal's tone as that she barely even hears him.

'I'd say the drink that the rest of this stuff was dissolved in was raw animal blood.'

A NICE CUPPA AND SOME
QUESTIONS

'And for you, DS Frazer, I have some nice chocolate bourbons.'

Mrs Dover thrusts the plate of cheap biscuits towards him, almost dropping them on his lap before Frazer reaches out to take the plate.

He's sitting on the sofa in Mrs Dover's front room, the one that looks out to Burrowhead, to the old fountain where Trish is gone, where she walked away from him again. The sofa is old and lumpy. He's sinking into it, slipping on the numerous hand-knitted blankets thrown over the back and sides, covering who knows what manner of stains, and there's a weird smell too.

There's no table for him to put the biscuits on. Is he going to have to balance the plate on his knee?

But no, Mrs Dover is coming back from the kitchen now with a tray containing a teapot, underneath a tea cosy, and two china cups. Beneath them, the tray itself has an image of a dog wearing a little Union Jack coat, some ribbons and a crown. From the coronation? Good grief. Now she's holding the tray precariously in one hand and unfolding a fold-up table that was leaning against by the TV.

'Can I...?'

Frazer stands, balances the biscuits on the sofa, and takes the tray.

And, breathe.

The table is assembled in front of the sofa. He puts the tray down on it. Remembers not to sit back onto the plate of biscuits just in time.

'You'll no get a proper conversation without a cup of tea, that's what I always say, DS Frazer.'

It's real tea, he's got to give her that – she's catching the leaves in one of those old tea strainers, with its own little metal plate to rest in afterwards. The walls are papered with something frilly and peach, patterned with climbing flowers of some kind. It is, in fact, exactly what he would have imagined the inside of Mrs Dover's home to look like. Until today, he's only seen the outside: the patch of concrete with roses in pots, the striped deckchairs she and Mrs Smyth sit on, when the weather's good, out front. The net curtains.

'Several people have recommended I interview you, Mrs Dover, about a particular line of enquiry.'

'Milk?'

'A dash.'

She clicks her tongue at that. 'You sound just like my husband, DS Frazer.'

'When did... Where is your husband, Mrs Dover?'

'Long dead,' she says, cheerfully, 'long dead. Sugar?'

'Er, no. Actually, yes. One. Thanks.'

'One sugar and a dash,' she says, handing over a delicate china cup balanced on its delicate saucer, gold-edged and floral-patterned, like the wallpaper. It's rattling as though the cup is the wrong size for the saucer. Or maybe it's her hands shaking, he thinks with a stab of pity. She's an old woman. Standing here in front of him, serving tea while he sits. Nearly as old as Betty Marshall in her care home – but here's Mrs Dover, living alone, taking care of her house and doing a good job of it too, all things considered. Aside from the smell, the place is clean, tidy. It's probably just old-person smell, anyway. That stuff they rub on, Vicks? Olbas Oil? Her hair is the palest grey and fluffy.

'So, Mrs Dover—'

She holds up a finger, then a miniature teaspoon. 'You'll need to stir.'

Dutifully, he stirs.

'Mrs Dover.'

She settles herself into the chair opposite him. Underneath all the blankets, the fabric matches the sofa.

'I'm trying to ascertain who might have organised and paid for the bench plaque dedicated to Abigail Moss. On the bench by the playground on the cliffs. You are familiar with the bench, Mrs Dover?'

'I am, DS Frazer,' she says, smiling.

'Good. Thank you. So, we're talking to anyone who might have information about dedication plaques being commissioned. I understand that you used to work at the garden centre in Crackenbridge.'

'Oh I did, yes, DS Frazer.'

'Good. It was your son who told me.'

'My Cal.' She beams. 'He's done well, hasn't he, my Cal?'

'He has, ma'am.'

She chuckles.

'Ma'am yourself, son.'

Frazer closes his eyes, allows himself a smile before continuing.

'So, you worked at the garden centre—'

'I did.'

'And when was this?'

'Before I retired, DS Frazer.'

'And when was that?'

'I retired when I was sixty-five,' she says, with another smile, as though the retirement was a happy occasion. 'They threw me a party, you know, and gave me my good china tea set and the orange rose beside the front door. Bessie Wilkie organised it.'

Frazer's interviewed Bessie Wilkie; she remembers nothing at all, just like everyone else.

'She worked there with you?'

'That is correct, DS Frazer.'

'And you liked working there?'

She nods. 'It made me sad when they closed down. Didn't seem right, that.'

'Yes,' Frazer says. 'That's the trouble, you see. They closed down over ten years ago, and it was an independent garden centre – no one to pass the records on to. If they ever kept them to begin with.'

He glances at her, but she's watching him earnestly and nodding.

'So we don't know if they sold the dedication plaque, you see. They did sell benches, I'm told. Did offer the service to create personalised dedication plaques.'

'Oh yes we did, DS Frazer. I always liked the idea, leaving a bench behind, so folk would remember your name. There's something special about that.'

'Maybe you might remember then.'

'Remember what?'

'If anyone commissioned the plaque to Abigail Moss. The one on the bench by the playground?'

Her smile is...what is he seeing? He can't tell if it's a smile of innocence, of interest, of having no idea at all what he's talking about. Is it possible she's deaf?

'Can you hear me okay, Mrs Dover?'

'I can hear you very well,' she says. 'Thank you, DS Frazer.'

'So do you remember anything?'

'Oh no,' she says. 'I'm certain I would have remembered someone ordering a plaque for Abigail Moss, if it had come in.'

Suddenly he's sitting straighter. 'What do you mean?'

'What do *you* mean?'

'I mean—' Frazer looks around for where to put his precarious cup and saucer, shifts the teapot over on the tray so he can squeeze them onto there, beside the chocolate bourbons.

'Do you know the name, Mrs Dover? Is that why you'd have remembered – or her, did you know *her*, did you know Abigail Moss?'

'Oh, I meant because that's my name.'

'What?'

Her eyes widen with alarm.

'Sorry, I didn't mean to shout... Your name is Abigail Moss?'

'My name is Gail, DS Frazer. Gail Dover.'

'And your maiden name?'

'Braxton, of course.'

She says it as though he should have heard of the name. He breathes, tries to fit it all together. 'I'm... I didn't mean to scare you.'

'You didn't scare me,' she says.

'So you're...you're *not* Abigail Moss?'

She throws her head back and laughs, and suddenly he can imagine her as a girl, a teenager – full of energy, full of life, all that potential. She was born just after the war, lived through rations, through the fifties and sixties, always here, always in Burrowhead.

'Don't you worry,' she says, still chuckling to herself. 'I still have my marbles, DS Frazer, and you've asked me about Abigail Moss before. All I meant was that we have the same first name, sort of. I'm Gail. So I'd have noticed another Abigail, if someone wanted to put her name on a plaque. Because if someone's putting a name on a plaque, that means they're dead, doesn't it? If there was another Abigail round here, and I found out she was dead – well of course I'd have remembered. Be like someone walking over your grave, that would.'

Frazer nods. He knows that feeling. He's getting to be familiar with it, out here.

And there's someone looking at him from the wall. Eyes staring, fixed, from an old photograph hanging over the mantelpiece. He stands. Walks over.

'What is this?'

'My father was their best man, at the wedding there. He took that photo.'

The young bride and groom are staring awkwardly at a camera they're not used to having pointed at them.

'I found it in her house after she died. She was my godmother, you see, so I... She never had any children of her own.'

Frazer's barely listening though, his gaze avoiding the eyes that are staring out from the photograph and focusing instead on the name written below in an elaborate swirling hand: *Mr & Mrs Pettigrew*.

Now that name he does recognise from Betty Marshall's statement.

Mrs Pettigrew was the housekeeper at Wyndham Manor, where Betty Marshall was working that summer. Mrs Pettigrew was the housekeeper there when Abigail Moss disappeared.

THE THING ABOUT BEES

Trish hasn't got her suit with her. Didn't know she was coming here, when she left the house; didn't even know where she was going after she walked away from DS Frazer but here she is, in the overgrown field by the disused community shed with Uncle Walt's bees. This is where he taught her to set up new hives in spring, to harvest honey, to protect the bees from winter winds; to care for them. Six years old and she'd watch every move he made, safe in her yellow beekeeper suit, entranced.

No Uncle Walt to insist she suit up today; no Uncle Walt keeping her safe any more. These are her bees now. Maybe they always were.

Her mam tried to forbid her from seeing them often enough, but Trish always found a way. Sneaking out when she could, when her mam was sleeping or working and wouldn't notice Trish gone missing for a couple of hours. Inventing school trips or friends' parties when she needed to. It wasn't a lie, not really: she always was visiting friends. She calmly reaches out an arm and a few bees land on the back of her hand then fly away. She feels her shoulders relax, and a bit of the tension she's been carrying for days finally leaves her skin. It'd be a good idea to equalise the populations soon. One of the hives seems too quiet for her liking and another's getting a bit too close to a swarm. They're glad to see her though, she knows that.

They could sting, her mam yelled in one of those fights with Uncle Walt when Trish was still a kid. Trish was listening in from upstairs where they thought she wouldn't be able to hear. She decided right then that her mam was afraid of bees and that meant Trish never would be. *I'm keeping an eye*, Uncle Walt had said after a silence that didn't make any sense, but it seemed to end that argument at least – when Trish ventured downstairs her mam was gone and Trish got to stay the night with Uncle Walt.

She never has been stung, not once. It never stopped her mam trying to keep her away from the bees, though, and that never stopped Trish wanting to be with them. Even today she's soothed by the sound, their steadying buzzing, their calming sense of purpose. It's almost enough to mask the sound of the engine. Trish wouldn't have noticed a car driving by, there's a few out on the road, but it's the stopping of the engine that catches her attention. The colour of the car that keeps her gaze fixed. She feels nauseous – but that's ridiculous, she has nothing to hide, does she, nothing to be afraid of. Since when has she ever been afraid of Georgie? And she's not afraid now. It's something else.

Why has she stopped her car right there? Is she watching her?

That thought's enough to make Trish stride away from the bees and over to the fence. Frazer probably called her, told her to question her or something. Fuck's sake. Georgie has no right, no right whatsoever to be watching her, to be spying on her. If that's what is happening, Trish is going to have words to say.

But Georgie's not even looking at her.

Georgie's turned away from the window and is staring at the passenger seat as though something's there. But no one's there. The passenger seat is empty, and Trish is staring at Georgie now from the edge of the field, through the horizontal wires of the half-fallen fence. There's grass to her knees, a crawling bramble stuck to her jeans and she's sweating through her vest top. Then Georgie turns. Looks at her like she's startled, scared almost, and something beyond that: she looks hurt.

That was how her mam had looked when she found her out here with Uncle Walt after she'd run away. Trish was eight, maybe nine. Too young to really get it, too young to understand. But before her mam had yelled at her and tried to pull her away and Uncle Walt had stepped in, she'd seen a look in her mam's eyes that she'd always remembered. Her mam had been angry at her plenty of times, angry at Uncle Walt just as many, but that time she'd looked hurt. That was the time Trish thought about the most, after she died.

Georgie's still staring at her. Neither of them have broken eye contact. It's the first time they've looked at each other since the funeral. Georgie looks tired, sad, and Trish can imagine herself stepping over the fence and getting in the car, sitting there beside Georgie and letting her talk. She looks like she needs to talk, and God knows Trish could use a friend. She doesn't move though. They both stay where they are, separated by a tumbledown wire fence, half a metre of scrubland, a couple of uneven paving stones and the car window's glass. A few of the bees have followed her over, are gently buzzing around her head. She loves them for that. She gestures back to the hives and Georgie gives the faintest half-nod and starts the engine again. Trish turns. Georgie slowly accelerates away. Once she is out of view, Trish climbs over the wire fence and strides back towards Uncle Walt's house.

No, towards her own house.

Everything he had is hers now, isn't it? It's about time she accepted it.

BEHIND A CLOSED DOOR

'Hello, Natalie,' Georgie says, sure to slip her foot over the threshold, to make sure Natalie can't shut the door on her.

She doesn't though; she opens it wide.

Georgie should have opened the window when she saw Trish. That's what she should have done. Why didn't she? She could have opened the window and called out to her, she could have got out of the car and given her a hug.

'Hello, Georgie,' Natalie says. There's a slight downward lilt to her tone, as though she's trying to convey humility with a touch of pity, and it's enough to snap Georgie into the present with something like irritation.

Georgie knows Natalie's befriended Fergus. You don't keep something like that quiet, not in the villages – she's even heard Fergus might be staying here. That he might have walked out on her to move in here. That's ridiculous though and she knows it. Even if he is here it's not like *that*, and she's not thinking about it anyway. She's not looking for signs of him, not checking the coat stand in the hall, not glancing round the kitchen for two mugs instead of one. It's bad enough she's close to breaking down in the office half the time, with only Si and Frazer there to see her. Bad enough Trish saw her having to stop the car because she kept seeing that little girl's pleading eyes in her wing mirror. Enough. She's here for work. Besides, Natalie's son is in hospital, still ill from whatever he took last night; her pity could be for herself and not Georgie at all.

With a quiet sigh and sweep of her hand, Natalie invites her to sit at the kitchen table. It's neat and clean and fresh. There are no half-drunk mugs of coffee in Natalie's house. No little girls clasping at Georgie's wrist.

'You'll be wanting to talk about my boys,' Natalie says, pulling out a chair for herself opposite the one Georgie has taken. She doesn't offer tea and biscuits, thank God – Georgie doesn't think she could have gone through the ritual with Natalie Prowle. No, she presses the heel of her hand against her eyes, then up over her forehead, through her hair. 'I will tell you anything and everything I know, Georgie. I want to save my boys, you see. I want to know who's responsible, same as you.'

'You've been to see Lee in the hospital?'

She nods. 'Lee was always the gentler one. Not just 'cause he was younger... You know the way brothers can be. But Lee was always a follower, not a leader.'

'You mean Aaron is a leader?'

'Aaron won't even speak to me these days. I don't know what he is, and that's the truth of it. Lee though, I'll not give up on Lee, not for anything. I think he's...'

'What?'

'He's vulnerable.' Natalie leans forward as she says that, almost whispers it.

As far as Georgie is concerned, there is nothing vulnerable about Lee Prowle. Or Natalie. She slaughtered Ricky Barr's horse with her own kitchen knife, claimed it was a ritual summoning the ancestors to rid the village of evil. 'Evil' meaning Ricky and his family. There's going to be a trial. Natalie's not just a worried mother, not by a long shot.

'People keep saying he'll be fine, the nurses and everyone, they say he's recovering well but—'

'He is recovering, Natalie. I spoke to the doctor myself.'

'You don't understand, I'm… I'm getting scared.'

'He's going to be fine,' Georgie snaps. 'Now, can you tell me who they've been hanging around with?'

Natalie looks stung, but she pulls herself together with a sigh. Behind her, on a shelf over the kitchen table, is a tall, brushed-bronze urn, engraved with three black parallel lines.

'I know the name you're looking for and you're right,' Natalie says. 'They were hanging round with Bobby Helmsteading before he got killed. That man had it coming.'

'How do you mean?'

'He was the one selling them the drugs – you must know all this, DI Strachan.'

'It's helpful to hear it from you.'

'Well, he came back from wherever he'd been at the start of this year, and all of a sudden was best pals with my boys. I mean, Aaron I could understand, but Lee was still at school, same as Andy Barr. Why would a man like Bobby Helmsteading want to spend time with schoolkids? But then it's obvious, once you think about it.'

'Did either Lee or Aaron tell you directly that they were buying drugs from Bobby?'

'Of course not. They're not going to tell me, are they?'

'So what makes you so sure?' Georgie fires back.

'Everyone knows it, don't they?'

'But he was only just back in the village, after years away – where would *Bobby* have been getting the drugs?'

A single beat.

'Ricky Barr?'

She doesn't sound sure of it though, not like she was a few weeks ago, when she was so certain of Ricky's guilt she cut an innocent creature's throat.

'And if it *wasn't* Ricky?' Georgie asks.

Natalie's hand rises to her mouth, then falls again. 'Who else is there?'

Georgie keeps the roll call of every one of the villagers to herself.

'Then if we could think back to the ketamine we found in your sons' caravan—'

'That wasn't mine, and it wasn't theirs.'

'We found it in the horse's blood.' Georgie stares at her and Natalie cringes.

'I don't know where it came from.'

'You have no idea?'

Natalie shakes her head sadly. 'You could try talking to Andy Barr. He's more talkative than my Lee – and you'll no get anything out of Aaron. Believe me, I've tried.'

'But you think Andy will talk?'

'He's been helping with my community food garden.' Natalie glances up and Georgie could almost believe she looks hopeful. 'Pami will have told you about that?'

It's Georgie's turn to cringe at the sound of Natalie using Pamali's nickname – Pami is what Georgie calls her, Georgie and Fergus and not anyone else.

'I thought it was Pamali's food garden.'

There's a clock on the wall that ticks each second that passes, and Georgie could swear she heard someone moving upstairs.

'I... I misspoke,' Natalie says. 'Pamali and I are working on it together.' She's getting defensive now and trying hard to hide it. 'It's not about me, it's for everyone.'

Georgie thinks Fergus is the person upstairs. No, she doesn't think it. She *knows* it. Fergus is here, upstairs, and Georgie feels every muscle across her back tighten.

'It's for the community,' Natalie says. 'It's a *community* food garden and...and I know Andy's had his problems. I'd not have given him the time of day six months ago, but Pami is helping him.' She swallows. 'Pami is helping us.'

'With the vegetables?'

'With the history of the village. She's helping us educate ourselves.'

Georgie wishes she had something to squeeze her hands around.

'Did you know these villages were built on the slave trade, DI Strachan?'

'Yes,' Georgie says slowly. 'Yes, Natalie, I did.'

'Well, it wasn't just the old minister that was a part of it, see, it was more…' She's gesticulating from one end of the kitchen to the other. 'What's the word?'

'Systemic.'

'No, no, like a normal word—'

'Widespread.'

'Yes. Thank you. It was widespread.'

'It still is,' Georgie says, but she can feel someone watching.

'My Aunt Nora used to tell the story of the old minister.' Natalie's eyes flick up to the urn, then back to Georgie. 'It's a good thing people round here tell stories to their kids, isn't it?'

That whispering.

'I mean, that's how they don't get forgotten, right?'

The little girl's standing behind her, words lost to the hiss of breath.

'Aunt Nora always said there was evil in these villages,' Natalie says. 'That it was our responsibility to keep it at bay. That's why she taught me about the threefold death—'

'So you *don't* know where Lee and Aaron are buying drugs?'

Natalie looks startled. No, not startled, something else. Georgie is suddenly here, focused, staring at Natalie Prowle.

'Or where they got that ketamine for you?'

'I told you, it wasn't mine. I promise you, DI Strachan. And it wasn't theirs.'

'Then do you know *what* they've been taking?'

'I've no idea. I never did that kind of stuff myself.'

'Never?'

'Never.'

Georgie can believe that. Natalie might have thought a dead horse would scare Ricky Barr away from the village, but she'd never want to lose control of herself. Too busy trying to control the rest of the village, like her Aunt Nora before her. She's not going to get anything more from Natalie Prowle. This is a waste of time.

'The community council are lucky to have you,' Georgie says, but the sarcasm seems lost on Natalie. She stands up to leave but Natalie reaches for her wrist.

'Wait, DI Strachan?'

Georgie yanks her hand away from Natalie's grasp, stays standing above her. 'What is it?'

'There's something…won't you sit down? There's something I've remembered.'

Georgie reluctantly sits down again. Imagines Fergus sitting in the room above. She stares at the table, clasps her hands in her lap. She will not lose her temper here, and she'll not lose her focus either.

'DS Frazer has been asking people about Abigail Moss.'

And what is Natalie up to?

'He asked me about her, back at the excavation. I'm sorry, Georgie, but nothing came to mind then. There was a lot going on.' She makes eye contact, and Georgie breaks it. 'I've had some time to think about it since.'

Like when she was in the cell for killing that poor horse. Georgie feels her phone vibrate in her pocket. Pulls it out and glances at the message.

'Georgie, I think—'

It's from Cal.

We're having a bit of a week, eh? Look, I'm no good at this, but I'm here if you need to talk.

'I think Aunt Nora might have mentioned an Abigail once.'

Georgie puts her phone away. Sits up straighter.

'What did she say?'

'It wasn't one of her big stories or anything. Not like the old minister who had to be punished. Not like the foster children she saved.'

A chill moves down Georgie's arms.

'But I think... You know how Aunt Nora was always taking care of this village?'

'Did she take care of Abigail Moss the same way she took care of Sonny Riley?'

'That was an accident,' Natalie says, her expression all hurt and sadness. 'I'll always believe that was an accident. That poor little boy.'

She does a good job of looking like she believes it, Georgie has to give her that.

'But from the one time she mentioned her, if I'm remembering the right name, I think Abigail might have been one of the villagers Aunt Nora protected.'

Natalie looks like she might cry. Georgie expects to see her eyes drawn to the urn again but instead her gaze lands on a door across the hall, open a crack, and she gets the feeling it must be Lee's room. Her son has been in intensive care. The other one won't even speak to her. It is haunted, this house. Lee, Aaron, Nora, all absent but here. Fergus, here but not.

'Protected her from what?'

'I don't know,' Natalie says. 'Aunt Nora didn't elaborate, and I knew not to ask for more than she was giving. I must have been fifteen or so and she was lecturing me – see, I'm not pretending she was perfect. I was seeing a lad, who became my husband. She was trying to warn me off. I should have listened, too. I wish I had.'

For the first time, it occurs to Georgie that Natalie has been nothing but helpful since she arrived.

'But what did Nora say about Abigail Moss?'

'She said, *You don't want to carry on like that Abigail did or you'll be needing me to save your life too.*'

NOW AND BEFORE AND
SOMEWHERE IN BETWEEN

Simon watches as Frazer stands there shaking his head, his eyes scanning the two lists, one held in each hand.

'This is...'

Simon doesn't have the words either. It's a match, that's one thing it is. The stomach contents they have from Lee Prowle – from the night he fell unconscious after a seizure, having been violently sick – match almost perfectly Rachel and Pauly's stomach contents from last year after their combined suicide that wasn't. Of course it wasn't.

'This is...'

It's concrete proof that the cases are connected. A way to move forward.

It's disgusting, too. Reading two lists of what those kids had ingested. Tree bark and roots, fur, raw animal blood.

'Well, it's a connection,' Simon says. 'Their stomach contents match. Whatever Rachel and Pauly took the night they died, it's the same thing that put Lee Prowle in intensive care last night.'

'I think this drug ties *all* these cases together,' Frazer says. 'Maybe even the animal killings too.'

'But how?'

'Betty Marshall saw a group of people dancing and chanting in the woods at midnight. She said they looked ecstatic in a way that terrified her. I'm going to say they sounded intoxicated. And she saw blood. She thinks the blood was Abigail's.'

'And you think?'

'I think...' Frazer's eyes lock onto Simon's. 'These kids are using animal blood in their drug, right?

Simon nods.

'Well, what if the people Betty Marshall saw in the woods were taking the same drug as Rachel and Pauly? Except Betty Marshall didn't see an animal being killed. She saw Abigail Moss being killed.'

'You mean...'

'Just because they're using animal blood now doesn't mean they didn't use human blood in the past.'

'You really think they might have killed people to use their blood in this drug?'

The door swings shut behind Georgie and Simon turns to face her.

'I hear what you're saying,' she says in that slow way of hers, her accent gentle. 'But all this is hypothesis. We follow the evidence, and we stick to the case.'

She's like the old Georgie again, and it's so bloody good to see her Simon could give her a hug.

'Our case is about drugs, here and now. There's something potentially fatal spreading through this village. It might have been what killed Pauly and Rachel last year, and you're right, some form of it might even have been used in the past. But whatever it is, we need to know where and how it's being manufactured *today*. Frazer?'

'Ma'am?'

'It turns out Nora Prowle might have known someone called Abigail.'

Frazer stands up. 'Good,' he says, almost clapping his hands. 'Good, another link. My news is that Mrs Dover knew the house-keeper at Wyndham Manor.'

'Now we're getting somewhere,' Georgie says. 'Keep following the links. And Si?'

'Georgie?'

'I'm thinking the kids might open up to you a bit. At least, I don't think they can accuse you of being too corporate... Speak to Terry, will you? And the new girl. Julie Alperstein. See if you can get them talking. Your job is to follow the drugs.'

A FRIENDLY FACE
WHEN YOU NEED ONE

When Trish opens the door to see Suze standing there with a tub of cookies and cream and a clinking bag from the Spar she could almost cry.

'Look,' Suze says, 'I know you were pissed off about the horse, but I didn't mean to land you in it or—'

'Shut up about the horse and tell me what's in the bag.'

'Six bottles of Budvar, and a merlot in case you fancied wine?'

'You get to come in,' Trish says, taking the ice cream and leading Suze through to Uncle Walt's living room. Her living room.

Suze sits in Uncle Walt's old comfy chair and Trish doesn't say a word to stop her. She gets some bowls for the ice cream – Uncle Walt's old bowls – spoons and a bottle opener she finds in the cutlery drawer. Trish needs to have a proper clear-out, put some of her own stuff in the kitchen. Choose what to keep and take the rest to charity. Next week maybe. Week after next.

'You going to sit down?' Suze grins at her, holding out a bottle.

Trish takes it, opens it, passes it back and takes another for herself before sitting on the sofa. Beside her, the drooping succulent has dropped another of its branches.

'I've got no food, and fuck all else to be honest.'

'Aye, but how are you really holding up?'

Trish snorts. Takes a few gulps of the beer. Lets herself breathe for a bit.

'Seriously, how are you?' Suze says, quieter.

'Let's talk about something else.'

'Like?'

Trish shrugs.

'Oh, I know. Elise saw Fergus Strachan and Natalie Prowle doing a grocery shop together, close as can be, all snuggled up.'

'That is gross, Suze.'

'I think it's happening…'

Trish scrunches her face but she's not laughing, not like Suze is. It would kill Georgie if it were true.

'It's not true,' she says. 'Fergus wouldn't.' He was trying to stand up for Georgie at the funeral, sounded to Trish like he still cared – that was part of what had pissed her off so much.

'Has Georgie told you something I don't know?' Suze says.

'I've not spoken to Georgie since I quit.'

'And here was I thinking you'd be able to fill me in.'

'You're on the inside,' Trish says. 'I'm way out.'

'I'm stuck up at Crackenbridge on bloody traffic duty.'

'Serious?'

'Well, patrol and paperwork mostly. I've requested the temporary transfer from my end too, so it might happen yet.'

'Transfer?'

'To help Georgie out with the drugs case here.'

Trish takes another swig of her drink. So Suze is stepping into her shoes already.

'Not in a bad way,' Suze says. 'Don't look at me like that. If you want your job back—'

'Don't be bloody ridiculous. I'm out.'

Suze purses her lips. Nods at the ice-cream tub. 'I'll serve then, eh?'

Trish softens a bit.

'On you go.'

It is good to have some company. She'd wondered if Frazer might turn up, but best not go there – at least with Suze there's no agenda.

'Truth is,' Suze says, 'I'll no be staying in the police forever.'

'No?'

'I've never done anything else, never been anywhere else. I mean, I'm only twenty-six!' She stands up as though to prove how agile she still is, and does a little spin.

'This is not me for the rest of my life.'

'What are you going to do then?'

Suze grins as she sits back down. 'Fuck knows. But it's like Cal says, you can't make a choice unless you've seen the alternative.'

'So go travelling, if that's what you want. See the world. Try out some alternatives...'

'Aye, but it takes money.'

'Everything takes money.'

Money. Trish needs money. Uncle Walt's bank account is empty, like she knew it was. She's quit her job. This house is all she has. What the fuck is she going to do?

'Hey, none of that,' Suze says.

'What?'

'That heavy look on your face. I mean, I get it, right? But you've had a shit time and you need to give yourself a break.'

'So your recommendation is that we get properly pissed this evening?'

'Drunk enough so you give me the low-down on you and DS Frazer.'

'There is not enough alcohol in the world, my friend.'

EMPTY EVENING

Georgie's key turns in her lock that was their lock. That is just hers now.

When Fergus lived here the door was usually open, and he'd be inside, pottering about in the kitchen maybe, in the garden, doing something or other with his drone. She never thought she'd see the day she could miss his drone. The drone she'd thought was so daft, such a waste of money, then verging on menacing as he started using it to map the history of the village – *his* drone had helped with the Sonny Riley case. Fergus had helped. He was always trying to tell her about the past, and she never wanted to listen. Then she'd called him a racist. And now he was gone.

In the hall, post lying underneath the letterbox. She picks it up, carries it to the living room. Nothing important. Gas bill. Frozen food. A flyer about the local elections. She sits on the sofa in the exact spot she always sits; dumps the post beside her.

Everything she'd said had been true. There was another way for him to react. A different way. He could have listened. He could have acknowledged it, that would have been a start. They could have rebuilt from that.

Now, according to Si, he's been going to the community council meetings in Warphill. Trying to lead some kind of archaeological campaign to discover the local stone circle. The village and the ancestors; the villagers who think they're the only ones who belong. He's not listened to her. He's dug his heels in and started leaning back the other way. It's hazy, when she tries to piece the timeline together, when she started feeling like Fergus was more interested in the village than he was in her, that he related more to the villagers than he did her. That he excused them. That he judged her. She wishes she could rewind it, watch it playing out in front of her eyes: her and Fergus, where they started, how they got here. If she could do that, though, there's someone else she'd need to see.

She doesn't know, even after all these years, if Errol would have loved it here or hated it. Prickled at every racist remark or gone running along the beach at midsummer, surfed the waves and enjoyed their crash.

Georgie picks up her phone and types a text.

I think I need a few days. We'll talk then. But thank you, Cal.

Then she leans back and closes her eyes, listens for the owls she can sometimes hear at night. Not tonight. Her house is silent, her garden is still, the heat is heavy and thick, and she lets it press in around her.

Then a single owl calls. One half of the pair.

A tugging on her shirt cuff.

She keeps her breathing steady. Tunes in to the whispering beside her.

'Are you here?' she says, forcing her voice out of her throat.

The whispers get closer, she can feel them moving against her skin.

'What are you trying to say?'

Please—

Her own voice again, echoed back at her and turned into a child's pleading.

Please help my mammy.

She tries to keep her face calm, her voice steady. She can't open her eyes, she mustn't.

'You said that once before.' Georgie takes another ragged breath. 'On the cliffs.'

Please help my mammy.

'But I don't know who your mother is. I don't know who you are.'

The little girl is stroking the back of Georgie's hand, her tiny nail tracing faint, impossible lines.

'Are you Abigail Moss?'

Nothing but the lines being etched on her skin.

'Are you Rachel?' Nothing. 'Rachel's mother died.' No whispers, no breath. 'Then Pauly and Rachel died too.'

PD and RT forever.

Shivers crawl up her arm from where the girl's cold finger is still tracing shapes.

'What does that mean?' Suddenly Georgie's legs are trembling. 'What do you want from me?' It's as though the floor is shaking, the shudders rising through her.

'Stop doing that.'

This can't be real.

'Stop it!'

She feels it in her eyes, in the way they're stinging, in the shame that pierces her as she forces herself to look. Her eyes wide and staring.

There is no one here. No one and nothing.

'I hate this place,' Georgie says, slowly and deliberately loud. Her voice fills the space, existing here and now in her empty home. 'I hate it here. And you're not real, are you. So leave me alone.'

THE CRACKS YOU CAN FALL THROUGH

Shona's never seen it like this before.

The rain is gone. The beach is still and shrouded. Low mist softens the sea, and the clouds are feathered and forgiving, masking the moon but letting through enough hazy light for them to see their way.

Kev is following her lead over the barnacled rocks, between the pools of warm salt water left by the tide. The clumps of seaweed are textured shadows in the glow. If Rachel were here she'd think they were being guided to a secret cove, a sheltered bay hidden until it's needed. She'd have been wrong though. Shona is following the path of the beach and it's leading to the cliffs, that's all, the deep red rise of rocks, sheer and jagged, and soon there will be nothing to do but turn round.

'What are we looking for?'

Kev, from behind her. His voice low, almost whispered, as though they're not allowed to be here at all.

'I told you, I don't know.'

'Shona—'

'Rachel used to talk about their place.'

'She meant the standing stone.'

'No, I think she meant something else.'

'Here?'

But Shona knows it's hopeless, it's dark, there's nothing but sharp rocks and smashed shells and the cliffs, their shadow lengthening across the beach.

'Okay,' she stops. 'Fuck this. Fuck all of it.'

'Wait—'

'Let's go back—'

'No, look! There's something here.'

He's leaning against the rocks, his hands following the shape of the cliff edge, catching trickles of moonlight like water and she doesn't understand, doesn't know how she didn't see it: the sliver of an opening, darker than the stone.

'It's a cave.'

He's standing beside the entrance and they know, they both know, they've heard the stories; everyone in the villages has heard the stories.

'Come on,' she says, but he doesn't move, and neither does she.

'Rachel thought—'

'Rachel's not here any more.'

But there's light. She can see light in the cave and it's not possible, is it, that deep inside the cliffs there could be something glowing? Beneath her feet is a smooth rock sheet, worn down by the weather, by the tide, by the feet of people who've been here before her and she follows them in, the walls stretching either side until the cavern is the width of her arm span and more. Overhead the steep rocks rise until they meet, obscuring the sky but filling the cave with air, giving it space enough to swirl while behind her Kev's breath is shallow, held, released.

'How was this not here before?' he says.

'It's always been here.'

'But it wasn't.'

'It must have been. The tide—'

'What's that noise?'

'Just your breath.'

'Not mine.'

'The wind then.' Though the air feels still against her skin, still and warm, and she's reaching out to the cave wall, tracing the shapes and curves with her fingertips and not looking to the back, to the strange golden glow from the rocks that must be a reflection off the water cradled in a shallow pool in the stone.

'Have you got your phone?'

Kev starts like he'd forgotten, then pulls out his mobile. 'You left yours?'

'It's in my pocket, but...' Her voice trails off and he doesn't push her as to why she can't take her hands from the cave's wall, he just clicks the torch on his phone and suddenly the light is a searing beam against the rock. The letters have been carved deep, edged in harsh shadow: PLEASE HELP MY MAMMY.

'What the fuck?' He stumbles back, nearly slips, but Shona stays where she is. She's following the words. They must be years old, scratched by a child decades ago.

'There's more,' she says.

His torch's beam sways against the wall, picking out letters, figures, low scratches in rock as if someone had been trying to claw their way out and she imagines him, poor Sonny Riley, the murdered boy, as her hands lead her further in. RIP, carved over and over again, RIP. It's written in different styles, etched deep or barely visible on the surface and further back, a stag, crosses of sticks wedged into rock, crosses tied with red ribbon around stones.

'Here.'

The beam lights a message more recent than the rest, clearer, lighter.

PD & RT 4EVER

'It's them.'

'It was them.'

And at the back, still the glowing, the light calling and the shadows moving.

'Turn it off.'

'What?'

But he does as she asks. The torchlight vanishes.

She can see clearer now. There are shadows in the rock, shapes undulating as she stares deeper, steps closer. Her hand reaching out. The rock face is smoother here, curved, and her fingers follow the shapes into the rock, into a barely perceptible crack in the rock, and they touch something fragile and damp—

'What is it?'

Her fingers reaching, struggling to clasp it, there's not space enough but she must, it's for her, it was left here for her and she has to—

'Shona?'

His hand on her shoulder and she has it. She stumbles back and he's putting the torch on again and light is everywhere, brightening the rock and the puddles on the stone floor, the stretch of the cliffs above them, the shimmering air and she can hear voices, whispered and gentle. Rachel's laugh like a smile snatched from the air.

'What is it?'

She looks down. In her hands, a rolled piece of paper, tied with a ribbon. She loosens it easily; the bow unravels. Rachel's writing. The torchlight on the page now, everything else in shadow.

Mam,

'Oh my God.'

Alexis wants me to write you a goodbye letter, but I won't. I need to see you again. No, I will see you again.

'Shona?'

'Be quiet.'

Everything you taught me was for this. I've been preparing for years and I'm ready for the next step. We'll be together, I promise you that, Mam. I'll never give up until I see you again. I can do whatever it takes.

'Oh God, Rachel, what did you do?'

Kev's hand is reaching for hers, but she can't let go of the letter.

'We know what she did.'

'She didn't kill herself.'

'But—'

'This is not a suicide note.'

'Then what is it?'

'Something else!' Her raised voice is wrong, in the cave, with Kev; she didn't mean to shout. 'She says she was preparing for years.'

He shakes his head. 'The churchyard? The candles?'

'She was trying to summon her mam back from the dead.'

She can hear their voices again, stronger now, whispering from the beach and she wants to see them, to see Rachel. Her feet carry her to the entrance, to the slit in the rock where the cave hides from the sea. She can feel water on her skin, taste salt on her lips. Then a sudden crash resonates through the cave. The shock pulses through her as she sees them. Rachel and Pauly. Their faces shattered. Every bone in their bodies broken against the rocks where they fell. Then they are gone.

LAST YEAR

When Pauly finds Rachel out by the standing stone, she's sitting with her back against it, facing away from Warphill, away from school, away from all of them. It's the far side she's leaning against and he only knows she's there 'cause he can see the long folds of her skirt to one side, the deep violet of the fabric, the daisies, the mirrors glinting in the middle of each one. She made it herself, found the fabric in a second-hand shop, designed the shape and flow of it, sewed it by hand. He loves that.

He doesn't go round to talk to her, though. If she'd wanted to talk to him she'd have come and found him. Instead, he sits on the opposite side of the stone, lets his head fall back and his eyes close against the light of the sky, and together they sit like that for a while, listening to birdsong and the soft buzz of insects.

She puts her hand out to one side, so he does the same, his palm lying over the back of her hand, and then it's the two of them, Rachel and Pauly, alone, against the rest; the only two people in the village who matter. The only two in the world.

'It didn't work,' she says eventually, so quiet it's barely more than a whisper. If he hadn't been listening, waiting for her voice, then he might not have heard her at all. 'I tried again, but it didn't work.'

'You went to the church ruin?'

He can imagine her there. Kneeling beside the candles scattered around the cherry tree. Her face streaked with mud and tears, with the shadow of branches through moonlight, the rising mounds of the graves around her. They say they're pushing up through the soil, those graves, and Pauly believes it. He's seen it happening.

'But she wasn't there.'

He gives her hand a squeeze.

'Maybe it wasn't enough,' he says.

Her hand pulls away and he feels the cold grass against his palm, his whole body falling closer to the soil. He turns on his knees to where he can see her face.

'Rachel.'

Above them, the stone is blocking out the sun. It reaches higher as he watches, obscuring the sky, and he wills it to happen, welcomes the feeling of being beneath something so eternal. He can feel the markings on the stone as though they were being traced with a nail along his skin.

'We need a way to get closer.'

'How can we get closer than her grave?'

He knows how important it was, to Rachel, that her mam be buried in the old churchyard. Hers was the last plot, her burial the final burial beside the ruin, so he takes a moment to breathe, to soften his voice before he speaks.

'A graveyard is just buried bodies,' he says. 'That's not what I mean.'

When Rachel speaks next, her voice sounds like it's reaching him from an underground chamber where her thoughts echo between the walls and there's the tiniest gap between the stones letting the light in.

'Maybe she's just dead,' she says. 'Just...gone.'

She doesn't believe that though, she's never believed that, and Pauly doesn't believe it either. He takes her face in his hands and kisses her forehead, her eyes, still closed against him.

'She's waiting,' he says, and he feels the shudder of it pass through her body. 'She's somewhere better than a graveyard. But we need to meet her halfway.'

'I don't—'

'No candles,' he says. 'No circle of people she didn't love. Just you and me.'

Her eyes are open at last, and her lips are finding his lips.

'Trust me,' he says between their kisses. 'We'll meet her.'

He undoes the buttons on her top, slips it over her shoulders.

'But I don't know how,' she says.

'I've found a way,' he whispers, as his fingers trace the curves and shapes of the standing stone on her skin and his kisses move down from her neck and she leans her head back and the air sighs slowly and a butterfly lands, unobserved, on the top of the menhir then flutters away.

WATER

WATER

OPTIONS AND HOW WE USE THEM

Ricky Barr's been up most of the night. He's getting fair used to it, the coughing, the choking, the walking. The air helps, the salt on the coast. He never thought he'd see the day. And Debs, having Debs home after all these years, having a sister, being able to let go of that tight knot of grief and blame.

Nothing's going to stop what's coming though.

Three months, they said. Two and a half now.

Hospital, hospice, palliative care, they said. Not for him. He'll die soon and he'll die at home and he's fine with it. He's made his peace. Ricky Barr is not someone who's ever seen the point in a drawn-out death, or old age either. Andy doesn't cringe when he enters a room any more. He's no saying that's enough, but he's saying it's a start. The villagers still think he's dealing drugs to their kids: idiots, the lot of them.

Ricky Barr is a man who knows things, though. He's always made sure of that. And his son – his son knows things too.

He clears his throat, spits on the grass, wipes his mouth with the back of his hand, as he always has, and strides back towards the farmhouse. It'll be dawn soon. Another day. He's got staff to cover the work, so he's not needed in the fields. They're scared enough of him even now that they'll do what needs done and then some. He's not concerned about that. And they're no lazy, that lot, not even the students – Ricky's always known that proper work, physical work, demands that you do it, and you come to like it at that. He wouldn't have it any other way. In fact, as he pushes the door to his farmhouse and Debs calls out in greeting despite the hour, he's alright with his lot. He's had options, much as he might once have denied it, and when your options become choices that lead you to right where you are, what's the point in regretting them?

She's at the table, their table, where they scratched their names with the point of his da's knife forty years back. Where he used to set a place for her years after she'd gone, until he gave up on the hope. She's been sanding it down. Says she'll make it like new yet, though if you ask Ricky that's wrong-headed thinking. He told her it could be worth more money looking old. She seemed to find that funny. The night's dark is still coming in through the windows, but she's got the lights on in here and she's cradling a mug in her hands.

Aye and she's changed a bit. All those years in the city, mixing with other people, not him, not their mam and their da, not taking the glares of the villagers. It's like she came back shinier than when she left. The years between have no done that to him.

'What you thinking about, all on your own here?' he says, taking his seat.

'That poor boy in the hospital.'

'Lee Prowle? He made his choice—'

'Ricky…' A tilt of her head, a plea for a bit of sympathy.

'He did, Debs.'

Her eyes flick away, then back.

'It's looking better, d'you not think?' she says, feeling the smooth surface of the big oak table between them. 'I might varnish it next. Or try some wax maybe. You can get this furniture wax these days…'

Falling into a silence, years between them again. It keeps happening, though God he's glad to have her back. Just wishes she didn't sometimes look like a total stranger to him. He clears his throat and the noise of it is disgusting, makes him feel self-conscious, ashamed.

'I've been thinking, Debs.'

'Oh dear.'

She smiles at him then and she's suddenly his big sister again. The windows are closed but the heat's not too heavy yet. His farmhouse – their farmhouse – always had a way of keeping cool. Thick walls and stubborn stone. He's never been too hot in here, he'll say that for it.

'Andy was in that caravan, Saturday night,' he says, voice dissolving into a cough even as Debs reaches for his empty glass, fills it from the tap over the sink. 'Now I don't know exactly what they were taking, and I don't know where they got it, but I reckon Andy knows more than he's letting on.'

'Are you sure?'

'No,' he says, hand across the back of his mouth, holding the cough in again. 'No, I'm not sure. That's why I need you to talk to him. If we can find out what they were taking, where they got it from—'

'Then we can go to the police,' she says.

Aye, forty years in the city have changed her. But she's back here now, with him.

'What I mean is,' he says, 'then we can get ourselves some options.'

THE DAWN CHORUS

It's getting light now. The sun's not visible but the haze through Georgie's window is undeniable; a mist of pink and green, fleeing from the predawn to claim the daybreak. She rolls over, checks her phone. It's 5.50 a.m. It's 6 a.m. It's 6.15 and her alarm is ringing and her legs are heavy, her stomach unsettled from the sense of falling that haunted her sleep all night.

A new hallucinogen, or an old one, something like DMT. But local, ingested, bringing on seizure and unconsciousness in Lee but not in the others. Vomiting, shaking, disorientation, in Lee but not in the others.

Case One, she tells herself.

Case One: What is the drug, who is making it and how.

Her head feels weighted, hazy, like she was drinking last night, but she wasn't – Georgie was never much of a drinker, never looked to drugs to lose herself. She never felt she deserved that. She had to remember Errol's death, to relive it over and over: her big plan when she heard about the protest, how she was going to make a difference and make damn sure Errol would too. You couldn't lie around being cute and charming and knowing your dad had your back forever.

She's never worked out how two people growing up in the same town, in the same household, ended up with two such different temperaments. Her instincts, when she was a teenager, were always to argue, to fight back, to risk it. Errol's were to smile and disarm, to let it flow over him. Decades of trying to learn that trick are failing Georgie now. All those years with Fergus, with his ability to see only the good in people – and what use is it? She needs to stay clear and focused, find out who's making the drugs and distributing them. Was it a trial run, with Lee and the others? Someone getting them to test a new product? They couldn't have had much money to buy it with.

The sky is losing its colour, rushing into the white heat of the day. She looks away, looking for something, for someone, then shakes her head; listens for birdsong instead, like she used to with Fergus, when they woke to hear the dawn chorus. Chaffinches today – there are always chaffinches in her garden – and the pair of blackbirds they have every year. Maybe siskins too. She saw one last week, an unexpected flash of yellow and brown. Then there's the screech of gulls. They're not in her garden but they're close: up on the cliffs, down by the beach. Through the spring, she'd felt like there were swarms of them gathering in the village, but they're all by the sea now, flocking to the coast. Even they want out. Georgie's not stepped foot on the beach for a while, but she needs to. Can't keep knowing there's something down there, knowing it with a shudder that tightens her skin, and not confront it. The hidden cave in the cliffs. She's sure Dawn Helmsteading was hiding in there at the start of the year, and Si found her. Then something happened to him and he let her go.

Perhaps she would have done the same.

Mrs Helmsteading says Dawn's safe now. She's safe and far away and she's never coming back. Georgie's glad. Must be good to be far away and never coming back. Frazer said Betty Marshall, his witness in the city, never returned to Burrowhead after what she saw: a young woman, Abigail Moss, being sacrificed in the woods, surrounded by masked people, chanting. At least, she claims that's what she saw. Sixty years ago. An old woman with dementia, living in a care home. It would be easy not to believe her, but for the fact Georgie knows Dawn was almost sacrificed on the cliffs, surrounded by masked people, chanting, twenty years ago. And Natalie Prowle sacrificed Ricky Barr's horse in the woods not two weeks ago.

Natalie and the horse she understands. It was a threat to Ricky Barr, because Natalie wanted him to leave. Because she thought he was leading her boys astray. Maybe she also believed the sacrifice would summon the Others to protect the village; maybe she still believes everything Walt Mackie told her. But there's no indication it had anything at all to do with making a drug – and Natalie wouldn't have been involved in anything like that. No, first and foremost it was a threat.

What is Fergus thinking?

Georgie suddenly stands, throws the duvet back onto the bed and storms through to the bathroom.

So why was Abigail Moss being sacrificed? If that's what was even happening – what was the motive, why *her*, why *then*? Could DS Frazer be right, could it have been to collect her blood to make the drug? And if someone cared enough to dedicate a bench to her on the cliffs, then why does no one remember who she was?

There it is, Case Two: What happened to Abigail Moss. And why.

She sets the shower to cold and lets the water wash over her.

The little girl is gone. She told her to leave, so she left.

And the birds are louder in the kitchen. Her flock of long-tailed tits, five, six of them, are all gathered at the feeder. Georgie loves those birds and they've not been here for a while; it's a relief to see them. She pulls out her phone to get a photo, texts it to Pami. She'll appreciate it. Fergus can find his own birds to watch now, and Trish never gave a shit about wildlife anyway.

Right. Her coffee smells good. She'll take her toast warm, with butter, today. Sometimes the simplest ways are the best. And she has a plan.

Case One: Who is manufacturing and selling the drug, today.

Case Two: What happened to Abigail Moss sixty years ago and why.

Case Three: Rachel and Pauly.

They fell from the cliffs last year. Did they jump? Were they pushed?

They'd been taking the same drug as Lee and the others – so they were connected to Case One. Except there was no sign of them getting sick like Lee.

They'd been dancing outside at midnight, like the group Betty Marshall witnessed – so they were connected to Case Two. But they weren't killing anyone. Were they?

There was animal blood in their stomach contents, though. Rabbit, Cal said. She feels a pull to the coast, a restless tugging at her insides telling her to run from the village and stand on the clifftop and she's falling again, the force of salt wind streaming against her face, the crack through her bones and it's there, the cave in the cliffs, where Rachel and Pauly fell, the hidden cave that needs her to see what happened to them.

Stop it!

It's an ordinary cave in the cliffs. It must be visible at low tide, and at high tide it is inaccessible. That's all. It's just a cave. There is no little girl tugging at her clothes, and right now she is sitting in her kitchen and she has finished breakfast. Enough.

She stands up, impatiently shoves what she needs into her bag. She'll call in on Pamali on her way to work, that's what she needs. Take her a flask of coffee and spend a few minutes with her friend. Spending time with Pami always gives her the strength to face the day. Then she is going to solve her three cases, because it's her job to do so.

PASSING THROUGH

Frazer has been to Wyndham Manor before, but he's not been inside it. The hotel where Betty Marshall was working when she witnessed the murder – or so she thinks – of Abigail Moss. The hotel where Abigail had been working before she vanished, her room emptied, Mrs Pettigrew the housekeeper silencing any questions about where she'd gone.

They had both been working here, in 1962, through the grand entranceway of Wyndham Manor, flanked either side by the crumbling statue of a sphinx.

That's where he starts, this morning. At the entranceway. Breaking and entering. Except it's not, seeing as he's police and the door to the hotel is literally hanging wide open. Nettles and brambles have already claimed the hall, though beneath them there's a carpet of buttercups; it would be easy to follow them and forget the danger of being stung or snagged by the plants that accompany them. Still, it's impressive, despite the heavy damp festering in the heat and the translucent brown fungi crawling across the plasterwork. The grand staircase rises from the entrance hall, splits in two at the landing and circles elegantly round on either side, still adorned by large portraits hanging on the walls. There must have been some serious money here, once. All gone now.

He tries the first step gingerly – it could collapse underfoot, who knows if it's stable or rotted to nothing. It feels like a staircase though, something solid beneath the moss. Another step. He doesn't want to hold the banister, doesn't want to touch it, not with everything that's growing on it. He's careful not to let his arm accidentally brush the sides, though keeping in the middle of the wide staircase has its risks too. If it's going to break, this will be where. Then he'd be falling, or trapped, and there must be things living in here, with all this plant life. When nature decides to take over it does so entirely.

Georgie might call that a comforting thought. Frazer would not.

Pausing where he is, he listens for what other life is in here with him.

The buzz of insects is the top level. Flies, bees, wasps, no doubt, in this heat – his skin itches, his neck, behind his ears – something small, biting him. But below that it gets worse. There are clawed creatures here, mice or rats, pine martens, something that could scamper and scratch. Trish now, she'd love it here. He slaps at his skin, scratches at the bites of microscopic insects, takes another step.

There's a knock.

Another step. It doesn't help to listen, he needs to see the rooms, get a feel for the place – though he knows he's climbing when he should be descending, looking for staff quarters, for the room where Betty Marshall would once have stayed, where Abigail Moss had slept.

Another knock.

Instead he's heading for the guest rooms, the luxury as it once was, the sense of rich tourists ordering the staff around, taking breakfast in bed, admiring that beautiful view. Stopping on the landing, he can see it through a triplet of wide arched windows over the grand entrance, smashed so long ago that even the shards of glass have vanished. The rain has lightened, finally, leaving only a light mist in the air. Elegant trees appear through it, following the slope of the landscaped gardens down to the stream. It must have been quite something to see, for Betty, aged eighteen. The first job she ever had, her first summer from home, four months as high-season staff here: serving this privilege.

Another knock.

Lee still doesn't feel like he can turn his head and he's no fucking idea why – they've took out that fucking tube and he's only got the IV in the back of his hand now but it feels like he's immobilised, plugged into so many drips and machines that he's no control over his own body any more.

Three knocks in quick succession.

Why the fuck are they even doing that? The door's no locked, they don't lock doors in this place, anyone could walk in – like his mam does several times a day whether he likes it or not. She even crept in when he was sleeping last night, finally falling asleep alone only to wake to her face, her eyes peering at him, all concern and love and, beneath that, judgement and questions, her questions, it made him want to scream *You killed a fucking horse you psycho, what the fuck do you know about real life?* He didn't though, just stared back, stared back and eventually closed his eyes.

Knock. Knock. Knock.

The others have gone, so the nurse told him, all discharged yesterday. Terry and Penny-Ann and Julie and his brother, so it can't be Aaron at the door. Or can it? Coming back to the hospital once he's out, that'd no sound like Aaron. Unless he's more threats to make. The door pushing open a crack, creaking like that, the breathing of whoever's behind it and he needs to turn, regain some control of his fucking body. It must be in his head. There's no reason why he can't turn to face the door but he can't, he fucking—

'It's little Lee,' says the voice, and Lee's not trying to turn around any more, he's staying exactly where he is, doesn't need to see, doesn't fucking want to.

'How are we today,' says the voice. 'Better?'

He can feel a scratch down the back of his neck, a fingernail, a knife, and he scrunches his eyes shut.

'I've no said a fucking thing to the cops.' His throat raw from the tubes, from the vomit, raw and scratching rough and burning. 'Of course you haven't, Lee,' says the voice. 'Of course you haven't. That's why I'm here. To make sure they're keeping you comfortable. Tell me, are you comfortable here, Lee?'

His eyes open to see the wall beyond his bed, the window, a sudden image of the glass shattering around his fist and how it would feel, blood spurting from his hands, his wrists, then the scratching returns and the voice behind him says, 'And have you had any other visitors?'

The care home told Frazer that Betty Marshall wasn't taking visitors. They said she was weaker, but comfortable. They said the best thing for her was to stay in her room, where she was safe. He'd called them as soon as he knew he was staying on to investigate – he'd thought it would be good to have Betty here with him, remembering, guiding him through exactly what she saw – but the new woman on reception refused.

'She's taken a turn for the worse, I'm afraid,' she'd said. 'She's barely left her bed this week, inspector, let alone the care home. And you want to take her out to the coast and make her relive these nightmares she has?'

Actually he'd thought Betty Marshall might want to be here. His memory had softened her frailty, her dementia, and latched onto her personality, her determination.

'Could be the death of her, something like that.'

'I understand,' he'd said, and he'd sent her some flowers, because everyone likes receiving things like that, don't they? Although looking out of one of the first-floor guest rooms, its bay windows opening over what was once a pristine lawn and looking all the way to the woods, he wonders if they were wrong in the care home. If sometimes we place a little too much emphasis on staying comfortable, on avoiding what scares us. Betty Marshall hadn't seemed like a woman scared of being scared.

He steps closer to the window frame and the salted air from outside tugs at him to leave the stale room he's in, to leave the mould and the damp and the king-sized bed to rot. And he can see the rot crawling all over the mattress. There are no squatters, no sign of habitation, no sense of anyone having used this vast hotel for anything. It's been left, abandoned in the truest sense, not only in a financial one but in a personal one too. There is no human life left here – and he feels it again, a tug at his chest, the promise of clean air and fresh grass, the image of what it must have been when they were here sixty years ago: Betty Marshall and Abigail Moss.

Betty's running through the crumbled walls of the rose garden to the woods, through silver birch and whispering aspen. Her legs are bare beneath her mini and the sweat's collecting behind her knees, in the dip of her spine. All the high-season staff are here. The boys are unbuttoning their shirts already, the heat barely dipping though it's gone midnight and the stars are out. The stream looks fresh and cool and such a perfect blue, like gemstones and ice and she can imagine it between her toes, the feel of cool pebbles underfoot. She closes her eyes and sways until she feels something calling her away and she has to go. She has to move through the trees, brushing bark with her fingertips, letting branches caress her hair, and she's barefoot, grass between her toes, mud slipping. Earth and soil shadowed by oak and there, the flutter of wings in the trees, the single call of an owl, unanswered, and a *tap-tap-tapping* and she looks up to see the impossible red and black streaks of woodpeckers in the moonlight and there are voices now. Sounds.

Voices she doesn't know.

Voices calling to her, raised in song but not in song, rising together and her skin rises in goosebumps and her legs want to run but her heart won't let her; she has to see, has to be a part of what they're a part of until, look, there: trees parting, hiding down among the shrubs.

Something turns, gold to grey. Shimmering water to solid stone. Their heads are thrown back unnaturally. Arms wide, a screaming chant rising from their throats. Words she has never heard, never known, as they surge from the shadows and in the middle, on the stone, altar-like and immovable. She knows that girl. It's Abigail Moss. Her head is hanging back. Her eyes are wide and non-blinking. There's blood. Betty feels warm liquid trickling down her legs. She needs to run. She needs to get away, back to the stream which is empty and deserted, back through silver birches and aspen and there's someone with her, someone running beside her, sending her away and through the rose garden, scratched with thorns, and Frazer finds himself running from the room, through the gaping door, down the stairs and out, out of the manor and into the rain, thank God, the rain is heavy, endless, like it never stopped and Lee is shaking, Lee's shaking, he's pressing the bell for help and he's screaming, a rough rasping in his throat still raw from the tubes and someone's coming, someone's here, the nurse, she's saying calm down, what's happened, have a sip of water, there's no need for this, you're safe, it's okay, there's no one here, you see? Roll over now and take a look around your nice room and you'll see, there's no one here. There's no one coming to get you, I promise you that.

No one at all.

MEETING, TALKING, SCRATCHING

It's stinking hot in here and the floor is wet with footprints. Trish
has no idea how the community hall – empty all night – manages
to greet the morning smelling like teenage sweat and stale cleaning
equipment. She wanted to meet them early, though. Best chance
of not being seen.

Fergus has not been invited, so the meeting won't be getting
back to Georgie. Though from what Suze said, there might be
nothing left between them – is that why Georgie had looked so
devastated when Trish saw her at the hives? Fergus has not been
invited so Natalie Prowle won't know it's happening either. Maybe
that's the point. Keep Natalie away now Trish has taken her place;
Trish doesn't need any more enemies facing her. She's glad Suze
is here, so she's got a friend among the old guard: Mrs Dover,
Mrs Smyth, June and Whelan, Bessie Wilkie, Colin Spence,
Camellia Taylor. Most of them remember when Uncle Walt ran
the community council and now Trish is standing where he would
have stood and she knows what he knew too: the village is in a
bad state, and Ricky Barr is dangerous. That's what she's always
known and what she's got to hold on to. Trish Mackie, running
the council like her Uncle Walt before her. He'd have been proud
of her for this.

'You'd no need to rush here, dear,' Mrs Smyth is saying and
Trish turns, startled. 'We'd have waited for you. We're very patient
here on the community council.'

'I didn't rush,' says Trish – although she did run, she needed
a run – pulling off her soaking T-shirt and not giving a fuck if
Mrs Smyth does raise her eyebrows at Trish's thin vest top as
though it's indecent. In her bag: a fresh shirt.

The community centre is made up of one big hall, a smaller
room used as a kitchen, and some toilets. The walls of the main
hall are beige, stained from tape and Blu Tack used for securing
posters long gone. The ceiling is made of Perspex panels designed
to let in some light; the effect is to stun visitors with the noise of
battering rain in the winter and drown them in the heat of a
greenhouse in summer. Then there's the fourth wall, opposite the
door. The wall with the single painting. It has been framed and
professionally hung, an original oil portrait of a woman sitting in
a tall-backed wooden chair. Her brown hair, streaked with grey,
has been combed into a tight bun at the nape of her neck. Her
high collar is buttoned up to the throat and edged with unexpect-
edly frilly white lace. There are three dogs at her feet, though no
one can remember her ever owning dogs. But the artist got her
eyes right. From high on the wall of the community hall, Nora
Prowle's teal eyes follow everyone in the room. Natalie might not
be here, but her Aunt Nora never leaves.

Lee has those same eyes, too.

He's still in the hospital, Trish checked first thing. He's not sleeping,
they say, still shaking, still keeping nothing down. They think the
muscle spasms might be psychological, something like PTSD.

'When you're ready,' Mrs Dover says.

Trish nods at her but doesn't speak yet. Trish is the one who
starts the meetings these days, and she's deliberately taking her
time. That's the power of Uncle Walt's old dagger. The dagger

WHAT DOESN'T BREAK US

that, so far as Trish knows, has only ever been used to kill Ricky Barr's dog forty years ago, but the villagers are so in awe of it they think more of her now than they ever did when she was police. She doesn't have it with her, but they don't need to know that. It's at the university being dated. Information is what Trish needs. Proof, not superstition. Uncle Walt was trying to save the village from Ricky Barr, and Trish is going to finish what he started.

First, she is going to prove Ricky Barr is the one bringing in the drugs. Not just whatever concoction put Lee in hospital, but the lot of them. Uncle Walt dying there on his farm *means* something. With Ricky Barr out of the way, maybe she'll be able to persuade the villagers to band together and buy back some of the farmland, or some of his properties even. But she's getting ahead of herself. With Ricky gone, Andy will be safe. He can stay with his aunt Debs and have a better kind of life. Folk round here can start to feel a bit hopeful again. And then she's going to save the village from itself.

Like she should have saved Uncle Walt.

They're not going to be so keen on that one, the villagers, and so she's not going to spell it out for them. But things have to change round here. Ricky Barr is not the only problem. She wants the superstition gone, the suspicion of strangers gone, the fear of change gone. She wants this place back on its feet. Strong, not scared. Forward-looking.

'Thank you all for coming,' Trish says, and is surprised that she means it. They all came when she called, every one of them. 'I realise this is early in the day—'

'We know there's work to be done.' That's Camellia Taylor. 'Could have been my Penny-Ann in intensive care, if she'd not been so steady.'

Trish is fairly sure Penny-Ann Taylor would have taken just as much of whatever was being passed around as anyone else.

'And what about Lee?' Whelan, holding hands with June beside him. 'How is the lad?' His face is full of more concern than Trish is buying, but still, she gets it. Local kids, overdosing like that, everyone is rattled. They've a right to be.

'He's going to pull through,' Trish says. 'He's stable.'

'And the others?'

'They're all okay.'

'They're not though, are they,' says June. Her hair is greying now – did that happen this year?

'That's what we're here to talk about,' Trish says. 'They might be out of hospital, but they won't be okay for long – not if this happens again. And we all know who's responsible, don't we?'

Mrs Dover's eyes are fixed on her and there's a grating noise getting louder. Trish has been trying to ignore it but what the hell?

'Ricky Barr,' Trish says. 'We know it, but we still can't prove it.'

It's like a low humming, fake and insidious. Is it those strip lights they have in here, or something else, power sockets? It's getting under her skin like an itch.

'But if we focus, not on stealing his pets' – she glances at Elise Robertson, still can't believe Elise got herself involved with Natalie Prowle and killing that horse, wouldn't have thought Elise even had the stomach for it – 'but on finding out exactly what drugs he's selling, and to whom, we can take control of this situation.'

'Meaning?' says Mrs Dover.

'She'll hand him over to the police,' Elise says, and the edge to her voice doesn't half remind Trish of old Art Robertson. Like father, like daughter.

'Maybe I will,' says Trish. Georgie never believed her though, did she? None of them ever believed her. Uncle Walt is the only one who believed in her, and he died gasping for breath on Ricky Barr's farm while Ricky was there, watching. 'Or maybe a different answer will present itself.'

'Well, it's lovely to have you in charge, dear,' says Mrs Dover, taking Trish by surprise. 'And I know I speak for everyone when I say the time has come for change.'

Is she expecting Trish to say thank you?

'But there is some outstanding business.'

'I—'

'Some things Natalie was trying to achieve.'

'I don't know what you mean, Mrs Dover, so you're going to have to tell me—'

'She wanted to put up a bench.'

'A bench?'

'At the playground,' Bessie Wilkie adds. 'Next to the one already there.'

'She wanted to dedicate it to her Aunt Nora,' Mrs Dover finishes.

Trish shakes her head. 'I don't really...' Trish doesn't know how to express how much she doesn't care about some pointless bench. Above Mrs Dover's head, she can see the old portrait of Nora Prowle hanging there. No one's taken it down. Maybe Natalie's been protecting it. Trish finds herself scratching at her arm, sits on her hand to make herself stop.

'So you don't want the bench?' Mrs Dover says.

'Look, I suppose you can have the bench if you really want the bench.'

'I think perhaps we should shelve the bench,' Mrs Dover says.

'Fine,' says Trish.

'Thank you, Trish,' says Mrs Dover, with a glance up at Nora's portrait, a fleeting smile on her lips. 'That completes the outstanding business.'

There is a murmur of satisfaction through the community hall and Trish feels a sudden compulsion to run out of the door. She doesn't do it, though. Where else has she got to go? Besides, she is here for Uncle Walt.

FOLLOWING FOOTSTEPS

Walt Mackie believed in the Others. The village ancestors. He was convinced they'd come back when summoned by the threefold death, to help him protect the village when it was under threat. Fergus Strachan doesn't believe any of that, course he doesn't. He's been reading about the threefold death, though. A traditional sacrifice by air, water and blood. It was thought to have been used by the Celts. Now that he can believe. The past is important, to Fergus. He's been thinking about it ever since he left Natalie's house for this thick rain – creeping downstairs, silently closing the door behind him. It wasn't till he was out in the sticky heat he realised Natalie hadn't been home anyway. She'd been at the hospital, with Lee.

'He's been biting his lips,' she'd told him last night. 'They're covered in bruises and sores. Why would he do that to himself, Fergus?'

He didn't have an answer, just shook his head and offered a useless arm around her shoulders. Today, though, he's not sitting around feeling useless. He's going to find the henge. Discover proof of a stone circle, if there was one – and he believes there was. He's got his survey photos from the drone, the Warphill standing stone's shadow at sunrise pointing him on a straight path between the motte and the cup-and-ring stone in Mungrid Woods.

He needs to walk that line all the way to Burrowhead, and once it leads him somewhere he is, quite simply, going to dig. He spent long enough on the excavation at the motte to know how it's done. The university aren't interested in exploring further, so he will.

This is what he's meant to be doing.

As he walks, he can feel scratching on his skin through the heavy air. It's the same as when he had his episode at the standing stone, that terrible migraine, when he imagined he could see the Others for himself. Their voices rasping at him as they rose from their grave. The murdered ancestors of the village. The family with their shattered teeth and desperate eyes. Walt Mackie was wrong. They weren't coming back to help the village; they were asking for help themselves. But they weren't real, obviously. He presses the heels of his hands into his eyes until the vision is gone and he's thinking straight.

He has plotted an accurate path. Right. He's going to do this like the scientist he is. It'll be good for the PhD application he's been planning while he's felt unable to leave Natalie's house. That couldn't go on, hiding like that. He'd even hidden from Georgie yesterday. Couldn't face the disappointment he knew he'd see in her eyes when she looked at him. Does she even care that he moved out? Of course she does. She'd tried to phone. Maybe she was worried about him. Maybe she wanted him to get the rest of his stuff. He can't face that. He can't even face her. It was good to hear her voice though, it really was. If she were here now, she'd tell him he's being ridiculous, wandering out towards Burrowhead to search for an ancient henge. She'd tell him to stop imagining things.

It wasn't just Walt who believed in the Others, though. It's Natalie too. She thinks they appear when the village needs help. Well, Fergus thinks they could all do with some help now. He's got the direction from the three menhirs: the standing stone outside Warphill, the broken stone buried in the motte, and the stone of the cup and ring. He has until four o'clock, when his shift starts.

He follows wet roads and soggy tracks, walks over yellowing grass drowned to mud. He can feel the height of the standing stone behind him as he pushes his way between gorse and cow parsley and on through the muggy rain. Not a person sees him. He could stretch out and touch the motte to his right and the cup and ring on his left and he's doing it, he's stretching his arms wide, one to the left, one to the right. A brush of leaves against his fingertips. The woods are calling but he won't go to them, despite the promise of shade and the cool shadows of birch and ash. He keeps them either side, the stone of the cup and ring and the mound of the motte rising against the blistering white sky and straight ahead, that's his route. Towards Burrowhead. Towards the coast.

THINGS THAT CAN MAKE
A DIFFERENCE

Si's been waiting at the garage for a while and he's had a shot of the rank espresso they sell from that self-service machine. He's sweating and fed up and Terry was supposed to be here to meet him for an interview and if he doesn't turn up soon he's a good mind to escort him down to the station and get this done with a bit of weight behind him.

Light touch, though, Georgie told him. 'He was in hospital too, remember. Could still be feeling a bit shaky. Let's not burn our bridges just yet.'

Well, he might have been in the hospital with them, and in the caravan, and on whatever damned trip they were on, but Terry wasn't a kid like the others – they were at school together, Terry and Si, in the same year. They weren't friends, exactly, though there was that kiss at a party, both of them fourteen and still figuring it all out. Then Terry started going out with Suze, which didn't last beyond school, and by then Si couldn't wait to leave anyway.

'Mate!' Terry calls from up the road, face all smiles.

Now Terry's seen him he's jogging the last few metres – through the heat, through the drizzle of rain. He's got a grin that always comes with a chuckle and a complexion that flushes easily to match.

'Sorry I'm late,' Terry's saying beside him now.

'It's no bother.'

'But I want to help.'

'You mean you'd have called us if I hadn't called you?'

There's the laugh, nervous, embarrassed, the flick of the eyes down then up.

'D'you want to come into the office?'

'Aye, sure.'

The office is a small desk with a computer in what Simon would describe as a cupboard behind the till in the garage shop. There's a chair for Terry and a fold-up one against the wall for Si.

'Coffee?'

Simon shakes his head. 'Thanks, no.'

'Right,' Terry says. 'Where do you want me to start?'

'How about the night of Lee's overdose?'

He seems keener to talk now Julie Alperstein isn't here telling him to keep quiet.

'Sure, sure.'

Simon doesn't get more specific, and Terry looks around again.

'Will I—'

'Whatever *you* want to say.'

'Okay, well, it was Lee who invited me along. And it was Lee who asked me to look after the gear the day before.'

Simon's taken aback.

'I know what you're thinking,' Terry says. 'And you've got a point. Aaron was right pissed off. But it was Lee who got the gear, and he didn't even trust Aaron to keep it in the caravan.'

'Lee?'

'Yep.'

'You're saying it's Lee gets the drugs, not Aaron?'

But why is he so ready with the accusations, so happy to land his friend in it?

'It was Aaron used to work with Bobby right enough,' Terry says. 'But Lee was giving the orders that night. Still had the bruise on his jaw his brother gave him, mind.'

'They'd fought?'

'Like they could have killed each other, aye.'

'So what was going on?'

Terry shrugs, gives Simon another grin. 'Wild guess? I'd say Lee's taken over whatever it was Aaron had going on. Doing it smarter too, I'd say.'

'Meaning?'

'He told me, anything happens, just tell the police. No lying, no taking the rap – no need. The stuff's legal. *I* know that, and now you know it too.'

Ah.

'And I've told Julie and all, she's no need to keep being so paranoid.'

That's where Simon will be going next – to interview Julie Alperstein and Penny-Ann Taylor. See if their story, if they will talk to him, matches Terry's.

'But I'm not saying it weren't weird. Mate, you should have *smelled* it.'

'What did it smell of?'

Terry's shaking his head then all of a sudden he slaps the back of his neck, like something bit him there, a mosquito or something.

'Fuck knows,' Terry says, looking at his hand. 'This weather, man. I mean, it's not normal, is it, not for around here.'

'It's not.'

'But tell you what, the closest smell is when there's a dead bird or something out on the beach, you know, like lying there rotting. All the flies swarming about it. The seaweed. The way that smell is heavy, yeah? It smelled like that in the flask he gave it me in. Told me to keep it cool and it was better, after a night in the fridge.'

'And you drank that?'

His laugh bursts out of his mouth like he didn't see it coming then abruptly stops. 'I held my nose and downed it, same as everyone else. I tell you what, though?'

'What?'

'Before Lee and that, before he had his reaction?'

'What?'

'It was worth it.'

The office itself smells of stale coffee and sweat; the shop smells of the two-day-old sausage rolls in the glass holder by the till; the garage, petrol spills and car exhausts. It's unpleasant enough, without imagining the smell of rotting gulls on the beach.

'You'd do it again?'

'I would that, aye.'

Simon doesn't know what to say. What is wrong with him? Drinking that revolting mix of animal blood and dirt, for what, a quick trip, to impress a bunch of teenagers who'd only invited him along so he'd take the risk of possession.

'Why are you hanging round with these kids, Terry?'

For a second Terry looks startled. Then he looks hurt.

'I mean...' Si shakes his head. 'What are you doing?'

'What else am I meant to be doing, eh? Everyone I know has fucked off. You, me, and Suze, we're about the only ones left here from our year at school, aren't we?'

It's true enough.

'Suze doesn't give a shit, and Bobby's dead.'

Simon blinks. He'd forgotten Terry and Bobby had been friends.

'Good riddance too, maybe, but fuck – who else is there? You?'

'Me?'

'Serious, where are you all the time? When you're not...' Terry gestures up and down at Simon, at the uniform. 'Friday night, never see you down the pub. Weekends – not a sign of you is there. Where d'you go, eh?'

Where does he go?

Waking up to realise he's not in his flat, not in his bed with the empty space left behind by Alexis; not with Alexis's pictures on the walls or photos ready to kick him in the guts with what his life was before compared to what he's trying to put back together.

Where does he go?

Waking up to a window in the wrong place but also in the right place, light streaming through, noise outside: traffic and voices and life, shops opening and people chatting on the street, the sound of cars, the beep of a pedestrian crossing. Even the disagreements – and Si's not one to kid himself on, it's not like everyone down on the street is best pals – but even the blare of a horn, the shout of *fuck you* as a car gets too close to a cyclist, the yelling at a bus that doesn't stop, all of it, has something comforting about it. The window open through the heat of the night. The sweltering sweetness of the city air, the cool white sheet tangled around his ankles and the smell of fresh bread. And he knows it's not like this all through the city. He knows this is the best part of the city, the rich part, but maybe he's allowed to enjoy this, to be in this moment, and beside him Orlando is stretching in his familiarity of it all, pulling him back to bed.

A rich kid, and Simon knows it.

A rich kid who knows what he wants and isn't afraid or hiding or apologising, not for one second. That confidence, that's a thing of privilege, isn't it? Is that where Simon's going, into that other world where he can relax into just existing instead of fighting. To a flat that's got wide windows and a view over the financial district to the lakes beyond, and yes, croissants from the expensive bakers on the corner that Orlando buys, coffee that Orlando grinds every morning, standing in his underwear in his kitchen that he owns – and Simon can't hardly get over this, twenty-two years old, final year at uni and he *owns his own flat* – as the smell of freshly ground coffee wafts through the air like he's in Paris or Rome. Lying naked in someone else's bed in the elusive West End of the city while at the coast Burrowhead and Warphill and Crackenbridge disintegrate into clumps of poverty and prejudice, with their smell of rotting seaweed and chips soggy with grease, and Orlando is reaching for him again, so sure of himself, sure of what he can get with that easy way in which he slows and why wouldn't he be, Simon's not saying no, he's smiling and Terry's looking at him with something like, what is that, envy?

'You get the fuck out of Burrowhead, I bet.'

It's true; Simon gets the fuck out of Burrowhead every chance he has. God but he needs it. Counting down the days till the weekend. The hours. Finally starting to feel alive again.

REASONS TO TURN AWAY

Natalie wants to reach out and stroke his forehead, like she'd have done when he was a baby; when he used to come toddling up to plant a kiss on her cheek, when he refused to nap unless she was there, sleeping beside him, the two of them in a muddle of arms and legs and warm breath.

She daren't, now.

How does that happen?

The hospital smells. It can't be sick, can it? No, it's the food and the way they clean the floors, the way disinfectant leaves the smell of something stale, like mildew lingering in the walls. But the place is perfectly clean. She can *see* that it's clean. So it must be the food – and the heat, everyone sweating under their clothes and their scrubs. Skin resents being hidden from the air like that.

Lee's skin is open to the air though, it's free to recover and still it carries the sheen of sweat that makes him look feverish, alien. It's glistening too much. For a second she finds it repulsive. Her son. She closes her eyes, knows she's going to hate herself for days for that thought, which clawed its way up into her mind, unwanted.

She should talk to him. Tell him she loves him.

'Lee?' she tries.

She's been sitting here so long without speaking that her voice sounds wrong in the room. How long? She doesn't know. Checks her watch. Forty-five minutes. Not even that long, then. Not halfway through visiting hours yet.

'Son?' Her number two son but always her number one.

She's a bad mother. She knows it every time she thinks that. Remembers how Aaron always scared her, even as a kid, how he'd jump to violence as a first resort, like his father. But not Lee. Lee was a gentle child. Her little gentleman.

Pamali says she's not a bad mother. Says she needs to stop thinking like that. Pamali thinks what's done is done and the only way to live is through what you do next.

Could she bend forwards, gently kiss his sweating forehead?

What would Aunt Nora do, knowing he'd taken some concoction of drugs that had put him in intensive care? Hit him, quite possibly, or try to; and that is no good. That's not how Natalie is, nor how she ever wants to be. She's seen enough punishment. She raised him better than this, though – she never raised him to be stupid. And he's not; neither of her sons are stupid. Maybe this will be enough to wake him up, this sickness.

'Lee,' she tries again, and this time she lets her hand rest on top of the sheet lying over his arm. 'Son.'

Natalie wishes boys didn't have to turn into men. Another failing, no doubt; surely a good mother would want her children to grow up. Not her. She'd have kept them exactly as they were at six and eight, if she'd had her way. That was a perfect year, that one. A year of sun and sandcastles and, later, snow dusting the village. The year Lee finally figured out how to ride his bike and simultaneously learnt to ignore Aaron's mockery, the year even Aaron joined in to sing carols when she took them round the villages. The pair of them had voices like angels, everyone said, standing at their doors, eyes glistening just a touch.

Aunt Nora never got to meet her boys, and maybe that was for the best. She was dead before they were born. Aunt Nora, who said her job was to protect her home no matter what, and sometimes that was going to mean protecting the villagers from themselves. Natalie was a child then, twelve, maybe thirteen – old enough to understand but not old enough to really understand – staring at the engravings on her Aunt Nora's precious, ancient knife. Tracing the shapes of the people, walking in a line that became, as she followed it around the handle of the blade, a circle, each of them in long cloaks, their faces masked, heads pointed, arms raised. They made her shoulder blades crunch together, sent a shiver beneath her hairline. Aunt Nora's eyes watched her all the while.

Do you understand?

Aunt Nora's voice like silk, making her feel special.

It is our job to protect these villages.

Her fingers cold on Natalie's face, drawing her gaze upwards.

If you need help, you must summon help.

'What the fuck are you doing?'

Lee's awake, struggling to sit, hitting her hand away and she hadn't, had she – was she tracing her own fingers over his face the way Aunt Nora had hers?

'Fuck!'

He's glaring at her with all the hate he can muster as he struggles to catch his breath, wiping his wrist over his head as though the glistening sweat there is a deposit from her, from Natalie.

'Hi,' she tries.

The air sucked into his lungs and held there, blown out through clenched teeth.

'How long have you been sitting there?'

The anger in him, what's causing that? Shock? Fear?

'Good morning, Lee—'

'It's fucking creepy.'

'Son, I had to see you, I want to—'

'What?' Yelled, accusing her of something, but what, what?

'I want to help you. You can talk to me. You can tell me…'

138

He snorts out another breath and it catches his throat and suddenly he's coughing, clutching at his neck as though every rasp is causing him pain.

'Is it sore, son?'

His eyes glaring through the coughs.

'I'll call the nurse.'

She presses the call button. Waits. Sunlight through the window, burning its way through the dappled glass they have there, like the patients shouldn't be allowed to see out, not completely, not without protection.

'They'll be a few minutes, will they?'

The sound of his cough, it's killing her.

'Son, I just want—'

'*What?*'

'I want to help.'

'Then please stop visiting.'

She's not going to rise to that; she's his mother, she loves him. Could she say that, to Lee, here, that she loves him?

'Where are the drugs coming from, Lee?' Her voice careful and pleading. She's his mother, she needs to save him.

'Fuck.' His head shaking, fists clenched, but she's saying names: Ricky Barr, Terry, Aaron, names from the village, names of the dead, Bobby, Pauly, Walt Mackie, every name she can think of, Art Robertson? *Elise* Robertson? Searching for a reaction, a glimmer of something in his eyes as she says names of people she's known all her life until he turns away, starts biting at his lips again and she can't stand it.

'Just get out of here, Mam.'

'I'm trying to help.'

'You're not helping!'

'You're in pain—'

'GO!'

The hate in his eyes, so sudden and clear and sharp and she can't take it. Something in her switches and she can feel the residue of his sweat on her fingers, she needs to wash her hands, get it off, get away from his spite and his blame and why is he like this, like Aaron, all full of rage at the world?

'You look like your father.'

'Please,' he says, his voice softer now but still rough. 'You don't know what you're doing, alright? You need to stay away.'

'Okay then.' She stands. 'I—'

'Just go.'

So she leaves the room, leaves the hospital, and something falls from her shoulders, though there was nothing there to fall, and something touches the skin on her arm, above the elbow, like an insect bite, sharp-toothed and malicious.

AN INFORMAL INTERVIEW
OVER LUNCH

'Another policeman,' Julie Alperstein says, standing in the doorway of the caravan Ricky Barr's given her for the summer. 'Lucky us.'

'I'm no wearing a suit though.'

'So he reported what I said back to you, did he?'

Simon just grins at her.

'No wait, is DS Frazer your boss?'

'Not exactly,' Si says. 'Can I come in please, it's raining?'

Penny-Ann appears at the door too.

'Alright, Si?'

She looks happy, Penny-Ann, positively bubbly, and she flicks the kettle on and starts chatting about how it's lunch break and does Si want a sandwich too 'cause she's got plenty hummus and red pepper and it's Julie's recipe and she loves it and he'd be welcome to share what they've got.

'I'm okay for now,' Si says. 'Thanks though.'

Julie, throughout all this, is sat quietly watching him, with her short bob, shaved up at the neck, and that sharp fringe halfway across her forehead.

'What exactly do you have against DS Frazer?' Si asks.

Julie shrugs.

'He must think he's better than the lot of you.'

'Because he wears a suit?'

'The whole attitude.'

'Dan Frazer's alright,' Si says. 'You might want to check your own privilege there.'

Julie goes quiet for a second, and Penny-Ann hands him a chipped mug of herbal tea.

'I'm hoping you might be willing to answer some of my questions, though.'

'Fire away,' Penny says.

He looks at Julie.

'Alright, we'll tell you what we can,' she says with a sigh.

Penny takes her hand and Julie seems unable to stop the smile lighting up her face. Simon thinks about leading in with something innocuous but changes his mind, takes a sip of his tea – it's peppermint. He likes peppermint.

'So who gave you the drugs?'

'Terry arrived with the flask,' Julie says. 'But he didn't seem to be in charge of anything.'

'Lee was the one who served up,' Penny adds.

'And all the while Aaron sat there looking ready to punch Lee's lights out,' Julie finishes.

So Terry might have been telling him the truth. It feels like they're all blurting out the truth now.

'And do you know where they got it from? Lee, or Aaron, whichever of them it was – who sold it to them?'

'We have absolutely no idea,' Penny-Ann says. 'And I'd tell you if I knew. I'd quite like to find out myself.' She glances at Julie with a grin.

There's only one more interview he has to do after this, and that's Aaron Prowle himself. Saving the best for last.

WHAT GEORGIE LEFT BEHIND, TWENTY YEARS AGO

Even though his face has become more familiar than any other, Georgie is still surprised by how young Fergus Strachan looks sometimes.

'How long has it been?' he asks her, gently, and there's no hint of accusation in his voice, it's not a judgement. In Glasgow he saw his own mother every week, every Saturday for dinner, and even now they've moved, with the drive, he visits twice a month.

'It's not the same,' Georgie says. 'Your mom's just up the road. My folks are in a different country.'

'You could fly over to see them, couldn't you?'

'I can't go back there.'

She phones, every month or so, she does that, even though it leaves her reeling and sick every time. The pauses in the conversation, the gaps where Errol should be, or her father – the gaps where he is, beside her mom but not wanting to come to the phone.

He's not a phone person, Georgie.

But it's nothing to do with the telephone. She can hear their grief down the line, doesn't need the lack of her father's voice to know what is lacking between her and her father. It's the weight of it she can't lift any more – she could have let it crush her, but she chose to let it fall in the sea between them and start living her life.

'They'll always be welcome to visit us,' Fergus says and just like that he frees her again, allows his meaning to shift from her broken family to their home – a shared place, his as much as hers. It takes her by surprise every time, the gentle reminder that she's no longer one person alone, that even this rented flat in Crackenbridge is something joint. 'Though I admit it would be a squash on the sofa and we could do with a spare room...'

'They're not coming, Fergus.' She smiles, reaches in for a kiss.

'I meant in general.' His hand stays resting against her face as he says that. 'Maybe we could think about...'

It's almost a game, the way she doesn't quite let him say it, just waits as he edges his way closer day by day. The truth is she can see it, clear as he can. Their life together. Of course they're going to have a life together.

'Cup of tea?' She smiles, lets it break into a laugh.

'Heard anything about the job yet?'

She shakes her head.

'I mean...no pressure.'

'Fergus, you couldn't pressure me if you tried.'

'Steady on.'

She pressures herself well enough though. He's doing well, Fergus, with his new position, a whole team under him, a career, a future. Georgie needs her own job, her own income, and more than that, a purpose. That's why she's making him wait. If they're going to buy a house it needs to be both of them buying it. That much she knows.

Somewhere on the coast, maybe.

Somewhere beautiful.

'You're going to make a great policeperson,' he says, and he's right about that. He's taking her hand, pulling her back down to the sofa but for a second her mom's words surface again in her mind and she has to push them down.

Your father's ill, Georgie.

'I'll make it,' Fergus says.

'Make what?'

'The tea.'

The concern flickers across his face. She doesn't want him worrying about her. Trying to save her.

'On you go then,' she says, and as he stands, he keeps hold of her hand as though he's going to lead her all the way through to the kitchen, and through her first job, through his proposal, her promotion, a wedding in Glasgow and two more rented homes until they make it to a cottage on the outskirts of Burrowhead where the garden flows with honeysuckle and montbretia and where they both think they're done with change, until things start changing again.

DEGREES OF SEPARATION

'Okay,' Georgie says, scrunching her eyes shut for a second then opening them again, wider. 'Everything we have. Who wants to start. Frazer?'

'Ma'am. As you know, interviewing the residents about Abigail Moss hadn't turned up any useful links, until yesterday. No one knew anything. But in Mrs Dover's front room I saw a photograph of a young-looking Mrs Pettigrew on her wedding day.'

'Mrs Pettigrew,' Georgie says, 'being the housekeeper at Wyndham Manor at the time Abigail Moss disappeared.'

'Exactly. So I've found a link from a resident of Burrowhead back to Wyndham Manor, and from today back to 1962: Gail Dover, to Mrs Pettigrew, to Abigail Moss.'

'Good,' Georgie says. 'And Mrs Pettigrew is where?'

'Deceased, ma'am. Twenty years ago.'

Of course she is.

'Family?'

'None.'

'Right.' Georgie sighs.

'Well...' Frazer says. 'None except Mrs Dover herself.'

'They were related?'

'Mrs Pettigrew was Gail Dover's godmother.'

'Gail Dover,' Georgie says, sitting down and leaning back in her chair.

'Yes, Gail Dover,' says Frazer. 'She's been here most of her life, from what I can tell. Can you both confirm that?'

'She's lived in that same house for as long as I've been alive,' Simon says. 'And I suspect a long while before. I think she was a teacher at Burrowhead Primary – that was in the 1970s maybe? It's closed down now. When I was a kid she worked at the garden centre on the road out of Crackenbridge, which also closed down ages ago.'

'It was the garden centre first got me interested in her,' Frazer says.

'Through the bench with the dedication to Abigail Moss?'

'Exactly. But she doesn't seem to know anything about Abigail Moss, doesn't even recognise the name. All we have is the link to Mrs Pettigrew.'

'And what other family does she have?' Georgie asks. 'Other than Cal.'

'Her one and only son,' Simon says with a grin. 'Our very own Cal Dover.'

'But if Mrs Dover has been here all her life, then that means Cal grew up in Burrowhead too?' Frazer says. 'I thought he was from...' He shakes his head.

Simon sips his coffee. 'Nope. He was raised here, went to Edinburgh to study, then came back to head up the forensics lab in Crackenbridge.'

'And what about extended family?'

'Well, this is Burrowhead,' Simon says with a shake of his head. 'Mrs Dover's family have been here forever. Her parents are both dead, but they used to live in the same house as she does now.'

'And she didn't have any siblings?'

'She was an only child. Probably why her and Mrs Smyth have always been inseparable. She's related to Camellia Taylor by marriage, through a cousin I think – though the cousin in question scarpered and left Camellia with three kids and debts up to her elbows. She had to sell up, take that council place in Warphill. And she's related to the Prowles, notoriously. Nora and Jacob Prowle and Gail Dover's parents had some kind of big fall-out, but they were family. This was back before Mrs Dover was married.'

'When her name was Gail Braxton,' Frazer says.

Georgie stands up again, finds herself walking over to the window. No grey eyes reflected there today. This restlessness in her legs, the muggy weight of the air. Maybe it's a good thing Crackenbridge couldn't spare Suze this week; another person in here and the heat would become unbearable.

'So the Dovers and the Prowles were both originally part of the Braxton family,' she says. 'Though there are no actual Braxtons left.'

'Braxtons...' Frazer says, but his voice trails off.

That cluster of birds fighting over something on the ground, the squawking through the glass. That must have been what pulled her over here.

'Are you okay, Georgie?'

That's Si, talking from behind her.

'Those gulls are back.'

And the little girl is gone.

'Oh good,' he says. 'They're not so bad, those kittiwakes.'

She glances at him sideways.

'D'you want a coffee?'

'No more coffee,' she says. 'But thanks.' Turning to face them again. Checking the room: she is gone. 'Okay, what have you got from today, Si?'

He smiles like he's pleased with himself and it makes Georgie smile too. The progress, the birds, whatever it is; it's the first time she's seen his face light up like that in a long while.

'Well, I've got Terry claiming that Lee was the one who gave him the flask of drugs to look after. Separately from that, I've got

Julie Alperstein and Penny-Ann Taylor confirming that Lee was the one who seemed to be in charge in the caravan.'

'They spoke to you then?' Frazer says with a raise of his eyebrows.

'They seemed happy to.' Si grins at him. 'But I think that was less about you looking suspiciously official and more about Terry convincing them there's no danger since the concoction they took was legal.'

'Well, he could be right about that.'

'No danger from us, maybe. Lee and Aaron had a bust-up a few days ago apparently, nearly punched each other's lights out. Putting it all together, it seems Lee was the one who got hold of the drugs, not Aaron.'

'Lee Prowle,' Georgie says.

'Lee Prowle, who's related to Nora Prowle, who's related to Gail Dover,' says Frazer.

'And what does Aaron have to say about all this?' Georgie asks.

'Aaron,' Simon says, 'appears to be avoiding me.'

WHAT THE RIGHT
PEOPLE CAN FIND

'You know, when Lee passed that flask to me, I thought it was going to be disgusting,' Julie says.

Penny-Ann's in front, leading her by the hand into the woods, and she glances over her shoulder. 'Fuck, me too. The way it was thick like black soup or something.'

They're passing through close-growing silver birch, tall aspens rustling in the breeze overhead and the rain's gone for now, the woodland granting them shelter, maybe, or just a break in the weather. The smell is fresh and healthy, and there's sunlight glinting between branches despite the heavy cloud covering beyond the trees.

'I only drank it 'cause you did,' Penny says. 'You seemed like totally confident.'

'As if!'

'You did though.'

Julie can remember almost walking out of the caravan actually. She probably would have if Penny-Ann hadn't been there with her. But when she put the flask to her lips it wasn't disgusting at all. It was earthy and rich and something else too, something she can't put her finger on. Then she saw Penny's eyes turning golden and starting to glow and her skin was glowing too, and everything became more intense, the colours, the need.

'What?'

She's stopped walking, the memory of it surfacing so fully, pulsing like the trees around them, and Julie pulls Penny-Ann to her and when she opens her eyes again the sun is glinting through the leaves like sequins.

'Well,' Penny says, kissing her softer. 'I think you like the woods.'

'They're alive, aren't they.'

'Come on. It gets better.'

Julie doesn't know if it's an after-effect, a hangover throbbing through her veins, but she feels like something profound is about to happen as her feet sink into the soft moss of woodland floor and Penny leads her deeper through the trees.

'It's not much further,' she says.

'I'm not tired.'

'Good to know.'

Her laugh is like a peal of bells and the canopy of leaves over-head has turned golden green, and they walk on, hand in hand, over moss-padded ground and feathery grass. There are no sharp twigs, no rough stones or gravel as the branches descend around them. Penny slows, reaches out, lets her fingertips brush the intricate leaves that encroach on their path, invites Julie to do the same. Julie doesn't know them; they look like they could be sharp like holly, but they're not, they're gentle as ferns, made up of dozens of smaller, fragile leaflets, curling in on her touch as if to protect themselves.

'What is it?'

She has never felt anything like it, never seen anything like it.

'Mimosa burnuiflora.'

'Never heard of it.'

Penny places her hand over Julie's, curling her fingers around one of the leaves.

'It only grows here, in these woodlands. We all know about it, it's like something kids whisper about. Rumour is you can smoke it, or eat it, like...'

151

She smiles again, like something forbidden.

'Like mushrooms?'

'But better.'

'You think it's what we had the other night?'

'I'm not sure. I guess it was part of it.'

'You didn't tell the police that bit.'

'Yeah, I thought you'd be pleased.' She grins. 'And I thought you'd like to see for yourself...'

Penny's hand is still clasped loosely around hers, the leaf protected in the soft cage of their fingertips, and Julie's eyes adjust as if she's stepped from the dark into bright light. They are surrounded by mimosa. There are no birch trees here, no aspen or elder, here the mimosa alone is thriving. She finds herself kneeling down, pulling Penny beside her. The branches hang low and the ground is rich and brown, no moss or grass beneath the thick trunks. Its bark is rough and Julie's sure she can see something carved into it, cuts made into the plant, deep below the leaf-bearing branches. Penny's hand follows hers, follows the trunk down to the soil, and Julie doesn't know if she can feel it, the heat, the pull to dig deep to the roots and she doesn't want to break the silence but suddenly Penny's hand is gone and she's scrambling to her feet.

'What's wrong?'

'What the fuck is that?'

Penny's pointing to a different mimosa, dense and unwelcoming, and there's something there, beneath jagged leaves – she's reaching her arm in through the twisted branches and pulling something out, a bag, a rucksack, placing it carefully on the ground between them and then looking at Julie.

'Whose is that?'

Penny shrugs.

'There's something inside.'

Julie pulls the zip and the air is humming with the buzz of bees and the drip of rain through leaves and they take out everything they have found, laying it all on the ground between them: a series of delicate blades, each one smaller than a penknife, three earthenware pots, and a pestle and mortar that look ancient and well used, stained ruddy with herbs and plants. On the handle of the largest knife there are words, scratched into the metal. No, not words, initials.

PD

'Who's PD?'

Penny purses her lips. 'Pauly Dawkes, I think.'

'Who's Pauly Dawkes?'

'He's a kid who died last year.' Penny looks like she's spooked, properly spooked, and Julie hasn't seen that before – the Penny she knows looks sharp and alert and unafraid. 'He killed himself.'

'Jesus.' Julie swallows, looks behind her, though there's no one there. 'So what do we do with this?'

Penny gasps. She's looking beyond the clearing, further into the woods, and that's when Julie sees it too. Hanging from an ancient half-dead oak, the arms snagged on gnarled branches.

'Shit. I thought that was…'

'A person. Me too, for a second.'

They both take a minute, catch their breath.

'Okay,' Julie says. 'You wait here, I'll get it.' She can feel her energy returning, her vision getting back to normal. She has no idea why she was feeling so spaced out, but she knows what she's looking at now: it's a hoody, that's all. Just a hoody snagged on a tree in Mungrid Woods. Except that it's smeared with something that looks like blood.

REASONS TO STAY

Fergus has left Mungrid Woods and the cup and ring far behind. The motte, with its brutal grave and its broken stone, is distant as memory. It's only the menhir, the standing stone outside Warphill he can still feel, like a pressure on the back of his neck. He takes a deep breath of the clinging, humid air. He's got a bottle of tap water with him and it's cool from the ice at its core; he put it in the freezer overnight, an old trick of Georgie's. He can take that idea with him, can't he? But his back is killing him. He crunches his shoulder blades together and something clicks, joint, bone, cartilage. There's movement up ahead, a shadow, a creature—

No, nothing, no one. He's alone.

Another gulp of water, then the bottle away in the side pouch of his rucksack and he's walking southward to Burrowhead: a small gathering of houses scooped together in a spoon of land between the cliffs and the farms, their low roofs a matching terracotta tile. The sky textured beyond the mist and cloud. It's so pretty it could be a postcard, from here. His legs are carrying him faster towards the village, but the angles are wrong, he has to cross the road to correct his course. The standing stone's not pointing to Burrowhead at all. The church ruin, that's where it's taking him. Then he's standing in the graveyard and someone's followed him, someone's here. He can't deny it, can't outrun them. Breath behind him, the crunch of footsteps but when he turns: no one. The old cherry tree beyond the gates, bits of fabric tied to the branches, fluttering in an absent breeze and he's touching them and behind him—

He spins, stares.

Nothing.

His arm has fallen to his side and with it came one of the offerings, a white and peach strip of fabric. He wonders what it was, before. A pillowcase, perhaps, somewhere to rest your head. He reties it in place, tells himself there must be more of a breeze than he can feel. The ebb and flow of breath through teeth is just wind through stone. The stones themselves are dissolving in the rain, crumbling against his fingertips and there's no one here, no one walking through the ancient graveyard. It's hard to avoid the graves, though, so many unmarked, so many overgrown. They're rising through the ground, the graves in this churchyard. He's heard people say that and he knows what they mean.

The pillars of the ruin were once magnificent archways all around the church. They're etched with lines, their tops carved with gargoyles, their faces eroded to shapes and hints at features, dips for eyes, protrusions where once there might have been a tongue, perhaps, a chin. The stone is dark grey now, mottled and lichen-layered and he's pulled closer, as he was once to the menhir, to decipher the marks. There must be meaning. Names carved into stone. Prayers barely visible – but no, he's imagining that. It's erosion, vandalism, a breath behind him. Whispers calling him to the church, to the pews filled with shadow. He reaches for the stone to steady himself but it's cold and damp and beneath his fingers the shapes are moving, shifting, and he falls against the wall and there are specks of gold, his head pounding, and through the stained glass he can see the old minister hanging where the villagers strung him up and he runs, he runs until he is beyond the church, down the trampled track that leads to the coast where at last he stops, hands on knees, gasping for air.

There's nothing out here. This is the end. The end of Church Street is the end.

His path didn't even take him through Burrowhead. It scratched the edge of the village then led him here. Fergus feels his skin tightening. It led him past the woods and through the church ruin to this desolate spot on the cliffs. The exact spot where Rachel and Pauly jumped last year.

'Fergus?'

His back jerks with fright and he stumbles closer to the edge.

'Fergus, are you alright?'

He regains his balance, turns. He knew he wasn't alone. Natalie is here. He should be pleased to have some company.

'Were you following me?'

He is pleased – he doesn't know why his voice is coming out all wrong.

'I drove here from the hospital.'

She looks out at the waves and he can see in the corner of her eyes, the raw redness there, that she's been crying.

'Oh, Natalie.' He reaches for her arm, stops short of touching it. 'Are you okay?'

'I'm going to tell you something,' she says. 'And I need you to make a promise.'

'What is it?' He waits but she doesn't reply. 'Natalie?'

'I want you to promise to help me.'

'Of course, after everything you've done for me, giving me a place to stay and... I'm always here to help.'

'No.' She closes her eyes, shakes her head. 'I want you to *promise* to help me.'

Fergus reaches for his water bottle again, but it's empty.

'Is it about the henge?' he says, but that's a stupid thing to say. 'Is it about Lee?'

'You need to promise.'

She looks at him and he was right, he's sure of it, she may have driven here from the hospital but there were tears streaming down her face as she did.

'Okay,' he says. 'I promise. Tell me.'

WHAT A SENSE OF
PURPOSE CAN DO

Shona used to find it annoying, the way Rachel believed in things that others didn't. It was a partition in their friendship, Rachel believing in things and Shona questioning them. But since she died, Rachel believing is one of the things Shona misses the most. She looks for it sometimes, in herself, but she has too many questions – and in Kevin, though the closest he seems to get is his belief in Shona. She was even looking for it in Georgie. It's not faith, exactly. More like a sense of purpose. A certainty.

'Kev?'

Shona puts her arm out and he stops rummaging through Aaron and Lee's caravan, returns a pack of dried noodles to the cupboard where he found them.

'Someone's coming?'

'Just stop for a minute,' she says.

He turns to look at her.

'I don't think there's anything here. Whatever it was in that flask, it's gone.'

'So that's it then?'

'That's not what I said.'

He stops then.

'Look, do you remember that night in the graveyard?'

'Of course I remember. Shona, what is it?'

'Remember what happened afterwards? The way Lee started spreading that crap about Rachel trying to summon the dead—'

'It wasn't crap though, was it?'

She looks at him.

'Alright, Lee was an arse. I was an arse. We all were.'

Shona swallows.

'It was all of our fault,' he says. 'That's why we're trying to make it right, isn't it?'

Footsteps outside, unmistakable. Someone's walking up to the caravan. It must be Aaron, shit. But no, they're walking past. Walking to Kev's caravan. Shona lifts a corner of the flimsy curtain, peers out to see Penny-Ann knocking on the door, Julie standing behind her on the grass, a rucksack slung over one shoulder.

Shona knows that bag, she's seen it before.

'Where did they get that?'

'What?'

'Come on!' She grabs Kev by the hand and they're out, running up to Julie and Penny-Ann. 'That's not your bag.'

'That's why we've been looking for you,' Penny says, her voice low and urgent. 'Where have you been?'

'Chill out, sis,' says Kevin.

'Shut up, Kevin,' says Penny, looking from Kev to Shona then back again. 'We need to talk. But not here, people could be listening.'

Kev scoffs.

'*Please.*' Her eyes firmly on Shona's now.

'Okay,' Shona says, looking up to the hill behind them, the scattering of buckthorn and sycamore. 'Up there?'

Penny nods, though it's Julie who leads the way, Shona beside her, Penny and Kev following behind. They look so alike those two, a stranger would be able to see they're brother and sister. Penny-Ann and Kevin Taylor. The rain's lighter up by the trees, and there's view enough to make sure no one's in earshot. Shona can see the coast, the cliffs drawing her eyes as she sits, back against a tree, and waits as Julie carefully opens the rucksack and pulls out a series of earthenware pots and some small knives. She holds one in her hand, rolls it over so the initials scratched on the handle can be seen.

'We were in the woods,' Julie says. 'We found this bag, and all this stuff, stashed under a mimosa. Penny thinks you might know who it belongs to.'

They're all serious now, even Kevin.

'The bag belongs to Pauly,' he says. 'I've not seen it since before he died.'

Shona nods. 'It's true. I've never seen the other stuff before, but that's his initials.'

Penny nods. 'That's what I thought.'

'Then what was it doing in the woods?'

'We've been trying to figure that out. It looked like someone had been carving chunks out of the mimosa.'

'Look, I don't even know what mimosa is,' Kevin says.

'Neither did I,' Julie smiles. 'But the internet does. Mimosa burnuiflora only grows here, in these woodlands.'

'It's supposed to have healing powers,' Penny says. 'And you have heard of it. Not as mimosa, but you've heard about something growing in the woods. Halloween stories, rumours about the spirit plant.'

Shona swallows. Kev beside her, she can almost feel the way he wants to reach out to the pots, to the knife.

'They say, if you eat it, you'll be able to see the dead.'

'Rachel,' Shona says, her voice almost a sigh. 'He got it for Rachel.'

'She was the other half of the suicide pact?' Julie asks, checking for Penny's nod.

'She was my best friend,' says Shona.

'Why would she have needed the spirit plant?'

'To see her mam again.' And just like that Shona understands it all.

'So they were, what, hallucinating? And they jumped?' Kevin says. He sounds almost scared.

Julie looks at Penny again, and Penny pulls something from her own rucksack. It's wrapped in a transparent plastic bag but it's clearly a jumper. It was light grey, but it's stained dark brown and rigid with whatever has soaked into it.

'Pauly's hoody,' Penny says. 'It was snagged on the trees beside the mimosa. There's blood on it. Why would there be blood if he was just gathering mimosa to get high? This could be proof that something else was going on, that someone hurt him.'

'No,' Shona says, and for a second no one else even breathes. 'Someone may well have hurt him, but that's not Pauly's jumper. That belongs to Lee.'

HOW BROTHERS CAN BE

'He's not stupid, my boy,' Natalie says. Natalie who Fergus has never seen cry, not like this, not when she can't control it. They're sitting on a bench with no dedication, sea-battered and salt-crusted, Burrowhead behind them, the church ruin behind them, only the sea with its layers of waves in front.

'That's what I can't get my head around,' she's saying. 'I mean Aaron, sure, he'd get into drugs, course he would. He was always angry about something, always—'

'Oh, Natalie—'

'He was always a thug.'

Fergus cringes, though it's not that he disagrees. Aaron is difficult and Fergus would avoid a confrontation with him, but he doesn't like to hear a mother say that about her child.

'Don't, Fergus.'

'Don't what?'

'Don't judge me.'

Fergus wants to know where Georgie is. What she's doing. What she'd think, if she heard a mother calling her son a thug.

'It was Aaron all along, you know. He was always telling Lee what to do.'

'What was?'

'That racist graffiti, on the Spar. On the fountain. I'm sure it was him forcing Lee to do it. I'm so ashamed.'

'Have you told the police?'

She looks at him like for a second she doesn't even know who he is.

'I've cleaned it, Fergus. All of it.'

'Yes, but—'

'I've cleaned it all up!'

Fergus swallows, says nothing more. What would Georgie have said? God but that twist in his stomach, he needs that to stop, leave him in peace.

'But Lee's not stupid. How could he do this?'

'Are you saying...what are you saying?'

Her hand is suddenly around his wrist, uncomfortably tight.

'Lee was the one buying the drugs, Fergus!'

He gently reclaims his hand.

'Sorry. But he's told me that much.' She pulls out a tissue, blows her nose, sniffs loudly. 'For years I've been trying to work out who was selling them. I thought it was Pauly Dawkes at first.'

'Pauly?'

'He was no good, always skiving off school – I'd see him wandering the woods, smoking away, shoulders hunched up like he was fighting off the world.'

'I always thought he was a sweet boy.'

That look she gives him. Fergus needs to stop talking.

'He was leading Lee astray, I'm sure of it.'

Fergus looks at her. It was here, on these cliffs, with this view.

'But then he died, and the girl with him, and my boys...'

'Took up where they left off?'

'It's getting worse though.'

'How do you mean?'

She pauses, sniffs again, clasps her hands in her lap and takes a deep breath. 'Since Rachel and Pauly died, there have been *more* drugs around, not less. Folk said Bobby Helmsteading was dealing, but then he was killed. Every time I figure out who's involved, they lead on to someone else, and someone else—'

'So you're trying to find out who's at the top?'

'After Bobby died, I thought it was Ricky Barr. That's why I…'

His horse. What Natalie did to his poor horse. The image of it appearing to Fergus so clearly he can't look away, its throat slashed open, hacked apart and Natalie did that; she was capable of that. He's tried so hard not to think about it since she offered him a room, gave him somewhere to stay when he couldn't go home, not knowing what Georgie really thought of him.

'But I was wrong. It's someone else.'

Fergus stares at her.

'Lee's got himself too deep into this. He's scared, Fergus.'

'I'm sure he's fine.'

'Are you even listening to me? Pauly is dead. Rachel is dead. Bobby Helmsteading is dead. And my son, my Lee, I don't know how he's got himself at the front but I'm telling you, he's lying in that hospital bed and he's scared.'

Fergus wipes a hand over his head, finds his hair damp with rain and sweat.

'I keep thinking about that horse, Fergus.'

His neck clenches again, his teeth ache.

'That poor horse and what I did to it. You do understand, don't you, how I had no choice, I thought it was Ricky hurting my boys—'

He's shaking his head to dissolve the image he keeps seeing, trying to hear the waves instead of her voice, the barely audible lapping of the waves against the barnacle-layered pebbles of the beach.

'Aaron could fight if he had to but Lee's the gentle one, he really is. Aaron used to pick on him something awful. Oh, Fergus, what do you do when boys are like that?'

Fergus doesn't know the answer; he never was a boy like that.

'But here's what I'm saying, Fergus. I'm sorry this is all coming out—'

'It's okay.'

'No, it's not. Lee is smarter than Aaron, always was. All he ever wanted was to earn some money, earn a living – that's not so bad, is it? You can understand that? Isn't everyone entitled to that? He wants to make something of himself. He only got angry with Pamali because she wouldn't give him a job, I'm sure of it.'

Fergus feels the cold crawling up his arms. She's talking about Lee and Andy's attack on Pamali, that racist violence and he's forcing his foot into the ground, sending a scatter of rocks crashing over the cliff edge.

'Not that I'm saying it was… I mean, it was wrong, what he did, I'm not saying it wasn't wrong.'

The smash of stone on stone.

'About a job, was it?'

Fergus saw what Lee did to Pamali, he was there in the hospital and he saw her dislocated shoulder, he saw her face and he's never going to forget it, never.

'What about Terry in the garage? He didn't give Lee a job.' His voice is like a stranger's, loud and angry, getting louder as more rocks fall and crash. 'What about the pub in Warphill? They didn't give him a job.'

'Stop,' she's saying. 'Please, that's not what I meant—'

The last of the rocks clatter onto the beach below. Fergus breathes deep, listens for the waves. He'd give anything to see Georgie.

'Lee's in over his head.'

She's still talking about Lee.

'Lee knows who's making this drug. And I swear to God, Fergus, he is terrified.'

'Okay,' he says. 'Okay.'

She is crying entirely now, not sniffing, not pushing away the tears, she has let her body slump forward and she's crying into her hands and hiding her face, so Fergus pats her back and mumbles something comforting till she's ready to sit up again.

'Let's go home, Natalie,' he says. 'You've got the car, right?'

She's nodding, swallowing, trying to get her breath under control.

'Let's go home and have a cup of tea and talk all this through calmly, okay?'

He wants to help, of course he does. Natalie has helped him these past weeks, he'll never forget that, and so he'll make sure they get home safe, home to where she'll feel better, feel comfortable. He'll make her a cup of tea and agree that she needs a lie-down. Then he'll phone Georgie and tell her everything he knows.

AFTERNOON HARVEST

'What,' says his da, looking over the produce covering his kitchen table, 'is all this?'

'Broccoli leaf,' says Andy proudly. 'Kale, pak choi, spinach and onion greens.'

'It's for me, is it?'

'If you like,' Andy says, a grudging look passing over his face before he shakes it away. 'Yeah, it is. It's from the food garden.'

'So…it's for everyone?'

'Me and Pamali grew it.'

'Is that right?'

'Yes it is.'

'Part of your community service for attacking her, eh?'

Andy scowls at that, his lips tight, but he'll not rise to it. His da is a fucking bully, that's the truth of it. Trish says so, Pamali too. So what if he's got cancer, only a bully would bring up something like that – the worst thing Andy's ever done – and use it to make what he's doing now feel fake, like it's worthless.

'My community service,' Andy says through the buzzing in his ears, 'was to clear the rubbish off the Warphill road and I've done that, done all my hours of it, and you know that as well as I do.'

'Alright,' says his da, pulling out a chair and sitting down. 'Don't lose it.'

167

'I'm not,' says Andy. 'That's what bothers you, isn't it.'

His da shakes his head at that and takes a leaf from the table, one of his broccoli leaves, and bites into it. Chews.

'Rabbit food,' he says, eventually.

'Don't fucking eat it then.'

'Actually it's no bad—'

'What?'

'Tastes like broccoli.'

Then Aunt Debs is here, pulling out a chair to sit beside his da, and Andy realises why his da has started being a bit nicer.

'What I meant was,' he says, picking up another leaf, 'she's letting you be part of her community garden, after what you did to her?'

He reaches out like he's about to touch Andy's arm and Andy winces, breath catching in his throat.

'I'm not going do anything to you, Andy.'

'You got that right.'

Ricky holds his gaze. Andy's not giving him any more though, not another single bit of himself. He's not telling him the truth, that he can't stop hearing it, that noise. The noise of when Lee dislocated her shoulder. The noise of Pamali screaming afterwards. He wakes up hearing that noise.

He doesn't say a word of that, but then his da nods at him like he understands, like he knows what it is to be haunted by his own actions. Andy's not forgiving him though. Why should he? Andy and his da, they're not suddenly going to be alright.

'And yeah, seeing as you ask, she lets me help with the gardening. I'm part a this community, and I'm part a the community food garden. I'm going to study it too.'

His words are coming out despite him – he wasn't even planning to tell his da, he was just going to leave, one day, up and leave, but he can't stop the words coming now.

'Sustainable farming,' he goes on. 'I've found a course and Pami's going to be my referee.' He couldn't even name his da's expression – not anger, not surprise even, something else, fuck knows. He's not going to stop him though; nothing is going to stop him. 'I'm not staying here, living your life.'

'Good.'

Then his da is coughing again and every time that happens they stop, in this house, stop talking and fighting and being what they've been to each other and become something else, something that's waiting for them all and Andy looks to the window, looking for some kind of fucking change but the sky does not oblige. It's still that same heavy-layered white and behind him the old tap is dripping into the wide sink like it always has.

Andy scoops up all the veg he'd put on the table and takes it over.

'I'll make dinner then,' he says. Tap on full blast now, wetting his T-shirt and hissing at them all.

'I'll help,' says Debs, standing up, getting a large bowl from the cupboard, bringing it over beside him.

'I'll lay the table,' says his da, a short, sharp laugh turning into a cough again.

He does it though, he lays the table for them. Like they're a family.

WAYS OF FEELING SCARED

Georgie rests her mobile against her forehead as it rings, letting the heat of it blend into the heat of her skin and thinking of Fergus on the other end, doing the same. Then she stiffens her back and answers the call, waiting for his excuses or his anger or whatever it is that's finally pushed him into phoning her.

'I'm calling about your case,' he says.

His voice is almost a whisper, but she can hear every word. She listens as he says he's in Warphill, on the street but there's no one about and she tells him to say what he needs to say, still wary of him, still raw.

'There's something else I need to say first,' he says.

She waits, doesn't speak.

'I heard you, Georgie. I need you to know that. I'm sorry it's taken me a while to say it.'

She feels her eyes sting then brushes at them, not wanting to be so soft – and so he should have heard her. God but it's good to hear his voice. The phone, pressing against her ear, is no substitute; she wants to hold him, see his big hopeful face and rest her head on his shoulder and let him engulf her in his hug. He's the only one who ever got that right.

'And, er, I've got some information.'

She needs to pull herself together, there's work to do. Her hand against her mouth, then pushing her hair back from her forehead.

'There are two things,' he says, voice still low. She can almost picture him glancing up the street, checking no one's within earshot. 'The first is that Natalie says Aaron's the one orchestrating the graffiti on the Spar and all around the village. All that racism. The overt stuff.'

She lets it sink in. She'll think about that, needs some time to think about what she's going to do about that.

'Natalie's been washing it off.'

Georgie waits.

'But she's also refusing to report her son to the police. So.'

She'd give anything to hold him.

'Closed ranks in that family,' Georgie says.

'Maybe not any more. That's why I'm phoning, love. Georgie. Sorry.'

Why did he move out? Why did he do it, only to talk to her like this, like she's the one who hurt him, like he's wounded – is he going to ask to come back? To see her, to talk over dinner, to walk through their garden and sit together for a moment?

'She doesn't think it's Aaron buying the drugs though. At first I thought you could use the graffiti to get more out of him, if that's the, eh... Sorry, I shouldn't try and think like police, should I.'

'The way you're thinking is just fine, Fergus.'

He goes quiet then and she's suddenly scared he might change his mind, hang up. But then she hears him swallow, take a breath, and she knows it wasn't doubt that made him go quiet at all.

'She's convinced it's Lee,' he says. 'She thinks Lee is buying the drugs, and that he knows who's manufacturing them. He's the contact.'

That's what Terry said too, and she's starting to believe it.

'And there's more, but this is Natalie thinking. I mean, it's her conjecture and I'm passing it on. I don't think there's any proof.'

She smiles at that, can't help herself, her own words coming back to her, that need for proof – and it's true and also not the whole story at the same time.

'She thinks Lee is scared of someone.'

'Lee Prowle? Scared?'

He pauses then, for a second.

'She said terrified. I know it seems unlikely.'

He wasn't terrified when she was there. He'd seemed more resentful than scared; ill, sure, but still carrying plenty of spite with it.

'I mean, he threw her out of his hospital room, refused to talk to her, so she might be...'

'Hurt?'

'Yeah.'

Oh, the space where they both breathe and don't speak.

'But, hurt or no, Georgie, she thinks someone's threatening him.'

'Like who?'

'That's the question, I guess. And that's what I wanted to tell you so that, well, I don't know. Maybe you could do something.'

'I'll look into it, Fergus. Thank you.'

That pause again and Georgie closes her eyes and imagines him there, beside her.

'I'd better go, Georgie. Got to get to work.'

Come here, come home – words crowding into her mind while she stays silent on the phone and he's doing the same, all those words not passing between them until the phone call ends without them being spoken and now?

No one reaching for her hand.

She has work to do, too. If someone were targeting Lee, could his reaction have been an actual poisoning? The others are fine, perfectly healthy. She needs to phone Cal. And keep it entirely professional this time. Walking fast to the bathroom, splashing her face, her eyes, scooping up a handful of water to tip over her hair, cooling at last and back to the office, nodding at Frazer and Si to follow. Three officers, waiting to hear what forensics might be able to tell them.

'But they didn't need stomachs pumped, the other lot,' Cal says. 'We got Lee's contents to go on, Lee's vomit, but that's about it.'

'You mean you didn't get bloods from the others?' Georgie says.

Cal's silence is very different to what Fergus's had been.

'No, ma'am. You didn't arrest them either.'

'We had no proof they'd done anything illegal.'

'Well, exactly.'

Georgie frowns at the phone but takes her time. 'So we've no way of knowing if there was something different in what Lee took compared to the others?'

'Only their combined word for it.'

'Known for their honesty, that lot.'

Her joke gets him back on side.

'So, Cal, have we *any* reason at all to think that Lee was being targeted or...' Her voice trails off. She knows the answer already.

'Seems more likely to me he was just the one had the bad reaction, Georgie. They were all drinking from the same flask, so that's all we've got.'

Georgie pauses. Simon's watching her, Frazer too, though they both look a bit confused. Why does she think there's something more here? Is it Fergus? Wanting to believe in him again?

'I'm pretty sure Lee Prowle is going to be fine,' Simon says, and she gets it. Lee's the one who hurts people. He's the one other people are afraid of.

'There was something he said to me, though,' she says. But was there? Georgie hadn't thought that until now, there hadn't been anything particularly unusual. He'd refused to say anything, he'd been the same spiteful boy as usual, except... The little girl had been clasping at her.

'What did he say?'

'No, it wasn't something he said.'

'Georgie, I'm—'

Busy, Cal's about to say, before Georgie cuts him off.

'Wait. Let me think.'

And they do. Cal, and her staff sitting beside her, they all let her think. She appreciates that.

'I think he seemed a bit scared when I was there,' she says. 'I didn't notice, but—'

'Lee Prowle,' says Cal. 'Scared of you?'

'Why not?' says Frazer. 'Of course he'd be scared of the police.'

'Oh aye,' says Cal. 'Imagine it. Lee Prowle feeling so sorry for himself he's getting scared of DI Georgie Strachan.'

And she lets him have his laugh, doesn't say a word more about it but she knows he wasn't looking scared of her. Cal's right, Lee Prowle is not scared of DI Georgie Strachan. He's scared of something else.

THE PULL OF THE COAST

Simon stares at the text, wonders whether to tell Georgie, then decides against it. He likes Shona, and she's asking for him and no one else. So he'll give her a chance. He finds them round the side of the station: Shona and Kev – no surprise there, where you see Shona you usually find Kev – but then there's Julie and Penny-Ann too.

'What can I do for you lot?'

Maybe it wasn't fear of the police so much as avoiding the gaze of the rest of the villagers made them want to meet back here. That he does get.

'We've got evidence,' Shona says. 'And we've got ideas.'

'Evidence first then.'

Shona nods at Julie, who slips a rucksack off her back and hands it to him.

'Found it in the woods,' Penny says. 'Carried it back here so it'll have our prints on and whatever.'

'You didn't think to call the police at the time?'

'It was just a rucksack in the woods.'

He looks at it, not opening it for fear of contaminating it further.

'But it was Pauly's,' Shona says. 'You'll see inside, pots, knives, one with his initials scratched onto the handle. Me and Kev both recognised the bag.'

'Pots?' Simon says. 'Knives?' Shaking his head.

'Well, here comes the ideas bit.'

Shona pauses, takes a deep breath as though she's rehearsed this. He wonders if that's because she didn't want to get upset. They were close, her and Rachel. She's been wanting him to reopen their case for a year now and she's got a good heart in her, Shona, even if she does want to be a journalist.

'Rachel thought she could summon the dead,' she says. 'Don't laugh.'

'I'm not laughing.'

'We saw her try, years back, in the church ruin. But after her mam died, she was devastated. I think she was trying to call her back.'

Simon waits – what has this got to do with pots and knives and Pauly Dawkes?

'But she'd have needed something more than candles in a graveyard, if she really wanted to see her mam. Or wanted to believe she did.'

'You said they were into drugs, the pair of them.'

'Well, I think Pauly made her something very specific. The spirit drug. Sometimes it's called ayahuasca. It's made from mimosa, in the woods, where we found this stuff.'

What they took was made from mimosa, that's true, and other things besides. He'll not forget that list of their stomach contents in a hurry. Ayahuasca is one version of it; there are others too.

'And where we found this.' Shona nods at Penny, who pulls out something else – an item of clothing, wrapped in plastic, stained by the look of it.

'I think there's blood on it,' Penny says.

'Blood on Pauly's old sweater?'

'No,' Shona says. 'It's Lee's jumper. There's blood on Lee's jumper.'

He's got to get this inside, packaged properly and couriered over to Cal.

'That's the thing,' Shona says. '*Lee* was the one using this stuff recently. Pauly's long gone. Pauly hated Lee anyway, he'd never have given him his knives or his bag.'

'So Lee found this stuff in the woods, started trying to recreate what Pauly had made?'

'More likely someone gave it to him,' Shona says. 'The same person who showed Pauly what to do, then moved on to Lee. Do you know who it is?'

'I've got to get this inside.'

Simon's adding it all up: they've got Rachel and Pauly's stomach contents on the night they died, and the matching stomach contents from Lee the night he ended up in intensive care, and now they've got the method of manufacture.

'Not just yet, Si.'

'You should go home, Shona. All of you. This is a matter for the police.'

'But I've got something else for you.'

'What?'

'And by you, I mean Si, not PC Hunter.'

The way she says it, so gently, he can almost feel whose name she'll say next.

'Alexis asked Rachel to write a letter.'

Alexis. All it takes is his name.

'She went to see him, after her mam died. He asked her to write a letter saying goodbye, but she did the opposite. She promised her mam she'd see her again.'

'Have you got the letter?'

Shona nods. 'And I'm keeping it. She was my best friend and I think she'd have wanted me to have it.'

'Then why tell me?'

He knows the answer, though.

'Alexis was trying to help her. I thought you'd like to know.'

He does like knowing that, though he's not surprised – Alexis tried to help everyone. Alexis was still helping everyone. But after Si has taken everything inside and shown Georgie and arranged for it all to be couriered over to forensics he finds himself standing outside the station, Shona long gone, being pulled to the coast again. He wants to stand in the playground where Alexis died, where he found him too late and held his body. He wants to walk the cliffs, to lose himself in the cave where once he wanted to fall into salt water and never come up for air; he feels the pull of it like a physical pain as he forces his legs in the other direction, to his car, to face inland. To drive away from the village and the cliffs. To arrive, unannounced, at a spacious city flat that's about as different from Alexis's home as anywhere could be. But all the way there he can feel the cave behind him, refusing to let go.

THE NEXT MOVE AND THE NEXT

Trish is on the road back to Burrowhead. She's focused on the drive and she's not thinking about what they said. She's not thinking about the superstition or the manipulation or the layers of lies; the way they see her, the way they see her home.

She's been to meet the research team at UHCN who've been looking at Uncle Walt's dagger. Drove out of Burrowhead up to Crackenbridge and then inland, all the way to the city. Trish doesn't like the city. She can feel the fumes on her skin every time she's there, half an hour on those streets and she can feel the dirt on her face, the grime of all that pollution. Uncle Walt used to say the same. As she walked from the car park she felt like she was moving against some force that didn't want her there, people knocking against her shoulders, banging into her bag, forcing her to edge away, sidestep, apologise – not that a single one of them apologised for barging her out of the way. Folk in Burrowhead, they make way for you on the pavement. If they accidentally bump into your shoulder, they stop and check you're alright then invite you round for a cuppa to make up for it. Not like the faceless swarm in the city.

Then there was the way the two PhD students had looked at her. She'd hoped at least the professor would be in charge, but it seems she delegated, didn't much care. None of them care

179

much about the villages. They weren't cruel, she'll give them that, but they were amused. Like she was quaint. Like Trish and her dagger, Uncle Walt's dagger, were quaint. The girl was pony-tailed and clear-skinned. The other one was older, scraggly beard, glasses. It was the girl who delivered the news.

'We've dated it to the 1830s,' she said.

Trish was so shocked she just looked from one to the other. The dagger was ancient; Uncle Walt knew the dagger was ancient. Didn't he? That was the whole point.

'But—'

'I'd say it might have been antiqued.'

'What?'

'The metal made to look older than it is. But it's not related to the burial site Anita found at the motte.'

'Who's Anita?'

'Professor McLeod.'

'Oh.'

'It is unusual, though, so that's good news. It might have a bit of value.'

'It was probably made to order,' the boy said. 'And the manufacturer had some skill.' He passed it over the table to her, like it was some ordinary thing they could wave around in the university canteen.

'It's not from the Iron Age?'

'I'm afraid not.'

'It wasn't used for...for rituals?'

God but she hated the way they smiled.

'We can't say what it's been used for, only that it's less than two hundred years old.'

'But there's a legend that goes with this. It's supposed to have been used for ritual sacrifice, for the threefold death—'

'That's not a legend, it's just a story.'

Oh, Uncle Walt. He'd treasured that dagger. He'd left it to her.

'And a ritual sacrifice would be a murder,' the girl said.

Why was Trish so shocked?

'No, it was...he...it was an animal, that's all, Uncle Walt would never...'

God but she'd give anything to have him back.

She can never have him back though, never, and the dagger he left her is nothing, a fake used to manipulate him. And it worked. He'd fallen for it, clutched onto the supposed power of that dagger as his farm collapsed and his life shrank and he watched the Barr family take everything he'd once had. She's driving back through the haze with tears burning her eyes, seeing Uncle Walt, alone, in an excavated trench on Ricky Barr's farm, clasping at his throat, his heart, unable to breathe—

Not alone. Being watched. Ricky Barr watching, his rifle held in his hands.

Her own hands clasp the steering wheel. She has to stop, pull in, force herself to piece it together. Someone had that dagger made. Nora Prowle's grandmother, or great-grandmother? They claimed it was ancient, that it gave them power to perform the threefold death as a ritual to summon their ancestors. By the time the knife came to Uncle Walt, he believed the Others would return the village to what it once was.

But it didn't work. The dagger, the animal sacrifices – of course they didn't work. All he did was make an enemy of Ricky Barr.

Someone has to hold that man accountable. Look at everything he's done to Andy, what he did to Uncle Walt; she has to fight back, she has to do *something*. She just doesn't know what. She doesn't even notice the police car that passes her.

The driver sees her, though.

It's Suze.

She's heading to the hospital, and when she sees Trish she sits up that bit higher.

Suze: the new police guard for Lee Prowle, on Georgie's insistent request.

She tells the receptionist they need to keep a close eye on who is coming and going, then positions herself on a chair outside Lee's room to wait it out.

When Natalie arrives, long after dark, the two women eye each other without a word.

Then Natalie walks into Lee's room and Suze stays where she is, sends a quick text and, leaning her head back against the wall, breathes in the muggy heat of the hospital and waits for the night to fall.

SUN GOING DOWN AT LAST

Pamali and Georgie meet by the playground as the sun sets, on the bench overlooking the cliffs. Abigail's bench. Both of them sitting with a deep breath, letting the sea lap quietly against the rocks for a few minutes before they start talking, before they try to unpick their days and make sense of it all.

'It's good to see you,' Georgie says at last.

'You see me every day,' Pamali replies.

'And it's good every time.'

Pami laughs, light and hopeful. Georgie smiles, but it's heavier for her.

'You haven't found her yet?'

She means Abigail; there's no need to say her name. She's here on the bench with them, after all.

'What have you found out, Pami?'

'Andy Barr wants to study sustainable farming.'

Georgie does laugh at that. 'Well, I guess that's good.'

'It's very good,' Pami says. 'And he's not so daft as everyone thinks.'

'I've not thought of Andy Barr as being daft since…' She doesn't want to say it, doesn't want to remind her but that's daft in itself; Pamali could hardly forget being attacked like that, by those two, Andy Barr and Lee Prowle. One coming back to ask forgiveness, the other ending up in a hospital bed of his own.

'Andy talks to me these days.'

'What's he said?'

'He didn't drink what the others drank, that night.'

Georgie nods. He'd been sober enough to make that obvious.

'But I *think* he might have kept some aside.'

'Are you serious?'

Pami smiles. 'I thought you'd like that.'

'That could be helpful, Pami. What has he done with it?'

'That I don't know.'

'Can you find out?'

'I can try. It's tricky to talk with Natalie around – he's not comfortable talking in front of her. He doesn't trust her.'

'Because of what she did to his da's horse?'

'Maybe… It's more like he doesn't trust her being around me. Doesn't want her on the community garden project at all.'

'Andy Barr, protective of you?'

'I know.' She smiles.

'You think he's genuinely trying to make things better?'

'We have to believe it's possible, don't we?'

Georgie wants to give her a hug. 'Well, Natalie might not be around so much now, with Lee in hospital.'

'She must be going through a hard time. And with the trial hanging over her—'

'What she did to that horse was vicious.'

Pamali purses her lips and nods. 'I'll find out what I can from Andy. And I'll keep my eye on Natalie.'

'You're an excellent spy, Pami.'

Behind them, Frazer is arriving. It's a good way to end the days, Georgie finds, meeting here on the bench dedicated to Abigail Moss; the same bench where Simon and Alexis used to sit; the bench where Frazer gives a sigh as he looks out at the expanse of the sea all the way to the haze where it blends with the sky, accepting a moment of peace. She gives him the space for that, before asking if he's got anything new.

'I've been following family links and land ownership,' he says. 'Most of the land round here is owned by a few families, half of them related to one another.'

'I'm not surprised,' says Georgie.

'One of those is Mrs Dover's family – the Braxton family, when you go back. It turns out they liked to keep their jobs close at Wyndham Manor. Mrs Pettigrew the housekeeper wasn't only Gail Dover's godmother, she was a poor cousin of the Braxtons. And that gave me the idea.'

'The idea?'

'There was no paper trail, you see. At least, any paper trail has vanished and none of their records were computerised – they closed down before that would have been a possibility. So, no record of employers or employees. But then I thought, there are huge family portraits hanging in the manor. I saw them this morning, just didn't realise at the time they could be helpful.'

'And do they show the Dovers?'

'The Braxtons,' he says with a smile. 'We're going way back now, before Gail Braxton got married and became Mrs Dover. That's where I've been – I had to go back to the manor to check. But I was right. One of the portraits hanging over the stairwell is of a George F. Braxton. Gail Dover's grandfather. I suspect, and I'm trying to get confirmation, he was the owner when Betty Marshall was there. I'm piecing together the dates.'

'There we were thinking Ricky Barr owned everything here-abouts,' says Pamali.

'He owns a fair bit of the land,' says Georgie.

'True – the farmland. But go back a generation or two and the Barrs were new, they had nothing. The biggest farms were owned by the Robertsons, the Helmsteadings and the Mackies. Meanwhile the Braxtons owned the village and, quite possibly, the Wyndham Manor hotel.'

'But what does all this tell us about Abigail Moss?'

'It tells me I want to talk to Gail Dover again,' Frazer says. 'She's the right age, and her family were connected to Wyndham Manor in more ways than one.'

'The right age?'

'She's only a couple of years younger than Betty Marshall.'

'We know her godmother was housekeeper at Wyndham Manor. And now you're saying her family might have owned the entire hotel where Abigail Moss vanished?'

'Exactly.'

'Okay,' Georgie says, letting herself talk slowly – it's a picture taking shape. 'Tomorrow. Let's invite her in for an official chat. Nicely, though.'

'Will do.'

'You'll be lead on that, Frazer. I'll be having a friendly chat with someone else. I'm going to get Lee Prowle to talk about ayahuasca.'

'How?'

Georgie shakes her head. 'Crackenbridge have put Suze on the door tonight at least, to make sure he's safe.' She had to put her foot down to get that much – but Georgie's team have been flat out and they're a person short as it is.

'You think he might not be?'

'I don't know. Now I've imagined him as scared I can't stop seeing it.'

And the little girl had been tugging on her arm.

So leave me alone.

'Scared of being caught, maybe,' Frazer says.

'Well, I'm being cautious. Besides, with a police guard outside his room all night, maybe he'll be a bit more willing to speak to us in the morning.'

'Do you think so?'

She doesn't know; she's never worked out how to speak to Lee Prowle, not since he was a short, pretty thirteen-year-old glaring at her like she was the enemy.

'What about Aaron?'

It's Pamali who says that, and it's a good question – what is she going to do about Aaron? No one's even been able to find him today. His mother says he's been vandalising the village. His mother says he's a racist. His mother said these things not to the police but to Fergus. Does Georgie have enough to arrest him? No. Can she keep questioning him; will that get her anywhere? You can help a kid like Andy Barr if you're lucky – no, not lucky; if you're willing to forgive, like Pami – but dealing with kids like Lee and Aaron Prowle is a different thing.

Georgie wonders what Natalie has tried so far. The soft touch, almost certainly. Natalie is one for protecting her boys against the consequences. But behind closed doors? Anger, or confining them to their rooms, or being *so disappointed* in them? She wonders if Fergus knows. She wonders, walking home, if he might be there to meet her. Imagines him waiting for her and as she walks the cliff path and sees their house come into view she is almost sure of it – but he's not there.

No one is there.

So she sleeps and wakes too soon, before any light can help her orient herself, and she rolls over and reaches out and misses him again, searches the room for the little girl but closes her eyes to see Trish running to the cliffs and so she follows her, to the edge, to where two teenagers stand hand in hand before jumping from the clifftop to break on the stones below. Their bodies are taken by the sea, by salt water that knows them and pities them and lets them die anyway and above them is Abigail's bench, moved from the playground to the cliffs where Georgie is sitting and watching Pauly and Rachel fall again, and again, unable to stop them.

INSOMNIA

'Ricky Barr, then?' Mrs Smyth says.

'I have no quarrel with Ricky Barr,' says Mrs Dover.

'Nor I.'

The two women are sitting in Mrs Dover's living room, though it's late – they neither of them sleep through the nights, these days, and a shared pot of tea brings more comfort than staring at the walls alone.

'They say his lung cancer is terminal,' Gail Dover says.

'They do.'

'It was good of Deborah-Jane to come back to look after him.'

'It was,' says Mrs Smyth.

'He'll not have the strength for much, these days.'

'Not like the Prowle boys.'

They fall into silence then, thinking about those Prowle boys, how angry they are, how they spit on the street, how they've vandalised the village. There are words scrawled on the walls these days that they've both read and will not repeat. It's not Ricky Barr doing any of that; it's not Ricky Barr with a stranglehold on the village and it never was.

'Seems to me, the more people try to clean up the village, the worse it gets,' Mrs Smyth says after a while.

Gail Dover nods and reaches for her tea. She's particularly fond of tea.

'It depends on what they mean by cleaning up, I'd say.'

'That it does, Gail.'

After all, to clean something up you've first got to designate something as dirty, and that right there is a part of the problem.

'We owe Natalie a debt of thanks for everything she's done,' Lori Smyth says.

'We do,' says Gail. 'We do, I'd never deny that. But owing her doesn't mean we've got to stay silent about that family.'

It's a dream that stops Gail sleeping these days; a dream of a little boy with matted blonde hair being trapped under floorboards, scratching against the wood as he gasps his last breaths.

'I remember Sonny Riley,' she says. 'I keep seeing his face.'

'I see him too, some nights,' says Lori Smyth. 'And Alexis Cosse.'

Gail relaxes back into her seat at the name, at the memory.

'I liked Alexis Cosse.'

But she can't settle where she is. She stands up from her chair slowly – back's too sore to get up fast these days – and goes to stand by the window. Heavy cloud cover tonight, no sign of the moon. It's not black out there though, more like purple. Like the heat's changing the colour of the sky.

'I saw your Penny-Ann out on the street with that new girl,' Lori Smyth says.

Gail smiles at that – she'd seen her too. 'Do you remember how we used to talk about free love?'

'I do,' says Lori, closing her eyes over. 'I do.' But after a few minutes her head droops to one side and she starts snoring quietly.

Gail stays standing at the window though – she's not going to sleep tonight. She's picturing what she might do if she could find a way to rewind the last sixty years and start again.

'That was before the husbands, Lori.'

The only sound in the room now is the ticking of her clock, which has been on her wall so long it barely registers as a sound at all.

'This weather,' she says to the sleeping woman behind her. 'The waves are getting louder. Have you noticed that, Lori? I've noticed that. There's less silence here than there used to be.'

There's no response, of course, but Gail is well used to there being no response.

'The truth is, Lori, I've never liked the silence. Never been able to settle with it.'

She turns to look at her friend, who is sleeping soundly now.

'Aye, you sleep well,' Gail says. 'I'll stand here a while longer.'

DEEP IN THE NIGHT

A gasp wracks his body. He's thrashing, trying to get to the surface but there is only darkness and smothering, raw pain and he can't breathe, he can't. He's kicking and thrashing but his arms are held and his legs are stone. No part of him can move. His lungs are burning and he can't breathe, can't see. Fuck, he needs air. Waves crushing him down but he has to rise, has to do something, twisting and fighting and choking against the burning grasp and he sees his brother and his mam and he sees nothing, stinging in his eyes, fight, kick, eyes wide and blind and gasping every time worse have to stop have to—

His body falls still. Completely still as the darkness around his eyes lifts and he can't hold it any more. He chokes and gasps and he's going to fucking kill and then, forced back, he sees shapes. Shapes hidden, masked in shadow and light and he can feel the bed is soaked, sweat, piss, his own piss and tears and sweat and whatever it is he is drowning in. This is how he'll die. But no, no, fight, fuck you, fucking fight and his eyes spinning, desperate, searching for shapes that make sense and he gasps a breath and it burns his raw throat and he chokes and coughs and spits and they gather, shadows, rasping, scratches burning his skin and he'll fucking—

Just let it happen, son.

191

And it is, it's happening again, the fear, gathering around him, voices and whispers he can't make out. He has to lift his arm. Has to make it to the buzzer, to call for help, but they're surrounding him, every part of him weighed down to drown, his body heavy with weight and it's happening again, the water, filling his nose, his throat, burning desperate pain but his arm, must lift his arm, fuck, fuck, his arm, the pain, the burning in his lungs in his throat and his arm is up, he's lifting his arm and he's pressing the buzzer, he's pressing and pressing it and his voice is starting to scream through whatever is in the way he has to scream with a rough rasping pain in his throat and colours and blackness. Eyes throbbing with the pain of it. Throat raw from the tubes and he's screaming for help, for anyone to help him; he's pressing the bell and screaming and no one is coming to help him and there is no one left. He knows it. Water fills his lungs and every breath is burning, thrashing, kicking and fighting but no way to stop his body retching and the water in his throat and nose and lungs and eyes, everything is water and there is no one left, no one coming; there is nothing, no breath no time no fight but raw pain and pity and rage and need and a reaching, a reaching for something, a reaching, for someone—

SALT WATER, TURNING

The nights have become some kind of hell where Trish is forced to remember herself, as a child, and her mother, before she was gone, and Uncle Walt, before he died. She doesn't want to see it any more, the faces in the dark, the ache of it. She used to be able to compartmentalise, to not think of her mam because her mam was gone, to not think of her childhood, to live in the here and now and just be Trish. Impatient, sure, smart, determined. Not someone who cried into their pillow at 3 a.m., curled in on herself like she was that twelve-year-old child all over again.

Get out of the house and run – that's what she told herself.

And she was right too. She gives good advice, Trish Mackie.

Though while her legs are pushing her to the limit, her feet stinging with how hard they pound the ground, she forgets she's not a police officer any more, thinks she could be running somewhere, for a purpose, not that she's running nowhere and she needs a job and a plan and a future, and soon she's going to need money too. Then it floods back. Georgie's suspicion and Uncle Walt's death and how she'd wanted to scream, and Georgie was the person she'd screamed at. Now all she's got is screaming at the sea, her hair thick with salt, wave-crushed in the dark.

DI Georgie Strachan. Why does she have to miss DI Georgie Strachan? She was always accusing her of jumping to conclusions, of suspecting the wrong people, of blaming the wrong people – her breaths are coming sharp now, pain in her chest from the pace – but when Trish forgave Andy, tried to help him up instead of sinking him into the system, then she was wrong too, wasn't she. Then Georgie didn't want forgiveness at all. DC Trish Mackie, always wrong. Until it paid off and Andy Barr came knocking on *her* door with what he had. She needs to remember that. He's not a bad kid, Andy, he was never a bad kid. Just a kid who made mistakes, like her. Maybe that's what they all are.

Her feet are soaked through now. The rain's relentless, but she'll not stop. She's running on the stones, ankles twisting against the slip of them, the slick black seaweed.

Ricky Barr doesn't deserve to be forgiven though, does he?

Her chest, her stomach; she'll have to stop soon but she won't.

Beating up his kid. That's not something Trish can forgive. She's clutching her side as she runs. Even if he's nothing to do with the drugs at all there's still what he's done to Andy and that's reason enough.

Her knees crack on rock as she falls.

Everything he did to Andy that Andy won't talk about. That no one can prove.

What he did to Uncle Walt. That no one believes.

She's well shot of the fucking police. She's on her own now and she can find the truth. She doesn't owe Ricky Barr any forgiveness whatsoever.

There's a sharp sting in her eye and before she can brush the salt out, she sees her mam out at sea. Not looking back; her mam leaving her behind. Fuck her. Fuck her. She tries to push herself up, but her legs are shaking. Hands on knees. She won't be sick. Just a fucking breath, a moment.

She needs to stop missing her. Where's it even come from, this missing of her mam, what good is it? None, no fucking good at all. She left, she died, the end. That's what she said to Uncle Walt once, still a kid and that hardened to it she was, and he cringed at her words like they hurt him, like each one was a kick to his stomach. She lets herself scream it out then, not a fucking soul on this beach, just the sea, nothing escaping from it and her words are no different, screaming out across the waves as her hands slip from her thighs to the water itself, to sink in broken shells. She can feel what's in her pocket: Uncle Walt's dagger, held close and pressing against her.

Uncle Walt wanted to save the village. He wanted to save her.

Uncle Walt is dead and gone, clasping at his chest in the dirt with the last man in the world he'd want to be watching; with Trish pushed away as far as he could.

That's not how you save someone, you stupid old man. She could throttle him. She wishes she could, right now. How do you save a village, anyway? What does that even mean? Maybe she should throw it out to sea, that dagger she's starting to hate, throw it out to the waves and let it drown like her mam did.

'I was out for a walk—'

'Fuck!'

It's Frazer. Trish is up, slipping, catching it, pulling her hoody tight, masking the knife she's holding. He's coming down the beach towards her.

'I was trying to warn you I was coming—'

'*Warn* me?'

'So I didn't make you jump.'

'Fucking hell.'

'I was out for a walk—'

'In the middle of the night?'

'It's dawn.'

It's true, infuriatingly. She's been here for – she doesn't know how long. She's soaked. It's still dark though, he'll not be able to see much, won't see her face, not really, or the shape of the dagger clutched to her chest.

'It's…' He waits, like always, while she searches for words, and that makes it worse. 'It's creepy,' she says at last. 'Are you following me?'

'No.' He stops a few steps from her. 'I called out from way over there.' He sounds defensive. 'I've learned how to avoid anyone thinking I'm following them.'

She blinks. Her eyes must be red in the corners. Wouldn't want him seeing that.

'I take your point,' she says. 'Sorry.'

'It's the middle of the night on a deserted beach so I'll let you off.'

Is he putting his hands in his pockets like he thinks he's cool now or something?

'It's dawn,' she says.

'So it is.'

'What are you doing here?'

Anything to keep him talking so he doesn't ask her that same question.

'I couldn't sleep,' he says, gentle again. And there it is: Trish remembering his wife, his sadness and the way he never seems to get angry about it, not like she does. Could he have heard her screaming? She hopes that was hours ago.

'It's okay,' he says. 'There's something about this beach, isn't there?'

'I thought you hated it.'

'It's more complicated than that.' He turns from her, his eyes scanning the cliff face behind them, the rocks black and smooth in the dim light, their veins of red and gold hidden. 'I've been looking for the cave,' he says, his voice hard to make out with him turned away from her like that.

Trish frowns.

'I saw it once,' he says. 'During that storm, months ago. I'm sure…'

'I thought you were here looking for Abigail Moss.'

He looks back, nods once.

'Any progress?'

'Trish, I can't talk about—'

'I know, I know.' But it's the first sting of dawn and couldn't he just once forget what he is and is not allowed to say. He's stepping closer though. Fuck, he's going to ask.

'Trish, are you okay?'

'I have a question. Not about the case—'

'Trish—'

'Just fucking listen.' Shit, why does she do it? 'Look, are you still watching Ricky Barr? Or is Georgie? I mean, is anyone?'

'You *know* I can't talk about it.'

'But there are loose ends, aren't there? I'm not imagining that. Ricky said in his interview, months ago, that he was going to visit a girlfriend in Warphill – he said that's what he was doing at the old flats where Bobby Helmsteading was killed. But who? There's no girlfriend. He must have been going to see Bobby. So why?'

'You know, Trish,' he says, quiet again, and the wind seems to have gone. 'If you want to come back to the police—'

'Who said anything about—'

'You could talk to Georgie. You should. I think she'll let you back in. She's still got your letter of notice on her desk, you know.'

'No.'

He doesn't hear though, because as she speaks his phone starts ringing. It sounds piercing, obscene, on the beach with the light spilling into the sea at the horizon.

'Oh God,' he says, answering. 'Yes.' She's trying to see his expression, but he's half turned away. She can't hear the other voice. She's as far out of the police as she's ever been. 'I'll be there.' He ends the call.

He's going then. She'll have the beach back to herself, just the way she wants it.

'Off you go.'

He looks at her, eyes depthless in the dawn light, and she wants him, wants him to hold her.

'Trish…' He's shaking his head, like he needs her too. Maybe he does, in his way.

'What is it, Dan?'

'Lee Prowle is dead.'

BLOOD

DEEP IN A DIFFERENT NIGHT

Abigail Moss runs fast through the landscaped gardens of Wyndham Manor. Outside, the evening is a cool, deep purple, no clouds to keep the breeze away, no mist to mask the stars. She's circling round the rose beds, jumping the ornamental displays of marigolds and allium, both caring and not caring that she might be seen – and who would be watching? Some of the other kids, all need and envy? Well. They can have their party and she's pleased for them; they can have their pills and their night swimming in the stream. She wonders what Betty Marshall is going to make of that. She's all nervous smiles and keen-to-please eyes, that girl, full of yes ma'am no ma'am. Abi likes her though. Or maybe that's the night talking, the whisper of leaves from the edge of the woodlands, the grass soft as rabbit fur beneath her bare feet as she runs.

Then: a low whistle, could almost be the call of a bird.

He's here, all the way from the city. She warned him his car would be recognised if anyone saw it – her mother or her father, the neighbours, the locals, all the eyes, all the watchers. *The likes of him round here.*

'Abi.'

Whispered, urgent. Like he wants her. She can hear the smile on his lips, the gravel in his throat.

'You're supposed to be at the clearing.'

'Couldn't wait.'

'Someone might see you.'

'Might see you and all.'

'Me alone is better than me with you.'

'Now that I'll never agree to.' Dougie steps out from behind the trees where he was hiding. Dark jeans. Leather jacket. Black skin. The speed of her pulse.

'C'mon,' she says. 'Let's get going.'

'Not so fast.'

His arms around her waist, lips soft on her neck and she loves the way he does this, loves the heat that spreads through her. She presses her hips forward, feels his hand rising up the back of her miniskirt.

'Not here,' she whispers. 'Later.' Slipping her hand down his arm to lead him into the woods. A glance over her shoulder.

'You think someone might be watching?'

'Old Mrs Pettigrew, maybe.'

She certainly likes to watch close when Abi's working – making sure the fresh towels are neatly folded, like so, hung smooth, like so. Everything has to be perfect in Wyndham Manor. And she's so grateful for her job, that woman. She seems *honoured* to have been tasked with keeping an eye on Abigail. For her part, Abigail feels more sorry for her than anything. This world is not the one Abi would have designed, but it's changing and she's helping it along.

'Come on.'

They weave hand in hand through hawthorn trees, through the scattering of cherry and silver birch at the woods' edge and delve deeper, between thick bronzed trunks and feathered shrubs and something startles in the night, birds taking flight, squirrels scampering through undergrowth. Something bigger. There are deer in the woods, though she's never seen them. Her pace slows as they approach the stream, follow the bank further from the manor. The distant voices of the other staff glisten as they taste the night air. Dougie slows. Puts a finger to her lips.

'Wait a minute. Just to be sure.'

His pulse is racing. Something flickers through her mind. Is he afraid? Worried Mrs Pettigrew might have followed? But it was Nora Prowle who'd caught her and Dougie in the church ruin; Nora Prowle who told her parents people were talking. *Abigail with that coloured boy.* Sticking her nose in like always. She was snooping round this afternoon, probably come to check a suitable punishment was being played out. Well. She's bitter, is all, and Abi's got to hand it to her father, working the hotel for the summer was hardly the punishment Nora Prowle was hoping for. She'd likely wanted to see her caned across the fingers – that's the kind of thing Nora would have liked to hear about, always pushing the school to be stricter, to weed out the bad elements.

As if Abigail would ever be seen as that.

'There's nothing to worry about,' she says, drawing Dougie's face to hers. She knows there's risk, but sometimes it's worth it to feel alive the way she does right now. 'We're there.' And as she says it, she knows it's right. Tonight, together in this clearing in the woods with the dappled moonlight falling on padded moss. She leads him to the low stone of the clearing where she's gathered everything she needs. Dougie's holding her hand as she whispers the words 'Trust me.' Their breath flows together and Dougie's thumb strokes hers like a promise. She led him here, to where her grandmother showed her the root and bark, to where she'd watch her mix berries and mint, and now it's her turn. She opens her eyes, barely breathing as she reaches for the mimosa root she has carved with her own hands and begins to combine it into something more. From now on she will be Abigail Moss of the woods, and this is the life she chooses. She presses the small blade into her hand.

'Trust me,' she says. 'It must be ours.'

And she is glad for what her grandmother taught her.

'It must be willingly given.'

And she is giving him the choice.

'It is a gift.'

The heat is like nothing else, gathering around her. A deep warmth as she invites him to kneel in front of the central stone, looks deep into his eyes. Knowledge passes between them. He accepts the blade. They hold their hands over the vessel and watch in silence as their blood collects together, as she stirs in the mimosa root and mint leaves, the sweetening honeycomb.

'Now we drink,' she whispers, welcoming the taste moving through her body.

'But what's it going to do?'

She is thankful for what she knows, what her grandmother taught her, and her grandmother before that.

'It does something different for everyone.'

She's thankful she has escaped what some in her family have become.

'It opens your mind,' she says. 'Some see the past. Some see the dead.'

His dark eyes widening, his luminous skin.

'Some travel to other worlds.'

'And you?'

'I want to see the truth of this world, with you.'

And she is here, in the woods, where the ground is soft on her bare feet and Dougie is tasting the drink on her lips. He's reaching out. He takes what she offers and then his eyes catch the moonlight, his lips are hot on her skin. She lets her head fall back and her body flow as Dougie unbuttons her shirt, slips it from her shoulders and they are dancing, they are dancing with their arms wide and the night free to flutter through the leaves. He catches her as she spins, she pulls him close; together they sing, their voices high and sweet and young, rising like they will never stop.

It's quieter now.

The rustle of leaves, the hush of the faraway stream over soft pebbles.

She knows every exhale of breath and beat of hope, the flutter of wings overhead, the stars like water droplets caught in light. Dougie is shining, he's glowing; they reach for one another's hands, vulnerable in their nakedness. This is their place now, their home. She is Abigail Moss, named for the soft moss beneath them, for their freedom. Hands linked; fingers intertwined. There's the call and answer of owls overhead and Abigail flies with them, through the shimmering purple night of midsummer. She is flying as she feels the tips of the feathers on her skin, as from far away she hears sounds that shouldn't be. Noise that doesn't belong here. Footsteps.

They are not alone.

There are others. Dark shapes, shadows. Cloaked. Eyes coming from the trees, out of trees. A deep shiver of dread.

Suddenly, there's screaming.

Her head is forced back. Nails clawing her skin. Screaming. Eyes like raw slits. Deep scratches at her neck and she's screaming.

She is screaming.

Skin clawed, sharp pain. Her head is forced and twisted and then she sees him, Dougie, lying crumpled on the ground. His face broken and smashed, bloodied into something that's not a face any more and still they don't stop. They don't stop. She tries to move but she can't. She tries to scream. There are hands holding open her eyes. Her screams die in her throat.

IN THE CITY

Simon's phone wakes him before the sun has made it over the skyline. It's quiet enough that Orlando can sleep on, but loud enough that he's up at the first ring. He moves fast, unplugging it from the charger, over to the window, looking out over the dark blue dawn. No stars here, not like on the coast; the city is lit, the warm fuzz of street lights, the square glow of others up as early as him. None of them on a call like this though.

Lee Prowle is dead.

He takes it in silence, feels like something's clasping round his throat. Another kid gone, another life. He's supposed to be stopping all this, making a difference, isn't he?

Georgie's blaming herself, by the sound of it, and he tells her he'll be there soon as possible, on his way now.

He always knew Rachel and Pauly weren't suicides, always knew there was more to come. Should never have let it go. He could have pushed more, got the case reopened, stopped it being closed in the first place – could he?

'What is it?'

Orlando's voice is fleecy with sleep as Si turns, phone still clasped in his hand and Georgie gone, on her way to the hospital already.

'I've got to go.'

'What's the time?'

'It's work.'

Orlando pushes himself up in the bed, leans back against the cushioned headrest. The sheets fall to his waist.

'Yeah, I got that.'

Si passes a hand over his mouth. He could do with a shave, a shower, but there's no time.

'I'll give you a call.'

He's pulling on his jeans, his uniform's out in the car. Three kids dead and they must be connected, they must be. Why does he feel like that's on him?

'Wait.'

'I've got to go.'

'Si, wait. I want to talk to you about something.'

'And you couldn't have done that last night?'

Simon turns as he speaks, not fast enough to stop himself speaking but fast enough to see the way Orlando cringes at his tone.

'I mean—'

'I assumed we'd have time for coffee this morning, that's all.'

Simon's back in the room. Dark wood beneath his feet, the large window behind him, letting enough light through the blinds now he can see details he hadn't noticed before: the colours of the old film posters on the wall, the twist of smoke from a 1960s cigarette, the crumple of clothes that are not his but that include his T-shirt, the phone chargers plugged in on both sides of the bed.

'I'm sorry.' He sits beside him, leans back too. 'This case is... I've got two minutes. What is it?'

Orlando pauses, looks almost nervous and Si has a sudden thought that whatever he's about to say might not be good. He wouldn't blame him if he wanted out already.

'Look, a couple of my friends, they need a flatmate.'

'What do you mean?' Simon doesn't get what that has to do with him.

'They've got a three-bed over by the river, top floor. Good views. You'd like it. Don't look so horrified.' His laugh is a little too sober. 'I thought, if you wanted to get out from the villages—'

'I live in Burrowhead.'

'Right.'

'I'm *from* Burrowhead.'

Si can hear the sound of traffic building outside, rush hour not so far away. You don't have to listen to traffic, in Burrowhead. This time of the morning you can hear birds waking up. Alexis used to be able to name them, from the calls they made. He'd lie in bed telling him, that one's a blackbird, can you hear it? And our robin's arrived. Guess who'll join them next.

'How could I move here?'

Alexis never wanted to be in a city.

'I mean, what would I do?'

'Live, I guess,' Orlando says quietly. 'We do have police here. You said the station was closing. I just thought—'

'Look, I'm not...'

But Si doesn't know how to finish the sentence.

'Not what?'

'I've not finished what I need to do there.'

'What is it you're trying to do?'

Si shakes his head.

'I've got to go.'

Stands up. Doesn't want to leave.

'You know, I've got work today too,' Orlando says.

Simon hadn't forgotten, not completely.

'Your new internship.'

'First day and that.'

Si looks at him, still sleep-ruffled and warm. Wishes he could get back into bed and not feel himself pulled away soon as his mind unfurls.

'Good luck, Orly. I'll—'

'Right.'

But Simon has this feeling, as he leaves, that they're never going to see each other again, and the tugging in his stomach that keeps drawing him home to Burrowhead twists into something else as he drives back to the coast, to the case, to Alexis.

ROUGH MORNING

The nurse is shaking. Mascara in streaks. Chewing on her nails as Georgie asks her questions then sitting on her hands to answer, as if that's the only way she can stop. She found him this morning. She does the wake-up, they get tea, she says, before the breakfast tray at eight and she thought he was sleeping or ignoring her, like he did half the time anyway and she was chatting away to him like a, like a—

'It's okay,' Georgie says. 'This is not your fault.'

'It's my fault,' says Suze, sitting on the chair next to the nurse, head in hands.

Neither of them contradicts her.

'But he was getting better,' the nurse keeps going, 'and he was supposed to be, to be going…but I was slow and stupid and if, if—'

'As far as I can tell, he's been dead for hours,' Georgie says, though it doesn't comfort the nurse, and Georgie thinks she'll need some help, counselling maybe, not everyone can absorb things like this the way she can. She's not proud of that, Georgie. She wants to go back to being someone shocked by death, turned inside out by it.

Instead she's asking herself if this could have been natural causes, or something worse.

'If I hadn't fallen asleep,' Suze says, 'I might have noticed something.'

Georgie shakes her head. She doesn't know yet; none of them do. She steps cautiously into the room.

His bed is neat. That's the first thing she sees, aside from the lack of colour on his skin and the fact his eyes are closed. So either Lee died in his sleep or his eyes were closed by someone. She'll have to ask the nurse if she did that.

It's not just the eyes though. His arms are laid neatly by his sides. His sheets have been tucked in. He looks like he's been put to bed by someone who cared for him, who loved him.

Fergus had said he was scared.

No, Fergus had said Natalie thought he was scared. He'd seemed scared to Georgie. She should have listened, to Fergus, to her instincts. She should have put two people at least on his door last night, taken it seriously – why hadn't she? Because it was Lee Prowle? Because most of the violence in the village has been committed by him or someone like him, one way or another?

The nurse, outside, is crying. Georgie can hear Suze trying to comfort her, putting an arm around her shoulders, showing some humanity while Georgie's mind is running through connections: Lee Prowle and Andy Barr attacking Pamali, painting racist hate all over the village, hanging round with Bobby Helmsteading, who killed Alexis, who was killed himself in return. Natalie Prowle, slaughtering that horse in the woods, hating Ricky Barr, hating anything that gets in the way of her perfect village, just like her Aunt Nora. No, not as bad as Nora. What Nora Prowle did to Sonny Riley was—

Footsteps: Cal arriving. She wills him to slow down, give her a minute.

Rachel and Pauly last year. Taking the same drug, or a version of it, the same ingredients. Their bodies broken on the rocks, bones shattered like ice smashed. Rachel and Pauly, Lee and Andy, Shona and Kev.

Six kids. Three of them dead.

'Let's see what we have,' Cal says from behind her. He's suited already and Georgie's not. She moves away to let him through then steps from the room, leaving Lee with Cal – no, leaving Cal with the body.

'I need cause of death,' she says.

'Don't we all,' Cal replies, not looking back at her. 'Did you shut these eyes?'

'Of course not.'

'Did someone else?'

He turns round then.

'I'll find out.' She pauses by the door though, something making her reluctant to leave. She doesn't know what it is, not until she feels something tugging on her hand. Not something; someone. The brush of a child's hair against her arm. It can't be. Can it? Georgie bites her lips, looks at Cal, only at Cal. They're supposed to be having a talk, at some point; they need to talk.

'He could have died in his sleep,' she says, as though that's the reason she's still standing here, watching him work. There's a noise, a shiver of breath. Georgie keeps staring at Cal, but she needs more people here, she needs to fill the room, where are the rest of his team?

'People don't sleep like this,' Cal says. He straightens up, hands on hips, like he needs to stretch out his back. 'My team are on their way.'

But she hadn't said that out loud, had she?

There's a hiss of half-formed words.

'Early start,' Cal says. 'They'll be here soon. They were sleeping. This kid' – he flicks his head towards the body – 'was not.'

That insistent tugging on her hand and a whisper too close to her ear.

Rest in peace.

Georgie feels her mouth dry out, her lips crack. She turns. There's nothing there.

'I'm saying we need to find out who closed his eyes, Georgie.' She has to reply.

'Frazer and Si are…they're on their way too, they can…'

'Ma'am?' It's Suze, behind her, touching her arm. 'Ma'am?' Suze is gesturing to the nurse, who has her head in her hands and is slipping lower, like she can barely hold herself up. 'She says she didn't touch him.'

'What?'

'She says she didn't touch the body. His eyes were closed when she found him this morning. But also…Andy Barr was here. Well, in there.' Suze points to the room. 'Yesterday, Andy visited Lee. Then on his way out, he got into a fight with someone.'

'Who?'

'They could hear voices yelling outside,' Suze says. 'Isn't that right?'

The nurse looks up, nods. A deep breath, juddering through her. 'Someone was yelling, you stay the…eff…away from my brother.'

'So Aaron was here too.' Georgie isn't surprised.

'This was all before I arrived though,' Suze says. 'After I arrived there was only the one visitor.'

Georgie moves to the chair beside the nurse and sits, offers an arm for her shoulder. She's trying to say something between the sobs. Georgie leans down to listen.

'Poor Natalie,' the nurse is saying. 'Poor Natalie.'

'At least she got the chance to see him,' Suze says, and Georgie glares at her before she realises what she's trying to say.

'You mean Natalie Prowle was the visitor you saw coming in?'

'She was in there for ages,' Suze says. 'It was late, pitch-black outside and I only closed my eyes for a second… Ma'am, I'm so sorry. Should I send my resignation up to Crackenbridge?'

'No, Suze,' Georgie manages. Beside her the nurse isn't even listening to what they're saying, she's still talking to herself. 'Poor Natalie,' she's saying, over and over again. 'Oh poor, poor Natalie,' and Georgie knows she has to go and tell Natalie that her son is dead. She has to do it now, and it has to come from her.

WHAT GEORGIE DIDN'T KNOW
HOW TO SAY, TWO YEARS AGO

'It's Thanksgiving, Mom.'

The phone receiver is warm against Georgie's face, her ear. It's always the landline she uses to call her mom; the only phone call she uses the landline for. Fergus knows. He's brought her through a cup of tea. He's leaving her space to talk but he's here, in the house.

'It is,' her mom says, and her voice is tired, more tired than usual. Georgie feels a sting of guilt, avoids asking if her mom has any plans, if she's doing a dinner, if the weather's fine.

The weather here is freezing. Frost on the car first thing, the grass crisp and inviting, the sun low through the window, making the world sparkle. The ice on the leaves. The intricate shapes of the tree branches.

'How are you, Mom?'

'I'm doing fine,' she says, like she always says.

Her mom's never asked her to move back home, not once. She's never hinted, never made one mention of how Georgie is the only family she has left. Georgie is grateful for that. But she's falling now, back to the last time she saw her, that static, dry heat she'd almost forgotten after so long on the coast, by the sea. It changes every day, this coastline, the salt on the breeze and the swirl of rich colours carried by the waves; she never tires of it. But for her father's funeral the air was thin and still. The kind of air that sucked the moisture from her skin.

Fergus had gone with her, to the funeral. She doesn't know if she'd have been able to get on the plane without him. They stayed in a hotel, treated her mom to dinner the night before, described the chill of autumn they'd come from, the rich terracotta of the land, the taste of the sea. Georgie couldn't go back to being land-locked, though there was no need to say that – her mom understood. It was a short visit, a few days. All Georgie could manage. The funeral in the middle of it. Being drawn back to the day of her brother's funeral, the same chapel, the same scent, the heavy pollen with nowhere to go in the stagnant air and the way people looked at her, stared at her. Georgie back in town after how long? How long?

Twenty years is a long time and no time at all, that's something Georgie knows. Twenty years can dissolve like salt in steam.

'How are you, Georgie?'

But that's the problem, isn't it – it's too easy to fall through the years.

'I'm fine too, Mom.'

Back to now, back to here. That's how Georgie does it, how she gets through the conversations and the guilt and the memories; she keeps herself rooted here, in her home, with Fergus, on their wild, windswept stretch of the coast.

'And work?'

'Busy,' she says. 'Good.'

She's started regular visits to the school and they're getting to know her now, those kids. It's doing some good. She wants them to reach for the horizon, not fall into boredom and where it leads – there's too much of that.

'You don't feel like an outsider there?'

Georgie blinks and all her focus is on her mom's words from across the Atlantic.

'Do you still feel like an outsider?' Georgie says.

'I am an outsider.'

She doesn't talk like this; they don't talk like this, Georgie and her mom, they make the best of things and keep their conversations light for both their sakes, so that they can say goodbye and get on with their separate days without the aching tug of the past and her mom knows it too, clears her throat, says something about dinner.

'So you're cooking something special?'

She regrets the words soon as they're out of her mouth.

'Happy Thanksgiving, Georgie,' her mom says, and she doesn't wait for a goodbye, she is gone and Georgie is holding a phone transmitting nothing but silence and then Fergus is there. He's asking if everything's okay, if it was harder than usual and she tells him that her mom is doing fine, just fine. Her mom's always fine. It's the first time she's lied to him in a long time. She doesn't even know why she does it. But the salt carried in the air this winter is sharper than usual and Georgie is starting to think that something might be coming. She can feel her body rebuilding the defences around her and for reasons she can't explain Fergus is standing on the outside, looking in.

PEOPLE BREAKING, PART ONE

Natalie hears the knock like a punch.

There is a bell – they could have rung the bell. But they knocked on her door instead. Why is it, how is it, that Natalie knows from a knock, from that single knock? She stands in the kitchen by the kettle, waiting for it to boil, waiting and not wanting to answer the door and then the knock comes again.

She forces herself to move. She can't know what's happened; she doesn't know. It could be anyone. But the shape at the door, through the frosted glass, is DI Georgie Strachan.

She knows why. Lee.

She can't open the door.

She's going to be sick. She's falling, shoulder at the door, knees buckling to the floor until she feels a hand on her shoulder.

'It's okay, Natalie,' Fergus says. He's helping her up, trying to, but nothing is okay; she knows that much. Her eyes are on the door but she can't open it.

'It's okay,' Fergus says again. 'I'll get it.' He reaches for the door, pulls it open. 'Georgie,' he says, his voice like an exhale.

Natalie knew it was DI Strachan and here she is. Natalie knows, she knows already: Lee is gone.

'Natalie. May I come in?'

Georgie steps inside, avoids making eye contact with Fergus. Natalie seems like she's in shock already, like she knows what's coming. It doesn't help. Georgie steers her through the house to where there's a seat, at the kitchen table, and Natalie sits down. Fergus sits down beside her. Georgie stays standing.

'Natalie. I'm...' She swallows, looks down at her hands, back up, forces the words out of her throat. 'Natalie, I am so sorry.'

She's ignoring Fergus but she has no idea what else to do. He phoned her, just yesterday, betrayed Natalie's trust to tell her what he knew and there was the silence shared, the hope she'd felt last night; what can she possibly say to Fergus here, now, with Natalie's son lying dead in the hospital?

'It's Lee, isn't it?' Natalie says.

'He passed away in the night.'

Natalie closes her eyes, rocks on her chair. Then she stares right up at her. 'From the drugs?'

Georgie hesitates. Gently pulls out a third chair and sits down opposite the two of them. 'We're trying to...we are going to determine cause of death. We'll find out what happened, Natalie.'

Natalie looks at Fergus. 'That means it wasn't the drugs, doesn't it?' Her voice breaking, desperate. 'Doesn't it? I told you he was scared.' Words rushing out now. 'I knew, I knew, I... Someone...'

'We don't know what happened, Natalie—'

'Someone got to him!'

'We're investigating, Natalie.' Georgie speaks quietly, trying to offer something, though she doesn't know what it is. Calm, perhaps. Maybe she can project that, even if she doesn't feel it. 'We'll find the truth, I promise you.'

To Natalie, DI Strachan's voice sounds like it's coming from somewhere outside. She can hardly hear the words. But here, inside, in her own kitchen, there's something on her hand. She's staring at something on her hand and it slowly takes shape into

Fergus's hand. He's here. Fergus is here with her. And who else has she got? His big eyes are soft and sad like they have been for weeks, but deeper now.

'Fergus.'

It's all she can say. She had wondered, with him staying here, what he thought, what he felt about her, but he'd never even suggested—

'I'm here.'

She can't look at DI Strachan, can't face her, she doesn't want to see whatever she'll see there.

'As soon as we know more...' DI Strachan says. She's still here, saying things and telling her things and Fergus's hand is on hers. Natalie's. On the kitchen table. She thought she would cry but she's not, why is she not crying? Why is she sitting here in silence letting Fergus hold her hand?

'Natalie,' Fergus is saying. 'I can make some tea, I mean, for the shock...'

Georgie stares at him. She can feel herself doing it but doesn't know how to stop. His eyes flick to hers, then away, then back again. Their conversation yesterday, he's thinking about it too. And he's mortified – Georgie can see that. He didn't want her to see him here, not like this. But what does that mean? He's not even dressed. He's wearing his pyjamas and his face is still creased from lying in bed. Natalie's smartly dressed though, like always, her shirt buttoned up and her hair blown dry, straight to her shoulders. They can't have been together. Can they? But his hand on Natalie's hand. She'd known he was staying here. She shouldn't be surprised but she can't look at Fergus, can't meet his gaze, so she says something about being in touch when they know more.

'I'm sorry, Natalie.' Her throat dry and sticky. 'I... I'm...'

Natalie tries to speak but it comes out as an inward gasp, a clenching of lungs. Fergus puts his arm around her.

Georgie stands up.

Fergus is staring at her, eyes pleading.

'Georgie—'

'I have to go.'

Natalie gasps again, like her lungs are tightening into fists, and Georgie can see the tears about to break.

'But Georgie,' Fergus says, 'it's not...'

Not what she thinks? That's what he's trying to say? Here, in front of the woman he's been staying with, whose son is dead. Suddenly, Georgie is furious.

'Stop it, Fergus,' she manages, stepping back from the kitchen. This isn't about her, it isn't about them. 'Look after Natalie.'

Fergus is pale, silent.

His breath shudders and he gives a nod.

Then Georgie turns to walk away, and sees the shadow of a little girl disappearing beyond the door.

PEOPLE BREAKING, PART TWO

The sound wakes Shona like the roar of an animal fighting for its life. It has them immediately reaching for something – clothes, for Shona, a weapon, for Kev, though all he finds is a bread knife and his work boots. Shona's breathing is fast, shallow; Kev's is slow and controlled. He's been woken up to threat more often than Shona has. He's not so out of his depth.

That noise, then the fracturing of wood and glass that follows: a caravan, splintered. Kev stands against the inside wall and kicks open their door.

It's not their caravan being attacked. It's next door. It's Lee and Aaron's.

Then she sees.

Aaron is yelling with everything he has, a wordless scream at the caravan as he hurls himself against it; glass everywhere, the window smashed, the caravan tipping dangerously to the far corner. Kev's running.

'Stop, Aaron, what the—'

'Fuck!' With a final scream he bashes against the wooden frame and crumples, back against it, head down, to the ground.

'What's happened?'

'Lee's dead.'

The way he says it, so quiet, under his breath, Shona hardly hears the words. He means Lee's in trouble, she thinks at first, they've had another fight, Lee's thrown him out of the caravan, he's hiding inside, cowering.

'He's dead?'

Kev's voice makes more sense but how—

'But he's getting out today.'

That's right, Lee's getting out of hospital today, he's fine, he's going to be fine.

'He's dead.'

'How do you—'

Aaron flings his phone against their caravan, where it bounces off the corner and thuds to the grass. 'My mother. My fucking—'

Other people have heard. Of course they have, a sound like that. Penny-Ann and Julie are coming, hand in hand, slower than Shona and Kev but still scared, she can see it in their faces. Penny-Ann's eyes are on Kevin as though it could have been him, but it couldn't; it could only have been Aaron, a noise like that. Julie's looking at her for an answer, but Shona doesn't know anything right now.

'My mother called. All cold and fucking—' Aaron lets out a yell that makes Shona want to run. 'She was so *calm*. That bitch, she said *Don't lose your temper*. Lose my fucking temper? My brother's dead.'

'She was probably trying—' Shona begins, but she stops with his glare.

'Don't.'

He's right, too, that's not helpful.

'The way she spoke to me, I fucking swear...'

She was probably trying to keep it together, that's what Shona's thinking. Trying to be strong for her son, trying to be strong for herself.

'She practically asked if I killed him.'

Silence between them all now. Words sinking to the ground.

'Fuck, man.' That was Kev.

'But it was a bad reaction, right, just—'

'The police are there. They're no releasing his body.'

Shona shakes her head. 'But why would your mam think you—'

'She thought everything was my fault all along. It was always my fucking fault.'

'We're only trying to understand,' Julie says, and something goes quiet though what it is Shona couldn't even say – insects, buzzing then gone, the crash of the waves, the rustling of something, around them, watching. 'What was your fault?'

Aaron looks like he's about to start punching the caravan again, but he doesn't.

'I was buying from Bobby last year, alright?'

'Bobby Helmsteading? Wasn't he one of the men got killed?'

'Fuck, man,' Kev says again, though Shona can see he's trying to calm things down. He pulls out a fag, offers one to Aaron. He takes it, doesn't light it.

'Fuck it all,' Aaron says, staring at the cigarette in his hand. 'It was just speed. Bobby was a mate. Of mine first, then Lee and Andy too. Lee started… Lee always took shit too far. And before you ask, Bobby had nothing to do with Rachel and Pauly, alright? *Nothing.*'

No one speaks.

'He used to stand up for Andy like no one else. He punched Ricky Barr right in the face one time. But he never said where he was getting the gear. Told us to ask him, whatever we needed. He was good like that. Gave me a decent cut too.'

'Until he was killed.'

Aaron bites his lip and Shona can see another shout building, has to stop herself from taking a step back in case it's her he lashes out at this time and not Ricky's caravan.

'I thought someone would find me after he died. Approach me, right? I was the fucking obvious choice.'

'To take over from Bobby?'

Kevin lights his cigarette.

'I thought, if I was here working for Ricky it would be easy enough for him to talk to me.'

'So Ricky was selling to Bobby like we thought?'

Aaron shakes his head. 'It wasn't him. At least, if it was, he sure hides it well. He's never said one thing to me. But then...'

At last he takes Kev's lighter. Shona's watching for a shake in his hand, but the flame is steady.

'But then Lee starts claiming he can get hold of—'

'Of the same stuff Rachel and Pauly were taking last year,' Shona says. She can feel their eyes on her, every pair, and she doesn't like it. She shouldn't have said anything, but it's done now. 'It's what we have to be thinking, right?'

The rain's getting heavier again. She's so used to it she almost doesn't notice the constant drizzle, but there's something sharper falling on them now.

'So that's what you and Lee were fighting about?' Julie says. 'That time when I saw you—'

'I wanted to know who was selling it to him. Who was making it. Thought we could be partners. But Lee, he was smart enough on his own, wasn't he. Said he could handle it. Why didn't he fucking listen?'

Shona is watching him, no colour left in his face, the bones of his hands standing out more than they should, knuckles prominent, nails bitten down. There's a sharpness around his jaw as he takes a drag. Kev's cigarette is burning down, unsmoked. Penny-Ann and Julie are quiet now, standing like they don't know what to do, like there's nothing to do – and maybe they're right. Shona, though, Shona's thinking about Bobby Helmsteading and Ricky Barr, about Natalie Prowle and what her Aunt Nora did to that little boy forty years ago. She's thinking about Lee dead in the hospital, forcing herself to believe the truth of it, and she's wondering if Andy Barr is going to appear soon, gangly and awkward as ever, or if he's not going to show up today at all.

ON THE WAY FROM ONE PLACE TO ANOTHER

Frazer's glad to get out of the hospital, the smell in there, the heaviness of the air. This weather, he tells himself, wanting to think about something other than that kid lying cold in a hospital bed, tucked in as though it were a cot. This weather. The heat, sticky and clammy with rain, always clinging to his skin. The sky is an unnatural bright grey, filled with layers of cloud but lit with sun refusing to be covered, edges of purple, green, colours coming through where they shouldn't, translucent and vanishing.

Lee Prowle had been tucked in. Like someone loved him.

Then he sees her, by the fountain. Not sitting on the edge the way Trish had, but standing looking in, an umbrella over her head, a transparent mac around her body, sandals on her feet. He pauses, tries to think straight. Not about Lee Prowle but about Mrs Dover.

Mrs Gail Dover who was Gail Braxton. Granddaughter to George F. Braxton, owner of Wyndham Manor, where Abigail Moss was killed.

Then there's Nora Prowle. Youngest daughter of George F. Braxton. Related but estranged. What she did to Sonny Riley. How Nora and her husband covered it up. How they ran the village as the hotel went out of business, as the Braxtons lost their money and the locals lost their farms. Locals like Art Robertson and Walt Mackie. Elise Robertson's father. Trish's uncle. He rubs his eyes.

'Mrs Dover…? Gail? May I?'

She doesn't look up from the fountain's basin. It's filled with rainwater, grey-white like the sky, the stone glistening. She holds out a hand and he sees she's clutching a bunch of feathers as though they were flowers.

'We're flooding,' she says.

He looks down; the street is wet, true, puddled but passable.

'It's not that bad.'

'Yes it is.'

When she says that it does seem like the rain's getting heavier – it's more than damp on his skin and clothes, it's purposeful.

'I suppose the fountain might overflow,' he says.

His voice sounds weird to his own ears, like he's having a fake conversation, like nothing he says bears any resemblance to the thoughts in his head.

'I've heard things,' she says. 'Since we last spoke, I've heard things I didn't want to hear.'

Her face is old and young at the same time and he can't focus on it. It's the rain in his eyes, soaking him where he stands, watching Gail Dover under her red umbrella. Gail Braxton, granddaughter to George F. Braxton who owned the Wyndham Manor, where Frazer saw things, where he heard things, where he ran and fell like Betty Marshall had before him.

'Is it true, DS Frazer?' she says.

'Is what true?'

'That poor boy.'

'You've heard?'

'That boy shouldn't have ended up like that.'

'Are you talking about Lee Prowle?'

She reaches out and takes a hold of his wrist. 'Do you ever feel like things are getting worse, DS Frazer? Worse all the time?'

'We're going to find the person responsible.'

She shakes her head at that.

'We will. Someone is making the drugs that are hurting these kids—'

'No, you don't understand.'

'I do, and we'll catch them.'

'But you don't understand at all, DS Frazer.' Her hand is still clasped around his wrist while her other reaches for his arm. 'It's powerful, the ayahuasca brew, but it's not harmful.'

He can't breathe. How does she know what they know? Who has told her?

'It's a form of DMT and it most certainly is harmful.'

'No, ayahuasca is different. You need to understand.'

He forces himself to breathe in the thick air. He's supposed to be taking her to the station, inviting her – nicely – he's supposed to be leading this conversation and asking her about Wyndham Manor, about Abigail Moss, but her smile has turned to something else and her hand is on his arm, raindrops clinging to her skin as though it were made of wax.

'First there was Nora,' she says.

'You knew Nora Prowle?'

'That woman was always telling people how to live.'

'Did she tell you?'

'Some of us didn't like her rules. I guess Lee Prowle wouldn't have liked her rules, even if he is one of her line.'

'What do you know about Lee Prowle?'

'Nora would have tried to save him. She always thought she could save people.'

'Save him from what?'

'She thought it was evil.'

'The ayahuasca brew?'

'She thought it was the evil in our village,' she says, eyes glassy.

'Can you come with me to the station? To talk about Wyndham Manor and, and this too, I just…it's hard to think out here.'

'The air is heavy today.'

'I'd like to record, I mean if you're willing to give a state—'

'It wouldn't have killed that poor boy, done right.'

'It didn't kill him.'

Her eyes on him, piercing. Shit.

'Lee Prowle was murdered then,' she says. Quieter, pulling him close. 'You shouldn't be investigating ayahuasca, DS Frazer. You should be investigating that family.'

'We don't know what happened to Lee Prowle, Mrs Dover.' Her skin, under the umbrella, is reflecting the red light. 'And we *are* investigating.' Her skin is too red, like it's radiating, it must be the light, the storm light searing through the fabric, that's all, he needs to breathe. 'Please, can we talk about Abi—'

'We have talked.'

'At the station.'

'I can't.'

'Mrs Dover, you need to make a statement.'

'About what?'

The rain's so heavy he can hardly see, it's in his eyes, stinging like salt, and the basin of the fountain is grey and murky and feathers are circling in the water as though there were a flow to it, as though it were a working fountain but the rain, the rain. The feathers sinking under the weight of it and when he looks up she's walking away, walking to the bus stop. She knows something about ayahuasca. The drug that Lee Prowle took; Rachel and Pauly too. She was connected to Wyndham Manor. All three cases, one two three. He has to follow her but his legs won't move and the bus arrives as he is standing there, watching it. Staring. It's bright orange and sordid against the pale buildings and lush trees, the roses, the vines and ivy, and there are people sitting inside. On the bus. Through the windows. None of them looking out as it drives off and he's still standing there and it's gone. Mrs Dover is gone to wherever she's going and

DS Frazer needs to sit and write it down, the faces he saw, the connections.

'Are you okay?'

Simon Hunter, on his way to the station.

'Where does that bus go?'

'Warphill. Why?'

At first he doesn't know why, doesn't know where his thoughts are taking him. He needs to connect it all together.

'Mrs Dover was heading to Warphill, on that bus.'

'It's not unusual.'

'And Whelan, I interviewed him the other day.' Frazer points to June and Whelan's house, their neat roses out front. 'He was waiting at the stop too.'

'There's not that many buses, so folk—'

'She knows about ayahuasca.'

He stares at Simon then.

'That doesn't necessarily...'

He keeps on staring.

'Penny-Ann read about it on the internet.' Simon stops, meets his gaze.

'The internet doesn't say anything about dissolving it in blood,' Frazer says.

'Did Mrs Dover?'

'No, no.'

Simon smiles, takes a seat beside him on the fountain's edge. 'I don't think Mrs Dover is our drug dealer,' he says kindly.

'I didn't say she was.'

'Okay. But you...you think something's happening in Warphill?'

Is that it, is that what he thinks?

'Frazer?'

There are connections.

'Trish was on the bus too.'

'Trish was on the bus too?' Simon echoes.

'I think they're all involved,' Frazer says, shivering uncontrollably despite the heat. He needs something, a sit-down or a drink, some food, something, because what his body's doing now isn't right, it isn't right at all. 'Mrs Dover and, and the Prowles and all of them,' he says. Trish, even Trish. 'They're all in it together, aren't they.'

GETTING THINGS HANDLED

Debs finds Andy sitting at the old oak kitchen table in the seat where she used to sit. He likes that spot, back to the sink, view out of the window. She can remember needing to see out. His long legs are folded under the table and he's drinking a glass of milk like a five-year-old, like Ricky used to do when they were children. She'll not tell Andy that. She's learnt that if she wants to build a relationship with him they both need to pretend Ricky's no part of it.

She's in her slippers. Floor's cold, these old tiles, cracked now. The once terracotta of them turned grey. Over by the sink is a dirty cereal bowl still there from breakfast, a plate and knife, Ricky's large mug. He's up then, up and out of the house. He spends hours out in the fields, her brother. Their da used to be like that and she used to be glad – away before she was up in the morning, their mam keeping to her bed, just her and Ricky at the table, cereal, milk.

'Morning, Andy,' she says, pulling out the chair beside him. That way they can both look out of the window, and there's no need to look uncomfortably at each other. Andy gets nervous if people look at him too much, doesn't like the eye contact. He's an anxious boy. Shy. She thinks most of the village have missed that about him.

'Hi Debs.'

This is how it starts every time, a gradual greeting, like two cats sizing each other up on the street corner.

'Sleep okay?'

'No bad.'

Only this morning is different, because she's going to have to tell him.

DI Strachan had rung her mobile, not the farm phone, not Ricky. His friend, the angry one who was in hospital. Andy thought he was coming home today. She swallows. Needs a drink.

'Cup of coffee?'

He flicks his head at the kettle and she puts it on to boil.

Andy's friend, Lee Prowle, was dead. DI Strachan had told her on the phone. Not what to do, what to say, but a hint at what she was hoping for and didn't feel she could reasonably ask. 'The two of them,' she'd said, 'they were close to Bobby Helmsteading. There might be something there.' She didn't say what though, just went quiet and Debs had wondered if something else was happening, if someone had walked into the room and she didn't feel she could keep going where she'd been going. 'He'll need an eye on him, after you give him the news,' was all she'd said, and Debs had promised to look after him – though that was not what DI Strachan had meant.

The kettle is whistling at her. It's high-pitched and sharp but she likes the sound, always has done, and the bubbling beneath, full of energy, the heat noticeable even from here at the table. Her mug is on the draining board from her morning tea – they each have their own mugs in this house that they use over and over again, though there's a cupboard with plenty of others in. The one she uses is the one Ricky gave her on her first morning back. It's wide, large-handled, sky-blue outside and white within. There's nothing special about it but she's used it ever since.

'Andy…' Sitting down, her voice soft. It's enough for him to realise she needs to tell him something, that it's bad news. With a shock of static she sees what he's thinking.

'No, your da's fine.'

His chest falls, though the rest of his posture stays the same, milk glass in hand.

'But your friend Lee…'

'What?'

'Andy, I'm so sorry. Lee died in the hospital last night.'

His face barely moves, just his eyes, darting. Then his head shaking.

'No—'

'I'm so—'

'No.'

'I'm so sorry.'

'But he's getting out today.' As he says the words he puts the milk glass down on the table, a slight shake to it, barely noticeable. 'He's getting out today.'

'Oh, Andy.'

His mouth has fallen open and he's staring at the table, staring at the solid old wood that can give nothing back.

Then, in a whisper, 'I went to see him yesterday.'

'You went to the hospital?'

'He was my mate!' A sudden flare of anger.

'Of course he was, Andy. It was good of you to visit. He would have—'

'What the fuck happened?'

All she can do is shake her head. He'd overdosed, maybe, had a bad reaction to what he took in that caravan; DI Strachan told her nothing, now she thinks of it, hinted that she needed to spy on her own nephew but gave her nothing to help him understand.

He's still sitting there at the table, like there's something he's trying to beat down inside of himself.

'I know what happened,' he says at last.

'What do you mean?'

His eyes on hers for a second, fleeting but unmasked, anger and hurt and beneath it something more, something dawning.

'It happened before,' he says.

'Do you mean...' She doesn't know if she should go there. 'Do you mean Bobby Helmsteading?'

It doesn't work; he's immediately tense, sharp, full of angles.

'Who's said what?'

'No one—'

'You need to fucking tell me.'

She could be afraid of him when he flares up like this but she holds out a hand towards him instead. 'I don't know what happened.' He shies away from her like she's seen him shy away from his da. 'I wasn't here then, remember.'

'I remember.'

'You know what this village is like, you hear things, that's all. I heard about how cut up you were, after he died.'

'He was my mate.'

'Was he?'

She leaves her words to hang between them. Doesn't like doing it, but she's watching his face, seeing the thoughts flicker across it – he's intelligent, Andy, but he's not learned to hide his expressions and she loves him for that. Ricky was the same once. Now nothing gets through the scowl.

'Can I...'

'Can you what, Aunty Debs?'

She feels the warmth she gets every time he does that, acknowledges who she is.

'Can I do anything to help you, Andy?'

'Aye,' he says, lips pursing and the anger pushing its way back into his eyes. 'You can trust me.'

He pushes his chair back, scraping against the tiles, leaves his milk half-drunk on the table and Debs is on her own now, cradling her mug in both hands and trying to understand what happened to this place until she feels a hand on her shoulder. That warmth again.

Ricky looks worse though. His face is so skinny she can barely see who he once was, the sagging at his neck, bones protruding; she can feel her eyes sting but he'd hate for her to cry, she'll not do it.

'Looking good, am I?'

He doesn't smile but it's as close to humour as he gets.

'I thought you were out.'

He shakes his head.

'You didn't sleep?'

'I never fucking sleep.'

'It's no wonder Andy uses bad language when you—'

'Give me a break, Debs.'

'Right.'

She smiles then; feels like she's smiling for this whole family sometimes.

'I heard,' he says. 'Lee Prowle.'

'It was the police called.'

'Not natural causes then.'

She shrugs, shakes her head.

'That phrase,' he says. 'What is a natural cause of death?'

Ricky never talks about his lung cancer; this is the closest he's ever got and Debs has been waiting for it, for an opportunity to talk, to think of the future. Though now he's given her the opening she has no idea where to start.

'I've made a will,' he says.

Her little brother. She's lost so much time, a lifetime.

'Andy's still a kid. I want you to...'

He clears his throat, and it turns, as it always does, into the awful hacking cough that keeps him awake all night and in pain all day; that she lies awake hearing, not knowing how to cope with the helplessness of there being nothing she can do.

'I'll look after Andy,' she says. 'I'll always look after Andy.'

He wipes his mouth on the back of his hand.

'That's good,' he says. 'Thank you.'

'You're welcome.'

These moments of softness between them, she feels like maybe that's what he's still living for.

AYAHUASCA

Georgie can't stop seeing the way Lee was tucked in. His eyes gently closed. He could have been sleeping, if he'd been the calmest sleeper in the world.

She can't stop seeing the way Fergus put his hand on Natalie's, without hesitating, without wondering if it would be allowed; then tried to tell her there was nothing going on between them. And even if there wasn't?

Cal says Lee was suffocated. Fibres in his mouth, his throat. He was suffocated with a flannel. The flannel right there by his bed, intended to wipe his forehead if he got too hot – it was stifling in there. This is a murder case now. She can't let HQ close her down until it's finished. And there are grey eyes calling her gaze towards them. A familiar tugging on her shirtsleeve; warm fingers curling around her wrist and she's here, she must be, she's here again and Georgie stands, the chair toppling over behind her.

Frazer turns calmly, surprised by the sudden noise but not wanting to show it.

'Are you okay, ma'am?'

Georgie picks up her chair but stays standing. Standing is better. Makes it easier to focus on the bewildering family tree Frazer has drawn on the board connecting Mrs Dover to half the residents of Burrowhead and Warphill. Including the Prowles. At the top is Nora Prowle, Nora Braxton as she once was. Gail Dover's estranged relative who married the police officer Jacob Prowle and kept an eye on everyone in the village. She killed Sonny Riley while he was in her care. She was Lee Prowle's great-aunt. Lee Prowle who is dead. Lee Prowle who dislocated Pami's shoulder with the words: *That's shut you up some. Not that it makes much difference round here. There's no one listening.*

'Nora Prowle,' Frazer says, 'was all about saving the village. Keeping it "pure" using the threefold death animal sacrifice. And, presumably, any other means at her disposal.'

'Same as Art Robertson and Jack Helmsteading,' Simon says. 'Same as Walt Mackie...' He lowers his voice as though Trish might be here.

'Same as Natalie Prowle always has been,' Georgie says.

Saving the village by slaughtering innocent creatures and bullying outsiders and blaming Ricky Barr for every damn thing. What is Fergus thinking? What is *Georgie* thinking, telling him to stay there, to look after her? But her son is dead. She needs someone to help her, they can both see that.

'Prowles, Robertsons, Helmsteadings,' Frazer says. 'All families known to have been involved with performing animal sacrifices over the years.' There's a short pause. 'Along with the Mackies.'

'Trish is not here,' Georgie says, folding her arms. 'You can both stop worrying about her.'

Then Georgie's worrying about her again, about Trish having no one left, Trish needing her and pushing her away; who has Trish got to help her?

'Now Mrs Dover, the sweet old lady who lives in her two-bed cottage in the centre of the village—'

'Don't tell me,' Georgie says. 'She's into ritual sacrifice too?'

'Actually, she's been telling me we need to *investigate* the Prowles,' Frazer says.

Georgie frowns. 'You think Gail Dover knows something?'

'I think she was trying to tell me something,' Frazer says. 'And she was talking about the ayahuasca brew. She's involved with it all somehow, I just can't see how.'

'Back up,' Georgie says. 'What exactly do we know about ayahuasca, in its original form? South American, a form of spiritual medicine, made from certain types of plants like vines and mimosa, what else?'

'Traditionally used as an entheogen,' Simon says. 'It's shamanic, it induces alterations in perception, consciousness, mood, behaviour—'

'In the US and here, a form is manufactured and sold as DMT—' Frazer says.

'But it can be made and consumed in different ways.'

'Though never, as far as we know, involving animal blood before.'

'And you think Lee and the others figured out how to make it?' Georgie says.

'No, we think they're probably just the ones taking it,' Si says. 'To test it out for someone, maybe...'

'You mean the same someone who is manufacturing this new variety,' Georgie says. 'It could be stronger than traditional ayahuasca, perhaps, with the use of raw animal blood. Riskier for the taker, but sellable for the manufacturer?'

'Both legal, for now, and highly profitable, ma'am,' says Frazer.

'And they're testing it out on local kids.'

'There could even be motive for murder in there somewhere. I've not been able to get through to Cal yet but—'

'Then bring in Mrs Dover.'

'She...got away from me.' Frazer hears his own words and allows himself a smile. 'Ma'am, I think she's gone to Warphill.'

'Why?'

'I think they've got a meeting there.'

'Find her, please, and bring her in. I want to be interviewing her after lunch.'

But how does it connect? Fergus taking Natalie's hand, the way Lee was tucked up in bed, the sheet neatly pulled up to his chin to keep him safe, the formless whispers beside her—

'Wait, what meeting?'

'The community council – that's what they call it, I think?'

'But Natalie runs that, doesn't she?'

'Not any more,' Simon says. 'We think...' His voice trails off and he looks at Frazer and Frazer looks back at him.

'What is it?'

'Trish is involved with them too.'

Simon is the one who speaks, who says her name. Frazer looks like he's lost someone he loves all over again. Suddenly Georgie can't breathe. Her throat tightens, her skin contracts. The little girl is here. She is solid and she is real. Her dress is ripped, her hair is matted and wet, and she is curled on the floor by Georgie's feet, shivering.

LAST YEAR

Pauly stands in Mungrid Woods, his eyes searching through the spindly silver birch, through low-hanging hawthorn and the head-high gorse barely visible in the dark. There have always been rumours, horror stories whispered in the dead of night about what happens if you find what he's looking for in Mungrid Woods. His parents call it evil. They like telling him about the evil in their village, insisting it must be kept away. But their definition of evil is upside down. What Rachel's trying to do, that's rooted in love. Pauly knows that sure as he knows he has to help her do it.

He's heard things in these villages, read things, learned about what the woods can give. There are deer, invisible until they dart through the trees then vanish, owls that call to one another overhead and pine martens that scratch through the undergrowth. His parents say the evil in these villages has been passed down through the generations and so, for once, he knows where he has to turn.

Even so, he didn't know until this moment that he would follow through; didn't understand where it was going to lead.

There, where the gorse seems to thin and the leaves on the ground glimmer deep golden brown against the twisting shadows. He pushes through, lets the thorns scratch his skin, forces branches away with his bare hands, the gorse retreating, the tall, thin aspen giving way to darker oak and sharper leaves, he kneels, as he was told to, kneels with his eyes on the ground and lets the night air engulf him. He can feel padded moss beneath his knees, and all around plants appear out of the gloom; he's surrounded by a shrub he can't name, the scent of honey and salted almonds, and he closes his eyes to breathe it in and then: the footsteps.

He stays where he is. Listens. Keeps his eyes on the dark brown trunks blending into the earth.

'Don't move.'

Pauly swallows, feels the air prickling at the back of his neck, wishes he'd pulled his hood up but it's too late for that. Then it's not the air on his skin, it's a knife. A blade. Sharper than the one he has in his pocket, making a shallow, deliberate scratch down his neck. He can hear something, a bee lost in the night, circling their heads. He keeps his eyes down.

'Dig through the soil.'

His fingers start working their way under the leaf mulch, under the earth, beneath the plant.

'That's right,' the voice says from behind him. 'Expose the root of mimosa.'

So he does, welcoming the mud and earth beneath his fingernails, scraping the soil from the roots that curve and grow between his hands, living things beneath his fingers. Mimosa.

'Now carve.'

Beside him on the ground lie a series of delicate knives, each one smaller than his penknife. Their blades catch the moonlight, reflect it to reveal earthenware pots in the shadows, a pestle and mortar that look ancient and stained.

He reaches out a hand.

'No, with yours.'

He imagines that the blade on his neck will follow his movements, take from his own body what he is taking from the mimosa. But it doesn't. As he carves, his neck knows the warm breeze of the woodland again. He keeps cutting at the root until he reaches the softer, inner vein, and he scoops the centre of the plant into his own hand.

His penknife is coated with the root's insides, yellow in the dark.

'Put it in the bowl,' the voice says, still soft and coaxing.

He tips his hand and lets the root and bark fall into the earthenware pot by his knees.

'Good. Now do exactly as I say.'

There is a smell, heavy and thick. Things start happening too fast. He feels a weight on his legs, but he can't look down. It sends a shudder of horror through his body; he mustn't look down. He's crushing the root with berries and leaves, adding bark with shaking hands, clasping the pestle and mortar. The night has turned brown and heavy around him and he can feel a wet warmth through his jeans. The warmth of a living thing. He mustn't look down. There are shapes between the trees that his eyes can barely pick out, through the gloom, beckoning him. He imagines Rachel, lying with her head in his lap, the warmth coming from her instead. He looks down. The rabbit lying in his lap must be sedated, but it's breathing.

'Now, you take the blood.'

The same knife he used to scrape the root, held in his frozen hand. The shallow breathing of the rabbit, still alive.

'I can't.'

There's a hissing too, coming from the woods, the trees beyond the shadows, like something sucking breath through teeth.

'Are you and I going to have a problem?'

He looks up at that, to the eyes watching him through the neat slits in the black balaclava. Shakes his head, feels the scratching at the back of his neck.

'You understood the cost.'

'I don't have any money.'

'We both know that. Take the blood.'

There was a time when Pauly thought he would tell Rachel everything. All that he was, all he had known, he would tell her. No part of him wanted to be secret. She can never know this though. She can know about the leaves and the bark, the root soothed from the ground by his fingertips; she can know the honey he will add to sweeten the taste, the inviting smell of wild mint. She can never know this.

He runs his fingers through the rabbit's fur, between its long ears. Watching his own skin meet with the skin of a creature he must destroy as the rasping gets louder, almost forms a word and it's close, the breath on the back of his arms, and he's not breathing any more, Pauly, he's not breathing. In one fast motion he turns his own arm over and presses the knife to the vein.

'No.'

'Why not?'

'It must be the animal.'

Pauly would rather offer his own blood. There would be a balance in that, after all the woods are giving them. But without knowing it he has sliced the blade through the rabbit's neck and his jeans are damp and there is a clawing at the back of his head and, beside him, the wide earthenware pot is being calmly held out to collect the blood.

A GLIMPSE OF WHAT THE LAND
CAN GIVE US

Pamali reaches an arm around Natalie's shoulders then pulls her in for a hug. Natalie doesn't say anything though, doesn't sob or cry; her whole body feels limp and hopeless.

'I am so sorry, Natalie.'

She pulls away at that, looks out at Pamali through small, raw eyes and in the silence Fergus starts to explain.

'She said she...we needed to get out of the house and I thought here maybe, a way of keeping busy, doing something...productive or...'

They are standing in the field between Ricky Barr's farm and the back of the village where there used to be nothing but neck-high nettles and creeping thistle but now there is a path through the length of it, cleared ground either side, four wide vegetable patches already filled and two more laid ready with compost. Fergus doesn't mention Georgie but he's looking intently at Pamali, like he needs her to understand but doesn't have the words to explain.

Pamali lets go of Natalie's arm, not to leave her alone but to look around the community garden, suggest where Natalie might like to work, but the second she does so Natalie drops like there's nothing holding her up any more, slumps on the path and just sits there. Pami is so shocked she doesn't move at first, doesn't say a thing. Fergus is the one who kneels down, starts talking to her in that gentle voice of his.

'Maybe you'd like to sow some seeds today,' he's saying, 'maybe some… I don't know…some beans or—'

'This is *not* what I meant!' Her arm swipes him away then drops again, listless and flat. Pamali kneels down, next to Fergus and opposite Natalie.

'I want to help you, Natalie,' Fergus tries again, though there's something hopeless in his voice. 'You helped me, when I needed a place to stay, and now…'

There's a noise, distant but carried on the wind, and Pamali looks round to see Elise Robertson waving at her from the track that leads into the village. She's looking a bit better, at least; she's had a hard time since her da died, though old Art Robertson was a difficult man. Another time Pami would have called her over, invited her to join in. It'd be good to have Elise Robertson part of the community garden. But Natalie's the one who needs help now.

'What is it *you'd* like to do, Natalie?' Pamali says. 'We can do whatever you need. We're here for you.'

'I need to find out who killed my Lee.'

'The police are—'

Natalie lurches forward and grabs Pamali's hand. 'I'm on the trail,' she says. 'I know it, Lee was giving me clues.' Her eyes up, over to the farm behind them. 'I'll make them pay.'

'Not Ricky again, please, the poor man's suffered enough.'

'Oh, not him,' Natalie says. 'I've got other ideas.'

Fergus is shaking his head. 'Then you should go to the police, if you won't tell us what you know.'

'You could be in danger,' Pami says.

'And so what?' Natalie, scrambling to her feet. 'What do I have left?'

'What about Aaron?'

'After everything he's done?'

'But he's your son too.'

'No, no, no!'

Fergus and Pami both fall into silence, watching one another, watching Natalie as she paces back and forth between the vegetable patches. Neither of them knows what to say. She's not okay, Pamali's thinking, Natalie is not okay at all, we have to do something.

'I have to make it right,' Natalie says. 'I have to make it all right. I'm going.' She glares at Pamali then turns and starts striding away.

Fergus scrambles to his feet, looking at Pami like he has no idea what to do any more. 'Georgie told me to look after her,' he says under his breath, glancing over his shoulder to Natalie. 'I... there's not...Pami, I...'

'It's okay,' she says. 'Call me if you need anything.'

He turns away, runs to catch up with Natalie, who doesn't slow her stride, and soon they're gone. Pamali watches until they're out of sight, a hand over her mouth and the heat of the sun pressing onto her shoulders. She needs to get going too, get back to work for the afternoon, but first she lets herself kneel on the ground and pick some leaves. A taste of beetroot and she finds that she's crying, just quietly. Beside the rainbow chard she lets her tears fall, lets her knees sink into the soil beneath her. Then she tries a small leaf of the peppery ruby mustard; sees fresh growth on the purple kale and a flower on her yellow courgette. Natalie is not okay, and she doesn't know how to help. Pami can't even imagine what she's going through. To lose a child, could there be anything worse? But what a world we live in – and this is how she lives in the world she lives in – that plants like this can grow up out of the ground and offer to sustain us.

INSECTS, GATHERING

Trish pushes her hand against her forehead. Her skin feels damp, seeping. The air in the bus is dense with moisture, the smell of sweat and rain. Her arms cling to the fake plastic of the seat. None of the passengers speak. Trish, Mrs Dover, Whelan, Terry from the garage. It's the way the villagers have always travelled to their community council meetings. It wasn't Natalie made it like that. It was their way before Natalie.

There are small, almost invisible flies along the tops of the windows – Trish thought they were dirt at first, before she saw them moving. She can hear bigger ones too, clegs, horseflies; there's one now, flying repeatedly against the window with a syncopated hiss and thud. She searches her pocket, finds a crumpled tissue and aims with a sudden, sharp movement. It doesn't work. Her tissue smears the window; flies swarm around her head. She thinks of the beach, this morning, Frazer walking away, phone still in hand, probably blaming himself for saying more than he should. She'd have found out soon enough anyway; everyone knows. Then, after he was gone, seeing Ricky Barr driving out of the village at the crack of dawn. She'd have followed if she could. There might be no proof he's selling drugs, but she's still got her instincts and she's listening.

The bus shudders to a stop and they walk on alone, rain gushing down their collars and soaking their clothes. Over the road, deep puddles at the kerbs ready to overflow, drains clogged with leaves and dirt. Opposite is the concrete building of the community hall. Down the alley, one by one. Trish pauses to let Mrs Dover go first, even though the woman has an umbrella and Trish doesn't. Trish wouldn't usually care about getting wet but it's different today, the heat of the rain, the clinging. She takes a deep breath but there's not enough oxygen for her blood, just the sticky taste of something lingering, pollen, wet leaves. She's the last one outside. She's pushing the heavy door; she bites the inside of her cheeks as she walks the few steps to the main hall. She's been worrying about money but when she checked earlier she'd been paid. Georgie has paid her. Why has Georgie paid her?

Mrs Smyth is standing behind a long table of sandwiches, telling folk what's been crammed in between each slice of bread. Cheese savoury, ham and tomato. They're on plates under cling film, though the flies are still trying to get in. Villagers are carrying paper plates and napkins, brushing insects away from their food with their spare hand. Saliva pools under Trish's tongue and not in a good way. She needs to cool the fuck down. She reaches to her bag, finds her bottle of water. It's warm, but it's something. She gulps, not even saving the last few mouthfuls for the meeting, then scans the hall. Elise arrives, late. The chairs are placed in a circle around a central point. That's her place. Like it was Uncle Walt's place. She sits. Breathes in the stifling air. Lee Prowle is dead. Uncle Walt is gone. Ricky Barr must be stopped. But she can't think in this heat, her clothes are clinging to her skin so tightly she can hardly breathe and they're talking already.

'So who gave it to him?' Whelan wants to know. 'Or *sold* it to him.'

She should be standing but Suze is on her feet first, saying something about Cal, something about a crime scene, and Trish needs more water.

'I saw something this morning,' Trish says, taking charge of her meeting. 'Ricky Barr was out at dawn, driving away from the village.'

'So?'

'So where was he going? What's he up to?'

Elise's laugh in the background, she's sure, but Elise is supposed to be on her side. Her father and Uncle Walt were friends, and more than that, they used the dagger together, they tried to save the village together – then she feels the stab of loss again.

'Why are you laughing? Ricky is still our strongest lead,' Trish says. 'We know he's the one behind the drugs, he always has been.'

'Ricky has cancer,' Mrs Dover says from behind her. Trish feels her shoulders clench. 'My dear, he is not what we're looking for.'

'What's that even supposed to mean?'

'Remember, it was Natalie who convinced us she needed to sacrifice his horse,' Mrs Dover goes on, her voice full of regret. 'An innocent creature.'

'And you all went along with that *madness*.' Trish's voice is raised and suddenly the flies are around her head and she's swiping at them, thrashing her arms.

'There's something I need to say about that,' Elise says, standing.

Trish doesn't know why but her stomach clenches.

'It's been on my mind,' Elise says. 'You see, when we were doing the horse—' A gasp passes around the room and Elise glances at Suze before continuing. 'When we were doing the horse, Natalie was...she was vicious.'

'Oh, come on,' says Trish. 'Why have you turned against Natalie all of a sudden? We're here to talk about the supply of drugs, about Ricky—'

'Natalie was the one who believed Ricky Barr was selling drugs to her boys,' Mrs Dover says. 'But maybe she just didn't want to see them for who they were.'

'Tell them about the horse,' Suze says quietly. 'Tell them what she did.'

What is Suze doing?

'She held that carving knife to my throat is what she did!' Elise shouts.

Trish stares at Elise.

Elise looks at the ground.

'Natalie Prowle is dangerous,' Suze says, eyes on Trish now. 'Look, I shouldn't be saying this, but you all deserve to know what we know.'

Why does Trish feel like she's going to be sick?

'Lee Prowle was killed, you've all heard,' Suze is saying, and murmurs through the hall confirm they have. 'He was smothered with a wet towel. It was by his bed for mopping his forehead. He'd been sweating.'

Mrs Dover, shaking her head at the tragedy. Elise, eyes down; hard to tell what she's thinking until she looks up, not at Trish but at Suze, hanging on her every word.

'But what you haven't heard is how his body was left.' Suze pauses to let the murmurs rise then die down again. 'He was tucked in,' she says.

Trish frowns; she shouldn't be saying this.

'He was lovingly tucked into the bed. His sheets were neat.'

She shouldn't be saying this. Trish might have left the police but Suze hasn't, this should be confidential, this should be—

'He looked like someone had kissed him goodnight. Someone who loved him.'

Trish stands. Suze holds up a hand.

'The last person to visit him at the hospital was Natalie. I saw her arrive myself.'

'You shouldn't be saying this,' Trish says.

Suze smiles and turns to her. 'I think the villagers have a right to know everything that's been going on. Don't you?'

Trish can feel her knee trembling, like there's a nerve caught; she'd hit her own leg if everyone wasn't watching. But they are watching.

'Our working hypothesis,' Suze says, looking around the villagers. 'And at this stage, it is just a hypothesis—'

It's useless, Trish knows, to tell people that. They'll believe it. They believe her already, whatever she's going to say.

'—is that Natalie couldn't cope with the fact that her sons were the ones dealing drugs. The shame of it.'

'How many years has she been trying to clean up these villages?' Whelan says.

'So many years,' says Bessie Wilkie. 'It must have felt like such a betrayal.'

Suze holds out her hand. 'Maybe we can all understand how desperate she was feeling. Maybe we all saw her slipping into… into something none of us wanted to see.' She lifts her hand to her mouth for a minute before clasping it in a fist at her chest. 'Perhaps we are all responsible.'

Elise lets out a sigh that's almost melodic, as though to express everything she's been keeping inside. 'That poor horse,' she says. 'Its eyes…'

'Natalie did that.' It's Mrs Dover speaking. 'She was copying what her Aunt Nora had done forty years before, using the threefold death against Ricky's dog. And we all know Nora was capable of killing more than animals. She murdered that little boy.'

Trish doesn't think she's ever heard Mrs Dover speak like this. She and Mrs Smyth tend to watch rather than participate. She thinks of them huddled together on a street corner, under their brollies, sitting together at community meetings with their flasks of tea and their heads close, present but separate.

Mrs Dover doesn't seem separate now.

'Natalie is capable of violence,' Trish says. 'We're not denying that, but so is Ricky Barr. He must be the one the kids are buying from, and after what he's done to Andy—'

'He's hardly someone who'd tuck a kid up in bed—'

'What are you doing, Suze?' They're getting sidetracked. They have to stop Ricky Barr, stop the drugs, that's the only way to give the local kids round here a future.

'What would Ricky's motive be for killing Lee then?'

But it's not just about Lee, is it? It's about Andy, it's about Uncle Walt. What if she's right and no one listens, none of them ever listen, no one ever makes him pay?

'Ricky was never even at the hospital,' Suze says. 'And if you saw him going somewhere this morning, he could have an alibi.'

Uncle Walt needs her to prove his guilt; she can't let him down, not now. Ricky must have had a reason to turn on Lee. Maybe he was talking, maybe—

'Natalie Prowle is our suspect,' Suze says.

But Suze is her friend, Suze *has* been her friend; Suze has seen her bloody well cry, fuck's sake.

'You're saying she killed her own son?'

Trish feels it rising from her chest, spreading around her neck, smothering heat like hands pressing against her skin.

'She thought Lee was the sacrifice the village needed.' Mrs Smyth, her voice quiet, almost a whisper. 'It's exactly what Nora would have done.'

'Air and water,' says Mrs Dover.

'The blood is hers.'

Trish could scream, she's standing, chair screeching. 'Stop it!'

All eyes on her, every pair, encircling her. The dagger is fake, she wants to yell, forget your stupid rituals – Uncle Walt was wrong! Then it hits her again, the loss of him.

'Of course,' Mrs Dover says. 'You are the one who keeps Nora's knife, these days, aren't you dear?'

'What's that supposed to mean?' Trish's head is pounding, suddenly, deeply; she can't even press her hand against the spot because it's everywhere.

'Nora had followers in this village,' Mrs Dover says. 'People who believed a threefold death would summon the ancestors to maintain our purity.'

As she says the word 'purity' Trish feels the skin tighten over her face. That's not what Uncle Walt was about, he'd never have—

'I,' says Mrs Dover, 'never believed that. In case any of you needed some clarity. There is nothing admirable about desiring purity.'

She looks at Trish and Trish can't even keep her gaze, the pressure behind her eyes, it's almost unbearable. Uncle Walt made some mistakes, she's not trying to deny that, but he wasn't—

'The threefold death was how Nora Prowle made sure everyone followed her rules. She chose to sacrifice animals, but there was always the threat of something more, something far worse. The knife was passed down to her through the generations, and she invited Walt Mackie to join her.'

Trish wants to be sick; something in her body needs to come out.

'Then Walt brought his friends in with him. Art Robertson. Jack Helmsteading. They were struggling. Losing money, losing their farms, hit by recession and disease. When old Herman Barr arrived and started doing so much better, buying up everything they had no choice but to sell, I understand why they wanted to fight back. Why they turned to the ritual, why they felt they needed to claim it as their own. But the threefold death tied them together.' Mrs Dover interlocks her fingers and Trish can see the strain in her arms as she fakes being unable to wrench them apart. 'And with Nora Prowle in charge of them, she was running the village. *Cleaning up* the village. Anyone stepped out of line, Nora Prowle sorted it out.'

Mrs Dover turns to look at Mrs Smyth.

'She beat her foster kids,' Mrs Smyth says. 'She killed that poor little boy. If any girl stepped out of line, Nora Prowle would see to it she'd be ostracised. And you know what I mean by stepping out of line, even you young ones.'

'Once Natalie was born, Nora started training her to take over,' Mrs Dover says.

'How do you know?' Trish's voice sounds distant, almost pleading.

'The villagers have always trained those who would follow.'

'Uncle Walt didn't *train* me.' Trish sounds so defensive; she hates it. 'And he hadn't done anything wrong, not for years.'

'Yet you're the one with the knife.'

'I'm making sure it won't be used!'

Over her dead body will anyone commit another sacrifice with that fake dagger Uncle Walt left her. Except no one even seems to have heard her.

'Things started to go wrong for Natalie,' Mrs Dover is saying, Mrs Smyth nodding along, picking up sentences where Mrs Dover offers them to her.

'After her Aunt Nora died, the knife was nowhere to be found—'

'Until it turned up in Walt Mackie's shed—'

'She couldn't stop her sons from taking drugs—'

'They got nasty, the vandalism got worse—'

'They took her talk of purity to mean attacking Pamali—'

'Poor Natalie has been losing her mind over it, we've all seen the signs—'

'That terrible violence with the horse—'

'She looked more desperate every time we saw her—'

'Until she couldn't take it any more. She'd tried everything to save Lee, until there was only one thing left—'

'Stop. It.' Trish is not shouting now, but she's standing and she's going to use everything she has to make them listen. Her voice is firm, not loud. Enough. She is going to speak the truth to these people and they are going to listen. 'We have no proof. The police' – she glares at Suze – 'will find proof and arrest whoever killed Lee.'

She hears her own words as she says them.

'What about Ricky Barr?' Suze smiles at her and Trish, for all the self-control she can muster, would like to punch her in the face.

'All I want is to find who's selling these drugs. Isn't that the real evil here?'

'No,' says Mrs Dover.

'What?'

'The drug is not evil. That's what *Nora* would have you believe.'

The heat spreading again, waves of damp clinging to her skin, to her neck; Trish wonders if she's the one going mad.

'What those kids drank, did it do them any harm?' Mrs Dover says.

'It put Lee in the hospital.'

'*Something* put Lee in the hospital. The others are healthy.'

Trish is seeing it now, the flask Andy brought her, hidden at home. She has something these people don't. That has to give her some power.

'Natalie's ritual was wrong,' Mrs Dover says, addressing the whole room. 'Her way was wrong, like Nora's before her. Walt Mackie was wrong. They used the threefold death to control the villagers. They killed using blood, air and water. Imagine it. Feel it on your own hands. Picture them, masked and cloaked, chanting in the dead of night. They used the dagger to slit those poor creatures' throats, they strangled animals, they drowned living things. It was violence used as a threat, violence used to spread fear. Now their time controlling our village has to end.'

Then her eyes are on Trish and Trish feels like she's being pushed, physically pushed until it hits her: she doesn't have to be here. It's like a blast of cold air right in her face and she sits back down with the force of it. She can leave. It doesn't matter what these people think. What is she doing here anyway, exchanging one institution for another? Uncle Walt wouldn't want this, he wouldn't want her dragged into village rituals, he'd always kept her away from them. So what did he believe? What did he do? She needs to know. She needs to go.

'Mrs Dover.' The voice booms into the room from the open door.

'DS Frazer,' Mrs Dover says with a smile. 'I think it's time for us to talk down at the police station.'

'Good,' he says. 'Shall we?'

His voice has changed everything. Mrs Dover is a sweet old lady again and the community council are nervous and Trish can breathe. He's brought the sea air with him and she was needing that, something crisp and sharp to cut through the tangled ties between them all. She was needing DS Frazer, but he won't even look her in the eye.

BELIEVING LIVES CAN CHANGE

'Georgie.'

All she says is her name. Pami can do that, convey so much with a single word.

'Am I looking that bad?'

'Come on through.'

Pami's just arrived, by the looks of it – June is on shift, manning the Spar and post office counter. Two days a week and Saturday morning, that's her hours. Georgie knows that but she'd forgotten today, forgotten what day it was at all. It's all seeping together through waking nights and the relentless heat in the air, the whispers, the words Georgie can't hear. Pami nods at June to let her know she's still watching the till and opens up the back room so they can talk.

'What's happened, Georgie?'

Pami thinks there's still a chance, for her and Fergus, for their marriage. She thinks Fergus needs some time, that's all. Thinks they both do.

'I saw Fergus earlier,' she says, like she can read Georgie's mind.

'He was with Natalie?'

Pami purses her lips. 'But I think he's trying to help her—'

'Then you know about Lee, too?'

Pamali nods, a deep pity in her eyes.

The little girl clutches at Georgie's sleeve, her eyes pleading. Her knees are dirty and grazed. Georgie looks away.

'I had to tell Natalie. I mean, it had to be me, with something so...'

'And Fergus was there?'

His hand, on Natalie's hand. Could it have just been kindness, sympathy, even with Georgie there watching? But *he* had created the situation, hadn't he? Fergus. He had made a choice.

'I told him to stay.'

'To stay with Natalie?'

And what else was she supposed to do?

'She's lost her son, Pami. Can you imagine?'

'No,' Pamali says.

Georgie's stomach twists.

'He was three years older than Errol, when he died.'

'Lee was an angry boy,' Pami says.

'Errol had more reason to be but wasn't.'

'Lee probably had reason too.'

'Well it was his own fault he ended up in hospital—'

The girl's wide eyes stare, her little hand tugs.

'He was the ringleader.' Georgie won't stop. 'Not Andy, not Aaron. It was Lee.'

And there's a horsefly, buzzing. Georgie scratches the back of her neck, under her hair, then suddenly it's Lee's face she can see, as clear as if he were here beside her. She can see the anger in his jaw, his nails bitten till they bled, his hatred of the police, of her, and beneath it she can see how scared he was. Then he is gone.

Beyond the door, Georgie can hear the muffled sounds of June ringing something up on the till, sharing a few words with someone.

'You've got a customer,' she says, more to break the silence than anything.

'It's been busy,' Pami says. 'I'm having a good summer. Might even be able to give Andy a part-time job soon.'

'You'd give *Andy Barr* a job?'

Pamali looks shocked at her tone. 'He's a great help at the community garden.'

Georgie shakes her head.

'And he's lost two friends, hasn't he?' Pamali's voice is quieter now, like she's telling Georgie what she hasn't voiced to anyone else. 'Bobby Helmsteading and now Lee. His two closest friends, both dead. That's going to change a person, living through that. Whatever their flaws.'

Georgie can see her remembering the vandalism, the attack, and consciously putting it aside, refusing to let it be the only thing she knows about Andy Barr.

'Has he told you anything new?' she manages. 'Have you found out what he did with the drugs he saved that night?'

'I'm sorry, Georgie.'

'Could you take a guess?'

'He spends a lot of time at the old church ruin.' Pamali pauses. 'It's where he used to meet Bobby.'

'Oh, I know.' When Georgie thinks of it she sees those gulls again, greedy and filthy, pecking at the discarded chip packet in the mud.

'He says he goes there to remember how badly he fucked up,' Pamali says, with a smile at the swear word. Pami tends not to swear. 'His words.'

'I'd say fucked up describes it pretty well,' Georgie says.

'Go easy on him, Georgie.'

'Why?'

'He's trying to change his life.'

'Then he should have brought those drugs straight to me.'

Pamali smiles at that.

'Going to the police might be expecting a bit much, Georgie.'
The little girl is smiling too.
'Anyway, he did the next best thing, didn't he?'
'What do you mean?'
'I mean, he came to me.'

THOSE WHO ARE GONE

Gail Dover is sitting at the table in the interview room and Simon and Frazer are sitting, together, opposite her. Everyone has tea, despite the drenching heat. The noise of the rain is amplified in here, it's not only pelting the window, it sounds like it's coming at them from all four sides of the room, threatening to break in the ceiling.

'Thank you for coming in,' Frazer says, his voice surprisingly quiet against the noise of the rain and when she smiles he follows with, 'I wanted to give you a space to talk. This is your chance, Mrs Dover, to tell us everything you know about Wyndham Manor, and about a young girl called Abigail Moss and what happened to her.'

'I've told you, I don't know anyone called Abigail Moss.'

'But you are familiar with Wyndham Manor. More so than you let on yesterday.'

He smiles and she smiles, and the scene strikes him as ridiculous: a little old lady, transparent raincoat, grey curls under a floral headscarf, soggy tan-coloured tights that have gathered around the knees, around the ankles.

'Did you see my old photographs?' she says, with a tease to her voice. 'I thought I saw you looking.'

'Mrs Pettigrew?'

'She was my godmother.'

'And housekeeper at Wyndham Manor.'

'We like to keep things in the family, hereabouts.'

Something in the way she says it makes him ask. 'You don't approve of that?'

'She's dead now, has been for years.'

'Yes, I know.'

'And you'll know that George Braxton was my grandfather? He owned the hotel.'

'Then who owns it now?'

Her hand strays up to her head and she touches the headscarf as though surprised to find it there.

'I'm sorry I didn't tell you before.'

Her fingers, trying to undo the knot at her chin, to release her hair. Frazer wonders if he should offer to help, but he doesn't – it would feel like too intimate a thing to do. She gives up though, after a minute, and leaves the headscarf in place.

'I own it, DS Frazer. For all the good it has done me.'

'You want to sell?'

'Nobody will buy, and besides, it was...'

'It was always in your family?'

'Something like that. It's all that's left, you see – no money to do it up.'

'You need to be careful. If it became unsafe, you'd be liable.'

'Oh, my son takes care of that.'

'Cal?'

She looks up at him. 'He's doing well, isn't he? Not many round here manage to do so well for themselves.'

Frazer can't help but smile at the thought of Cal being her son, having Sunday lunches with her, tucking her hand in his elbow on the way to church. He'd never really thought of it before, despite the shared surname – such totally different people. Still, we all contain multitudes. It'd be good if he'd answer his phone though.

He glances over at Simon but he's not smiling and Frazer realises he's not been taking Mrs Dover as seriously as he should be. At least, not as seriously as Simon is. Simon's frowning and Frazer waits for him to glance up, to give him a nod to ask his question.

'There was money, though, wasn't there,' Si says at last. 'When Cal was growing up? So some might say he had something of a head start.'

'We all suffered, in these villages, over the last fifty years, PC Hunter.'

'Like old Art Robertson, losing his farm. You remember that?'

'I do.'

'And Jack Helmsteading, he lost all his livestock, lost his business.'

'That was the plagues did that, one after another.'

'The plagues?' Frazer has that sense again of none of this being quite real, of a whole different language spoken to keep him out, keep the village closed and secret.

'Mad cow disease,' she says.

'Foot-and-mouth,' Simon says.

'We all remember the smell of them burning.'

That at least is true – he's checked the dates, read the reports, though he was a long way away and he never smelled the burning animals himself. He's glad of that.

'Then there was Nora and Jacob Prowle,' Simon says. 'They were struggling, weren't they, financially?'

'I wouldn't know about that.'

'Wasn't that why they took in foster kids the way they did?'

'Like I say, I wouldn't know.'

'You were related to them as well, though, weren't you?'

'We rarely spoke.'

'Why was that?'

'She fell out with my father.'

'Over what?'

'Over the money.'

'What money?'

Watching Simon hammer away at her like this, despite her being an old lady, despite knowing her his whole life, he can see Simon making detective, in charge of a station maybe, one day. He'd not seen the confidence before, not recognised it for talent. He's getting through the grief in a way Frazer's not managed – doesn't seem to be struck silent by it in the middle of a day, a case, a sentence the way he still is.

'She inherited nothing,' Mrs Dover says. 'But it was hardly my fault.'

'No one is saying anything is your fault.'

'Well, there it is then. My grandfather owned the Wyndham Manor hotel, the old cottages on High Street, even the local grocer's in Burrowhead, before it became a Spar. My father inherited it all. I inherited it all. Nora never forgave us. She was a bitter woman, that's what I can tell you. And all that inheritance, all that grandeur she hated us for? Falling down and rotting away with no money to do a thing about it. So that's the end of the Braxton family, PC Hunter. No Braxtons left. The end of the line.'

'And Abigail Moss?' Frazer says, so quietly he thinks she hasn't heard. Then her face lightens, and Frazer could swear she's suppressing a smile.

'There's nothing I can tell you about Abigail Moss,' she says.

'So you did know her?'

'Absolutely not.'

'There's something you're not telling us, Gail, and I'm not going to stop asking questions.'

'We've all got to do what we've got to do, DS Frazer.'

She's so polite, the way she says it, he regrets using her first name.

'Now,' she says. 'You have my full family history, so I assume I am free to go?'

'I have one last question,' he says, clearing his throat. 'What do you know about the ayahuasca brew?'

'It's like a herbal tea, DS Frazer.'

'It is not like a herbal tea, Mrs Dover.'

'All the ingredients can be found here, in the woodlands. The recipe was passed down to me by my grandmother.'

'And the blood?'

'Don't be absurd,' she chuckles. 'It's a herbal infusion using all natural ingredients. Mimosa root, vines, mint, honeycomb. It helps me sleep.'

'That's not what you said before.'

'It's exactly what I said. There is nothing dangerous about ayahuasca, I promise you, DS Frazer.'

He looks down at his own hands on the table.

'Don't be downcast,' she says, and for a second he thinks she is about to reach for his chin, lift his face up to hers like his own grandmother used to. 'You'll always be welcome round at mine for a cuppa and a biscuit.'

THOSE WHO ARE LEFT

Shona sends the message. Keeps it to their original group, plus one.

Tonight, at the church ruin.

They make their way separately. Kev, on the bus from Warphill, telling his mam he'll be late back. Rain thrashing at the windows, heat sticky as old gum. Aaron, drenched before he makes it out the caravan park, kicking at stones as he walks the track, hiding the pain with all the hate he can muster. Teeth clenched tight. Nails digging into his palms. A flock of crows scattering. And Andy, coming from the farmhouse where Aunt Debs and his da are talking about him, where he couldn't take the pity in her eyes. She looks at them both like that, Aunt Debs, him and his father, as though they have the same story. She's wrong about that. His story is going to be different.

As he gets to the gate he remembers, this is where he fell, that time. A coffin pushing its way out of the soil in the old graveyard. No edges visible, no wood or bone, but it's the shape he can see – a rectangle of land rising in a curved hump, a body hiding under a bed of earth. He hopes they're sleeping, whoever the fuck they were; hopes he didn't disturb them back when he came here to meet Bobby and Lee. The smell of the sea smothered by fags and weed. The memories of what they planned are so raw he doesn't want them, but there's something else there too, a sense of purpose, of being in it together, fighting for something. Maybe that's why everything Bobby said used to make sense to him, even when he knew it was wrong. Is it better to be wrong but doing something with folk for a reason, than to be right and on your own, doing nothing?

But he's not doing nothing. Andy's got plans, his own this time, and they're bigger than Bobby's ever were. Besides, he used to come here long before meeting Bobby. It was six of them once: Rachel and Pauly, Shona and Kev, Andy and Lee. Half of them gone now. Half of them dead.

That's what makes him stop, at the corner of the church ruin. There are beetles crawling through the cracks in the stone, scuttling down to the soil by his feet. He needs to hold something solid, grabs the side of what would've been an arched window. He could see the whole church when he came here that night, with Rachel and Pauly, when they sat on the grass and held candles and he felt eyes watching him. The flame's heat against his skin. A breath that shouldn't have been there. There's a scratch now and he slaps his arm, looks down to see a mosquito squashed against his skin.

That's when Shona finds him, standing on the threshold of the empty space that should have been a stained-glass window. He looks spooked and it reminds her of who he was back then, when they first came here, the six of them. It feels distant, eroded like the stones themselves, but Andy was terrified that night; she was sure of it. The night Rachel brought them here, told them to sit in a circle and hold their candles as the flames flickered closer to their hands.

'Andy?'

He knows her voice and immediately changes, not that vulnerable boy any more but someone older, self-contained and determined.

'Aye. What we doing here, Shona? I'm not lighting any fucking candles.'

'I'm not asking you to. This is different.'

They hear someone else arriving and they know it's him.

'What's different?' Aaron's words come out weaker than he'd intended, less bite and more pain. His fucking voice betraying him along with everything else.

'It doesn't matter,' Andy says. 'We were talking about something else.'

'Then why the fuck am I here?'

Andy looks at Shona as if to say yeah, why the fuck is he here, he never hung out with us before – and he didn't. Aaron wouldn't have been seen dead hanging round with his little brother's mates, his little brother who he didn't even like when he was alive, even if he is acting all cut up now he's dead. Andy saw the way they'd fought, no holding back, no hesitation. Aaron had gone at Lee like he'd wanted to kill him.

'I know why we're here,' Kev says, joining them.

'What the fuck are you talking about?'

Kev's brought more rain with him, heavy and stagnant, all the way from Warphill – his hoody is soaked, clinging to his body.

'There were six of us once,' Shona says.

'But now there are three.'

'Four, with him,' Andy says. 'But he's not a replacement for Lee.'

'You think I'm trying to replace my brother?'

Aaron's voice does that thing again, fucking cracks when he needs it strong and he clenches his fists; he could knock Andy flat and walk the fuck away from all of them. He doesn't though.

'We're here,' Shona says, 'because someone pushed Rachel and Pauly.'

They're standing in a circle now. Standing in their soaked T-shirts and hoodies, their mud-splattered trainers, their sweat and anger.

'Rachel and Pauly killed themselves,' Aaron says. 'Their choice, their right.'

'Then Lee died of natural causes in that hospital,' Andy fires back at him, the sudden cruelty of it making Shona wince.

Not Aaron though, he barely reacts. Stands and takes it as the others wait. Something is coming though. It must be. Then slowly he steps towards Andy and Andy stumbles back, falling against the old church wall, the eroded stone that's stood for hundreds of years, that crumbles now against his weight. He rights himself fast enough, sending pieces of flaked stone scattering among the grass and moss. Aaron's breath is ragged. Shona doesn't think she's ever seen him like this before, like he's on the edge of tears; would be hard to believe it was even Aaron, if she wasn't witnessing it.

'He was my fucking brother,' is all he says.

It's enough. Andy nods, purses his lips, and they all know it's an apology.

'I think someone taught Pauly to make that drug,' Shona says, quieter, though her eyes are pulled to the stone walls of the ruined church. They look different, somehow. For the first time in her life look like they might fall.

'Well, someone was teaching Lee too,' Andy says, and they can all believe it.

'It was the same thing,' Shona says. 'The way Penny-Ann and Julie have been talking about it... Penny says it's like being connected to everything that has ever lived.'

Aaron doesn't speak but he nods; he must have felt it that way too.

'Rachel was trying to summon someone who'd died,' Shona says. 'Her mam. She wanted to see her mam again.'

'Lee was testing it out,' Andy says. 'That's what he told me in the hospital. He didn't even have to pay for it, he was right pleased with himself. Said you were jealous.' Eyes on Aaron, waiting for the punch that doesn't come.

272

'I'm not jealous now.'

Around Aaron's feet are crumbled stones. They look old, to Shona, moss-covered and half buried in the soil, but where the church wall once ran a large stone is still standing, unmoved. There's another opposite it. She moves closer, leaving Kev and Andy behind, standing next to Aaron but not looking at him, her eyes fixed on the stone, her hands drawn towards it. Through the heavy rain it looks like it's been carved, like—

'What is it?'

'Nothing.' She shoves her hands in her pockets, turns back to the others. 'Rachel, Pauly and Lee. The drug didn't kill them, a person did. *Someone* killed all three of them.'

The sudden gust of wind blows her hood back from her head, the rain pelting her face, hot and rough, and through it she sees a car arriving, beyond the gate.

'It's the police,' she says and Aaron bites his lip so hard Shona can see the blood.

'Fuck this,' he says. 'I'm not speaking to the police.' He strides off, hood low, hands in pockets, as though DI Georgie Strachan wouldn't dare follow him. Except that Shona knows she would. And she does. They all watch as Aaron's paces get faster, as Georgie tracks him through the graveyard, running towards the coast, then it's just the three of them left: Shona and Kevin and Andy Barr.

'Georgie thinks it was Aaron,' Shona says.

'You mean she thinks he was getting the drugs?' Kev's hood is pulled low over his face and Shona can't see his eyes. 'Or that he killed his own brother?'

Andy's pushing his foot into the ground, into the mud and sodden grass by the collapsed wall, not angrily but insistently, like there's something he wants to uncover.

'What is it?' Shona asks, and she can see him as that boy again, vulnerable, lost.

'Lee told me,' he says, his voice almost snatched by the howling wind.

'Told you what?'

His eyes though, not the eyes of that scared boy, bullying others to avoid being bullied himself. He's someone else now.

'My whole life,' he says. 'All of it, leading here.'

'What did Lee tell you?'

'I've lost more than anyone, haven't I?'

Shona takes Kev's hand, and they let Andy go where he needs to go. The clouds are sinking lower and Shona could swear there's a swarm of something overhead.

'I lost Bobby,' Andy says. 'I lost Rachel and Pauly. I lost Lee. My aunt was driven from this village before I was even born. And I'm about to lose my da, too. So if anyone's in the middle of all this, it's me, aright? Me.'

LAST YEAR

'Did you get it?'

Rachel's voice is breathless and warm, whispered in his ear, her lips against his neck. He'd climbed up to her room, in through the window. It's dark, only just dawn.

'I've got it,' Pauly says, closing his eyes against the memory of what he had to do. 'I understand now.'

The scratching at his skin, even as he says it. He pushes the feeling away.

'Can we go tonight?' Her eyes are glowing.

He pulls her closer, their lips finding each other's, and he thinks only of her, of the warmth and promise of her skin; he ignores the scratching on the back of his neck, getting deeper, sharper.

She pulls away, holds his face.

'What is it?'

A nail clawing against his skin, something unseen, insistent and there, in the corner of her room behind the door – but it can't be. The room is dark, that's all, and he's shaken, reeling from what happened in the woods and he'll never tell her, she never needs to know.

'Shall we go to the woods?'

'No.' It comes out faster than he means, more afraid. 'I mean, I think we have to leave the woods behind. The village, the church ruin, all of it. We have to leave it all behind.'

'We'll go to the cliffs then,' Rachel says. 'It's perfect – Mam loved the cliffs.'

'The cliffs,' Pauly whispers, but his voice catches and Rachel hears the fear.

'What's wrong?'

'Nothing, so long as we're together.'

'Pauly.' She pushes against his shoulders, creates some space between them to show that she's serious. 'Where did you get it?'

He shakes his head.

'How did you pay?'

'I told you, I'll keep you safe from it.'

Something scratches against his jaw and he feels it move inside him, pull at his teeth.

'But it must have cost—'

'Stop it.'

And he feels it again, like in the woods, he's back there and it's dark beyond night and eyes peer at him from neat holes in a balaclava, colourless and empty. Shadows move between the tree trunks. Growing and stretching out towards him, becoming shapes of people, smashed and broken, and they are reaching out with their long arms, their sharp nails carving lines against his skin, their eyes deep and weeping.

'Pauly?'

Rachel is here, Rachel is holding him.

'We have to leave the woods behind.'

'I can get money,' she says.

A flick of her head and he knows she means her da, not showed his face for years but here now, full of false promises.

'If you owe—'

He puts his hand against her lips and she stops talking, doesn't start again as he moves it to gently push her hair back from her face.

'We have to leave the village behind.'

It's about more than money, he wants to say, but can't. The creatures in the woods, melting from trees and shadow and the scratching that won't stop, pulling at him even now, clawing at his skin.

'I think we'll be safe on the cliffs,' he whispers.

'I'm going to see my mam again.'

'You are,' he says. 'I promise.' Though he can still hear the voice, the words, after the blood had all been drained and the knife he'd used was in his rucksack, hidden beneath the mimosa. *You work for me now.*

'I'm scared,' he says at last, his voice a raw whisper, but Rachel doesn't hear him. Her eyes are alight, her face glowing in the dawn, and her hair is dancing in wisps by the open window.

A TRUE COMFORT

Gail Dover doesn't go home after she leaves the police station. There's someone she needs to help first. She finds her sitting at her kitchen table with that oaf Fergus Strachan. She's holding her hands in her lap and stroking the back of each, over and over, with her thumb.

'Natalie,' Gail says. 'Oh, Natalie.'

Natalie looks up slowly, like the words are taking time to be absorbed.

'How did you get in here, Gail?'

'The door was open, my dear. I'm here for you now,' she says, taking a seat at the table beside her. 'I'm here.'

'We're doing okay,' Fergus says. 'Right, Natalie?'

Gail glances up at the urn Natalie keeps up on the wall: Nora Prowle's ashes.

'You're a good man, Fergus,' Gail says. 'But could you give us some time, please? We women need to stick together.'

He looks at Natalie as if he thinks he can't leave her, but Natalie nods her head, shivers as Fergus's chair scrapes back form the table and soon enough Gail has her alone.

'I am so sorry,' she begins. 'Oh you poor, poor girl.' She takes Natalie's hands in her own, copies her motion by gently rubbing the back of each one.

'Aunt Nora used to do that,' Natalie says, her voice wistful, as though she misses her.

Natalie loved her Aunt Nora, Gail knows that. But where did she lead her? To the slaughtering of dogs and horses, that poor little boy buried out in the field.

'Don't you think about what she did to Sonny Riley?'

Natalie collapses, hunched over her kitchen table, making a noise like a wounded animal – like the noise the horse must have made when she killed it.

'I'm sorry, my dear, I shouldn't have... It's so hard, having a legacy like yours,' Gail says. 'Nora's shoes are too big for anyone to fill. It would destroy every one of us.'

She smooths Natalie's hair while she lies slumped on her kitchen table there, her body heaving with sobs.

'And with the court case hanging over you, too, when all you were trying to do was help. You poor, poor thing. No wonder you...' She sighs, lost for words.

'What?' Natalie stammers through her sobs.

'No one could have foreseen what your boys would get caught up in, Natalie. What they would become capable of. It's not your fault. That's what I came here to say. I thought you might need to hear it—'

'But it is my fault.' Her words come out as a horrified whisper.

'No, no, Natalie, none of it is your fault, I promise you that.'

The silence shudders between them as Gail pauses.

'If you want to...but no, no...'

She lets it hang as Natalie's sobbing stops and the air resonates between them, heavy and loaded with promise.

'What is it?'

'I thought I should warn you, that someone should...' Her voice drops to a whisper. 'I think the police are coming.' She touches her hand for human contact, for kindness.

'They're coming here?'

'There's forensic evidence.'

'Oh God, no.' Natalie clasps at her stomach and rocks back and forth. 'Please say it's not true.'

Gail could almost feel sorry for her, deeply sorry.

'I can't do that, we both know... But Natalie, you have a choice.'

Natalie sits straighter then, though she is trembling along the length of her arms.

'What do you mean?'

'I mean, there is a way to make it right.'

HOW THINGS THAT CONNECT
CAN BREAK

The run does something for Georgie, helps her in a way she wasn't expecting; flashes of matted hair streaming in the wind, propelling her over muddy gravelled puddles to the cliffs, chasing Aaron Prowle. Catching up with him, in fact, taking the breath deep into her lungs and living every pace. She could keep going, not even bother to question him, give up trying to unravel the connections between these villagers who never wanted her here; these villagers who still whisper, when they think she can't hear, where *is* she from?

Her eyes on the back of his head, that hood, grey and drenched. She can hear his breath, gasping like his lungs resent him.

'Aaron,' she calls, her voice sure and strong.

He looks over his shoulder once, twice, to confirm. The shock when he sees she's nearly caught him. Arrogant kid, always has been. The way he looks at her, at the police, at women, at everyone; he stops suddenly and Georgie nearly goes crashing into him.

'Fuck.' He puts his arms up like she's trying to knock him to the ground.

'Sorry—'

'What?'

Breath racing. Wind from the sea keeping the insects away. There's salt on her lips and heavy warm rain soaking her and she loves it; for a second she forgets what's happened, and she loves it here. The little girl stops at the cliff edge, turns to look at her.

Then it all comes back.

'Aaron Prowle.'

'*What?*'

'Some reason you're running from a police officer?'

'Didn't feel like talking.'

But there is something different, though. He's not the same kid he was, two days ago. It's changed him already, Lee's death. She can understand that. She gives him a nod and is glad for the rain in her eyes, soaking her hair. There's a bench overlooking the beach, and she points to it.

'A sit-down?'

'Alright.'

There's something in his voice too, his throat raw, his words quiet, like some bit of him has been forced to grow up.

They walk in silence to the bench. The tide is high, almost at the cliff face itself and the colour is a strange, dark grey, sinking to purple further out. Aaron pushes the hood off his head, wrings it out, seemingly unaware that the water cascades down his neck.

'I'm sorry about Lee,' Georgie says.

'Right.' Flat and angry, as if her sympathy could ever make a difference.

No one's sympathy will, though. Georgie knows that. The little girl is standing beside her now, soaked to the skin, her dress clinging.

'I want to go back to last year,' Georgie says. 'Back to when Bobby Helmsteading was around.'

Aaron lets out a noise, too short to be a laugh, too unimpressed.

'You were buying from him?'

'Everyone was.'

'But before he turned up?'

Aaron shrugs.

'This is a murder investigation, you understand that? I'm not going to—'

'You could get stuff around, up in Crackenbridge and that. Car park off the high street. Toilets in the pub. Whatever.'

'But there wasn't one person?'

He swallows, looks out to the water. His nails are bitten down so far they've been bleeding, she can see it in the cuticles. 'Not that I know of. Not till Bobby.'

'He was new though, right?'

'Aye.'

'So who was running him?'

'I don't know.'

She thinks about pushing him but changes her mind. It doesn't feel like he's lying to her, and if he is, police insistence won't get him to change his mind.

'What did he sell?'

'Coke, speed, meth…whatever.'

'Heroin?'

'Not to me.'

'And the ketamine we found in your caravan?'

'I told you at the time, that wasn't ours.'

'Where did it come from?'

In the silence the little girl climbs up on the bench beside her. Her grey eyes are older than the cliffs.

'Does your mother visit your caravan much, Aaron?'

She doesn't expect him to reply. One thing, telling him to give her what he knows about a dead dealer, another expecting him to talk about his mother.

'My mother and I are not on good terms,' he says, and the formality tells her he's angry enough about it not to say much. 'She came that week, though.'

Georgie is so surprised she doesn't speak; besides, she doesn't need to.

'Brought Suze along too. She was pissed we were working for Ricky, convinced he was selling us drugs. Lee was doing too much speed, and my mam liked to blame me. Suze was there to threaten us with police involvement I guess, though given your face it was unofficial.'

Natalie never did tell them where she'd got the ketamine to sedate the horse. Could she have hidden it in the caravan so she wouldn't be found with it? Risking her own sons, though – would she have?

'Has she spoken to you about Lee, about his…'

'Called to tell me he was dead.'

'She *phoned* you?'

'Cold, right?' He bites at his thumb, then thrusts his hand into his hoody's front pocket. 'Still, she's better than my da.'

'You're in touch?'

He makes that noise again, almost a snort, lips turned down, face turned away. Now they've been on the bench a while the insects are gathering, attracted by their bodies probably, the heat of them, the sweat. Georgie could swear there are more every time she sets foot outside the station, every time she opens her eyes.

'I remember him from before Mam got rid,' Aaron says. 'We never talk about him, but some things I remember.' His eyes dart at hers, daring her to ask, then flick away to the edge of the cliff.

'When was the last time you saw him?'

'I was like seven years old. He'd been out, fuck knows where, came home all bloodied and stinking. Mam was upset and I mean, I hated him already. You do, when you see things as a kid. So I told him he stank.'

Georgie watches his face, says nothing. Between them, there's a woodlouse crawling along the wooden plank of the bench.

'He took my hand and slammed my fingers into the door. All four broken.' Aaron holds up his left hand. 'Spent the night in hospital and the next day he was finally gone. And do you know what I did?'

Georgie shakes her head.

'I did the same thing to Lee a couple weeks later,' he says. 'Just because I could.'

Georgie stares down to the shoreline. Gulls, like always. Grey and white, black-headed, some of them, with their hooked yellow beaks. The squark of common terns on the rocks. Oystercatchers too, a clutter of black, white and red on the waves. For a second, she envies them being down there.

'You were seven,' she says.

He doesn't respond, just looks out at the sea with that scowl on his face.

'What about last year...' she begins, softly, after a while.

'Last year?'

It's like he's forgotten why she's here, who he's talking to.

'What happened after Bobby died?'

His shoulders jolt like a shiver's running right through him.

'I mean, where did you buy—'

'Been low.'

'Until?' For the first time she wonders if the chewing of his lips, his skinniness, is more to do with withdrawal of drugs than drugs themselves. He seems sober right now.

Then he closes his eyes. He speaks like that, not looking at her, not looking at his feet or his hands or the cliffs, the darkening sea, the white layers of sky spilling rain.

'Lee started getting hold of stuff. He was the one got the brew. That's what you want to know, right?'

'Well,' Georgie says slowly. 'We want to know where he got it from.'

Aaron shrugs. 'I tried to make him tell me. He wouldn't. He thought this was his big chance. Stupid kid.'

Georgie cringes – the pain in the way he says it.

'So no, I don't know where he got it. No one's approached me. I'll no be taking it again.'

'Thank you, Aaron,' Georgie says, and he scoffs. 'I mean it. Thank you.'

'Right.'

'Is there anything else you can tell me, anything at all?'

'Try Andy,' he says.

Georgie feels something in her sharpen. She needs to get through to Cal, find out what he's got. But there's something she needs to tell Aaron first.

'I lost my brother, too,' she says, and the little girl takes her hand. This time Georgie doesn't pull away.

'My brother was killed,' Aaron says, 'not lost.' There's anger in his voice, like how dare she even compare, and she can see clear as anything, he's breaking.

'So was mine,' she says. 'He was shot.'

His eyes on hers, properly, for the first time. Shock. Deep shock, then something changing. She's not leaving, not yet. She needs to spend a bit of time here, sitting with Aaron Prowle in the pouring rain. Aaron Prowle, who always looked at her like something he could hate, whose brother Lee used to do the same, the pair of them internalising every bitter comment they heard and regurgitating it into violence, whose brother Lee is dead; she's going to sit here beside him and let the waves keep lapping at the seaweed-encrusted strip of stone down on the beach until it's gone.

TOGETHER AFTER
ALL THIS TIME

'Chin up,' says Suze.

She nudges Elise as she says it, but Elise is walking along with her eyes on the flooding pavement even as she drags her feet right through a deep puddle. She doesn't even wince as the water makes it up over her shoes. Suze is glad she's wearing her boots.

'I mean it,' Suze says, softening her voice a bit, pushing further. Ignoring the rain running from her hair down her neck. 'He'd be proud of what we're doing here, your da.'

'Would he?'

'Course he would. You told me yourself he never liked Nora.'

As they pass the overflowing bin on Main Street a pigeon swoops at them, low and fearless, and Suze swipes at it, swears, though Elise seems oblivious.

'He told me a lot of things, towards the end,' she says, her voice faraway and fading. Her steps have slowed so much they're barely moving at all, just standing on the street in the drenching rain and Suze is trying very, very hard not to get impatient.

'One month, that's all it's been,' Elise says. 'One month since my da died. It feels longer than that, doesn't it?'

Suze nods sympathetically as she links her arm through Elise's and tries to guide her with a bit more urgency towards June and Whelan's place.

'It'd be good to speak to him again.'

Suze turns away, eyes up to the sky. At least the clouds are fucking serious – not much daylight getting through there.

'It's so hard, Elise,' she says, turning back, giving her arm a squeeze. 'Everything you've been through this year, it's all so hard.'

'Natalie used to bring me muffins.'

'Natalie's done a lot of good things for this village.' If they could just pick up the pace a bit. Is she going to have to drag Elise all the way there? 'That's why we're helping her now.'

'Is that really what you think? That we're helping her?'

Suze gives up and lets go of Elise's arm. If they have to do this standing in the pouring rain on Main Street, that's what they'll do.

'Are you sure about what she did, Suze?'

'Look, I'm not supposed to—'

'Tell me.'

Elise looks like she could cry, though quite what her problem is today Suze doesn't know.

'There were fingerprints, Elise. Natalie's prints, her DNA on the flannel. I saw her myself... I'll never forgive myself. But the least, the very least I can do is help her find peace now.'

'I do keep thinking about the way she tucked Lee in.'

'And I keep thinking about the way she slashed that horse's throat.'

A sharp shock, will that get her moving?

'Now come on, you know we're doing the right thing.'

Finally Elise is moving again, wiping those tears from her eyes, thank God, taking a deep breath as they approach June and Whelan's, pulling herself together.

'Should I wait or...?'

'What now?' Suze doesn't mean to snap. 'Sorry.'

Elise looks hurt. 'It's just that we always go separately.'

'Not today,' Suze says. 'Not this time.'

June and Whelan's place has a new wooden fence round the front garden and there are pecky little birds perched all along the front of it.

'Trish won't be there?'

'No Trish, and no Fergus,' Suze says. 'Only the people we can really trust.' She takes a deep breath. 'Only the people who still believe. You believe, don't you, Elise?'

'It'll be good to talk to him.'

Good God, is she talking about her da again?

'I need to ask him things.'

'Of course you do.'

'There are too many things he never said.'

'Uh-ha.'

But they're at June and Whelan's front door and Suze is ringing the bell and telling them to come, now, over the road and Terry is here too, parking up past the fountain with Camellia Taylor. Elise blows her nose into a tissue and Suze sidesteps, just a touch. Just to get away from any unnecessary germs, and she could swear that's Natalie's voice she can hear, distant and muffled, from somewhere behind her.

PEOPLE WE HURT AND PEOPLE WHO SURPRISE US

'I could paint the alley for you,' Andy says. 'If you like.' His fingers intertwining and uncrossing the way they do, like he's never quite sure what to do with his limbs when he's standing or sitting or existing in a place with other people.

'I suppose it could do with a bit of brightening up, that side alley,' Pamali says.

'I could do you a picture? A landscape, maybe?'

Every time he speaks Pamali can hear two versions of his voice. The one here, now, eager to impress, wanting her to like him. Then the other one, growled through a balaclava, her own screams a distant backdrop, with GO BACK TO WHERE YOU CAME FROM scrawled across the counter. It wasn't the worst bit of racism graffitied on her shop, but it hurt her the most. Andy wanted her to go back to where she came from. Where did he imagine that was?

'Pami?'

'That would be nice, Andy. You go for it.' She doesn't ask if he has his own paints; she knows full well that he does. But there he is, nervous, smiling at her, twisting on his feet like he needs perpetual movement. Georgie told her once he reminded her of a daddy-long-legs. She can see that. He's not leaving though, not heading off to get paints or choosing a can to buy or anything, he's just standing there, awkward as a kid.

'Is there something you need, Andy? Not that I don't appreciate the company.'

He nods, repeatedly, his head bouncing back and forth on his neck as he chews his bottom lip and looks over his shoulder as though someone had come into the shop. No one has though.

'See... I think I got to tell someone.'

'Do you want to come in, Andy?'

He looks confused, until she lifts the hatch between the shop and the till, opens the door to her office with her computer and her bag, her own pictures on the wall.

'You're inviting me back there?'

'Sure, if you have something important you need to talk about.'

She doesn't know why she didn't think of it before. He stands taller as he walks though, not so ashamed he's folding in on himself all the time. Maybe being in the shop jolts him with the memory, with visions of the attack, like it does her. She thought she'd shown him he was forgiven by inviting him to work on the community garden, but then her office is a more private space.

'I think,' he says, standing in her office and looking at her sketches on the wall – pencil on paper, nothing finished. 'I think I've found a way to make things better.'

'The gardening?'

'That too,' he says, smiling. 'But I mean to properly make things better.'

That's what the community garden is for – to properly make things better in these villages. She doesn't say that though; even Georgie doesn't see how it might work, so maybe it's too much to expect a teenager to have faith in it. He's working on it, with her. That's enough for now.

'I mean, after Rachel and Pauly and...and Lee...I need some justice.'

'Andy, you need to leave the investigation to the police.'

'Do I though?'

'Yes, absolutely.'

'I've made mistakes, Pamali.'

She looks at him then until he returns her gaze. 'I'm aware,' she says.

'So it's up to me then, to make things better.'

'I'm not sure what you're talking about, Andy.'

'There's information I have that I need you to keep safe, Pamali. It's a...like...'

'An act of good faith?'

She sits down and he folds himself onto the spare chair, the one where Georgie normally sits.

'Thing is,' he says, 'I need someone I can trust.'

'You can trust me,' she says.

'I need to know you'll not tell anyone, *anyone*, unless something bad happens to me tonight.'

'Andy, what are you—'

'Can you promise?'

'Yes,' she says, 'yes, I promise. But I'm worried about you, talking like—'

'Listen, it's important.'

For a second she's back there, tied on the chair, twine digging into her skin, the smashing of glass and she lets herself remember; she'll always remember. And she'll always bring herself back to here and now and her feet on the ground and Andy, anxiously twisting his fingers together on one hand and biting at his nails on the other.

'The night I called the ambulance...'

'When your friends ended up in hospital?'

'You know I didn't drink mine,' he says. 'Well, I hid it. I gave it to someone for safekeeping.'

'Andy, that could be helpful for the investigation.'

'I needed to see how it were playing out, aright?' Biting at his thumbnail, biting so hard it must hurt. 'So I gave it to Trish,' he says.

Pamali blinks.

'So, if something happens to me tonight, if something—'

'Please tell me you're not going to do anything dangerous.'

'Aren't you listening?'

'Or illegal, Andy, we're past all that, aren't we?'

'Pami!'

Her name, that only her friends use and his voice, the desperation in it, the way something in him wants to give up and cry and be comforted like a child; she can see it all, though he's battling not to let it show.

'Okay,' she says. 'You have my word. I'll tell no one unless something happens to you tonight.'

His head, nodding back and forth again, the frown on his forehead. 'Thank you.'

'But I'm worried about you.'

Suddenly he's not that little boy any more, he's older and intensely sad. 'You know that stuff we wrote?'

'The graffiti?'

'Yeah, all that racist stuff. Someone gave it to Bobby, and he gave it to us.'

'What do you mean?'

'Someone else told us what to write. It was like payment, for...' He's shaking his head and his lips are forming around words he can't say, and she waits for him to get there, to spurt it all out like he needs to. 'Nah, not payment exactly, it was just the deal. We accepted it and it was intense and it felt like it mattered but what I mean is, it was written on notes, like, these bits of paper that Bobby gave us along with our stash, right? He told us to read them and burn them at the old church and graffiti them on the Spar and I thought you should know. I thought you should know it all now, in case.'

'In case what?'

'In case something happens to me. I'm the last one, see? Bobby's dead and Lee's dead so it's just me now.'

'Andy, you're scaring me.'

'You're safe.'

'That's not what I mean. Please don't do anything stupid, Andy.'

It was the wrong word. She should have said dangerous, not stupid.

'I'm trusting you,' he says. Then he unfolds himself from the chair and Pamali is deeply afraid for Andy Barr with his awkward limbs too long and thin for his body and his careful way of gardening. But he's gone, he's left the office and she can hear the bell jangling over the door and her phone's ringing, it sounds distant and muffled but she can hear it – her mobile is ringing in her drawer where she keeps it out of sight. It's Fergus. Fergus is calling her, but she doesn't want to speak to him. She waits as the screen dims and the noise stops and then she makes the call to Georgie.

THE RIGHT AND WRONG OF IT

Gail Dover stands in her floral living room and no one quite knows why but they all hold their breath, as though something is about to happen and they can do nothing to stop it.

Sitting behind her is Natalie Prowle. Her eyes are red from tears, the corners of them weeping. Her clothes are crumpled and stained. From the smell they know she hasn't showered or changed; this is what she is without any of those superficial things, what she has been since the moment Lee was killed. Since the moment she killed him.

And it was her that killed him. They all know this, though not a single one of them says it. No one needs to. Her boys were the evil in the village; that's how Nora would have seen it, that's how Natalie must have seen it. They were the ones bringing in the drugs, scrawling hate on the shops and littering the beach – Natalie herself used to clear it up and they all saw her, washing graffiti off the Spar, and why would she do that, if not for the guilt of knowing it was her own boys?

She did what she believed she had to do.

So now there's only one way for the village to be free of it all. Washed clean. A mother killing her own son: that can't go unpunished. That's one thing they all agree on, the villagers of Burrowhead and Warphill, every wrong has to be paid for.

'Natalie,' Gail says to the room, which is hushed and stinging with static, 'has something she would like to say.'

Natalie shivers in the heat. Exhaustion is dragging on her skin like mud; she feels it clenching around her, dried and crusted. When she breathes, the air sticks to her tongue and leaves it thick. Her hand rises to her hair and her nails dig into her scalp, scratching with both hands, oblivious to those watching.

And those watching her see a woman sweating and scratching at her own hair for no reason other than the heat – and they're all suffering that without making a spectacle. It's enough to make them queasy. They see her clothes, wet through, and remember how she looked just days ago. Neat and coordinated, clack-clack heels to let everyone know she was coming. There's not a one among them hasn't received one of her looks, a note about keeping their front porch tidy, their kids in line, telling them to join a beach clean-up, to collect – with their own hands, as though they themselves were guilty – the used condoms and stale chewing gum that sticks to the rocks on the beach like barnacles. And despite all that, there's not a one of them hasn't seen her sons dragging their feet through the village, dropping wrappers and cans, spitting on the pavement, up to no good and they all know it. Natalie more than anyone, so they can understand the shame.

On her feet, Natalie feels a little stronger than she did sitting on Gail's sofa. Fergus wanted her to stay home and rest; Fergus who has no idea what it's like to lose the way she has lost. No, it was Gail Dover who helped her. Showed her a way. What other way could there be, for someone who knows that her first son killed her second. That's what happened, she knows it deep within herself. Aaron killed Lee. Somehow she's known, from the day they were born, this is how it would end. Aaron showed her when he was a boy, and she never could forgive him. She couldn't stop him either. So now she's the one who needs forgiveness. She's supposed to be speaking, but when she opens her mouth she fears she'll be sick here in Gail's peach-coloured living room.

It's Suze who speaks, instead.

'The police are planning an arrest,' she says, and she doesn't even stand, she doesn't need to. She speaks from her chair in the corner, quietly and sadly, as if she wishes there were some other way. 'We have forensic evidence.'

Natalie sways, held up by something she doesn't understand. She feels hands on her shoulders, fingers curled hard as bone. There's a rasping in the back of a throat, close behind her.

'We don't talk in terms of good and evil, in the force,' Suze is saying, 'but here, among one another, we can speak the truth.'

Aunt Nora used to talk about good, and evil.

'We have fingerprints—'

Aunt Nora used to tell her to stay pure.

'After all,' Suze says, 'only family would have tucked him up in bed like that.'

There is evil in these villages, Aunt Nora used to say.

Her own son, her blood. She always knew how it would be. Aaron killed Lee. And so she loses them both.

'An arrest,' Suze is saying, 'a prison sentence. But *we* know that's not the cure.'

There's something in Natalie's hand. Soft and warm. She looks down, sees Gail Dover's wrist so thin the joints stick out like driftwood and the veins pulse with the strange colour of the sea.

'That is why Natalie's here,' Gail says, giving her hand a squeeze. 'Because she is strong, and brave, and one of us.'

All their eyes.

'Natalie, it's your turn.'

All waiting for her to speak.

'I...'

As Natalie starts and stops and looks lost and broken Gail Dover keeps hold of her hand, tight in her own. Natalie Prowle's small, neat hand. She strokes the back of it with her thumb, soothingly, to remind Natalie she's not alone, just like she had when she went to her home, when she showed her the way. Though Natalie's holding her palms out now, standing up straight, held by nothing but her own will.

'I am choosing this,' she says, her voice stronger, almost resonating. 'Don't feel sad for me. Please, don't blame me any more. I'm making it right.' And as she speaks she remembers her boys, as they were once on the beach, one perfect summer's day, when they had new buckets and spades, a set each so they wouldn't fight, and the sea was turquoise and the seaweed had washed away with the tide instead of rotting on the rocks. They'd decided to bury her in the sand. 'Mam,' they'd yelled, 'Mam, get in,' so she'd climbed into the hole they'd dug for her, helping them fill it in, scooping handfuls of sand onto her legs. She'd asked them if she could get a mermaid's tail and they looked at one another, weighing it up, before speaking the same word at the same time: 'Yes.' She has a photo of that day. Someone from the village must have taken it for her. It was after their da left. A real photo, not a snap on an iPhone. A perfect photo she still has at home in an album simply labelled *Lee and Aaron, childhood.*

EVERYTHING CARRIED
IN A WORD

'Cal, I've been trying to get you on the phone for ages,' Frazer says, and it's true enough, none of them have been able to reach him all day and it's late now – they need to know, what did he get from Lee's hospital room, from the cloth that was used, from his sheets, his bedside table? What did he find on Lee's jumper from the woods?

'I've been working,' Cal says, slowly, 'on Lee Prowle's body.'

'Of course, sorry…' Frazer regrets the apology seconds after he uttered it. It's his job to follow up, for goodness' sake, and it's Cal's job to answer the phone and keep them updated, as frequently as they need. Thank God Georgie's coming.

'Wait for the boss, shall we?' Cal says, suddenly back to his usual cheerful self.

Frazer has trouble matching his mood, but he agrees with the words. They'll wait for DI Strachan. It's a murder case and there has to be some evidence, something more than what the villagers are saying and family trees connecting like tangled yarn.

There's air conditioning here though, in the lab, none of the sweltering heat and moisture-streaming windows they have to deal with in Burrowhead. The lab won't be getting shut down, not like the station. Maybe that's why Cal's following his own leads, less inclined to report in; more arrogant than Frazer remembered.

He's all smiles for Georgie, though.

'I've been flat out,' he says. 'Trying to get you something, Georgie.'

'What do you have?'

'Nothing but circumstantial evidence, I'm afraid.'

'Prints?'

'All over the side table, on the bed frame, but none of them surprising. He was visited by hospital staff, by the kids from the caravan – we got Andy's prints, and the others all admit to popping in to say hi, including Aaron – and by his mother.'

'Then it could have been one of them,' Frazer says.

'Could have been, not necessarily.'

'But Suze was right outside—'

'She was asleep,' Cal snaps, a little too quickly for Frazer's liking.

'So we've got Andy Barr, Aaron and Natalie, all visiting,' Georgie says. 'And no other evidence.'

'That's right, Georgie,' Cal says, looking straight at her. 'His friend, his brother and his mam.'

'And his mother was the last one in,' Georgie says.

'Unless they crept past Suze,' Frazer says, though neither of them replies. 'We know Lee and Aaron were fighting, maybe Aaron came back to finish the job?'

Georgie's frowning, but she doesn't speak.

'Or,' Cal says, 'ground-floor window. I've had my staff test it, and it's doable. So someone could have got in that way.'

'The frame?' Frazer says.

'No fibres, no DNA, but that just means they were good.'

Georgie takes a deep breath and they both stop talking to let her say what she needs to say: 'What about the jumper, Cal, from the woods?'

'There was blood on it, right enough. Fox.'

'Fox blood?'

'And we have a match to the stomach contents too, it was fox blood.'

'Where would Lee get a fox?'

Cal shrugs. 'Creature could have been caught in a trap.'

Georgie winces.

'So I can place Lee in the woods,' Cal continues, 'with his hoody, the gear in the rucksack, and the fox blood. I think we can safely say Lee was making the ayahuasca. But we don't know who killed him.'

'I need a sit-down,' Georgie says.

Cal chuckles and Frazer has no bloody idea why.

'Through here.'

A decent seat each, a table, a coffee machine in the corner that none of them suggest using. Georgie holds up her hands.

'Give me five minutes, okay?'

'Sure thing, Georgie,' Cal looks round. His eyes fall on the paper and he reaches for it.

'Actually…' Frazer speaks just soon enough to stop him picking it up. 'I have a few questions for a different case. Do you mind?'

'Questions for me?' Cal leans back. 'Fire away.'

Frazer leans back too, copying Cal's pose. 'They're about your mother.'

'My mother?'

'I understand she owns the old Wyndham Manor hotel.'

Cal chuckles again.

'Why is that funny?'

'That old dump? She owns it, it owns her, no way of selling it and no money to fix it. It's a stone around her neck is all.'

'But you do know that's where Betty Marshall was working.'

'Who's Betty Marshall?'

'My witness,' Frazer says, sitting straighter again. 'I spoke to you about her before. You didn't say anything about your family owning the hotel then.'

'Look, I can't remember what you said or what I said back then, I'm working on an actual murder case here and I don't know anything about any Betty Marshall.'

'No need to get—'

'I'm not "getting" anything,' Cal says. Smiling again. Reaching for the paper. 'It's been a long day for all of us.'

'This was just a couple of weeks back.'

'What was?'

'I've been here, interviewing everyone. I interviewed you.'

'And?'

'You didn't tell me your mother owned the Wyndham Manor hotel.'

He opens the page at the crossword, runs his thumb over the fold to flatten it.

'*That* is where Abigail Moss was attacked.'

He looks startled then. 'You didn't tell me—'

'Yes I did—'

'It didn't register.'

Frazer leans forward, takes the paper from Cal's hands. 'I have a witness, on the record, who believes she saw a murder, and you didn't think to tell me the location was owned by your family?'

'Okay.' Cal's sitting straight now. 'I apologise, I was clearly not focused on what you were saying when you interviewed me. I didn't hear you say anything about Wyndham Manor. Since then I've had my hands full. An oversight.'

Frazer swallows.

'If there's anything else you need to know about it, son, just ask.'

Frazer doesn't move. Everything in him is prickling with static and his mind, flashing with all the things he should say but doesn't. *Son.*

Enough.

'What did you just call me?'

'Sorry, *DS Frazer*. We're very informal round here, you'll have seen it.' A wave of his hand like it's nothing. 'Old habits die hard.'

Frazer is not smiling. Georgie is not smiling.

'Do you understand what I'm saying?' Frazer says.

And there it is, the flash in Cal's eyes that tells him yes, he understands exactly what Frazer is saying, he knows exactly what he said himself, too, and it's nothing to do with being informal, and then it's gone and he's pressing a hand to his heart.

'I meant nothing by it, I promise you that.'

Frazer waits.

'It won't happen again, DS Frazer.'

Georgie's silent, but Frazer knows she was watching, hearing every inflection, and as they walk out to the car their steps are in time. She starts the engine. Keeps the gears in neutral. He looks at her, and she looks back, and they both understand it.

'There's something else going on here,' Georgie says.

'There certainly is.'

She puts the car in gear.

'Frazer?'

Keeps her foot on the clutch.

'When did you last see Trish?'

OLD HABITS DIE HARD

Trish is kneeling on the carpet by Uncle Walt's bed as her hands drop to the floor, as the note flutters out of her grasp. The pain crunches against her ribs, forces her to clutch at her stomach. She was wrong about everything. All of it. Oh God.

Uncle Walt, what did you do?

She reaches for the page again, picks it up. The shoebox on her other side is open and empty, its lid upturned and ripped at the corner. The letters she found inside are strewn around her. Each of them written in Uncle Walt's barely legible hand, each of them addressed to *My dear Isabella*. Returned to him. Saved, by him, all these years.

Hidden from Trish along with what she'd most needed to see all her life.

There is only one Isabella that Trish has ever heard of: Isabella Barr. Ricky's mother. Uncle Walt had been in love with Ricky's mother, before Ricky Barr was even born. But she'd chosen someone else. She'd chosen John Barr and returned Uncle Walt's letters and he'd never been able to let it go.

It was jealousy. The Barrs had never done anything to Uncle Walt, it was just his jealousy. Was that why he'd killed Ricky's dog? Persuaded himself the wretched threefold sacrifice was 'for the good of the village' when really he was lashing out at the family who'd hurt him? He'd even encouraged Natalie Prowle to kill Ricky's horse. That crunching in her chest. It was petty and spiteful; who even was he? Turning again to the single page in her hand, the last thing she'd found in the shoebox, the last and the worst.

She was looking for evidence against the Barrs. Something solid showing they'd pushed Uncle Walt and the others into selling their farms; maybe something showing illegal payment or driving the farms' value down or something, anything. What she'd found was a shoebox stuffed under his bed behind bundles of old clothes. Inside: letters wrapped in red ribbon. And this one final note, addressed to herself.

Trisha

It's her mam's writing. She left a note, and Uncle Walt had it all along.

I am sorry, but I can't stay here any more. I can't stand it.

It's her mam's writing, but it's Uncle Walt who's back from the dead to kick her in the stomach. It's that physical a sensation, the sudden knowledge that he'd hidden this from her, stuffed in a shoebox under the bed and left there like it was nothing.

After what they stole from me.

A note from her mam, what she'd dreamed of for so many years, and her mam has something to tell her. There was a reason; there had always been a reason.

After what your Uncle Walt did.

She should have known, she should have suspected there was something – it was Uncle Walt that her mam never trusted, it was Uncle Walt that her mam always looked at with blame and anger and hurt. She was never trying to keep Trish away from the bees, it was never about the bees; it was about Uncle Walt. She was trying to keep Trish away from Uncle Walt.

I can't bear to stay here any more, and so I'm leaving.

But what did he do? How had she never asked, why had she never pushed him? A deep anger suddenly crushes against her grief and then he's gone; he was never her Uncle Walt at all. He was a liar. Everything about him was a lie. Oh God, she's been so stupid.

Just know that I love you, Trish. You have been the best part of my life.

She feels it again, not the love but the anger. Clutches her stomach and lurches.

'What did you do?' Said out loud followed by a gasp of the thick air and she could choke on it, gorse-sweet and clinging to her throat. 'Come on then, what did you do?' The weight of her blood and her eyes burning. '*What did you do?*' Her voice raw and loud in the empty house, a scream she barely recognises as her own and she's on her feet, slamming the door. Out. Out, through the silent, heavy village, roads streaming with rain, drains clogged, paths flooded, clouds low and clinging to her skin as she runs.

Uncle Walt, spending his life trying to protect her, and what did he leave her with? No one. Nowhere to fit. A fake dagger and the knowledge that he'd hidden what she needed the most. How could he have done it?

Leaving the streets to head round to the disused shed that was once a community hub, that's now rotten and crumbling. It's hidden through gorse and nettles high as her head, but she pushes through, thorns gouging at her skin, doesn't slow her pace. A left before the shed – she doesn't want to step foot in that shed again. She is here for the hives. This is what Uncle Walt left her. These bees. She just wants to be around them, to see them, to know they're here.

But they're gone.

Her hands rest on the hives and she looks away from the village to the hill, dotted with Ricky's caravans, then back at the hives. The bees are gone. She needs to breathe. Then she pushes back through the nettles, heads round the village and out to the farm, not even knowing why she's doing it. Her skin is stinging and scratched, her lungs heavy. She's in the caravan park. There's no one there either. It's as empty as the hives. The silence thick as the air. Every caravan locked. No kids on the steps smoking, no voices inside – where the fuck are they? Shona, Kev, the students working on the farm, what are they all doing, away from here, as night falls?

And it falls fast, around Trish's shoulders. The sky turning dirty blue, the trees dark shadows in the texture of the land, the caravans, creaking. The track down. Her phone out as a torch and she almost falls in the mud, grit in her eyes and she's running again, until she reaches the fence, wooden posts, wire, sharp where it's been cut and attached. A handmade fence. Ricky Barr's fence. His land. His farm, beyond. Because it wasn't always about Uncle Walt, was it? It was about Ricky's violence. It was about him driving round in the middle of the night. More than that: there was evidence. Ricky met Bobby Helmsteading before he was killed. He was seen by the old flats; his alibi was a lie.

She pushes a mud-soaked trainer into the wire, holds onto the top of the fence post to pull herself over. Lands with a knee in the dirt and ankle throbbing but she doesn't care. Across the next field, through the trees, she can see lights, windows: the farmhouse could look almost welcoming, from this distance, in this rain.

And she'll have to do this alone.

The mud is up to her knees now, she can feel it through her jeans, the heavy dirt clawing at her skin and it's darker, round the back of the farmhouse. Dark but for the slanted crack of light spilling onto the ground from Ricky Barr's back door.

So this is where she needs to be. Here is what she needs to see.

And maybe she has been wrong about everything.

But if she hasn't?

TRUST IS A MISTAKE ANYWAY

Georgie pulls up outside Frazer's B & B in Warphill. The little girl's been with her the whole journey. She was sitting on her knee as Frazer hammered away at Cal. Waiting.

'We're getting somewhere, ma'am,' Frazer says, and his tone reminds her of Pamali, of the way she talks to her softly, with kindness. 'I mean Georgie.'

She nods, tries to return his smile as the little girl's whispers get louder.

'Are you okay, Georgie?'

'I'm... I'm worried about...'

She's trying to say something, to tell her something.

'Is it you and Fergus?'

Please help my mammy.

'My mother?'

'You're worried about your mother?'

Frazer looks surprised; Georgie is surprised.

'Yes, maybe that's... She's on her own and I think she needs some family around.'

'Is there someone nearby?'

'I'm the only one she has left,' Georgie says, the truth of it striking her as she speaks.

'She's in the States?' His words hang between them. 'Have you ever thought about, I don't know, going back?'

But there's something else, the little girl is trying to say something else.

'I'm sorry, it's none of my business.'

'It's not that, I…'

Georgie doesn't know what to say next. She looks out of the window, sees two figures walking up the street towards the car. Their hoods are pulled up, their hands held, and even in the dark something tells her who they are before she can see for sure. Mrs Taylor's house is just up the road, that's where they must be going.

'Can I do anything to help, Georgie?'

'Thanks, but you head on in,' she says. 'I'm fine. Really. I'll see you tomorrow.'

As Frazer opens the door, the spill of light confirms it's Penny-Ann and Julie heading up the street. Frazer spots them as he gets out, waits for them after swinging the door closed and they stop to chat despite the rain. Georgie doesn't mean to stare, but the three of them, chatting away, openly, it's not a scene you see every day in Warphill. When did Frazer win them over? He even looks a bit younger, loosening his tie there as Julie starts laughing at him. They've become friends. Then the tugging on her sleeve, more insistent now:

Please help me—

'You?'

Frazer's knocking the window, waving goodbye. Georgie nods and turns the engine on. Checks the rear-view mirror. She has to drive, to go somewhere. The sky's dark and her lights fail to light the emptiness on the road behind. She doesn't like what she's about to do but she knows she's going to do it. She'll be breaking the rules and breaking a trust and breaking herself, a bit, but she's made the choice. She's thought of nothing else since Pamali told her what Andy said and suddenly Georgie misses Trish with something sharper than guilt.

'How can I help you when I don't know who you are?'

Georgie clenches the muscles across her shoulders, then consciously releases them. She needs to be thinking straight.

'You're not Rachel, you're not Abigail Moss. Who else is there? Are you Dawn Helmsteading?'

This is ridiculous. Georgie stares at the road, wills it to challenge her, to force her into the relentless rain of the present. Is that Simon, heading out towards the coast?

'I visit Mrs Helmsteading in prison, sometimes.'

The sudden blaring horn of a car too close and Georgie swerves, curses, drives slower, eyes fixed on the road until she is back in Burrowhead, parked at the station. She has to park at the station. People watch, around here, they watch *her*, they always have; Georgie, with her brown skin and her accent, DI Strachan who's not from around here and never will be, no matter how long she stays. It clings to her like the damp in the air, in her lungs, in her veins. The pavements are flooded. The little girl's pulling urgently on her sleeve so she avoids Main Street, glances up the alley beside the Spar to Alexis's empty flat, then hurries on until she gets to where Walt Mackie used to live, before he died. To where Trish has been staying since.

The flies have gone. The moths and midges, the insects that have been gathering all day – where have they gone? Georgie looks up, sees nothing but purple haze and, further out, a bird of prey circling high over the cliffs. In front of her the house is dark, breathing shallowly to welcome her in. The back door is open. The little girl's hand is in hers. Georgie is inside.

Walt's kitchen, where he used to make tea, pile custard creams onto a plate before taking them through to his comfy chair. There are drooping plants on the windowsill, yellowing leaves and dried soil. There are cupboards that swing open with her touch, that contain tins and pasta and flour and salt. There is a fridge. Trish is so logical sometimes. Georgie wishes everything were different and she could laugh about this, maybe give Trish a hug. Instead she takes the flask off the top shelf and closes the door, resting her forehead against it and picturing her friend, Trish Mackie.

She wishes she knew how to help Trish. Imagines the long, padded coat Trish disappears inside every winter, the way she spikes her hair up when she's on edge, how kind she was to Si after Alexis died, the way she used to blush from her neck to her cheeks every time DS Frazer walked into the office. The way she loved her Uncle Walt. Then she opens the flask, inhales, seals the lid again. The little girl smiles up at her. She's found what she was looking for. She takes the track round the edge of the village back to the station, and she's in the car and driving home by the time the next visitor to Walt Mackie's house arrives.

They are not so gentle.

They throw cupboard contents to the floor, pull a cabinet door off by its hinges, upturn Walt's old comfy chair and cut into the lining underneath. They pound up the stairs like it's their right to be here, and they go through Uncle Walt's bedroom, ignoring the letters strewn on the floor. Then Trish's bedroom. The one that was hers when she was a little girl, the single bed, the wallpaper of bees; the room where Trish has been sleeping ever since her Uncle Walt died. They find the roll-top desk Walt must have got her when she was a kid, when she first started needing somewhere to sit and do her homework, to keep her things in the little drawers. That's where they find something wrapped in a silk scarf that doesn't look like anything Trish would ever wear. Suze is the one who pulls it out. Lets the silk scarf fall. Elise is the one who takes it. The handle fits neatly in her palm, smooth and strangely warm. She runs her thumb over the carvings and imagines her father doing the same. Then she feels a hand on her shoulder, and the knife slides from her grip.

LAST YEAR

Rachel touches her lips and smiles as Pauly lifts the flask, hesitates. Then he twists the lid and the smell reaches her, warm and earthy and strong, like honey and almonds and sweet mint and the deep soil itself, life and sea combined. His hand trembles as he pours, as it flows, thick and viscous, into the bowl, becoming a deep swirling well of dark red that draws her towards it. High feathered clouds flow across the moon and Rachel knows tonight is the night; she can feel it beginning already.

'Now we drink,' he says, and they drink together as her skirt shimmers between night blue and gold and terracotta, the greens of mimosa leaves, deep electric green and Rachel wants to touch the sky; wants it on her skin, in her hair, flowing in her blood. Her arms spin and her back arches and she's looking up to the sky and there are diamonds glittering like sunlight on the sea. Heat flows from the ground, Rachel can feel it, the earth and rock, the warmth of a planet pulsing beneath her feet. She reaches out to Pauly, his head back and his arms wide, to the right, to the left, arms wide and palms open, swaying in the warm sea breeze.

Pauly's mind is unfurling, releasing at last and he can feel how much he needed it. Like the lapping of waves on his toes, pebbles shimmering, flowing away the tightness that's haunted him – he won't look – his eyes on the sea, clear and sparkling and free, rolling out and back to them and only them and the rocks of the cliffs and the earth, the grass between his toes. He's kneeling like a child and Rachel's laughing, running her fingers through his hair, blowing dandelion seeds to watch them dance on the breeze.

'This is it,' she calls from far away. 'This is the place, we're here.'

She's singing from beyond him and beside him and she's dancing; he's lying down gratefully and she's dancing, eyes wide, palms open, she is calling her mam and she is here, and she always was.

'You are colour,' Rachel sings.

'I am colour,' her mam answers, 'I am here,' and Rachel's face is silver wet and glowing. Pauly rises from the ground to join them and they're dancing together, above the ground, raised by fine silk threads while around them something else rises, too, solid and thick and ancient, lined and carved with lives that intertwine like their fingers until there is a circle of stones around them, rippling with colour. Rachel and her mam are swirling together, glowing with light and air. Pauly lays his head down on the cool moss of the ground between the stones.

'Someone's watching us,' Rachel says from far away and whispers in his ear.

Her voice is like a stream, sparkling, she is sparkling colour and light like her mam, but her mam is looking beyond them, beyond the stones to something coming closer. Rachel reaches for his hand and she's not laughing as she speaks. Pauly is saying stop but his lips move too slowly and in front of his face there's a moth, a moth out at midsummer. He can see every flap of its wings and his voice is deep and absent and Rachel's pulling on his arm, her eyes piercing, urgent. He turns. He sees them, emerging into the light. Their faces are rotting with decay. Their teeth shattered and sharp, fractures of bones sticking through lips and the noise, the noise that comes from their throats. But they are not reaching for him.

They are not reaching for Rachel, glowing like embers, like the last of a fire. They are reaching between the shadows, melting against skin.

'He's watching us!'

'Rachel,' Pauly says, his voice still slow. 'Rachel, no.'

'But I know who that is!' Words spoken that can't be undone. 'Is that who you're afraid of?'

He can't stop it, the weight of the sky pressing against him, pushing him into soil and mud and rock.

'You think you can watch us?' Rachel shouts at the figure Pauly knows, the man who is watching them. Eyes raw slits through black fabric.

'I own you,' he says and Pauly is sinking, sinking further until Rachel pulls him up, pulls him to her.

'I know who you are.' Rachel takes a step back. 'I'm going to—'

'You're going to what?'

Together now, stepping backwards, fingers intertwined. The flicker of the sea, a lick of salt.

'I'm going to report you,' Rachel says. Her voice is the fluttering of moths and it's gone before Pauly can catch it.

'No you're not.'

He's peeled off his balaclava and he's staring at Pauly, straight at Pauly and Pauly can see the creatures moving through his skin, their broken teeth becoming his, their vacant eyes claiming him.

'I own you.'

Pauly looks at Rachel because he wants to say sorry, but Rachel's eyes are alight again, like when her mam is here. Her hair is shining curls bright as gorse flower and delicate as fritillary.

'I. Own. You.'

Another step back and they are standing on the edge of the clifftop. There's a fluttering of wings around them, lifting them up. They can feel lightness beneath their feet, the air where the rocks used to be, the solid ground freeing them at last. They are holding hands and no one can touch them. There is nothing to be afraid of any more. Rachel reaches out to her mam and Pauly says *I love you* and his voice blends with the rush of sea wind against the cliffs as they fly.

TONIGHT AND ALL NIGHT

Georgie can't deny the silence in her home. There's no shaking it. It's not just that Fergus is gone. It's the knowledge that despite it all, he's still the kindest man she's ever met, and what does that say about everyone else? That no one is innocent? That when a society is broken perhaps it's not possible to heal?

That maybe it will never be possible for her and Fergus to heal.

There's a noise beside her, a whisper of breath.

Georgie came here wanting to see the best in people. A complement to Fergus's gentle optimism, a counterpoint to Trish Mackie's insistent anger. Trish used to think she chose to see too much of the good, not enough of the bad. Georgie's gone the other way now and she's not sure there's a way back for either of them.

Then a warm hand, taking hers. The girl's eyes are piercing against her pale skin and her hair is dark twists around her face.

'I'm listening,' Georgie says. She still doesn't know who she is, Dawn or Rachel or Abigail or all the lost girls of the village, but she's looking at Georgie with hope, pulling her gaze through the village and away to the church ruin.

It has been used for so many things, that church ruin: a meeting place for teenagers, for bullies, for kids wanting to smoke and drink and tell each other who they hated and why; for other kids too, to light candles and call the dead, the missed; where Simon used to go as a teenager, knowing no one would see to judge him – so it's not all bad, the church ruin, just a place for things hidden. Left to ruin after the villagers took their own revenge on a minister who brought a slave among them while they pretended not to see. The minister who invited them to watch while he murdered her, then asked they forget while he walked among them. But it's easier to forget things once they are buried in the earth. The villagers knew that then and they know it still. Georgie's been avoiding the past so long there's a release in falling towards it, though the further back her mind goes the more she's straining through the dark. The church was built in the Middle Ages, though she can't name a century. Built with tall stones carried from the cliffs.

The little girl is smiling now, pulling herself up on to Georgie's lap.

Yes, she's beyond the church, she's at the coast, the cliffs; the standing stones were taken from the cliffs, dug from where they stood.

The girl's hand has wrapped tightly around her own.

They are etched with intricate markings. Are they prayers, scratched into the stone? Are they a warning? A curse, a threat to make people stay away, stay silent? She can't see any more, can't see any further back, and she is so thirsty. Her mouth is aching for a drink. For something rich and earthy, not from a tap, sanitised and swirling with chemicals, but there, through her window, there's a light.

It's the outside light, over her back door.

Fergus put it there so they could see the step down to the garden in the dark, head out together to watch constellations moving across the sky. Looking up is like looking back, he'd said, deep into the past. Fergus had always wanted to see the past and Georgie had always resisted. Now in the light she can see moths fluttering against the glass, dancing and vanishing, and the little girl is stroking her face. It's such a beautiful feeling everything else starts to melt away. The little girl's hand is wrapped around her own as she clasps the lid of the flask and the pressure inside her dissolves. She kisses the little girl's hair, then turns the lid on the flask and lifts her head to drink.

HOPE

LOST

Georgie feels a hand take hers. No, it dissolves into something softer. Her brother's blood slipping through her fingers, a haze of heat, a scream, and her knees crack on concrete as she falls. Then, sudden rain, cold and sharp on the back of her neck and she sees Alexis Cosse and Dawn Helmsteading, standing together at the rusted playground on the cliffs six months ago. Wind is whipping her hair into her eyes; Georgie feels the sting of it like a paper cut. Dawn is crying. Alexis holds out his arms to her but then, falling backwards, she sees Dawn held down against the stone when she was a child. Her small arms are forced wide, her wrists crushed. Around her people gather. Their eyes are red and fleshy through slits in fabric, their bodies cloaked. Georgie feels their nails against her skin, tears her gaze away and when she looks down there is soft grass and dandelion seed. She hears soft singing.

Rachel and Pauly are standing on the clifftop, their hands together, fingers intertwined. The moon is layered with craters and valleys, golden like the flowers embroidered into Rachel's skirt. There's a pull on Georgie's hair, soft but insistent. She turns to see him arrive: his face masked, his voice rasping needles of threat. Pauly has turned the sick grey of the sea. Then Georgie is falling with them to break on the rocks as a voice whispers from the cave, calling her inside.

Please help—

The entrance is tall and narrow, glinting with quartz in black-red rock.

PD & RT FOREVER

The little girl takes her hand and together they trace the words. *It's Pauly and Rachel.*

'I know.'

Looking up there are only cliffs and stone; the floor is the stillness of puddles collected in the footsteps Georgie follows. Stale seawater, the smell in the back of her throat. Dawn is here, crumpled on the rocks, but the little girl points to another shape. Georgie kneels to see his face, his desperate eyes, his nails scratching at invisible wood above his head. Sonny Riley, the murdered boy. His breaths are fast and shallow. The girl sits cross-legged beside him as they watch him fight for air under Nora Prowle's parlour floor.

Rest in peace.

It is scratched on the cave's wall: RIP. Letters etched into stone over centuries, lives gathering here deep in the cliffs. There's something sweet in Georgie's mouth, sweet and sick and sharp, all gorse flower and stale seaweed and her eyes are following the messages now, the desperate prayers. The little girl's lips move as Georgie reads her words: PLEASE HELP MY MAMMY.

There it is, being carved on the cave's wall by the little girl standing on tiptoes. Georgie knows her but doesn't. She knows the expression behind her eyes, the shape of her face but the throbbing in her head is pushing her further into the cave and there's something there. Someone is there but the stone floor melts into yellow buds, bursting open with the smell of coconut, spilling out against dark green thorns. Georgie's bleeding but she has to stay hidden among the brittle tangle to see who's here. Two teenagers, their clothes abandoned on the woodland floor, their faces gazing up at the sky. It is a night full of glistening silver.

They're singing, passing a drink between them. Georgie can taste its sweetness in her own throat. *Abigail.* Then people appear, masked and cloaked, and a cold knife passes through her. Georgie stumbles, but someone touches her shoulder. Offers a hand in comfort.

She has reached the back of the cave. There's someone here. Her eyes are a depth of sadness. There is lace up to her neck. Her dress is corseted and made of fine silk but drenched and torn and clinging. She is the woman murdered by the old minister, the slave buried and never spoken of, and the Others are gathering around her. Georgie has seen them before, but never like this. They melt from the rock to show their faces. They are young and scared: a whole family, cowering in their home. Georgie falls as the door is kicked down. A mother, a father, punched and smashed against the floor until their teeth shatter, their bodies dragged through soil and dirt. A young woman holding a baby until it's taken: the baby, its throat cut with a knife, its neck tied with rope, held into water, and then she is standing at their grave, the motte, and the villagers, eyes down, are walking away. Never talking, never telling, as the murdered rise from their graves to witness what no one is willing to see and she has to destroy this place, this can't go on.

Please help us.

Georgie is falling again until she lands surrounded by a circle of tall stones. Each one is intricately carved. They have been carried here, positioned with care and strength. The markings are exquisite. They show silver deer flitting between swaying trees, an eagle soaring gracefully through dappled cloud, boats on oceans, coastlines, people arriving, dancing, inviting her to join them. They have travelled so far to get here. They have eyes like her eyes and her voice is rising with theirs—

Please help us.

Cold fingers clasp her wrist. The song dries on her lips, replaced with sharp dread. She is on the cliffs. She is standing on the clifftop with the church ruin behind her and the rusted playground creaking through the dark; she is here, now, and a circle of shadowed people surround her. She can feel the slip of blood between her fingers and she wants to fall but she won't. She knows these people. She has lived among them. They are the villagers, and their masks are gone.

FOUND

Andy waits till his da's in bed and Debs is upstairs, sleeping. The house has turned that heavy clinging quiet that happens out here, in the summer, when the light finally falls and insects settle on tables and floors and skin. The window reflects his own face back at him, drawn and skinny. He pulls a hoody over his T-shirt and opens the door silently. Enough nights creeping away from here to know how. He's seen the shadows, walked in them. He's not scared of the hiss of wind through trees.

Outside, a slip of light sneaks out from the open door. He follows it, pulls his hood low over his eyes. He thought about wearing his balaclava, the one Bobby gave him, but that's what he was wearing in the Spar when Lee did what he did and he doesn't need the reminder of that night; needs strength, yeah, but not that. It's not so quiet out here, louder than in the house, what with the wind and the rain. Cloud's been so thick it had to break. Andy gets that. Everything reaches breaking point eventually.

He scratches at his chin where he can feel something, a moth, or maybe sweat, the edge of his hoody; keeps his head low and his back hunched as he follows the track away from the farm. The insects don't land on him out here, that's something, though he can hear the buzzing of them as they pass. Where the fuck they're going he doesn't know. He's keeping his eyes low, keeping his

325

mind focused. It means he doesn't see Trish, where she's been watching the back of the farm. But she sees him.

The sight of him does something to her, the hood pulled down, the way he's creeping. He's got a good heart, Andy, she's believed it, these past months, stuck her neck out for him, but now there's a shudder of something thin and sharp cutting her skin. She's got so much wrong. She scrunches her eyes shut, doesn't want to be seeing Andy like this, and when she opens them it's not Andy in the crack of light spilling out from the back door of the farmhouse. The muffled sound of a cough smothered against an arm. Ricky Barr, less hidden than Andy, no hood, no hunch other than his own body struggling with the weight of his head, he's that weak these days.

But he's still Ricky Barr. Trish knows that.

She waits as he follows the same track Andy took, waits in the muggy heat of the night, her arms shaking. Fuck's sake, Trish, pull yourself together. She lets her head fall back, eyes on the sky; the nothingness of dense cloud and no moon, no substance save the clawing mist and as she opens her mouth to drink it in, a creature lands on her tongue. She lurches, stifling her own cough, spitting it out, something winged and legged in her mouth. She wants to throw up, but she needs to stay silent, stay hidden. She scratches at her own tongue to get the sense of it away, spits again and waits till the shadowed shape of Ricky Barr is at the edge of the village before she follows him.

The rain's pelting water like fists by the time Andy has skirted the village and joined the track that leads out to the church ruin. He chose it. The church ruin where Rachel took them to face the dead. The church ruin where he used to meet Lee, where the graves are clawing their way out of the ground and Andy knows every step as well as he knows the fields on his da's farm. He knows how to avoid the lumps of the rising graves, which stones crumble against his weight and which ones last.

Now he's approaching, though, there's something wrong about the ruin – more than the graves rising and the crumbling stone. The walls look too tall and he stops, forces his fists into his eyes. When he looks again the church is as he remembers it. Grey stone, collapsed, corners blunted with erosion and the trees in the graveyard, twisted and easy to break. He takes a branch off by the gate, snaps it with his fingers then regrets it not because of the noise but because the tree is a living thing, that's what Pamali would tell him. He just snapped off its lung and he doesn't even know why. He thinks, at first, that it's the thought making his feet stop and his legs prickle with static, like a shiver in the heat. Then he sees the figure. Hooded, like him. Face masked with a balaclava. His eyes, through the eyeholes, darting and amused.

This is Andy's meeting. Andy's choice. He needs to remember that.

'You came,' Andy says, his voice too high, too young; he hates himself for it.

'You called.' There is almost a laugh underneath the words.

Andy needs to scratch his neck. Can't seem to lift his hand. His meeting. His choice. His fucking plan. But there's something else here. It's supposed to be just them, he said come alone, he fucking said but they're not alone, are they, there are shapes moving between the ruined walls of the church – he blinks, can't rub at his eyes again, has to keep them open, stay in charge.

'I have an offer,' Andy says.

The man steps closer and Andy can smell his breath, coffee and food, something sticky and fried.

'First things first.'

Andy can only turn his head away as the man reaches his gloved hands inside his pocket. Andy's pocket. The front pocket of his hoody. Andy is so stupid. He can't move his hands, his arms. The man takes out Andy's mobile phone and looks at the screen. Andy's breath catches in his throat. There's a rasping sound from behind him but the man is in front, calmly swiping.

Andy is such a fucking idiot.

The man holds out the phone so Andy, too, can see the red button on his own screen. The timer flicking on seconds, the phone clearly set to record everything. Then his gloved hand presses Stop. Throws the phone, face down, onto the stone. Stamps on it, not quickly but deliberately. Picks up the pieces and puts them in a transparent bag that he pulls from his pocket. Andy has to speak. This is his choice, his meeting. His life.

'I know who you are,' he manages.

There are shadows from the stone, elongating, stretching out towards him, but they're not real, they can't be.

'Oh, I know who you are too, Andy Barr.'

He's peeling off his balaclava. The man who killed Lee is peeling off his balaclava. Underneath it his eyes are blood red, teeth smashed through his lips. Then the image is gone as fast as it came, and the face Andy is looking at is white and unblemished and smiling.

HERE AGAIN, IN THE DARK

Simon's standing at the tideline of a sea so angry it's fighting the air. This is where he fell, once, to his knees, the sea drenching the pain he couldn't process. He doesn't fall to his knees today, doesn't need the jolt of his bones hitting rock or that scream he made. He'll let the surging crash of the waves smother his thoughts.

Alexis's smile, though.

It's physical, whatever is holding him here, when logic tells him the dead have no reason to want the living to stop. Alexis would never have wanted that. But here he still is, Orlando's text unanswered in his pocket. The promise of the city drowned out by wind whipping against his face, the pull of the cave behind him. There's no chance of seeing the horizon tonight, no light from the sky for the sea to reflect. Just the weight of the cliffs, the clamouring of sea on rock. And a voice, low and raw beneath the waves.

When he turns the cave is so close it startles him. Its entrance is even taller than he remembers, glistening with damp red rock and quartz. He almost calls out her name: Dawn. She led him to the cave, showed him how to see it, so perhaps she's the one who can help him leave. But Dawn's not lying huddled on the stone any more; he's here alone with nothing but rock shadows on the cave's floor and the way the noise is dampened inside, the wind a whisper rather than a screech. The tide's getting higher, though. It moves fast, when it's on the turn, and it can cut anyone off from the village. He turns from it, lets his hand follow the scratched words, though it's so dark he can barely see.

PD & RT 4EVER

He knows that one well. Dawn showed him, and he's been back here since, to remember Pauly and Rachel, to read their words. Lives cut short, like Lee, like Alexis. He can feel the shadows moving, clenches his teeth against them; he is alone here. Then his phone vibrates, and something startles at the back of the cave.

'Who's there?'

A movement, a scuff against stone. Then words.

'Can you just fucking go?'

Simon knows that voice. He searches the shadow for a face. His eyes fail him at first, the dark is so complete, but then words appear, scratched deep and glowing in the rock.

PLEASE HELP MY MAMMY

Words and prayers, hidden in stone. Not everyone can find this cave, but he's not alone in here.

'Aaron?'

He feels the chill of salt water at his ankles. The sea has reached the threshold.

TRYING TO GET ONE
LAST THING RIGHT

Trish can see four immense stones where the walls of the church ruin should be. Uncle Walt used to talk about standing stones, but she never listened. This can't be right. She's hallucinating. It's the heat, the rain seeping through her clothes, the haze making her throat burn. She can see the shape of Ricky Barr, beyond the gate of the churchyard. She feels sick. Like she's breathing in something her body must reject, something toxic and sweet. There are voices, low, gravelly, but she can't catch the words. This is what she's been waiting for, so many months, wondering if everyone else was right, Georgie and Si and Frazer, the fucking council. This is it. She leaves the tree she's hiding behind. On to the next one. Pause, listen.

Two voices; there are two voices. One low, anxious, nervy. It's Andy.

On again, reaching the gate, keeping her knees bent and her body low. The old rope that holds the gate shut is disintegrating, comes off in her hands. She has to catch the gate to stop it swinging open and hitting the cherry tree beyond. It's covered in large leaves, black in this light and drooping like hair and the voices are louder now, they're inside, between the huge stones that used to be the church ruin. They're covered in shapes, symbols. No, they're etched with erosion, that's all, lined and crumbling – but that voice. Andy's not talking now, it's someone else. She needs to get closer. That voice. The curl of amusement. It's not Ricky. Pressing herself as flat as she can against the nearest of the stones. Ricky Barr is gone, she's no idea where he's gone, she's lost him, but she can hear Andy now, Andy, what are you doing?

'He chose me,' he's saying.

Andy, no.

'So why the phone recording?'

'That was like, a backup, like insurance, aright? Fucking forget about that—'

Shit, Andy, what are you doing?

'Lee chose me, he chose me to take over from him, and here I am—'

'Here you are.'

That voice, light and dancing. Trish wants to be sick.

'Yes, here I am, so now you deal with me—'

Too fast, Trish knows, he's talking too fast, he's scared, he's a kid and he's lying, scrambling to find a way out.

'—because I've taken over from Lee, aright? Me.'

'I saw you at the hospital.'

'So?'

'So I'm wondering how much Lee has told you.'

'He's told me enough, aright? I'm here to do the job and you got to take that, aright, you got to deal with me now because—'

'Because, because.'

That laugh, that smirk.

'What's that?'

What's what? Fuck. Andy. She needs to get closer; she can't see. Then, between the stones, the flash of a blade catches the only light in the sky. There's a long, rough yell and the sound of running, of bodies slamming, screaming. Trish is running too, crashing over crumbled stone and pulling herself up, fast. There's a tangle of bodies past the stones. Andy's screaming. Then she sees Ricky Barr. He's fallen, clutching his stomach. Blood pooling everywhere, on his clothes, his body. Andy's frozen in fear and shock and there are hands on Trish's shoulders, clasping too tight. A knee in her back and she falls. Pain from her head shoots down her neck and the ground is hot and wet against her face and everything goes black.

WHAT WE SEE AND
WHAT WE DON'T

Si thinks he hears Aaron hiss *fuck* under his breath, but he's not sure – could be the waves clawing up to the cliffs and they can't stay here for long, they'll be cut off. Dawn should have drowned, hiding the way she was, Simon knows that. All those days she was huddled in here, soaked and shivering. But the sea left her be.

'I'm sorry about Lee,' he says, still standing near the entrance. His shoes are soaked and Aaron's right at the back, but Si doesn't want him to feel trapped there. Besides, he can't see where to put his feet, how to find a path in through the dark. He moves slowly, his hands following the walls until he reaches the back, knows the smooth damp of the rock and leans against it. Beside him, Aaron is hunched. Si leaves plenty of space between them.

'Tide's coming in,' he says.

'I know the fucking tides.'

'You here to drown, are you?'

Aaron doesn't reply to that. He smells of sweat and cigarettes and Si can just make out the way he's staring at the waves in the darkness. The noise of them is fading to an impression and the air has settled, thick and still. It makes Simon miss the sharp whip of the wind. He tries to imagine the spite on Aaron's face, his scowl, but something about it seems off.

'We used to come here when we were kids,' Aaron says.

Simon turns to face him, but he's shrouded in the dark. What he sees instead is the carved shape of a man and a stag on the wall, etched through the black surface of the rock to something lighter beneath, something harder to scratch.

'Did you do this?' he asks.

'No,' Aaron says. He doesn't ask what Simon is referring to. He's seen it.

'What about the messages?'

He doesn't reply so Simon listens to the cave instead, to the quiet breathing of the rocks. It doesn't scare him as it did before. It fills Simon with calm. Even the words are familiar; he feels something release as he reads them.

'Please help my mammy.'

'That was here before us,' Aaron says, his voice rough. 'And she never needed helping anyway.'

Simon thinks Aaron's mam probably did need help, probably still does, but the lack of help never stopped her being Natalie Prowle.

'I've a knife with me tonight though,' Aaron says, a threat in his voice. 'That allowed, PC Hunter?'

'It's not up to me,' Simon says, ignoring the sarcasm. 'Carve your message.'

Aaron straightens up and Si can see the shape of him moving, touching the rocks behind them, finding a patch where no one's carved before. Then he takes out his knife and starts scratching something on the stone. Si can't see what it is, but the metal of the blade catches some light that nothing else in here had been able to grasp.

'Dare say no one gives a fuck that he's gone,' Aaron says.

'I do.'

He's carving Lee's name; Simon doesn't need to see it to know that.

'He was a vicious little shite who constantly fucked up and no one ever cared why, so they're not going to start caring now, are they.'

'I care,' Simon says.

'Fuck you.'

'Fuck you too.'

Aaron's knife catches harder stone, screeches against the surface then finishes its final line. Lee is here then, etched into the rock, despite everything he's done.

'Any of them yours?' Aaron says.

The question takes Simon by surprise, but when he touches the cave's wall it feels warm and smooth beneath his hand.

'No,' he says. 'No, I don't need to write anything in here.'

It happens just like that. Alexis isn't keeping him here at all; he never was.

Si follows the shape of the stone across the back of the cave, allowing its ridges to scrape against his skin and the shallow dips to stir beneath his fingertips. He hears scratching, like fingernails on wood. Breath drawn through teeth, then harsh air rushing in, the noise of the sea crashing furiously against the rocks and Aaron stumbles back, eyes darting around, breath ragged.

'What the fuck?'

Suddenly the cliffs shudder, the floor they're standing on jolting with the force. Simon stumbles, falls against the cave's wall, pain shooting down his arm. Everything is in darkness, everything, and nails claw at his face as the rocks shake again and a deafening creak slices through the cave.

BEGUN

Gail Dover is standing on the clifftop as it shudders. All around
her she can sense the weight and height of the rock, the power it
contains. She led the villagers here, where the haze captures the
moonlight and light itself vanishes into the black night and reap-
pears through cloud. She holds her arms wide and opens her face
to the sky, to the heavy night air, and she is standing on the cliff
edge and remembering how she stood, once, in the woods as the
moon shimmered in a clear, cloudless sky. That girl is long gone
now. The shame is gone, too. All that's left is the anger of a lifetime
and the truth of this moment as the villagers form a circle around
her. This is where the stone circle once stood, inside the ancient
henge on the cliffs where their ancestors gathered. The strength
of the land; she can feel it in the rock beneath her feet, tensed and
ready, in the rain drenching them and the air rushing beyond her
to the sea, while in front of her they're all here, watching.

She sees them and she knows them: Lori Smyth, her oldest
friend; June and Whelan, her neighbours in Burrowhead all these
years; Camellia Taylor melting from the mist and back again;
Elise Robertson, her eyes pleading through the slashed white of
her father's cloak, a cloak that Gail would rather see hurled from
the cliff than standing among them. There's Terry from the garage
and Ben from the pub, Colin Spence and old Bessie Wilkie, there

she is – Gail is glad Bessie's here to witness what's coming, she needs to see it through to the end – and within the darkness Gail sees their eyes.

It was eyes she saw before, too. Nora Prowle's eyes. Eyes like those she sees now in Natalie Prowle's face, peering up at her from where she's kneeling in the mud. Eyes spilling with rain and tears.

'Don't be afraid,' Gail tells her. 'There will be peace at last, my dear.'

They are starting to sing.

She doesn't tell them to begin; she doesn't need to. She lets her head fall back and her voice rise, pure and younger than her years, as she welcomes the thick cloud spilling purple across the land and the sweet smell of the sea.

It has been done wrong so many times. Tonight she will do it right.

'Air,' she sings.

Beneath her voice she can hear Natalie sobbing.

'Water.' And she remembers the eyes and the hope, the guilt, the hate, she remembers it all.

'Blood,' she sings, her voice rising higher in the centre of the stone henge where her ancestors would have sung and danced, and between the words Natalie is crying and broken and Gail is holding the knife. Its etchings are warmer than the air. She runs her fingers over them, feels their stories, their lives and deaths; feels the Others gathering, waiting for her to call them from the shadows. Their rasping whispers cling to the edge of sound as the ground slips beneath her feet. Rocks creak far below. A shudder of stone jolts her bones. It is time. Her fingers tighten around the dagger that was Nora's once, used unjustly, that at long last has come to her.

'Welcome,' Gail says, and the villagers hear her as though she were standing beside them, whispering in their ears. 'We have come full circle.'

Beside her Natalie is compliant, holding out her right wrist.
'It is time to see the truth.'

Gail feels the engravings on the dagger's hilt in her palm: air,
water and blood. A land renewed and a debt paid. She passes the
knife to Natalie, and Natalie draws the blade along her wrist.

'Arise,' she sings, her voice rising with the air as they emerge
from between the shadows, their long limbs melting from rock
and forming in the haze. 'Arise!' she calls, as she holds the vessel
to collect the blood and allows it to blend with all that nature has
given. She closes her eyes as she drinks, sways on her feet as the
rocks shake, and then: she's back there. She is a young woman
again.

She is Abigail Moss.

She's standing in the shimmering woods at midsummer and
Dougie is reaching for her hand. Their fingers intertwine at last.
His smile softens her breath and reminds her of how young he
is; how nervous. They fall together onto soft, padded moss
surrounded by the silver bark of birches. Owls call to one another
through the night. Elegant brown deer emerge from between the
trees. His gentle hands are on her skin as his eyes dance and a
moth lands on the stone beside them. She knows every flutter of
its fragile wings, the true colour of her hands against his black
skin, twinkling droplets of light suspended in the night air and
he whispers *Thank you*, his words for rustling leaves and fresh
water and the warm sweet air. But she needs more, now, right
now. The vessel has returned, the villagers have drunk, and Natalie
is holding out her left wrist. Gail takes it, lets the blade call more
blood. She needs to get back to Dougie; she should never have
left him – how could she have left him? There is rasping breath
in the night, startled cries, song turning to screams but she drinks
again, again, again, as the shadows stretch from the stone and
scratches claw at her skin and beside her Natalie slips to the
ground.

WHERE WE FALL

Fergus lets his bike clatter against the stone. Natalie's not come home. She's not answering her phone, she sent him away and when he came back she was gone, she was nowhere in Warphill. So now he's in Burrowhead, ringing doorbells, knocking on windows and trying to see in but every house is dark, not a light in one of them – no one's here. The villagers are gone, Natalie's gone and he was supposed to look after her and something's happening, he knows it. When he feels a touch on his elbow he almost screams as he spins around.

'Oh thank God, Pamali.'

'Who did you think I was?'

'I can't find Natalie.' Words tumbling out: he checked the hospital, Lee's room and there was no sign of anything, like it had all been wiped clean and buried, like, like—

'Fergus, what on earth is wrong?'

'Where is *everyone?*' His arms waving wildly around him as Pamali takes a step back and she almost looks afraid of him then, but it's not just the people, it's everything. The insects, the birds, they've vanished. Fergus is so used to seeing them, groups of wrens under the rose bushes, the pair of collared doves by the fountain, even on a night like this there are always seabirds flying overhead, but tonight there's nothing, not even gulls, where have they gone?

'I spoke to Georgie,' Pamali says.

Fergus realises how he must sound, how he must look. It's late. The rain. He's soaked. What has Georgie said?

'I was trying to support her, that's all. Natalie, I mean... After what she'd been through, and Georgie looked at me like...but that's not...she asked me to look after her, Georgie did, but I don't know where she is.'

'Georgie?'

'No, Natalie.'

Shame pulsing through his body, the way it sounds like he cares more about Natalie than Georgie and it's not that, it's just that Georgie will be fine, Georgie's always fine. He's doing what Georgie asked him to do. Isn't he?

'And everyone has gone, *everyone*.'

Pamali looks around, at the dark houses, the curtains. The fountain is overflowing with rainwater, flooding the pavement, and around them street lights are pulsing and his head is throbbing from the intense pressure behind his eyes.

'And I don't know where Georgie is either,' he says. 'She came to Natalie's house.'

'I know.'

'But something's happened to Natalie. Or she's going to do something or...*everyone* is gone. They're always here, aren't they, watching, that's what Georgie says.'

Suddenly the rain is everything, the weight of it, he could lie down and let it drown him. But Pami is talking to someone on the phone, held close beneath her hood. She's calling Georgie. Georgie's coming here. Georgie's coming to help him. He leans against the fountain and glances up and there: a herring gull. It's ghostly white where it's caught in the street light, then gone. A feeling overtakes him, like it was the last one in the village and now there's nothing left and the stone of the fountain slips beneath his fingers and he falls, the fountain's edge crumbling with him.

'Oh my God, are you okay?' Pamali's saying, helping him up, but the ground is shaking, splitting beneath him. 'Come inside, out of this weather.' Leading him to the Spar, shutting out the relentless rain. 'Georgie's on her way, she'll know what to do.'

'But Natalie could be anywhere.'

'I'm sure she's fine.'

'Was she fine the last time you saw her?'

Pami's face falls and Fergus regrets it. They both know she's not fine. Pami means she's safe. Not in danger.

'This storm...' Pamali says, turning to face him.

'There's nothing going on with me and Natalie.' He needs to explain, but she's shaking her head.

'We all make our choices, Fergus, it's not my business—'

'I've not made any kind of choice!' Then every hair on his neck is standing up and he knows: Georgie's looking in the window, rain running down her face and her eyes glistening. He almost rushes out before Pami opens the door and pulls her in; but something's wrong.

'The road,' Georgie says, her voice alive and ringing. 'The pavement—'

They need to see out. Pami's standing by the window, flicks the switch. The three of them are plunged into darkness. The night glows with the fuzz of street lights caught in torrential rain and they all see it now: tarmac fractured and bursting, paving stones upended, serrated, grasping for the sky.

'Oh my God.'

Georgie's leaning her head back and gazing at the ceiling, here, in the Spar, and Pami is staring out at the devastation and Fergus can hear Georgie's breath next to his own. Her eyes are golden in the dark and he wants to hold her face, wants to kiss her. Pami flicks the light back on and Fergus is staring at Georgie, staring into her eyes that are glowing like he's never seen them before, and her skin is luminous, more than wet, it's more than the rain, she looks extraordinary.

'Why am I here, Fergus?' she says.

'I... I was worried...' Pami touches his arm and he's so grateful he could cry. 'Natalie's gone missing.'

Georgie seems so far away; he wants to pull her back, hold her close.

'I've checked the museum, the hospital,' he says. 'She's not answering her phone.'

'She's a grown woman.'

'Her son just died,' Pami says, that kind voice of hers, gentle with Georgie like she was with him. 'She's not in a good frame of mind.'

'And Mrs Dover was round at the house wanting to... I don't know, but if something happens, and I hadn't said... You told me to look after her, Georgie.'

'I know.' It's Georgie speaking but it's someone else too, someone different.

'There is *nothing* going on with me and Natalie, Georgie, I promise you that.'

She seems so distant, beyond him.

'I was staying with her for a few days, that's all, there's not, she's not... God, Georgie, I think she's in danger, I... Georgie?'

'What is it you know, Fergus?'

'I don't... I think Gail Dover has taken over the community council. I'm not sure what they're doing, but sometimes...' His voice falls to a whisper. 'Sometimes Natalie talks about the three-fold death.'

Georgie is shaking her head but not at him, she's looking down at her own hand as though something's there.

'You think they're planning another sacrifice?' Pamali says.

Fergus feels sick. 'I think this time it's worse.'

'In Mungrid Woods?'

343

'I don't think so.'

'Then where?' Pami's voice is clear and sure but why is Georgie not speaking? Why is it Pamali answering him while Georgie sways on her feet and looks through him?

'The henge?' He sounds hopeless.

'But there is no henge,' Pamali says and Georgie's eyes glide from his to something else – what is she seeing there, by her hand? Her eyes are reflecting the light and her fingers are trembling, Fergus is sure now, she's shaking.

'The menhir is pointing past the village,' he says. 'Through the church ruin—'

'To the cliffs,' Georgie whispers.

'Georgie' – her name, the feel of her name on his tongue – 'are you okay?'

'I think they're on the cliffs,' she says. 'Where Rachel and Pauly fell.'

'Natalie went there before,' Fergus says.

'Then we go there now.'

Georgie's already moving away and Pamali's pulled on a waterproof and Georgie isn't even wearing a coat, she just steps out into the storm, shirt open at the collar, trousers drenched and clinging, and he follows. Picking his way over fractured paving stones and smashed gutters and soon they are running from the village and out along the track to the cliffs, where thousands of gulls are screaming.

WHEN WE RUN

Shona has to stop. Leans down, hands on knees, gasping. They ran from the church ruin, ran away and didn't look back. She can feel vomit rising up her throat. Kev's beside her, struggling for breath, for words.

'His eyes...' She feels her stomach crunch inside her.

Kev falls to his knees.

They're on the track leading away from the ruin, the trees giving them a bit of shelter. Her pulse is hammering. Suddenly Kev grabs her arm.

'What the fuck?'

'Shhh,' he whispers, low and urgent.

The dark is clinging to them, their clothes clinging to their skin, and the heat, alive and clawing. She needs to breathe. Fucking breathe.

'He's following?'

Kev is straining to see back to the church. 'I don't think so. It was just a bird,' he whispers, letting go of her. 'Gull.'

She looks up but there's nothing, darkness and heavy clouds and nothing else. She swallows, tries to spit the acid taste out of her mouth.

'He doesn't know we were there,' she says. 'He didn't see us.'

'You sure?

'No one knows we were there. Except Andy.'

Andy, who left her that message, told her what he was planning, when and where, insisted she stay hidden to witness everything. *If he sees my phone, you're the backup.* She'd barely taken him seriously.

She forces her hands into her eyes and away again, trying to get the rain out, the water. The sight of that knife slicing Ricky Barr open. Andy, screaming like that and Trish, fuck she's sure that was Trish hitting the ground and she'd run, they'd both run. They'd run away. She's down in the mud now, like Kev, the both of them shaking.

'We should have stayed—'

'Don't, Shona.'

'But he stabbed Ricky!' Her words make her throat clench. This is not who she is or who she thought she'd ever be. 'We were there, Kev, we should have—'

'Stop it,' he says, more forcefully. 'It could have been you ran into that knife.'

'Instead we ran away.'

She can hear him inhale.

'Yes.'

There's shame in his voice too and it helps.

'We had to, Shona.' His eyes look to her hands, to what she's still clutching tight in her pocket. 'We had to get away, or else what was the point in any of it?'

Her grip tightening on her phone.

'You got it, right?'

She pulls her hand out, checks her screen. Nods at him, their eyes holding one another's. The recording worked. She emails the file to herself, then to Kev. Ever since Rachel died she's been searching for proof of who sold her the drugs, who was responsible.

'D'you think Ricky's dead?' she says.

The nausea again, the burn of it in her throat, pooling under her tongue. Kev just rocks back on his heels, takes a breath and holds it.

They got away. It's sinking in now, the fear slipping down a notch.

'What do we do now?' he says.

She straightens her back, pulls her legs out of the dirt.

'I think we call the police.'

'The fucking *police*, are you kidding?'

But who else is there? What's she supposed to do, write a fucking story? Post her evidence on the internet and hope for the best?

'The police are *in on it*,' Kev says.

And they are. Maybe they all are. There's no one she can trust, not the villagers or the police. But there's someone not from around here. There's someone who was never from around here.

'DS Frazer,' she says.

Then she makes the call and they wait in the torrential rain, in the mud, because they can't get up and they can't move on, they both know that; they can't leave, not until this is finished.

WHAT CAN BREAK US

The first thing Trish knows is the sodden mud beneath her face. Pain in her head, shooting down her neck when she tries to move. Then sounds come into focus: Andy's juddering breath, the sink of footsteps into drenched soil. She's on the ground and there's someone by her feet, someone else beyond her head.

'Natalie has gone mad,' the voice behind her says, not addressing her – they think she's still unconscious. He's talking to Andy. 'Look, she's stabbed your da. Poor Ricky Barr, what a tragedy.'

The sound of his voice scratches at her skin.

'If only we could find her to ask her why.'

A smirk, beneath the words. So, their plan is to frame Natalie Prowle.

Trish can't open her eyes. They feel glued shut with something, mud, blood, but she needs to open her fucking eyes. The wind is shrieking through the ruin's walls.

Then there's another voice. A woman.

'Is Natalie going to kill her too?'

A foot on her back, giving her a nudge. She rolls with it, gets her face out of the mud. Grit in the air, on her skin. Rain stinging raw. But she knows that voice. Fuck, her head. The blood is coming from her head, that throbbing pain.

The man behind her hasn't answered. But she knows there are two of them. The woman and the man. One standing over her, the other still in the shadows. She has to do something. Has to force her eyes open. Has to do that, at least. Mud in her mouth, on her teeth, but she can't lie here waiting for them to decide to kill her too, what would that make her? She is Trish fucking Mackie.

She opens her eyes, flickering open then closed, but it's enough. It's enough. She's going to be sick. She has been wrong about every last thing.

'Hello, Suze,' Trish says.

Fuck, pain, shooting pain as Suze kicks her, yanks her arms behind her back and clasps them together at the wrists and her face is forced down into the gushing mud again but she needs to speak, fucking *speak*—

Suze's knee forces down onto Trish's back and all she can do is make a rasping noise from her throat, a desperate gasping for air and that's not who she is. Forcing her head up. Spitting out mud. She's not trying to speak this time; she is fucking going to.

'I thought it was you,' Trish says, lifting her head.

A sharp punch into her face. She takes it. Readies herself again. Beneath the pain she can hear the waves thrashing at the coast.

'I want in.'

Her wrists are free and she's turning, slowly, onto her side. Taking in a slow breath. Letting the rain wash her face of the mud.

'I'm not falling for that,' Suze says and suddenly her knee is on Trish's throat, pressing down, and Trish's vision is turning red, that desperate choking noise coming from her lips again. Breathe, fucking breathe. Then the pressure's gone and her lungs fill and she takes her chance.

'Why the fuck not?' she says. 'I'm serious, Suze. I want in. Get the fuck off me.'

Andy's voice comes from between the stones: 'Fuck you, Trish.'

Shit, Andy, be quiet.

'*He* killed them,' Andy spits out between sobs.

'Your stupid da just killed himself,' Suze says.

'Fucking listen, Trish. *He* killed Rachel and Pauly.'

'They didn't have to jump, did they?' the voice says from the shadows.

That laugh, that fucking laugh. Trish knows that laugh.

Suze's face is grey in the darkness and someone's moving closer. Shards of rain, sharp as steel. Suze is looking up. Looking for instructions. Suze is not in charge here. Another screech of the wind and Trish is ready, she's going to do this. Head throbbing, she sits up slowly, calmly, and turns to face him. He is drenched, his hair plastered to his face; he looks so very ordinary she wants to be sick.

'There you are, Cal.'

He smiles at her then.

'Want in, do you?'

WHAT CAN DROWN US

'Wait!' Simon screams as the cliff is wracked again, a violent crash of rockfall overhead throwing him against sharp stone.

Aaron stumbles, his breath shallow and fast, but doesn't stop.

The wind is howling through the cave, snatching Simon's breath as he tries to speak, to call Aaron back, but Aaron won't be called. He is running to the entrance, wading through the waist-high waves thrashing at his chest. Another crash and rocks fall at the threshold, smashing into water as though they could crack it open and even Aaron turns away then, hiding his face from the force of it.

'Aaron, please!'

Simon has to yell to be heard above the din of the waves, the splintering of the cliffs around them.

'Get back here!'

Aaron's eyes dart to his for a second before he turns back to the sea and it's enough for Simon to know he won't stop. Over the water, the sheets of rain are dense and furious, heavy as fists and the rock face behind him lurches with the force of another tremor and Si falls forward, stumbling through the flooding cave floor.

'Aaron, you don't want to die!' He's trying to call him back into the cave but Aaron turns instead, hair whipped in the wind and eyes red with salt grit.

'You mean *you* don't want to die,' Aaron yells, and the cave shakes with another violent cascade of rocks and Aaron's falling, he's falling into the sea and Simon's grabbing his hand as they are both thrown into the waves and all he can do is choke and thrash against the weight, the depth and rage of it.

BLOOD

Georgie stumbles into the circle of people gathered on the clifftop, their voices screeching against the howling wind and their faces desperate, hollowed in horror. She knows them; she knows them all. She's gasping for breath, the salt raw in her throat. She knows these people, she has lived among them, but they're staring through her as though she doesn't exist. There, the broad shoulders of Whelan, his head hanging back in the rain as though his neck were broken. Beside him June's face is upturned, her mouth wide in a silent scream and there: Colin Spence from Warphill, old Bessie Wilkie beside him, clutching onto each other. Terry's eyes are desperate, searching the haze. Elise Robertson is grasping at her neck and Camellia Taylor has fallen to her knees, a shriek coming from her throat. Then, in front of them all, Georgie sees Gail Dover and Lori Smyth. They are standing tall, unlike the villagers, their arms spread wide and their heads thrust back, either side of Natalie Prowle. She's lying limp on the ground. There is blood on her arms, her wrists.

That's why Georgie's here. Isn't it? To find Natalie Prowle.

Gail Dover doesn't see Georgie arrive, doesn't see Natalie's fallen body; she doesn't see any of it. She is lying on padded moss and Dougie's head is on her chest and they are breathing soft air that flutters through the leaves. But then there are faces in the dark. A sudden desperate flight of birds and Nora's eyes are peering at her through slashed fabric. Disgusted fingers grab her hair, pull her neck back, and the shock pulses through her as she screams. They're kicking him, kicking and beating Dougie there on the ground, and he's naked and helpless to stop it. His teeth are broken, sticking through his lower lip. Eyes swollen to bloody sockets. His back crushed, his ankles stamped, and her neck is forced to twist and watch. The ground is shaking. She's shaking, she's screaming as Georgie falls, her knees sinking into the mud, blood slipping between her fingers.

No, she is not back there. Georgie will not watch her brother die again.

She looks up. Between the villagers, she can see standing stones stretching to the sky, covered in deep intricate marks. The air calms as she stares at them; the wind lets her breathe at last. Someone is beside her. It's the little girl, she's here to help. No, it's Pamali. And Fergus. Pami and Fergus are here beside her but the ground shakes again and Rachel and Pauly appear through the dark. They're on the clifftop, arms outstretched between them like paper decorations. Georgie lurches forward but they fall, she can't save them, she failed to save them and in the mud by her feet Sonny Riley is lying on his back, clawing at the air. Georgie falls to her knees as all around her the circle of villagers watch the old minister drown his slave in shallow salt water and Georgie can't stand it, she can't stand it any more.

Gail Dover's voice rings out through the dark.

'Destroy us!'

The land is ripped with a violent shudder. Georgie stumbles up, falls again. Rain gushes through the widening cracks in the ground but she has to see, she has to face the rasping breath behind her, the shrieking wind, and the villagers are stretching, their fingers clawing out at her; no, no! She can't believe it, forces her hands into her eyes, but from their feet the land is cracking into jagged shafts of rock, carving the villagers from each other as shapes gather from the stone, the dead melting into the living.

'Destroy us all!'

Georgie's hands are clenched over her ears, arms bent against the wind to shield her face from the onslaught. Deep fractures are running through the rock and it's going to break, the cliffs will fall, and there on the edge are Gail Dover and Lori Smyth, arms wide and faces upturned. Between them, Natalie Prowle is unconscious and bleeding.

The little girl's whispering, *Please help, please help, please help us—*

But Georgie can't move. Gail Dover's eyes meet hers.

'Destroy us all,' Gail whispers in her ear.

Then from beside her and far away, Fergus says her name.

'Georgie?'

Like he knows her. Like he expects something from her. Like he is asking her to make some kind of choice.

AIR

'Yes,' Trish says, as the wind surges. 'I want in.' Salt air whipping her face, her skin raw, but she stumbles to her feet, falls against the wall of the church ruin as the rocks disintegrate beneath her.

Cal is watching, smiling.

She tries again, pushes herself up against what was a pew and it crashes to the ground, sinking into mud. The wind is howling in her ears now, eyes streaming.

'Tie her up before she manages to stand,' Cal says, and Suze yanks her arms behind her back and ties her hands. Trish ignores the pain.

'So you had Ricky dealing for you?'

'Of course not.'

'But he was meeting someone, we could never explain—'

'He was buying,' Cal snaps. 'You want in, you'd better get less stupid.'

Trish blinks, grit in the corners of her eyes, but she takes it, forces the world back into shape. She can do this. She is Trish fucking Mackie.

'Buying what?'

'Cannabis oil.' Cal laughs, loud. 'For the pain.'

He pushes his foot into Ricky's stomach but Ricky is too far gone to move, to make a sound. Andy has tears streaming down

356

his face. Trish forces a laugh out, just as loud as Cal's had been and even through the slashing rain she can see Andy looking at her like he wants to kill her himself. But then she hears the sound, the swarm pulsing in and out of the air, and through the pain in her head she knows it has to be now. She is Trish fucking Mackie and fuck the pain, it has to be now now *now*. She kicks with all her might, catching Suze in the stomach again and again as Suze stumbles and she keeps going, screaming, kicking, fast. Suze reels back with pain, with the shock, clutching at her stomach and slipping on the gushing mud. Trish needs her hands; she's straining against the rope tying them then kicking Suze again, keeping her down, curled on the ground and screaming through the buzzing and they're everywhere, the bees, her bees. Trish can't even see through the swarm, but Cal is flailing, his skin covered in them. She screams as she rams her body into him with all the strength she has, and Andy's shouting and Cal's flailing at the air as beneath it all she hears footsteps, running, no, yes, someone's here. Frazer's here, fighting beside her. Cal's down. Trish is kicking and screaming and Frazer's kneeling on Cal's chest, holding him down, telling her to stop, Trish, you can stop now, but Trish is kicking and screaming and wall after wall of the church ruin is crashing down as the ground shudders and the air shrieks through the church ruin and out to the coast, to the cliffs.

WATER

Georgie is moving, she's up, she's screaming.

'Now! Go, now!'

Pamali stumbles forward, Fergus too—

'*Go—*'

Pami grabs Lori Smyth, Fergus lifts Natalie, stumbles, carries her back inland as Georgie races past them to the edge, the final cliff edge and Gail's outstretched arms. She's reaching out, grabbing for Gail but she can't do it; she's not going to make it. The cliffs shudder again and Georgie lurches forward. This is it. Blood slipping between her fingers. Not like this. She grasps at Gail's clothes, her nails ripping, but she's got her, the ground shuddering beneath them and Georgie throws herself back from the edge with everything she has as the rocks they were standing on crash down the cliff to shatter on the beach below and she has her, she has her, they're on the ground, they're alive.

'No!' Gail cries, pushing against Georgie then slipping in the mud, thrashing as Georgie grabs her ankle, holds her back as the land shakes. 'We have to end it!'

'That's what I'm doing,' Georgie screams, trying to hold her still. 'Gail, that's what I'm doing!' But the land hasn't finished. The fractures rush towards them, scoring through the rock, leaving jagged scars of broken stone and crumbling earth. Georgie sees it happening in slow motion. The cracks destroying what's left between the villagers, the ground itself separating Georgie from Fergus, June from Whelan, isolating Pamali and Terry and Gail as though reclaiming every part of itself not touching us, not ruined by us, and Bessie Wilkie has fallen, Camellia Taylor is clutching at mud, Elise is crying, her voice a series of desperate sobs, 'Da...don't...da...no...' and then a strange stillness descends as the cracks in the land move beyond them towards the village.

First, they destroy the track that leads from the cliffs to the old church, carving it from the coast then flooding it with mud and grit and broken branches until the track is buried beneath the uprooted remnants of the land. What's left of the church ruin shakes and crumbles as the earth beneath it disintegrates, walls folding in on themselves, pews curling down to the mud, ancient stones sinking deep into the graves below as Trish and Frazer watch in stunned silence. Further inland, uneven grey pavements shatter like glass and the old concrete flats crumble to their foundations and in the heart of Burrowhead the fountain bursts, exploding through the village square, showering it with smashed stone that glints, even now, with quartz, and all the lost fragments thrown into the fountain's cracked basin over generations: rusted coins and discarded toys clatter into gutters, rotting feathers and birds' bones fall between the serrated edges of broken tarmac. Buildings shudder against the force of it. Terracotta roof tiles crash into splintered paving stones and trees heave and fall and there, there, looping back to the coast, to the peeling red and yellow playground: the swings are moving in the wind, their metal links creaking like the call of distant gulls. The horse and donkey lurch back and forth. The rusted roundabout screeches as it spins, falls silent, screeches again and the whole playground is lifted from its tarmac and floating in the air. For a moment, the swings hang suspended over the sea. The faded yellow paint of their bars, the chipped red frame, the split grey seats swinging high over the crashing waves. Then metal clatters against rock until the water below engulfs it and the cliffs are suddenly silent and still.

The playground is gone.

Georgie can taste clear, cool mist rising from the land like breath released.

The cliff edge is gone. The church ruin and the standing stones and the fountain are gone and Georgie rises to her feet because the bedrock has stopped threatening to break her. The ground is steady again, the grass feathered and soft beneath her feet. If she wanted to, she could step across the cracks; there is amazement in the possibility. Fergus is looking at her from where he fell, and she allows herself to see him. The rain is fresh as spring water. It's washing the salt grit from her eyes. She stands at the new edge of the cliff and below she can see a cave.

She can see the cave at last.

Its entrance is clear in the night air. The gentle curves of it eroded from smooth rock over centuries. The waves are close but calm, water lapping at the pebbled shore as the sea retreats. Georgie looks down expecting to see the souls who scratched their desperate messages on the cave walls, but instead she sees two figures. Two figures in the cave's entrance, drenched but standing, looking out at the new tideline in the moonlight.

Around her, the villagers look like themselves again. Almost, but not quite. June and Whelan are sitting where Georgie had seen one of the standing stones rise. Whelan's face is drained of all colour. His arm is around June's shoulders, June's face pressed into his chest. Georgie thinks she's crying. Bessie Wilkie is rocking on the ground, knees clutched to her chin, muttering under her breath. Terry's face is streaked with mud, the horror of what he's seen flickering through his expression.

Suddenly Bessie shouts, 'I'm sorry, Gail,' the words bursting from her like she couldn't contain them any more. 'Abigail.' She dissolves into tears, her head folding into her chest. 'I'm sorry, Abigail.'

Fergus is trying to stand, Natalie held in his arms; her clothes are drenched in blood. Pamali helps him up, then reaches for her phone to call an ambulance. Beside them, Camellia Taylor struggles to her feet. She's walking towards Georgie with her hands held out, as though she wants Georgie to arrest her. All Georgie can do is shake her head. Camellia touches her shoulder, and Georgie can feel how badly her hands are shaking. She looks exhausted, filthy, barely able to stand.

'I thought I was going to die,' Camellia whispers, as the tears add their streaks to the dirt on her face.

'No one here is going to die,' Georgie says, surprised at the strength in her own voice. They're watching her now. All the eyes of the village. Even Gail Dover. She looks so frail, slumped in the mud. Georgie reaches out a hand and Gail takes it, stumbling to her feet. 'Do you hear me?' Georgie says, quieter this time, though they all hear her perfectly. 'Every one of you is going to live.'

TO BEAR WITNESS

Fallen tiles lie cracked and shattered on the pavement around the police station, on the fractured stretch of tarmac that serves as a car park, on the concrete paving stones rising vertically like gravestones to separate the station from the patchy grass beyond. Georgie picks her way through them carefully and takes a moment to look at the fresh turquoise sky, soothed with high-feathered cloud, before opening the door.

Inside, a thick crack runs through the plaster on the corridor wall, from the reception all the way to the cell at the back, widening into a hole the size of a fist opposite Georgie's office, then drawing in on itself to streak down in shards. But the building is still standing. Its structure remains. It was not always a police station and soon it will not be one again and so: a reprieve. They have a chance to do this.

In the box room at the end of the hall Frazer has set up a desk and two chairs. He'll be sitting on one already, Georgie knows, his back to the wall, his eyes facing the door. Opposite him will be Abigail Moss, who grew up to become Gail Dover. He has found her at last.

But Georgie walks straight to the interview room where Simon is waiting for her, three cups of water on the table. Staring at him is Cal. He barely glances up at her as she enters, takes her seat.

He looks the same.

It's hard for Georgie to get her head around, the way he looks exactly the same. Then he smiles at her like he's here to fill them in on the latest forensics.

They were drenched and filthy when they came in, every one of them. Cal and Suze going in the cells, Trish bruised and shaken but standing, Simon escorting Gail Dover home and staying out there, watching her door. There was a felled tree lying across High Street. Church Street was knee-deep with the flood, dirt and debris floating by like belongings. The roads were pitted and fractured. The villagers were told that if they attempted to leave they'd be arrested. No one tried. Some even offered to help, to stand guard in the wrecked streets of the village, but in the end they all went peacefully into their homes.

They couldn't have started the interviews last night. Georgie couldn't. She needed to drink some water, let sleep clear her head. The little girl slept beside her, curled against her body.

Fergus stayed in the hospital with Natalie Prowle; Georgie had asked him to.

He woke with the dawn and it seemed at first like it wasn't real – the landslide, the floods and wind, Natalie's limp body – but there she was, in the clean hospital bed. Unconscious, tubes grating in and out, sheets tucked neatly around her.

That was how they'd found Lee, wasn't it?

The light is coming through the window, the flimsy curtains letting in a diffuse shimmer and the crack between them allowing a fresh glint of sun to fall across the floor and onto the bed, up to Natalie's wrists. They are bandaged and deeply cut but, the doctors said last night, they have a chance to mend.

In the interview room, Georgie grinds her teeth.

'My foolish mother,' Cal says, shaking his head as though he's fond of her.

'Meaning?'

'She thought the ayahuasca brew was *real*.'

Georgie sits back and waits – this is not going to be an interview where she presses and questions and has to navigate a maze of lies. She's going to let him speak. He *wants* to speak.

'She thought, if it was made with willing human blood, it would show everyone some kind of truth,' he says. 'She honestly believed it would reveal the past.'

Georgie takes a sip of her water. Was it the past she was watching last night, when she saw the crimes of the village clearer than ever before?

'I tried to tell her,' Cal says. 'I said, Mother, the old ways are irrelevant – human blood can be traced.'

A piece slots into place. The animal blood. That's what Cal was using. That's the drug *he* was developing. A powerful hallucinogen, unknown and untraceable. Based on the ayahuasca brew but modified with animal blood; that's what he was testing on Lee and the others, on Rachel and Pauly.

'But she was so set on Natalie Prowle.'

He shakes his head and rests his back against the seat again, his knees accidentally bumping the table.

Fergus jumps at the knock, the silence had been so regular – silence with the whir of hospital machines and the click of a trolley being wheeled down the hall, with distant muffled voices that were a comfort to him. But then he turns and knows it's time for him to leave. He was here as a caretaker, that's all, and now the right person has arrived. He's not afraid Aaron Prowle will do the wrong thing by his mother. He can see in his eyes, in the nervous movement of his hands, he's here for better reasons than that.

Aaron for his part doesn't even notice Fergus closing the door, though he was glad he left without trying to speak to him – Aaron's in no mood for talking. He's going to sit here, and he's not going to pretend anything is okay 'cause it fucking well isn't. He's not spoken to his mam in a long while now and there are reasons for that, reasons he and Lee grew up to be so angry and they've no gone away and there's no sense pretending like they have. There's plenty things he needs to say. He's not afraid of a fight, not with her or anyone, and nor is she, so they'll shout at each other, no doubt, and blame too, and he's fine with that. But first she needs to wake up. The doctors are hopeful, so. He'll wait here until his mam wakes up and the first face she sees will be his.

'Look, it wasn't personal for me,' Cal says. 'I just thought, seeing as how Natalie had been asking too many questions, it would be a neat way to tie everything up.'

'To frame an innocent woman.'

'Natalie's not innocent.'

'None of you are innocent.'

'Is anyone?' He smiles, catches her eye like he's trying to remind her of their friendship. 'After the way she killed that horse, it was only a matter of time before she hurt someone—'

'She *didn't* hurt anyone,' Si says.

'But would the world really have been worse off without her?'

'So you'd have framed her for Lee's murder,' Georgie says, 'and then killed her?'

'I didn't think I'd have to.'

'You thought your mother would see to that?'

There's a flicker in his eyes. Regret, maybe, but not for what he's done.

'My mam would never want to hurt anyone,' he says. 'She truly did believe in ayahuasca, in the whole ritual as a means of… atoning.' He lowers his voice for the first time. 'She told me Natalie wanted to do it, she volunteered. It would have been suicide.'

'Maybe so, thanks to you manipulating the lot of them,' Simon says. 'You got Natalie to believe Aaron had killed Lee – knowing full well how badly that would mess her up – and you got your mam to believe Natalie herself had killed him.'

'Look, all Natalie had to do was leave well enough alone, and I'd have left her be,' Cal says, his voice still calm, reasonable. 'But a woman like Natalie Prowle can't leave people alone, can she? Always keeping an eye, always poking her nose in. I've had Suze watching her since last year.'

At the mention of Suze, Georgie feels a wave of sadness. Suze had been the one passing Cal's lies on to the community council. She'd let Cal know when the coast was clear in the hospital, she'd even been the one to knock Trish unconscious. All because Cal was paying her to do it.

'And Elise, was she working for you too?'

'Hardly. Suze had her monitoring the villagers, reporting back, but she'd no idea what was really going on. Elise Robertson is... well, clueless.'

Georgie purses her lips, thinks of Elise's tear-stained face last night, her apologies, her pleading to help. She said she'd drunk the ayahuasca because she wanted to see her da again. She'd just wanted to talk to him but instead she saw what he'd done. More than slaughtering animals; he'd kidnapped Dawn Helmsteading along with Bobby, nearly sacrificed her on the cliffs. It was a hallucination, it would be no use in any court, but Elise was shaking from the truth of it. She didn't know, she kept saying, she hadn't known. Georgie had felt sorry for her.

It's time to change tack. She glances at Simon and gives him a nod.

'So what really happened to Rachel and Pauly, Cal?' Si says, and he does a good job of sounding conspiratorial. 'We've got their stomach contents.'

Cal exhales as though it's ancient history to him, an unfortunate series of events that he handled as best he could.

'The girl was trying to speak to her dead mam. The lad was a scared kid. He wanted to buy at first, came looking for the "spirit drug", so I told him I had something better. Turned out he couldn't pay, so the deal was I'd teach him to make it for me – keep my hands clean and give him a bit of a future. But he was freaking out, threatening to run away. Didn't like the idea of owing me, apparently. I went up to the cliffs to talk to them, explain the situation, that's all. They worked for me.'

'Whether they liked it or not?'

'It wasn't my fault they jumped.'

'What would have happened to them if they hadn't?'

Cal shrugs as though it's not his job to answer that sort of question. 'I didn't want them dead, did I – what good did that do me? I had to call Bobby Helmsteading in for a while, and he was not discreet. Then Lee bloody Prowle...' He shakes his head like everyone in the world is a disappointment.

'So if Rachel and Pauly hadn't died, Bobby Helmsteading might never have come back to Burrowhead?' Simon says.

Georgie looks at him, then down at the little girl sitting cross-legged on the floor beside her. If Bobby Helmsteading hadn't come back to Burrowhead, maybe Alexis would still be alive. Maybe everything would have been different. Or maybe not.

Maybe none of them can know what would have happened if Rachel and Pauly hadn't died.

THAT THE PAST BE KNOWN

'It's time for the truth now,' Frazer says, and opposite him Gail Dover thinks he's right. She likes his face, DS Frazer. It's not often she can look at a man and see right into kindness like that. 'Tell me about Natalie Prowle.'

'Oh no.' Gail almost reaches over the table to take his hand, before realising that would be the wrong thing to do. 'We have to start long before that. We have to start with Abigail Moss. That's who I was back then.'

'You were working at Wyndham Manor.'

'A punishment for my wayward behaviour.'

'An effective one?'

'No,' she says, her eyes glazing over as though she can see something beyond him, before they focus again. 'No, that came later. That night.'

'Tell me what happened.'

He speaks gently, and Gail Dover's gaze doesn't leave his, not even as she tells her story. When her eyes fill she pauses until they're clear again; she doesn't want to speak while she cries, he can see that. She wants to be calm. She wants to get it right.

'They made me watch as they attacked Dougie,' she says. 'They kicked him to within an inch of his life. Then they carried me back to the village, claimed they found him raping me. It was a lie – I told everyone it was a lie, but no one would listen. Not my parents, not anyone in the village… Abigail Braxton *could not* have chosen to be with a black boy.'

Frazer feels his throat tighten, doesn't trust himself to speak.

'I don't know what happened to him after that,' she says. 'I never saw him again. My parents made me marry a local man to keep me right.'

Her eyes are piercing in the way she looks at him then.

'He knew how to keep a woman right, my husband. But that night, Nora Prowle was leading them. They were all wearing hooded cloaks and masks, as though we were going to be sacrificed – except they kept us alive. Maybe they thought it would be more of a deterrent that way. Maybe they didn't want the inconvenience of a dead body. Either way, I could tell who they were. I knew Jacob Prowle at once, the way he kept beating Dougie even after he was broken. The Robertson brothers were part of it, all three of them. They were vicious. But they're long gone now. Bessie Wilkie was there, watching. She was supposed to be my friend. I never told her I knew. Never. All our lives, every time she's been nice to me, I've known it was the guilt doing it. Even young Walt Mackie was there with his father – can you imagine? He was just a child. His father was training him to take over, so he could lead the threefold death one day.' Her mouth twitches, as though the thought disgusts her. 'The truth is, all the villagers were there, watching, and I had to spend the rest of my life living among them. But Nora Prowle was the leader. She was the one held my eyes open to make me watch.'

'Why did she do it?'

'You tell me. Because we were unmarried, or unapologetic, or because I was white and Dougie was black. Because I did whatever I wanted – and Nora preferred to tell people what they were and were not allowed to do. Or maybe because I'd inherited what she thought should be hers, and it was one way to take a little bit of that back.'

'All of those reasons, I expect,' Frazer says. 'And it's possible she was made into what she became, too, isn't it?'

'She was the ringleader,' Gail says, shaking her head. 'She...'

'It was the men who performed the violence,' he says quietly.

Trish closes her eyes again, doesn't want to face the morning. She'll be called in for a witness statement soon enough. That's all she is now, a witness. She's not sure if that's a weakness or something else, but she's not much of a detective any more, that's for sure. It's hard to believe she'd been right there at the community council meeting. She heard what Gail Dover was saying but she didn't get it, did she, didn't realise what it meant even though she was right there listening. She wishes Uncle Walt were here, sleeping in his room upstairs. She wishes he were here to explain, tell her everything he did. To confess. Maybe then she'd be able to forgive him. She almost wishes Georgie were here, but she doesn't know how to face her.

'It's hard to forgive,' Frazer says, in the cell turned interview room, in the station. 'I do understand that.'

'Then you understand why Natalie completed the circle,' says Gail Dover.

'No,' he says. 'I don't. You're saying she had to pay for Nora's crime? You wanted Nora's blood to make the ayahuasca, so you decided to murder Natalie with a threefold death?'

Gail's eyes are filling again. 'Oh no, the threefold death isn't—'

'I know it's supposed to summon your ancestors to *purify* the village,' Frazer says, though he doesn't mean it to come out so angry.

'No!' Gail shouts, actually shouts, and Frazer is stunned by the noise. He's never even heard her raise her voice before. 'I needed to right a wrong,' Gail says. 'I was trying to right all the wrongs.'

Frazer just stares at her; none of it makes sense.

'The threefold death has been twisted into something unrecognisable,' she says. 'It's been used as an excuse to kill innocent creatures, to threaten and control these villages for generations. It brings out the worst in us, again and again. The Others were never coming back to *save* the village – they wanted revenge, and who could blame them? The village had destroyed them.' Her eyes search his. 'Every time the Others were summoned with that violence, they saw more hate, they *felt* more hate, it was turning the villagers into...' She shakes her head as though she can't bear to describe it. 'But that was not the original way, DS Frazer, and it has *nothing* to do with ayahuasca. Nothing. Nora even told people ayahuasca was evil. She didn't want anyone seeing the truth.'

'What you did to Natalie was—'

'Natalie wanted to see her boys again, before she... She was willing, don't you see? *That* was the way of our ancestors. A choice, DS Frazer. A willing sacrifice to produce the most powerful form of ayahuasca – a gift to reveal our past, the truth about our own natures. And once the truth was known, the Others could finally be free. Even Natalie was given peace. She saw the happiness of her boys before the end. There is beauty in that.'

'Natalie,' says Frazer, 'is still alive.'

Gail looks stunned. 'She's still alive?' she says quietly. 'That's beautiful, too. Ayahuasca is powerful.'

'I'm pretty sure it was people who saved her.'

'Oh yes,' Gail says. 'It's always people who do things. That's why I had to make them see. I told everyone Natalie's sacrifice was to save the village – they're familiar with that idea, thanks to Nora – but really it was to confront the villagers with all the guilt they'd buried. Natalie understood. After what her boys had done, what *she'd* done... She killed her own child. She knew her blood would reveal Nora's crimes and all the crimes that had come before. That's why she was willing. That makes a difference, DS Frazer. That's why what *I* did wasn't wrong.'

She doesn't know yet that Cal is the one being interviewed for Lee's murder. Not Natalie, but her own son. His voice comes out sadly when he next speaks.

'Every version of your ritual is wrong.'

'But DS Frazer—'

'You could have helped her instead, Gail.'

'But…' she says, shaking her head. 'But after what Nora did…'

'Guilt isn't passed down generations like that.'

'Here it is.'

'No, it's not.'

'But you're… You're not from around here,' she whispers.

He leaves it for a moment, while Gail Dover looks at the ground as though she's watching it all happen again, and when she looks up somewhere within her Abigail Moss begins to cry for all the things she once knew.

'You put up the bench dedicated to Abigail?' he says quietly.

'I needed to do something,' she says. 'To remember her, as she was.'

'And do you remember who you were, now?'

She closes her eyes and doesn't reply. He wonders if he might be able to arrange a meeting between her and Betty Marshall. Maybe help them both find a bit of friendship after all these years.

'Is there…' Frazer clears his throat. 'Is there anything I can do for you, Gail?'

She looks bewildered when he says that, as if no one's offered to do anything for her in a long, long time. She wipes her eyes with her hand, so he passes her his handkerchief. Trish would laugh at him for that; for having a handkerchief in his pocket. Wouldn't she?

'There's a portrait of Nora Prowle hanging in the community centre,' she says.

He nods; he remembers it.

'And it's not just of Nora Prowle,' she says. 'Jacob Prowle is in it too. He's standing behind her, in the shadow. His hand is on her shoulder.'

Frazer feels his breath moving through his body, allows himself to exist with it.

'Will you take it down for me, DS Frazer?'

'Yes,' he says. 'Yes, I will.'

THE PRESENT SEEN

'But why did you kill Lee?' Georgie takes over again. She's told Cal what they have, the new forensics: his DNA on Lee's hoody, the one Julie and Penny-Ann found in the woods and Shona brought to the police. A hair soaked in fox blood, enough to place him with Lee, and the equipment used to make the ayahuasca, in the woods. And they have Shona's recording, Cal's voice on her phone – he'll not be able to wriggle out of that. Maybe that's why he's not even trying. Thank God for Shona.

'Lee Prowle was about to talk,' Cal says. 'What was I supposed to do?'

'So you put something in the brew? Gave him a different batch, what?'

'No, no, Lee took the exact same as everyone else. He had an allergic reaction to it, that's all. It was unfortunate. It freaked him out so much he became a liability, started saying heaven knows what to his mam in the hospital. So yeah, I had to... He backed me into a corner, okay? Come on, *no one* is going to miss Lee Prowle, are they? I'm not—'

'A killer?' Simon says.

Cal doesn't answer. Lee dead and Ricky Barr dead and still he can't see what he is; Georgie's not sure how you get through to someone like that.

'Okay,' she starts again, her voice slow, her accent a comfort to her today. 'So how did he know you were making it in the first place?'

Cal shakes his head. 'I needed someone after Bobby died.'

'So it was all about getting kids dealing for you. Why? To make money?'

He holds his hands out as if to say there was no other reason for anyone to do anything.

'My family had money, once,' he says. 'I'm just reclaiming what should always have been mine. All of it. The money, the land, the hotel, the shop—'

'The shop?' asks Simon.

'Do you mean the Spar?' says Georgie.

She knows the answer, though. She knows the answer before he even replies. He ordered the vandalism, the graffiti, the attack on Pamali. It was him.

'Look, no offence to Pamali, alright, but the fact is this is not her land.'

And there it is.

'That shop, that should be my shop.' He says it likes he's stating the truth, like he believes it. 'This land should be *my land*.'

His finger pointing at his chest, stabbing at where his heart should be, while outside the station, along the track and all the way to the field on the outskirts of the village, Debs has her arm around Andy's shoulders and Pamali's eyes are filling with tears. They're telling her that Ricky couldn't be saved, didn't want to be – his DNR request, his death early this morning. She tells them how sorry she is, but Andy shakes his head, so she stops and lets him talk. It's not often Andy needs to talk.

'I just want to do a bit of work here,' he says. 'Keep my hands busy.'

She looks down at the patch they're standing beside. Runner beans neatly winding their way up the pyramids of canes Andy built for them. A lot of the villagers have been by today, wanting to help, offering to do a bit of planting. June and Whelan were working on the brassica patch all morning. Whelan said he was sorry he'd wasted the last forty years on roses, but there's a place for roses too, Pami told him. There's a place for everything that grows.

'Of course,' she says. 'It's yours, Andy, it's ours. That's the whole point. It's the community garden.'

But Andy is looking at Debs now and Debs is the one who speaks next.

'Well, that's the thing,' she says. 'Technically, this field is part of our farm.'

Pamali's heart falls then and it keeps on falling while in the station Georgie knows they have Cal.

'You'd have killed Trish too,' she says. 'Even Trish.'

'No,' Cal says, shaking his head as though finally there is something he cares about, something he needs known. 'I'd never have killed her, not Trish. She's one of us.'

'So were Rachel and Pauly,' Simon says. 'So was Lee – they're all villagers.'

'Oh no.' Cal smiles at that. 'I don't mean the villagers. I mean the police.'

Si goes quiet then and Georgie can see he doesn't know how to counter it.

'Well thankfully,' Georgie says. 'Whichever tribe you're talking about, I don't consider myself a part of it.' And she's not certain but she thinks, out of the corner of her eye, she sees the crack in the ceiling stretch over to the wall, turn a corner and start edging its way down towards the door – a millimetre wide, that's all, but it's there. Like the fracture in Main Street that's crumbling the stone, leaving a mess of gravel and uncertainty, and there's a shaking in Pamali's hand as she waits until Debs speaks again.

'You see, Ricky made a will,' she says. 'He told us both about it – he wanted us to understand. He was...'

'Ready,' Andy says.

'And we, Andy and I, we inherit everything jointly.'

'So then the community garden is yours,' Pamali says, backing away now.

'No, wait,' Andy says. 'You don't understand. We're giving it to you.'

'What?'

'This field, all the way to the edge of the trees there, and up to the village on that side, it's yours now. You can do whatever you want with it.'

'All I want is to build a community garden.'

'Yes, I thought you'd say that. It's why I'm here to help.'

She can't process it at first. It doesn't make...not sense, it's something else she's reaching for. But she can see Andy needs to start work. He needs to do something with his hands, for the grief, to keep him going, he needs to be in among the soil with things green and alive. That she can understand. Debs is saying something about drawing up a contract, and Pami is nodding but not really listening because it doesn't matter to her who owns what, as long as she can build the community garden, and as Debs says, 'This is your land now, Pamali,' she kneels beside Andy and starts showing him how to support a fallen pea stem with gently threaded twine.

TO START FRESH

Shona keeps a little way from the edge. The rain has stopped and the air is clear, but it still feels like a few rocks could slip down to the beach, if folk get careless. Behind her, the church ruin is nothing but rubble. The whole place looks like it'll be overrun by grass and wildflowers before the end of the season, and the old graves have pushed their way up through the soil like they've been wanting to do for years. It's not as creepy as it sounds. There are no coffins, no bones risen through the earth, but the church-yard has become a patchwork of low mounds and dips, like a fairground for insects. The buried have been moved to the new graveyard, Rachel's mam among them. So they're together now, Rachel and her mam. Meanwhile, under the cliffs, the hidden cave is open to the beach at last. She can almost imagine Rachel and Pauly down there, not broken and shattered but landing on some-thing soft and forgiving, settling down there at the cave's entrance for a picnic. Or a seance, maybe. Rachel always was determined to speak to the dead.

'We know they didn't mean to die,' Kev says, taking her hand. 'They jumped 'cause they were being threatened by that...' He has not yet found the word he will use to describe Cal, that smiling arrogant man who bullied their friends to their death.

'It's okay,' Shona says. 'I mean, it was...' She shakes her head. 'They should still be alive, but I'm okay. I just wanted to stand here for a bit, you know? To remember them.'

'I know,' he says.

They can hear gulls down on the beach, chattering away to each other. It's peaceful, the noise of them over the lapping of the waves.

'They've offered me the job,' she says. 'Starting right away.'

'The paper?'

She nods. It makes her feel lighter, thinking about it, talking about it: a possibility, away from here.

'You'll take it? Get a flat in the city?'

'That's what I'm thinking.'

'Please tell me I can come,' he says.

She smiles at that, though she was expecting it. 'What are you going to do in the city, while I'm chasing stories?'

He laughs. 'A course maybe. A job. I'll find something.'

They hear Simon's footsteps behind them but neither of them turns; they know who it will be.

'Thanks for the message,' he says.

'Thanks for reopening the case,' Shona replies. They found the truth, between them, and she'll never forget it. 'I thought you might like to say goodbye.'

Simon keeps his feet slightly back from the edge, as Shona did, though he likes how the wind is starting to pick up, that hint of autumn to come. Alexis's favourite season. He's fond of it himself, too. There are some guillemots down by the shore, he can see them bobbing on the waves.

'They really closing the station?' Shona asks.

'Oh yeah. Don't know what they'll do with the building, it being government-owned and that, but I'll be moving up to HQ.'

'Detective's exam?'

'Could be,' Si says, though he's considering his options. He's not sure he wants to go around arresting kids; he'd rather talk to them.

'Might see you in the city then?' Kev says.

'Will do.'

Kev pulls out a cigarette and lights it, offers one to Shona, one to Si. They both shake their heads.

Simon's been craving a cigarette for years, but today the feeling's gone. He wants to smell the sea, the salt, the wet soil still drying, so he gives them both a nod and steps away a little, lets his eyes stray to where the playground was, to the strange arc-shaped ragged line of cliffs left in its place. There's a cormorant perched right on the edge, stretching its wings. And below him: the cave. Once hidden in layers of rock now carved open by the land itself. Messages scratched into stone for everyone to read. The crimes, the prayers, the lives. Fading cries for revenge like the scratch of claws. A shimmer of golden eyes, of lace. *RIP.* Screams, sometimes, and rasping breath. *PLEASE HELP MY MAMMY.* But love, too. *PD & RT 4EVER.* And hope.

But he can't stay here, he knows that. He'll be back, for visits and that, no doubt, but Burrowhead will always be about the missing, for him. Missing Alexis, missing the life they'd barely started together.

'Bye then,' he says, and he turns, doesn't walk the cliffs towards the hole left by the playground's collapse, just heads into the village until, where Church Street meets High Street, he pulls out his phone and makes the call.

'Alright,' he says, 'I'll take a look at the room.'

There's a pause on the other end of the line. He thinks he can hear a smile beyond it, though.

'If it's still available?'

Then he waits.

'It is,' Orlando says. 'I'll tell them you're interested.'

'Thanks.'

Si's walking past the fountain now, still lying broken and lopsided in the middle of the village square.

'Just the room you're after, is it?'

And past the Spar, still standing, the one building in the village undamaged by the landslide: the building where Alexis lived.

'No, it's not just the room.'

Turning off High Street, away from the Spar, heading out of the village now. A family of wrens under the laurel hedge there; Alexis would have loved that.

'No?'

'Course not.'

Up to his own front door, turning the key.

'Then…can I see you tonight?' Orlando says.

'You're in luck,' Si laughs. 'I'm coming round for dinner.'

'Cheeky bastard.'

'See you then.'

And with that he lets the front door swing over behind him, takes the stairs two at a time and starts packing up his stuff.

TO LET GO

Fergus is standing in the museum, in front of the central display where there used to be an Iron Age cauldron that was taken out and used to collect Natalie's blood. He came here for comfort, but it's not working. He's surrounded by posters and pictures that are all telling stories, but as he reads them the burning in his eyes gets worse and his stomach clenches against words. They're wrong. Over and over again, the text avoids the most important information. It talks about rituals without acknowledging killing, leaps over human atrocities to celebrate steam trains and cotton mills and it's so completely wrong.

In the hospital, Natalie had said she wanted nothing more to do with it. She was passing it on, she told him, as she lay propped up with pillows and surrounded by flowers and fruit bowls and chocolates. She insisted he take a pack of biscuits away with him. Said the villagers were falling over themselves to take care of her.

'Short memories,' he said.

'I don't think it's that,' she replied, her voice still raw and husky but getting stronger. 'Mine is pretty long. And Aaron isn't about to forget anything.'

It made Fergus shiver, that, despite the warm sun coming in through the window, but he decided to leave it. For now anyway.

'Look after the museum for me,' she said. 'Though, there's no money, so just give whatever time you have. If you think…'

'I'll look after it, Natalie,' he said.

It's part of his PhD application too, so if he's accepted he'll be spending a lot of time here, working through it all. She was right about the money, of course. No money for his time, no money for updating or changing any of it. There's the basement, though. All the boxes she'd told him about, full of donations, photographs, antiques. The villagers have been dropping more off, since that awful night on the cliffs. Leaving boxes of donations by the door, family albums and heirlooms and old crockery and maybe even artefacts among all that. Like his figurine. He's holding it now, his Iron Age figurine, and he knows he needs to show the truth. When they put the cauldron back, when they add the engraved dagger that Trish is donating, when his figurine goes into a glass cabinet, the bodies must be here too, the bones they excavated from the motte – the truth about how they were killed.

He will make sure of it.

The bones will be displayed, and he will tell their stories. The family murdered. The villagers complicit. He can see the words taking shape as his gaze follows a tiny moth over to the poster about the Second World War: *Our Boys Go to Fight*. But that picture is changing, too, in his mind, missing faces appearing, the girls, the women, living here and fighting and dying and he needs to start earlier, of course he does. *The Industrial Revolution*. But nowhere does it say a word about the slave trade it was built on, nowhere are the ships that docked along this coast filled with human beings packed among the dead and he has to fix all this, he has to get it right and he'll need money from somewhere, it's going to take money. Further along: *Life in the 60s and 70s*. Actual photographs of the village, of High Street and Main Street, of the fountain, of the villagers. They look poor. They were poor, mostly. And they are all white.

He searches the photographs, leans close to look at *The Village Shop*, which was there, which was being run by Pamali's uncle and aunt, but they're not in any of the photos. They're gone, erased from among all those rugged white faces.

What is a history so selective it describes a society that never existed? Not a history at all. A lie.

But he's going to change it. He has the keys, doesn't he?

Suddenly he's moving, restless, striding past display cabinets and posters and through to the hall. The keys, thrown on the front desk. Looking around: old curtains, dirty windows, faded carpet. Taking a seat behind the till, switching on the old computer to search the records, to see what's there beneath the dust. Standing up again; his legs won't let him be still. There's something else. The keys, catching his eye again. The keys to the door and the cabinets, the displays and the stories they tell. They're his now. His. Fergus Strachan. A middle-class, straight, white man. He's picking them up. He's holding the keys and it's worse than a lie, isn't it?

Georgie was right about everything. And all he did was feel sorry for himself and hurt her.

He's moving again, throwing open the door and then he's out in the street, in the light. A gust of air blows the door over behind him. He turns, locks up just in case – Fergus Strachan is nothing if not cautious – and at last he starts to run.

FOR CHANGE

Georgie can hardly believe what Pamali is telling her.

'You've accepted the land from Andy? Like a...like a...'

Like a pay-off?

'Like a gift,' Pamali says.

'That's not what I was going to say. That kid dislocated your shoulder.'

'He's sorry.'

'But what they did to you...' Georgie shakes her head.

'Lee was a kid too, a mess of anger and—'

'Don't excuse them.'

'I'm not excusing them, Georgie. I'm forgiving them.'

'Some people don't deserve to be forgiven.'

She's thinking about Cal, awaiting trial, the lives he stole and the things he made those kids write, the racism they acted on; the way he'll smile and appear so reasonable and educated, the way he'll talk to the jury, the way they'll see him. But Pamali is looking at her with such sad eyes she can barely stand it.

'But without forgiveness, what is there? Punishment? Death? Is that a helpful resolution?'

'There's no such thing as resolution.'

'Well, I tell you what,' Pami says. 'Penny-Ann and Julie have joined the community garden.'

They'd come by yesterday evening, wanting to know what it was all about. When Julie knelt down to touch the feathered leaves of the heritage carrots, Pami knew they'd be back, that they were here for the long term.

'That makes nine of us now,' she says. 'Ten, with you?'

Georgie raises her eyebrows at that and Pamali feels a surge of warmth for her friend.

'I think it'll take more than gardening,' Georgie says.

'Then you could try forgiving yourself.'

Pami knows it's a push, but she thinks maybe it's time.

'You mean for what happened to my brother.'

Georgie knows she's pushing her, too, and she's grateful for it. There's a tugging on her arm, the girl's small fingers intertwining with hers.

'It wasn't your fault, Georgie.'

'I know. It was the fault of racists who were firing guns on a crowd of protestors, and a police service who didn't stop them, and the society who enabled them—'

'And it was *not* your fault you weren't able to save him.'

Georgie takes a breath.

'That's what my mom always says.'

But it hasn't stopped Georgie spending her whole life trying to make sure that the next time, when it happens again, to someone else, she'll have the power to stop it. And does she?

'How is your mam?' Pamali asks, lighter, and Georgie looks down at the little girl.

'She's...' Georgie begins. 'I phoned her.'

'You don't speak often, do you?'

'It was the first time this year.'

Pami nods and the year passes between them, everything that has happened, still carried in the air, in the salt from the sea.

'I think I should...' Georgie begins.

'What, Georgie?'

'I think I'm going to invite her over here,' she says and the words, the absurdity of her mother here, the wonder of it, is almost enough to make her cry. 'I think she'd like it here.' She doesn't cry though; she starts to laugh. 'I think it might do her some good.'

'Well,' Pamali says. 'It is very beautiful here.'

Beside Georgie, the little girl isn't saying anything any more. She's just waiting.

'A bit of company in the house might be alright too...'

'And what about Fergus?'

Pamali is smiling, and it almost looks like she's about to grab her for a hug. Georgie wouldn't say no to a hug. The last time she spoke to Fergus, he'd asked her if she could love him again. As if she had ever stopped.

FOR CHOICE

Trish texted Frazer to meet her at the broken fountain because, well, because once they shared a sandwich there and also she likes the way it's collapsed, the edge of the basin crumbling down, the central statue fallen on its side and propped up against a street lamp by some helpful passer-by. They'll have to remove it or replace it or something. People are talking already about what to do. People in the village, that is, but the council will have to get involved too – not the community council, the real one. The roads will need fixing and the remnants of the fountain removed and the village square could become some other kind of village square. Maybe they could have some plants. A cafe. Some tables. She can imagine it, though she's no idea if they'll do it.

Frazer arrives without a word and sits down beside her, on a low stone that was once part of the fountain's bowl.

'How are you, Trish?' he says, and the concern in his voice is a jolting reminder of how she was when he last saw her; drenched, bloody, screaming, kicking. Terrified and furious and she thinks she might have really hurt Cal if Frazer hadn't been there to hold her back.

'I'm going to save the village,' she says.

He looks at her, his deep eyes glancing at the bruises still on her face. She finds her hand rising up to her hair, spiking it a bit.

'You still plan on saving the village?'

'Yes, I still plan on saving the village.'

Why is he smiling at her?

'How?'

He is oh-so-clever isn't he, DS Bloody Frazer.

'I have no fucking idea.'

He starts to laugh and she's glaring at him, stony-faced Trish, and she was perfectly fucking serious.

'It's not a joke.'

'Oh, I know.' His laugh quietens but he keeps some of it to himself, like he's going to be saving it up for the next time he needs something to smile about. Well, fine.

'Look, actually I do have some ideas, I just—'

He's grinning now.

'Would you fucking stop!'

'I'm sorry, I—'

'What?'

'It's just so good to see you like this. Back to your old self.'

'What is that supposed to mean?'

'I was worried everything might have...'

His voice trails off though and she doesn't finish the sentence for him. She was out for a drink with Si last night, but she's still not spoken to Georgie. Not for what feels like a very long time.

'Look, I want to set up like a community centre or something. Maybe a social enterprise so people have got a place to go. Is that so ridiculous?'

'Not ridiculous in the slightest.'

'And it'll give other people a reason to visit too, right? From wherever. We need to bring more people into the village. Open up. And we'll need information.'

'We?'

'Education, I mean. But in a good way. I'm no teacher, and it can't be too preachy. We've got to take people with us. These people.' She looks around as she says it, as if the full implications are sinking in. 'We've got to take these people with us.'

'Right.'

'And you're going to help me,' she says to Frazer. 'That's why you're here.'

'What?'

'You heard. I think you should—'

'Help you?'

'Be a part of it.'

Fuck, she can feel the red spreading up her neck at that. Her body is such a disappointment sometimes.

'Are you asking me to resign from the police force and set up a...a community arts centre to promote diversity with you in Burrowhead?'

'Yeah,' she says. 'Yeah, something like that. With me.'

'I've got to go back to work.'

'You want to stay with the police?'

He hesitates.

'Seriously, you want to stay with the police, after all this?'

'Look, I'm not saying the force is perfect—'

'But?'

'It's easier to effect change from the inside than the outside.'

'Is it though?'

'I need a job, Trish.'

Trish is disappointed. But only for a second.

'Well then.' She straightens up, fires a piercing glance at him. 'You'll just have to help out at weekends for now. And we'll see.'

'Okay.'

'Okay?'

'Okay.'

'Good. Come on then.'

'Where are we going?'

'To look at the Wyndham Manor Community Centre.'

'Hell, no! I was thinking you could.'

'Me?' Georgie laughs. 'I think grassroots is more my style.'

Trish takes the stone that Georgie was offering her. 'Yeah, I can see that.' She smiles at her again, warmer this time. 'It's mine too, you know.'

'I know.' The sea is a beautiful colour, over the sand bed out past the rocks, almost emerald in places. 'You think we can make a difference here, Trish?'

'Oh, we're going to make a difference.' She glances sideways, nudges her shoulder. 'You and me, Georgie.'

Georgie nods, places a hand on the little girl's head. Her hair is soft and warm, and Georgie is soothed by it, by her presence.

'I'm truly sorry about your Uncle Walt,' Georgie says. 'I never wanted him hurt.'

'I know,' Trish says. 'And he made his mistakes, I know that too.'

'He was a kind man, at heart.'

'Not always, I don't think,' Trish says, though Georgie can hear the loss in her voice. 'I won't be following in his footsteps.' She pauses for a second, her thumb rubbing against the sea-smoothed stone. 'I found a note from my mam.'

'Oh, Trish.'

She shakes her head impatiently, like she doesn't want Georgie's sympathy.

'I think he did something to her, a long time ago. Uncle Walt, and the rest of the villagers. I don't know what, but it was still hurting her. She had her reasons for...'

Georgie knows that she still can't say it – she's never heard Trish say that her mother is dead.

'For leaving?' Georgie suggests.

'For doing what she did.' Trish purses her lips. 'She needed some help, and no one helped her.'

Please help my mammy.

'It was you, who wrote the message in the cave?'

As Georgie says it she feels the breeze against her hand and looks down to see that the little girl is gone.

'Trish?' Georgie whispers.

'I always thought she'd come back,' Trish says. 'I mean, I wouldn't have said it out loud, but somehow I thought it. She's not coming back, though, is she.'

Georgie shakes her head.

'But don't you worry about me. I'll not be following in her footsteps either.'

Trish is staring up the beach, to the cave. Now it's open to the elements the scratches will be eroded away, the messages freed by the salt and wind; their edges are being softened already. Georgie resists the urge to put an arm around Trish's shoulders, for now at least.

'I was thinking,' Georgie says. 'We could put up a monument or something, in the village square, to remember the people who've been killed.'

'Like Sonny Riley?' Trish says. 'I've been thinking a lot about him, with Uncle Walt dying right where he was buried. People should remember that little boy.'

Georgie always will; they may never know who his parents were, or where he came from, but she'll always remember him.

'And Alexis too,' Georgie says. 'And Rachel and Pauly and... and your mother, if you'd like that?'

Trish nods, staring down at the stone still nestled in her palm.

'I think it should be for all of them,' she says, and she throws the stone so it makes a gentle arc into the water and disappears.

'You don't want to leave the village then, Trish?'

'No, I'm not leaving. No way. This is my home.' She pauses. 'Have you thought about it?'

Georgie smiles; she's thought about it a lot. 'I'm staying right here,' she says. 'This is my home too.'

396

'Good.' Trish is staring at her now, serious as can be, and determined too. 'I mean it. There's work to do here, isn't there?'

'There is a lot of work to do.'

'And I've got ideas, Georgie. Like I was telling Frazer, I've got plans, and I'm going to need some help because this' – she waves her arm from the sea to the clifftop and the village beyond – 'this is not over. Nothing here is over.'

Georgie feels a welcome restlessness in her legs as Trish says that. There is work to do here; and there's the autumn to look forward to. Georgie loves the colours here in the fall, the rich golden reds of the leaves, the exquisite layers of the sunrise. As she looks out, the sea turns from that deep turquoise over the sand bed to a shimmering silver green haze at the horizon. There are clouds, too, satin lenticular clouds, her favourite, and above them a layer of feathered cirrus travels high through the atmosphere.

Looking down again she sees a group of kittiwakes gliding over the water.

'Si was right about them,' Georgie says.

'What?'

She points at the birds. 'They're beautiful gulls.'

Trish just snorts at that and stuffs her hands into her pockets.

A little further along the beach, unnoticed by either of them, the year's first sanderlings dart in and out of the waves building on the tideline.

ACKNOWLEDGEMENTS

The creation of a trilogy involves a huge amount of work from a huge number of people. The knowledge that you have all worked so hard to bring these stories into the world is humbling. My editor Jenny Parrott and copy-editor Sarah Terry take such care of my words, and work with such insight and thoughtfulness, that they've not only made these books better but have made me a better writer. Thank you both. The whole team at Point Blank and Oneworld is full of talent and skill, and I am deeply grateful: Julian Ball, Thanhmai Bui-Van, Lucy Cooper, Francesca Dawes, Jennifer Jahn, Juliet Mabey, Laura McFarlane, Anna Murphy, Paul Nash, Aimee Oliver-Powell, Mark Rusher, Tom Sanderson, Molly Scull, Ben Summers, Harriet Wade, Matilda Warner, Hayley Warnham and Margot Weale – it is an honour to work with you all.

My agent, Cathryn Summerhayes, is an inspiration. Thank you, Cath, for your support and advice, for always listening, and for being the kindest most genuine badass super-agent I could wish for. The whole team at Curtis Brown work tirelessly for books and for authors; thank you, Jess Molloy, Luke Speed and Anna Weguelin. And I want to say a particular thank you to Alice Lutyens and Sophia MacAskill for looking after my audio rights brilliantly, and to everyone at Bolinda for their flair in producing and promoting the audiobooks, read beautifully by Julie Maisey.

There is a network of support in Scotland that I want to thank. I feel so lucky to be here, and to be part of the Scottish literary community. Thank you to Scottish Book Trust, Creative Scotland, Publishing Scotland, Highland LIT, Moniack Mhor, Tain Library and Book Group, and to all the book festivals, residencies, publications, libraries, bookshops, literary events and groups across Scotland that have found ways to keep supporting books and writers throughout a global pandemic and beyond.

My writing process simply would not work without feedback, and there are a few people whose advice is invaluable to me.

I would never have been able to write these books without Viccy Adams and Jane Alexander. They lead me gently through the chaos, time and again. Thank you both for your discerning insight, friendship and support. It has meant more to me than I can say.

Liz Treacher's thoughtful advice always gives me exactly what I need to keep going. Liz, there were times I felt like giving up, and you pulled me through. Thank you.

And I think I am unusual in having family members who can give such helpful feedback, so a special thank you goes to Ally Sedgwick and Chris Sedgwick. Your perceptive editing of my works-in-progress made these stories better, and the published books mean all the more to me because of your involvement.

I have been supported in many ways by friends and family while writing this trilogy, and it's been a tough five years, so without that I doubt I'd have finished a single draft. Margaret Callaghan, Aoife Lyall, Mairi MacPherson, Seamus MacPherson and Kate Tough – thank you. Kelsey Ansbro, Claire Askew, Ali Braidwood, Nick Brooks, David Duguid, Merryn Glover, Maggie Hope, Kirsty Logan, Katy McAulay, Laura Morgan, Philip Paris, Debbie Ross and Gill Tasker – thank you. Mary Gallacher, Ari Lugo, Brigit Sedgwick, Lindsay Sedgwick and Steve Sedgwick – thank you.

Michael, it goes far beyond gratitude; none of this would be possible without you.

I will end the Burrowhead Mysteries by saying that these three books have been dedicated to three women from three generations of my family: for Mavis, for Brigit, and for Hazel, with love.

© Michael Gallacher

Helen Sedgwick is the author of *The Comet Seekers* and *The Growing Season*, which was shortlisted for the Saltire Society Fiction Book of the Year in 2018. The opener to her Burrowhead Mysteries crime trilogy, *When the Dead Come Calling*, was published in 2020, followed by *Where the Missing Gather* in 2021. She has an MLitt in Creative Writing from Glasgow University and has won a Scottish Book Trust New Writers Award. Before she became an author, she was a research physicist with a PhD in Physics from Edinburgh University. She lives in the Scottish Highlands.